LIBERTAS

BOOK ONE

LIBERTAS

Pocket Full of Seeds Trilogy

DANUTA PFEIFFER

LUMINARE PRESS
WWW.LUMINAREPRESS.COM

Luminare Press
442 Charnelton St.
Eugene, OR 97401
www.luminarepress.com

LCCN: 2020923802
ISBN: 978-1-64388-519-3

For Robin

Table of Contents

Fredericka

⸻◦∞◦⸻

Fredericka had never seen herself in a mirror before. Never all in one piece. She shot a glance around the room as if she needed permission, as if her reflection was forbidden. This was not the watery image of her face in the creek or her shadow in the Big House windows. The mirror reflected her clearly, from head to toe, at fourteen, still a stranger to herself.

The girl in the looking glass was tall, thin, and brittle as a stick-built chimney. She touched her brown hair swirling to her shoulders in a mist of curls and stared back at her eyes, glinting green and gold like sun-shocked river pebbles. These were not innocent eyes, not cunning or sorrowful, but a combination of features gazing at her with the undiscovered strength of an old soul.

Leaning in, she examined her complexion: neither the pure white of the Master's dinner plates nor the char black of her mother's hearth. Her skin had the varnished hue of unspun flax powdered with freckles. Everything about her seemed delicate except for her feet, which were flat and broad, having never been corralled by shoes. She ran her hands over her budding chest and fingered her protruding ribs, observing her limbs, appraising her parts and their connection to the whole.

Then the horror of her days rushed back at her.

It began on a hot South Carolina day in 1841, an event that would shape all of her days to come.

The night was young, the morning had come early, and the four o'clock bell tolled for the day to begin. Field workers rose from their shabby bedding, stooped and bent like under-watered plants. With the listlessness of slow starvation, they gathered their baskets and hoes and shuffled barefoot into the predawn rows of cotton. Each carried a small pouch of cornmeal soaked in water for the midday meal, never enough for tilling 583 yards in the dawn-to-dark days of labor.

The tabby crew had already begun making the cement, swinging their mallets behind Fredericka's hut, crushing piles of oyster shells. Others tended the smoky burn piles, reducing the crushed mounds to lime. A third crew was busy mixing the lime with water, sand, and other shells to make concrete for foundations and walls and columns. The order for concrete work promoted rumors the Master might build newer huts with floors off the ground, sturdy chimneys instead of stick-builts, roofs that didn't leak, and walls that didn't let in the draft. Rumors without promise, but false hope was better than no hope.

Fredericka had carried pails of grain to the horses and mules, fed the pigs, and drove the cows to pasture before hurrying out to the cotton field. At fourteen, she was a three-fourth hand, worth three-quarters of full labor, who had twelve rows to till every day. The blisters on her young hands were reminders of the drivers' scolding, "a child who don't work got no value."

The clay ground was hot and hard, and the sun boiled everything. The only salt she ever tasted was the sweat on

Danuta Pfeiffer

her skin. Hunger cramped her hollow insides, and food was always on her mind, even if dinner was the same boiled cotton seeds thickened with cornmeal. Scarce fuel favoring quantity over quality, a diet that fills the belly but betrays the body. The belly was all that mattered now. Like everything else on the plantation, Fredericka was part of the muscles for the field and bones for the grave.

She worked fast enough that day to finish her task before sunset. She took to her small pleasure of wandering through the gardens, tipping her fingers over the magnolia blossoms and the yellow jessamine, and tucking new seeds in her pocket. That was her secret—a collection of seeds hidden in a tin pot. She loved the whirling butterflies with its tall spires of pink flowers spinning in the wind and the white-flowered lantana.

Her favorite was sage in all its colors—red, purple, blue, and yellow—a handsome flower tall enough to kiss and with a perfume that spoke of magic. Though she didn't know any of their names and couldn't read or write, she drew their pictures on slips of paper foraged from the garbage and wrapped the seeds in bits of burlap and cloth. Each tiny spore gave a dormant hope for a sunny flower or a plump tomato. These were her prized possessions, seeds awaiting a new season.

That season hadn't come. It might never come, but Fredericka would know it if it did. It would arrive like a lost relative, a familiar face of someone she had never met. Still, she'd know them anyway, just like she would know meat even if she never tasted it, or new shoes even if she had never owned a pair, or freedom, even if she had never had it.

She found her spot in a grove of lacy mimosas where the grass was thick, and the air carried the scent of flowers. Flowers reminding her of feathers, of birds, of flying away, where she could almost hear the wind rushing past her ears and she could trace her trail through the clouds. She had slipped an early black-eyed Susan into her pocket, a reminder to draw it later in the hut, and turned to study a single file of ants marching in a tireless line. Curiously, the ants began to scatter in all directions, as though they were puzzled by their journey.

Before Fredericka could detect trouble in their colony, she heard her mother scream her name. The urgency tore across the manicured gardens and through the praying magnolias and bolted Fredericka to her feet. Her Mamma never called her name, not like this.

She raced barefooted, past the stables, past the slave shacks, past the storage sheds, and past the fishy smoke of oyster shells toward the gleaming white columns of the Big House. The air was sullen and flecked with no-see-ums that chewed on her skin, but Fredericka took no notice; she only wanted to find her mother.

By the winding entrance to the mansion, she stopped to scan the grounds. In the twilight, the massive white columns of the sprawling veranda seemed to hold the Grafton Plantation house skyward, signifying the graceful living of the upper-class in the Carolina lowlands. Panic set in when Fredericka spied her mother at the bottom of the steps, rumpled on the ground, hardly distinguishable from a pile of clothing tossed nearby.

"Good girl," Annie said, gasping for breath as Fredericka helped her stagger to her feet.

Her mother had never looked disheveled before, but now her calico dress was torn and her apron undone, her white head wrap crumpled in the dirt, and her hair a fright of wild wires. Blood streamed from her temple.

Fredericka's balance faltered. "Mamma? Mamma?" she asked. Even to a plantation child, born and raised on blood and blisters, she could not absorb her mother's crisis.

Annie wanted to believe in balance, even at the cost of pretending. That was all she could give her daughter. The woman tried to straighten her apron and give purpose to her bewildered hands. She retrieved her turban with a groan. "C'mon, now," Annie said as her hands fought against the knot that tied the ends together.

Fredericka tried to help, but Annie insisted, "I have it. Just a knot."

"What happened, Mamma?" Fredericka asked, fearing the answer.

Annie concentrated on untying the knot on her head wrap and did not look up. "Child, you know how I told you I was a 'particular' house servant?"

The girl nodded, staring at her mother's hands tearing at the fabric.

"Masta' Frederick Grafton, he your daddy, and our masta', right?"

Fredericka nodded.

"He own this here plantation, right?"

Fredericka bobbed her head again.

"Well now, Masta', he say, now time for you to be his particular." Annie tried to sound casual, but her voice caught in her throat. "You understand, child?"

Fredericka shook her head, no.

Annie picked up the bundle of clothes from the ground and faced Fredericka. "Time now for you to wear a head wrap, like your Mamma. And a long dress, like me. You fourteen years now. Time for you to be a woman. Masta' say you no longer little now." She extended the clothes to her daughter.

"Mamma, what you sayin'?" Fredericka fingered her homespun jumper, searching for the black-eyed Susan she had picked earlier, but it had hidden into the seam of her pocket. One part of her brain struggled to remember what the flower looked like, while another part scrambled to understand her mother's meaning.

Annie offered the bundle of clothes again. "You put on this here dress, apron, an' head wrap, an' you do what Masta' Grafton say. That way, we stays together. Masta' say you shoo the flies off him at night, and he won't sell us."

Darkness had closed in, but every sense in Fredericka's body was on high alert and accentuated. The nocturnal arias of crickets had become shrill, and the throated drumming of frogs throbbed in her head. A cockroach scratched across the ground, and despite the suffocating heat, Fredericka felt cold.

"Shoo the flies, Mamma?"

"That's right. When he call, do as he say. An' then, just close your eyes and shoo the flies off him. Masta' Grafton say he keep us together this way." Annie searched Fredericka's face, begging for understanding behind the words.

Fredericka didn't want to understand, but whatever her mother meant, she recognized danger lurked in that duty. "But I don't wanna shoo the flies, Mamma."

Annie's voice was hoarse but as fierce as her fingers clenching Fredericka's shoulders. "You wanna get the whip? You want scars like your mamma? You wanna get us sold at auction? Standin' on a wood box, all greased up and shiny in pig fat and naked with White men puttin' they fingers in your mouth, checkin' your teeth, or up your privates? Listen, child, I not in the Big House no more. You is."

Fighting back the tears that would only frighten her daughter more, Annie dabbed at the blood on her face with the fringe of her apron. Her tone softened as she explained with false assurance, "We just tradin' places. Thas all, just tradin' places. You get to live in the Big House and eat all the food you want. I go to the field."

"But…"

"Ain't no buts, now. You gotta do as you told, you hear, or else we be in a heap a trouble. You put on this here dress. And you shoo the flies anytime he say. You wait for him to come and give a little cough. Means he hot. Means he want you to cool him off. You got that? Just close your eyes. You got a special gift, child. You sees the world different. Use that way. He be done with you soon enough."

Annie caressed her daughter's freckled face, stained with tears. "Is not what I want for you child, but when the Good Lord made you pretty, almost White, with them green eyes, it a curse for sure. I try hard to change Masta' Grafton mind. But he be drinkin' something awful, put the devilment in his head. He kick me down the steps, 'bout kilt me. So you do as he say, and we be safe."

Her mother's words fell upon Fredericka like cold, hard rain as her childhood dissolved. Was it only moments ago she reveled in the scent of flowers and the dream of wings?

"C'mon now, let's get you dressed," Annie said. "He waitin'."

As Annie dressed her daughter, a shadow on the verandah moved and melted into the darkness of the Big House. Waiting.

Horace

⟨⟨⟨⟩⟩⟩

orace could read, a rarity for a young Black man, even more so for a former slave. He was purchased as a toddler to provide companionship for Spencer Redburn's young son, Jonathan. Redburn was a widowed multimillionaire who made his early money in the fur trade. The pelt of beavers built his Skylark Hotel, New York's finest, complete with running water. The family occupied an entire floor in the hotel where he raised the boys. Nannies and tutors taught Jonathan and Horace to read and write, and the boys challenged each other in the skills of arithmetic, French and Latin.

Inseparable playmates, they could sometimes be found playing hide-and-seek with the hotel staff, or with Jonathan's father. "Ready or not, here I come!" Spencer would call out, pretending to search high and low. A giggle from Horace or Jonathan, and Spencer would pull back a curtain. "Got you!" he'd say.

"Oh, sir, let us hide again!" Horace would plead.

"Yes, please, Father," Jonathan would say, laughing. "Another round!"

Their favorite game was stealing apples. They'd sneak the fruit from the kitchen, roll the apples down the long hotel hallways, and bat them with sticks in creative games of croquet. They used Latin to conspire against the adults by waging battles behind chairs and camping under tables. When scolded or trundled off to bed or frightening an imaginary foe, their call to arms was, "*Sic semper tyrannis!* Thus always to tyrants!"

"*Adiuva* me," Jonathan would shout as he lashed out with his wooden sword. "Help me, Horace! The tyrant is upon us!"

By the time the boys turned nine, Jonathan was due for boarding school and college, and although the state of New York had outlawed slavery six years earlier, Horace had remained on as part of the family. The sting of reality was that Horace would not be joining his friend at school.

Redburn tried reasoning with his son. "Jonathan, you know that's not practical. Horace is…"

"Colored, Father?" Jonathan's expression soured. "He's like my brother."

"You know I don't think of him as Colored. He's part of the family. It's just that he wouldn't fit in with all the other boys. Where would they put him? Where would he sleep?"

"He can sleep in my room! I won't go if Horace doesn't go."

"That will do, Jonathan. You're going to Princeton, and Horace is staying here with me. I promised your mother, may she rest in peace, that you'd get an education. I'm not going back on my word, and that's final. Horace'll be waiting for you when you get back."

The night before Jonathan left, the boys sat on the edge of Jonathan's bed, bags already packed and sitting on the floor. "I wanted you to come with me," Jonathan said, swinging his feet.

"Yeah," Horace said. "But I heard them talking in the kitchen, and Cook said nobody is going to let a house nigger go to school."

"She shouldn't have said that," Jonathan said, but they both knew Cook was right.

From a small knapsack on the floor, Jonathan pulled out a little gray book. "I want you to have this."

"Your Latin book?" Horace gently held it in his hands. "We'll write to each other in Latin. Our secret code."

⁓⁓

FOR THE NEXT EIGHT YEARS, HORACE REMAINED CIRcumscribed by his status as "a private butler," as Redburn described him. Horace consumed the books from Redburn's vast library, determined to educate himself, and corresponded with Jonathan, practicing their secret Latin code. Jonathan came home for vacations and holidays, but as the years wore on, Jonathan's letters and visits became less frequent.

Although formal education was not Horace's birthright, Redburn took pleasure in showing off his literate Negro as a testament to his progressive ideals. He had Horace parrot Shakespeare and poetry to the amusement of New York's elite at grand galas and dinner parties.

During one of these entertainments, Horace had a fateful encounter with a plantation owner.

It happened one night after dinner. Redburn and his hotel guest, Frederick Grafton, were lighting up cigars. Redburn called for brandy. "Bring the good stuff, Horace."

Horace appeared with a handblown glass bottle with a pale yellow label. "Renaud & Dualle, 1795, sir?"

"My boy knows a good calvados," Redburn said, laughing. "Straight from Normandy. Bought it directly from their wine merchants. What do you say about that, Horace?" He was a man in his fifties whose starched high collar seemed to be permanently affixed to his chin. He dug his thumb into his red-and-black paisley vest, and took another puff off his cigar; the smoke of his satisfaction dissipated into a gauzy cloud above his head.

"Just as you say, Master Redburn, some of the finest apple brandy in the world, sir."

Horace poured a few ounces into two crystal goblets. He cut a dynamic figure, leading with his shoulders as his arms caught up with the motion of pouring. In his gray suit and white shirt, but for his caramel complexion, a casual observer might have thought Horace was himself a dinner guest. His features were amplified by a certain self-confidence which did not go unnoticed by Grafton, who studied him for a long moment.

Horace set the drinks on a silver tray and served the men who were seated by the fireplace. He then took a position in the room just out of sight and ready for any additional needs.

Grafton clutched his goblet and raised it above his head. "A toast! To a man who spares no expense!" He unbuttoned his waistcoat, liberating the meaty paunch of a well-fed man, and swigged down the brandy.

Redburn responded, "And to you, sir, welcome to the Skylark."

The two men sat back in their velvet chairs, smoking cigars, taking in their comforts. The fireplace cast a warm glow upon the dim room—the flickering light from matching Italian torchères animated the walls filled with fine Japanese prints. A massive French tapestry muted by antiquity and embraced by a gilded frame filled an entire wall. In the corner, a Ming vase rested on a shelf. Next to these possessions stood Horace. His face, illuminated by the amber light, gleamed like highly polished copper.

"So, what brings you to New York, Grafton?" Redburn asked, pouring himself and his guest another brandy.

"Niggers for the plantation, Redburn. The rats are off the ship up North here, escaped slaves from the South runnin' free through the streets, taking jobs from good Christians, infecting White culture. Well, I like to say, the slave drain is my gain. I need every last nigger I can catch. I buy 'em cheap and sell by the dozen. Gotta business to run. Cotton prices are high, but slave labor—now there's the future."

"New York is a free state, Grafton. No slaves here."

"Free state, you say? Ha! I have my constitutional rights. The Fugitive Slave Clause. A slave is a slave even if they escape to a free state. And the Fugitive Slave Act gives me every right to hunt down escapees. You know that as well as I do."

"Even if they're not yours?"

"Hell, Redburn, who cares if they're mine or not? A sign of a pen and the law takes my word for it."

"That's tantamount to legalized kidnapping. Northern states don't take kindly to bounty hunters."

"Tell that to the judge. I have eight men hunting the streets now and a wagonload of darkies ready to transport South. I don't see anyone giving me crap for it."

"How many slaves do you own now?" Redburn flicked his cigar in a bronze ashtray on the side table.

"Three hundred, give or take. Numbers vary, dependin' on the breedin' program. Sold twenty-some pickaninnies last year. All fine stock from one to fifteen-year-olds. Try to get 'em just after they're weaned most times—that way, they don't get stuck to their mammies. More loyal to their owners. More manageable that way. Sometimes I wonder if I'm selling coons by the bushel or cotton," Grafton said, snickering. "And it comes with benefits. I got myself a host of "elbow relations" as you might call 'em in polite society, out of the pretty ones, you know, the concubines, if you get my drift."

Horace bowed his head, ever so slightly.

"Nasty business." Redburn shook his head. "Abolition rules New York. Times are changing, even for the South."

"Nonsense, Redburn. South Carolina has thrived on the economics of slavery for two hundred years. Had us nearly six million darkies come through Charleston harbor alone. It's good business."

"I understand the business aspect of slavery, but opponents here made their arguments—fortune and misery were synonymous with wealth and privilege. Made New York prosperity look bad. We were forced to make hard economic decisions back in '27. Like it or not, slavery's outlawed here." Redburn tapped at the ashes from his cigar.

"Not in the South, Redburn. Hell, niggers float the boat for the whole damned economy. Pickin' cotton, breedin', and sales. That's what they're for—muscle and rough work. It's all they know. They're dumb as mules and just as stubborn. The savages need White folks just to keep 'em alive, ain't that right, Horace?" The warmth of the room and the brandy had turned Grafton's cheeks crimson, and he loosened his cravat.

"Not so," Redburn said. "Horace reads and writes, recites poetry. Come over here and recite something for our guest, Horace."

Horace quickly took his place between the two men. Eager to prove himself and directly addressing Grafton, he asked, "Anything, in particular, you want to hear, sir? A sonnet? Shakespeare, perhaps?"

Grafton's eyes narrowed to slivers. "I don't like niggers staring me in the face, boy."

Cowed by the snarl, Horace averted his eyes to the ground. "Sorry, sir. Yessir."

"But go ahead, recite somethin'. Let's see how good you really are," Grafton said.

Unaccustomed to the Southern demands of submission, Horace almost whispered now, "I learned a new poem by Percy Shelley." He paused.

"Well, go on then, let's hear it," Grafton said, gulping down more cognac.

Horace began softly, still staring at the floor, but his voice rose with each line:

I met a traveler from an antique land
Who said: "Two vast and trunkless legs of stone
Stand in the desert…Near them, on the sand,
Half sunk, a shattered visage lies, whose frown,
And wrinkled lip, and sneer of cold command,
Tell that its sculptor well those passions read
Which yet survive, stamped on these lifeless things,
The hand that mocked them and the heart that fed:

And on the pedestal these words appear:
'My name is Ozymandias, king of kings:
Look on my works, ye Mighty, and despair!'
Nothing beside remains. Round the decay
Of that colossal wreck, boundless and bare
The lone and level sands stretch far away.

The walls resonated with Horace's sonorous tone, and the poet's warning hovered in the air.

"A colossal wreck, boy? Who's a colossal wreck?" Grafton rose and strode toward Horace—the plantation owner's bulbous face tipping up at Horace.

The butler's stature took Grafton by surprise, as if he recognized the dimensions of a large tree only after leaning against the trunk. This factor ruffled Grafton even more.

"Just a poem, sir, that's all, just a poem by Shelley. People can interpret it as they wish." Horace plowed his eyes into the floor.

"That'll be all, Horace." Redburn dismissed him with a wave of his cigar.

"Well now, he's one uppity nigger, ain't he?" Grafton clenched his cigar in his teeth, and made his way back to his chair, eyeballing Horace, who melted back into the room's shadows. "I don't cotton to niggers readin'. Spoils a good nigger. Makes 'em unfit. Makes 'em discontented and unmanageable. No tellin' where that leads."

"Bought him when he was a pup." Redburn took a sniff of his brandy. "After my wife died, I purchased Horace from a trader such as yourself as my son's companion. He's a good boy. Kept him on after manumission."

"So, how many slaves did you have?" Grafton asked.

"Well, Horace," Redburn said. "And I kept a stable of sixty or so Coloreds for the Skylark here. But now, I pay wages and room and board." Redburn chuckled and poured another drink.

Grafton pushed his back into the soft cushion of his chair, giving a spread to his voluminous belly. "City slaves were a spendy proposition, no doubt about that. Had to feed 'em regular, clothe 'em. Hell, they practically had the privileges of freemen compared to plantation slaves." Under his breath, "Some city slaves just needed a good nigger-breaker to put 'em in their place."

Then Grafton made his move. "How much you want to sell him for?"

The equilibrium in the room shifted, and the pause that followed lasted long enough to stop Horace from breathing.

Grafton

⸺⧼⧽⸺

He came in the night, a dark silhouette in the doorway. He cleared his throat. Fredericka clutched her blanket. Maybe if she didn't move, he might think she wasn't there. He stood for agonizing minutes, and then he was gone. Night after night, Fredericka didn't know what frightened her more, the shadow of him, or the reality of what was to come.

During the day was no better. Whether she was in the kitchen or cleaning out the fireplace, he prowled around her, coughing into his handkerchief. When he came close, he murmured foul words that made her cringe and always ended with, "Don't make me wait, child."

He didn't wait long. As usual, he stood in the closet doorway where Fredericka huddled on her cot, and he made the same small cough into his handkerchief. Fredericka still refused to move, but this time, he didn't disappear. His dark shadow grew into the room, soaring above her. Fredericka shielded herself with her blanket. The shadow bent over her. A hand wriggled between her legs. The shock jolted her upright on her cot, legs curled beneath her.

Then, the dark whisper, "Come on, now, all I want is a little sugar." The hot, wet silt of his tongue licked her neck. She squirmed further back on her cot, wiping his slime off with the back of her hand.

Danuta Pfeiffer

In an instant, he was on her. Fredericka clawed at him, kicking and scratching as they tumbled to the floor. He was on top of her. His weight pinned her down and crushed her lungs. His face smeared hers with sweat and the sour stink of whiskey and smoke. His hands fumbled between her thighs. She turned her head and bit his face, nipping his lip. He flicked back just enough for her to twist out from under him and scramble to the wall, breathless, wide-eyed, and nowhere to run.

He sat opposite her, breathing hard. His shirt was open, pants undone, bloated belly heaving with every word. "Ain't you a little cherry?" He licked his bleeding lip. "I'll teach you to bite!" He grabbed her leg and yanked her toward him.

She let out a soft cry and then closed her eyes. Above her, the sky roared blue. Instead of the stale smell of whiskey and sweat that engulfed her, she inhaled the honeyed perfume of flowers, reminding her of feathers, of flying away. From that dark room, she could almost trace the sanctuary trail through the clouds and the wind rushing past as she flew away.

The Bet

⸺⸱⸱⸱⸺

Redburn didn't like him. Grafton was an uneducated, ill-bred man who slugged brandy as if it were grog and he reeked of a rancid odor. But he had money, lots of it, enough to make Redburn overlook his contempt.

"Horace is not for sale," Redburn said.

"But every nigger has its price. Even for a man who spares no expense."

Redburn wafted out a slow curl of smoke from his cigar. "Not Horace. He's like a son to me. Been a free man for years since abolition."

"Holy Mother of God!" Grafton slapped his knee. "I'd sell my own nigger daughter for the right price. Come, Redburn, you're a gambling man, made a lot of money betting on furs and land. If you don't want to sell him, how about a wager? Or have you lost your nerve?" Grafton pulled out a stack of playing cards from his waistcoat and waved them in the air.

Horace felt the ground beneath his feet begin to sway. He transferred his weight from one foot to another, fixed on every word.

"You want another slave that badly?" Redburn leaned back and took another puff on his cigar.

"Just that one." Grafton sneered at Horace.

"It's against New York law."

Danuta Pfeiffer

"Look Redburn, you and me, we're some of the biggest toads in the puddle. We understand business opportunities. The law is of no circumstance to men like us."

"Still, the law is the law."

"Dang it, man, the law is for poor critters who don't have the balls to rise above it. Wealth is power. That's what makes men like us special." Grafton stood and poured himself another healthy shot of brandy.

Redburn tasted an acrid bile creep into his throat, but managed a grimace disguised as a smile. "I'd rather think of my position as noblesse oblige," he said. "The obligation of one in a high station to act honorably to others."

Grafton flopped back in his chair. "You can take all that noblesse shit and hang it." He took a swig of his drink. "Don't tell me, you ain't never cut corners, a little horn-swoggle here and there. Never got caught."

Redburn thought about the man he cheated out of the New York plot for his hotel, about the underpaid builders, and the favors he paid for under the table. "Perhaps, to an extent," he said, "But…"

Grafton pushed on. "Then, after a while, you probably done bigger and badder things that ain't necessarily legal but you told yourself it was just good business."

"But wagering a free man…"

"A slap on the wrist, a pilfering fine. Most of the time, the law looks the other way. Shit, we're untouchable! Besides, with blackbirders and kidnappers prowling around, darkies disappear from New York streets every day. Get sold downriver. And I'll bet you ain't never raised a ruckus about that before."

"Well, no, but…"

"No buts about it. Wealth is our religion. We're the Church of the Privileged, outside the reach of common law. We follow our own doctrine. And government don't interfere. Hell, we can follow laws we think are right, but if the law goes against our gain, we can ignore it. I say go the whole hog, man, if you got the grit."

"I have no deficit of grit, sir."

Horace listened from the corner of the room, as still as the peasants woven into the wall tapestry. His mouth had gone dry, but he dared not go for water fearing he'd awaken the wolves in the room to his presence. But the wolves were ready for meat.

Grafton leaned forward. "Then let's liquor on it." He lifted his glass in a toast. "I'll wager ten thousand dollars against your nigger."

Redburn stared at Grafton. Horace struggled against gravity. And the grandfather clock drummed out the seconds.

Grafton seized upon Redburn's hesitation. "You've got little to lose, just that boy over there, but a lot to gain."

"You have a point," Redburn said. The room was warm. The stakes were high. He could win either way. "But what's in it for you?"

"If I win, I get a chance to break a horse I want to ride. If I lose…" Grafton shrugged. "I get the satisfaction of knowing I'm no damned coward." He bit down on his cigar, and with a menacing glance at Horace, began to shuffle the cards.

Redburn shot up out of his chair. "If you are suggesting that cowardice precedes my reluctance to your wager, you are mistaken, sir!"

"Not at all, Redburn. I was simply speakin' for myself. I meant no disrespect." Grafton continued shuffling the cards.

Redburn began to pace. "Well then, as a gentleman, and I too mean no disrespect, how do I know you're not going to cheat?"

His nerves were running north and south, head to heel, excitement triggering small explosions of adrenaline. A game was afoot and with it the scent of risk and the delicious defiance of defeat. These were the thrills of his success, the addictive pleasures of the hunt. He was not about to lose face to this Southern scum. And at worst, all he had to lose was Horace. Grafton knew he had him. He'd seen men like Redburn before, whose conceit was only of value in his rival's eyes, achieved with a generous display of bravado. Now was such a time for this pompous New Yorker, Grafton thought to himself, when honor is corrupted, allegiance is forsaken, and money talks. He'd played this game a dozen times before with his own cards that were sure to stack the deck in his favor.

"No disrespect taken." Grafton rose and slapped his deck of cards on a large round table in the center of the room. "Let's have Horace deal the cards." The bait was set.

Redburn fixed his eyes on Grafton. He could smell blood in the water, but it sure as hell wasn't going to be his. "Horace!" He barked for his servant.

Horace crept forward, posture buckled, knees unable to lock, his anxious gaze unsure where to land. "Mr. Redburn, sir," he whispered, "I'm a free man. Don't do this, sir, I beg you. Think of Jonathan. We're like brothers. Master, please!"

Redburn and Grafton faced each other like two gunslingers twitching at their pistols, ignoring the man's plea.

"Poker. Five-card draw. One hand. All or nothing," Grafton said, pulling his chair to the table.

"You have the money?" Redburn asked.

"You know I'm good for it."

"Deal," Redburn said, dragging his chair to the opposite side of the table.

"But, sir!" Horace clasped his hands together. "Please!"

"Cut the cards. And deal, damn it." Redburn kept his eyes drilled on Grafton.

Grinning through his cigar, Grafton thumped his fingers on the table.

Horace inched forward. He reached for the cards, clenching and unclenching his hand as if the cards would bite. Dizzy with dread, he divided the stack in half.

In a flat, controlled voice, Redburn said, "Now Horace, deal the cards. One at a time to each of us, until we each have five cards."

The muddy haze of cigar smoke engulfed the scene in the sickly sweet scent of that male hormone. Avarice and ego devoured the walls until all that remained constant and true lay in the balance of the cards.

A small bead of sweat trickled down the side of Horace's face. Hands unsure, he dealt the cards—each card falling to the table in a slap of humiliation, each an indictment against dignity. Grafton and Redburn had passed the threshold of that virtue and took up their cards, their faces stony. Horace stood between them, his heart pausing in its rhythm as these men, slaves to their own vapid lives, sought refuge from their tedium in a game for his freedom.

"Give me three cards, Horace," Redburn said, disposing of three from his hand.

"I'll take two," Grafton said.

Horace scanned each man—one, and then the other— desperate to learn his fate.

Almost imperceptibly, Grafton parted his lips and leered at Redburn over his cards. Redburn did not return his gaze but stared hard at his hand.

Grafton laid down first. One card at a time. Redburn sagged. He had taken the bait, hook, line, and sinker, and all that was left was the reeling in. He dropped his cards on the table.

Grafton gave out a whoop.

"Master Redburn?" Horace cried. "Did you lose me?" He picked up the cards, trying to decipher his fate in the clubs and diamonds. "What do they say?"

In a time like this, it takes guts for a man not to show remorse for a self-inflicted wound, and Redburn was not about to offer Grafton that satisfaction. If he sensed that Grafton had cheated, he was not about to lower himself to make that accusation. He got what he bargained for—nothing. Redburn sniffed. "Wasn't in the cards for me today, Horace." He stood, stamped out his cigar in the ashtray, and left the room with a singular thought: how to explain to Jonathan that he lost Horace to a game of cards.

Pocketing his cards in his jacket, Grafton swiveled around to face Horace. "They say a pair is at the losing end of a jack-high straight. They say you're mine, nigger!"

Half an hour later, Horace was in shackles.

Henrietta

⊶⊷

Henrietta Grafton married Frederick two decades earlier, and she still attended the same church where they were married. As a devout Christian, she occupied her pew up front, nearer to God and the gospel. This position also allowed for visibility. The Graftons loved to be seen as pious and prompt for the morning service, steadfastly arriving half an hour early to greet neighbors and friends, as though the couple owned the stones and stairs of God's house. They may well have owned them, consistently out-tithing the other congregants so their name always topped the church's annual donor ledger. No one would dispute the Graftons' fervent adherence to the Holy Book and the church. For Henrietta, the church was her sole purpose.

Henrietta was the daughter of an itinerant preacher who often preached the medicinal value of gin. Hawking its effects against scurvy and malaria compensated him for the time spent spreading the gospel. Her disturbed mother, on the other hand, displayed both cruelty and neglect toward her child. At a young age, Henrietta vowed she would never marry a man who imbibed spirits, and she would never be like her mother. She failed on both counts. Compounding these failings, a miscarriage, and her inability to have children doused whatever dreams Henrietta may have had for Frederick's love and devotion. She lost those dreams in her bitter well of self-reproach. What was the necessity of the marital bed if there were to be no children? The church, then, offered her a single-mindedness, an identity, and a safely guarded position of respect in the ranks of the faithful, a position not to be found without the pure force of her will at Grafton Manor and Plantation.

Henrietta knew about Frederick's proclivities, as if he tried to hide them from her. She told herself she didn't mind that he took out his hankerings with the slaves, relieving her of such indignities. She said to herself she didn't even care if nigger babies came from some of those "happenstances." However, she loathed seeing the cream-skinned chattels clinging to their mothers' breasts, flagrant reminders of her husband's infidelities and weakness. And her barren womb.

The slave traders were more than willing to buy the mulatto children, and sometimes their mothers, which made for an unspoken pact between her and Frederick. He could have his dalliances with his Negro whores, and she could sell them once they left the house. She didn't mind, she told herself.

But she did mind, very much, the day Fredericka moved into the mansion. She carried the same name as her husband, her golden skin glowing with the pretense of whiteness, her hair bobbing on her shoulders. She hated the way the girl moved through the house, pilfering her husband's affections. Fredericka was Henrietta's greatest humiliation, by far. He was obsessed with the slave girl, watching Fredericka, following her, whispering in her ear. On too many nights, Henrietta heard his drunken footsteps shuffling down the hallway and the muffled sounds coming from the closet. She hated the girl for it—for all the longing, and all the years Henrietta had become invisible and powerless around Frederick until all she had was the appearance of propriety. But power was something she craved, like water to thirst, and her desire to feel the tingle of vitality came at the expense of the lives around her.

That's why she sold Annie. The day the slave traders made their rounds couldn't come fast enough for the plantation's mistress. Frederick had already culled his crop of those slaves he could do without and still get a decent return. He did not need a dozen misshapen, damaged, or otherwise bothersome Africans either too young to be serviceable or too old to work the fields. And Annie was like a bad dream. Henrietta had wanted to get rid of that black nightmare for years. She had made a show of it too. Calling Annie from the fields on a pretense of needing her at the house. Making sure Annie's whore of a daughter, Fredericka, would watch as the mistress of Grafton Plantation staunchly asserted her role. She was unmoved by her chattels' wails and tears as the traders loaded them into the cart. She smiled into their misery as Annie pleaded, "But Masta' promised! He promised!"

Henrietta found comfort in knowing that by sheer force of her will, she could provoke intensity. She took great pleasure watching Fredericka suffer after her mother—grasping her flailing hands, running along with the cartwheels, crying out, "I talk to Masta', Mamma! I get you back!"

Henrietta knew her husband would not dare interfere. Indeed, he showed little remorse when the slave cart rolled down the carriageway, choosing to turn his back on the scene, closing the door behind him. Henrietta had shown them all who was really in charge.

Fredericka ran after the cart as it rattled down the road until the cart became smaller. The knot loosened, and when the carriage finally disappeared, the tie to her mother came undone.

Now, only hollowness followed the girl, the days and nights knitting into an endless weave of despair. That didn't stop Henrietta from flexing her fist upon Fredericka when she thought her husband wasn't around.

"Fredericka!" Henrietta sat on the settee with a teacup in her lap, drumming her index finger on the saucer.

The girl hastened into the room.

"The tea is cold."

Fredericka made a move toward the side table and the teapot just as Henrietta swatted the tray, sending the china crashing into bits against the wall.

"Now look what you've done." Henrietta rose and dropped her teacup into the shattered clutter.

"Sorry, missus." Fredericka's anxiety was on display as she knelt and began to scoop up the pieces into her apron.

"Stop that and bring me a bucket of water," Henrietta ordered. "A big bucket."

A few minutes later, Fredericka came back, lugging a five-gallon bucket of water, and placed it next to Henrietta.

"I'll teach you to bring me cold tea." Henrietta had an odd smile that twisted up one side of her mouth. "Now drink it," she said.

"Missus?" Fredericka reached for the seeds in her pocket, scrambling them with her fingertips.

"You heard me, drink it. All of it."

"But…"

Henrietta pointed at the large wooden container. "Drink! Or so help me God, I will lash you with the cowhide until blood puddles at your feet. Now drink!"

Fredericka knelt and cupped her hand in the water.

"Not with your hands, with your face—get your face in there and drink!"

Fredericka hesitated, trying to understand the order, and then put her face to the water and pecked at it. She accidentally inhaled and reared up, coughing and choking. Before she could catch her breath, Henrietta grabbed Fredericka by her hair and shoved her head back into the tub. Choking and panicking, Fredericka involuntarily inhaled again. Her lungs flooded, and the water frothed about her head. She tried screaming, but more water filled her mouth, nose, and throat. She flailed her arms, clutching her hands for air, but the woman held her down. The edge of the bucket cut into Fredericka's chest; her legs scraped at the floor.

Henrietta, now on her knees, shoved Fredericka's head down even further. Fredericka's flailing began to slow, and her arms slumped. She could not fight death. It would come. Darkness swarmed through her, and in that obscurity, the slow dissolution of pain, a dull ache, and a curious lightness of being and in a sublime moment, the sweet sense of letting go.

And Henrietta began to sing: *Nearer, my God, to thee!*

The Bucket

⚬⚬⚬

Fredericka felt gravity give way. She was cradled high above the earth, against the swirling sky, toward her bright path through the clouds. Rocking gently home. Feathers.

"Sweet child," a whispered chant called her back, "Sweet child..." But she would not be found in these cool drifting ethers; she would not succumb to that hard and heavy ground.

"Sweet child." Again the beckoning call and an elusive tug to see what lay below: a body, somewhat pretty but lacking radiance, a wet strand of hair across a pale cheek. Two men attended a dead girl. A White man moaned, "Sweet child!" while an African kneeled, bearing the girl up, rocking her torso, pounding at her back. Pounding, pounding her back.

Why do they rush so? What do they want? Why should I care? But they seem to care.

She slipped from her lofty harness. *A closer look would do no harm.* The White man had become quiet. Why did she know him? The African persisted with a strange sense of passion. His face glowed like a copper pot. He swiped the hair from the girl's face with a gentle purpose. Who was this Colored man with the soft hands who shored her up so relentlessly? *A closer look would do no harm.*

A sudden burn of air shocked her lungs. Gravity resumed its agonizing pull, and an excruciating weight descended upon her. Sensation and pain. Sputtering and choking. Clutching the African's arm for all her life, she breathed.

"She'll be alright now, Master Grafton," Horace said. Gently resting Fredericka's head down, he whispered, "You'll be alright now." His eyes washed over Fredericka, who clung to his arm as if by letting go, she might fly away again.

"Good, good," Grafton said, patting Horace's shoulder, both men smiled at each other, forgetting for a moment all place and privilege. No sooner had he done so, Grafton jerked his hand away as if he had inadvertently placed it over a flame.

"Don't think I'm going to take it easy on you, boy, just because you happened to be in the room here." His words came out tight and hard. "You're going to the fields, and I'm going to work you hard."

Grafton had only just arrived at the mansion with Horace, his poker prize, when he heard the commotion in the living room and found Henrietta singing. His sweet Fredericka was drowning in the bucket.

"What have you done?" he hollered at his wife, who was still on her knees, holding the slave girl's head down. He shoved Henrietta aside, careening her backward on her rump, her black dress and petticoats tossing in the air like an upturned weed. At that moment, he could only think of the motionless girl, his sweet child. He knelt on one knee, and with great tenderness, scooped Fredericka up and cradled her in his arms. Her limp body seemed weightless and insubstantial; her hair dripping wet, soaked into his shirt. A painful ache tore through him, a raw and unaccustomed sentiment he could not name, a vulnerability that made him breathless and, for the first time in his life, uncertain.

"I might be able to help, sir." Horace was standing at the doorway.

"Then, for God's sake, help her!" Grafton wheezed, gently laying Fredericka back on the floor.

"Let me loose, sir, and let me try." Horace held his cuffed hands toward the overwrought man.

Freed from his bonds, Horace pummeled the girl's back and rocked her back and forth like a rag doll, as Grafton called out to Fredericka, over and over, "Sweet child, sweet child!"

Days later, Fredericka drifted in and out of consciousness. Feverish hours mingled with voices and faces hovered above her and collided back into nightmares of suffocation and engulfing rivers of water. By the fourth day, she awoke to find herself in a real bed with a feather mattress in a large room with a window. She pulled back the covers and slipped out of bed. She fingered her long, clean cotton gown. Stepping to the window, she peered below to see giant magnolia trees and beyond, small wooden huts, and people feeding pigs.

Her days and nights came flooding back to her. *I'm in the Big House, in the guest room, wearing Missus's gown! What if they find me here?* She stripped off the nightdress to search for her clothes, and for the first time, saw all of herself in the mirror, a stranger in the looking glass. Fredericka had never seen herself in a mirror before, had never seen herself all in one piece. She shot a glance around the room, as if she needed permission, as if her own reflection were forbidden. This was not the watery image of her face in the creek. This was all of her. She touched her auburn hair and examined her freckled, not exactly White face. She brought her hands to her chest and stomach, and observed her legs, appraising her parts and their connection to the whole.

The moment passed quickly as the horror of the past tumbled upon her. She couldn't be caught here. She rummaged through the closet and under the bed, searching for her own rags.

Just then, Martha, the cook, walked into the room carrying a tray of food. "Child," she said, putting down the tray and retrieving the nightgown, "Get yourself back into bed before Masta' sees you all naked. He be thinkin' ole Martha not takin' good care of you, now."

"B-but I don't b-belong here. What's h-happening to m-m-m-me?"

Martha froze with the girl's nightgown in her hand when she heard her stutter. "You had yourself a fright, thas all." Martha quickly tossed the nightgown over Fredericka's head and tucked her back into bed. "You rest now and eat somethin'. Masta' worried somethin' fierce over you. Says you to have the White doctor come lookin' at you every day. Lordy! I ain't never seen a Colored girl treated like a princess. But you is. He say the Missus can't talk to you no more. No sir. She can't lay a hand on you no more."

"B-b-but, what happened?" Fredericka grabbed Martha's arm.

"Girl, you don't remember?" Martha sat on the bedside. "The Missus, she done try to drown you, thas what. And Masta' Grafton, he done saved your sorry self, thas what."

Fredericka struggled for words. "He saved m-m-m-me?"

⸺※⸺

GRAFTON HAD MADE SEVERAL DECISIONS. TO PUNISH his wife for abusing his favorite slave in his absence, he had Fredericka installed into the mansion's guest bedroom until the girl recovered. Afterward, he decided to move Fredericka into her own cabin near the estate, one he had built especially for her.

The day he showed her the cabin, he made a surprise announcement. Standing in the room's modest center, he tugged on his handkerchief from his waistcoat pocket and wiped his face. Then taking a deep breath, he made his proposal: "I want you to come to me, on your own, Fredericka. I care for you. You know that, don't you? I want you to care for me. Do you think you could do that?"

He spat a wad of tobacco to the side and mustered a smile showing his yellow teeth. Just before stuffing the linen cloth back into his pocket, he made a self-conscious little cough into the hanky. Fredericka squeezed her eyes shut.

"I d-d-don't wan' it." She backed out the door and onto the porch.

"Are you stuttering?"

"Not," she struggled to say, "s-t-ttuterin'."

"Well, hell, I don't mind about any of that," he said, laughing. "I don't need you for c-c-conversation!" Grafton spit a wet brown wad of tobacco between them. "I just want a little companionship every now and then." He threw his arms open. "The whole thing, it's just for you, a nice fireplace, your own rope-cord bed, fresh corn shuck bedding, even some pots and pans. I can get you curtains! You want curtains?" He spit again.

"I don' wan' any of it."

"Now, don't be like that, Sweet Child. Tell me what you want, and I'll get it for you." He moved toward her, but she backed down the wooden steps, leaving him on the porch.

"N-n-n-no." She walked to the shade of a tree where she began to gasp for air. "Can' can' breathe, can' breathe!"

He stomped down the steps and marched toward her. As Fredericka struggled to breathe, Grafton pressed her with his intentions. "But I have everything you want right here." He pointed at the cabin. "You understand, girl, it's for you. My gift to you. It's what I've been working on. All I want is for you to come to me." He pointed his finger to the sky. "I swear to God, I will never force you again, but it's your choice. You live at the mansion with the Missus, or you be with me every now and then. It wouldn't be so bad, would it?" He spit again, tore his hat off his head, and wiggled out a handkerchief, wiping the sweat off his red face.

"Masta." Fredericka tried to gather herself. "I can' do it, s-s-sir. Out here, front of all the people. Watch you come, and g-g-go. Hate me more than they do now. I would rather d-d-d-die."

Grafton slapped his hat on his thigh and placed the straw brimmed hat back on his head. He moved closer to her, chewing his tobacco in her face as if he couldn't choose whether to spit at her or to kiss her. Seconds went by. Then he lifted her chin up to his face. In a raspy, deep-throated voice that rattled her, he said, "You have the most beautiful eyes I've ever seen." Brown spittle collected along a thin line on his lower lip. "And you will move into this cabin, Sweet Child, or you will regret the day I ever pulled you out of that bucket." He hawked the sputum on the ground between them and stalked away.

Fredericka and Horace

Fredericka moved into Grafton's cabin. Although she still worked in the mansion and took precautions to duck out of Grafton's way when she spied him, he had not made any more advances toward her. An uneasy truce.

Someone did catch her eye from time to time, a handsome copper-colored man who occasionally nodded to her. He looked familiar, but she couldn't remember why. One day, just before dusk, Fredericka saw him sitting against the wall of his shack reading a small book. He didn't notice she had walked up beside him.

"Better not let J-J-Jimmi see you readin'," she said, referring to the night watchman. "It not allowed."

Startled at first, but then Horace recognized her, the half-drowned girl from the bucket. Softening his shoulders, he said as casually as he could summon, "Jimmi, that scurvy-ridden excuse for a man? I'm not afraid of him. Besides, I'm not reading. I'm studying."

She liked his voice. "Studyin' what?" She sat next to him.

"Latin," he said, without looking up.

"What that?"

"An old language. The root of all our words."

"What you mean r-r-root?"

"I mean, like a carrot. The greens on top are English words, and the carrot is the root of the words." Horace turned the page in his book without looking up.

"Words are carrots? You talk funny. I ain't never hear a c-c-c-Colored talk like you."

"Ain't isn't a word." He continued reading.

"If it ain't a word, how come people say it?" She giggled. "You so s-s-smart, teach me a word in your Latin. What is freedom?"

Horace looked up from his book and stared into the distance. "That's easy. *Libertas.* In any language, it means sovereignty. I almost had it."

Catching his self-pity, he meant only to glance at Fredericka to see if she registered his lapse of self-confidence. Instead, he drifted into her eyes and fell into them.

"*Libertas,*" Fredericka repeated, staring back at him. A strange sensation welled up in her, and feeling self-conscious, she trilled off a laugh. "Now I know you c-c-crazy with your big words."

Horace broke from his trance, tucked the book into his coarse linen shirt and said, "I am crazy sometimes. Knowing things. Things I've seen. Things I can't have. Sometimes I think it's better to be stupid, like everyone here. I envy their stupidity. They don't know how wretched they are." He hurled a small stone away in frustration. "They haven't had freedom come close and be taken away. I smell freedom in the wind. I see it in every second of every day. Out of reach. I don't wish such torment on anyone."

"I like birds. Sometimes I dream of flyin'. And findin' my Mamma. That's like freedom, ain't it?" She let out an embarrassed chuckle. "You don't think I'm s-s-stupid, do you?"

"It's better you don't think." Horace kicked at the dirt with the back of his heel.

"You sound like a sad b-b-bird."

"Yeah, and you laugh like a hyena." He shot her a frown.

"What's a hyena?" She wasn't sure she liked being compared to something she'd never heard of before.

"It's like a wild dog."

"You think I's like a wild d-d-d-dog?" Fredericka snapped to her feet. "You think you better 'an me, 'cause you can read? Well, you ain't better 'an me or any other Colored here. We're all dogs here—even you."

"No, I only meant you had a high pitch, I didn't mean…" Before he could finish, Fredericka stormed back to her shack, resolving she would never speak to him again.

NIGHTMARES CONTINUED TO HAUNT FREDERICKA. While Grafton hadn't yet made further advances toward her, sleeping in his cabin was as much an ordeal as the slog she endured during the day. Chest pains plagued her. The very sight of Henrietta caused her heart to palpitate, and her lungs refuse to breathe. Henrietta forced her to work sixteen-hour days, rationing her weekly food to a half-pound of rice and half a peck of corn. The only compensation was work—hard, never-ending, tedious, and unrelenting work—fetching water, cleaning pig stalls and chamber pots, polishing silver, washing floors, and mending clothes. On little sleep and less food, she became as brittle as a bone.

Horace, meanwhile, toiled in the fields. As an urban free man, he was unaccustomed to the plantation's harsh life. His delicate hands bled from the prickly bolls that lured his fingers with white cotton puffs and sliced his flesh each time he reached for the bait. From sunrise to sunset, food, water, and mercy were rationed by the whims of those who owned him. Together with other slaves, he ate a diet of corn mush and slept on hard ground. Soon his shoes wore out, and like the rest of the broken and subjugated, he went barefoot. His body ached and craved sleep and nutrition, but every now and then, his eyes would set on heaven with a glimpse of Fredericka.

Although she vowed to ignore him, her sad eyes yielded to his stolen glances the same way she watched birds fly, spellbound at first by their soaring nature yet cruelly reminded of her own earthbound despair. He became for her all those things she could never attain, the solace she would never know, the safety she could never trust, and love she could never have. The sight of him made her ache inside, arousing desires so far beyond her reach that avoiding him was the only way to elude the pain.

Horace well understood the landscape of despair and did not press whatever feeble advantage he had in her green eyes. Rather, he spoke to her in the words of a poet who had long ago formulated keys to unlocking the reluctant heart. He took a chance one night, avoiding the night watchmen, sneaking out of his hut to crouch outside her cabin, just under the window where her bed lay. He whispered a poem to her through the clapboards that separated them. "She walks in beauty, like the night…"

She was alarmed at first, thinking the night whisperer was Grafton. Still, the voice was velvet and the words like music, and she eased into the soft sounds attending to every murmur. "Of cloudless climes and starry skies / And all that's best of dark and bright / Meet in her aspect and her eyes…" Then he stopped and traced his way back to his quarters. Fredericka lay repeating his words in her head, *She walks in beauty, like the night.*

As often as he could, Horace made a rendezvous to the side of her cabin, breathing the same poem, never calling her name, but she knew it was for her all the same. She would scratch the rough boards with her fingertips, and he would speak into the wood, moistening the fibers with his breath. The night became their bond as surely as the day exposed their desperate lives.

But desperation feeds betrayal. While Horace and Fredericka believed the night held their secret, an overseer had been eavesdropping on their encounters and made a play to his advantage.

William had been Grafton's slave since he was a boy and had long ago learned how to survive. He was a driver, currying favors by pointing out potential runaways, revealing hideouts in the swamp, and watching for thievery. William had a foot in both worlds, but honor in neither. While his snitching ostracized him from the others, he had earned himself a pass from field worker to driver, a pound more rations per week, and for one in his circumstance, an uncommon sense of purpose.

William had seen Horace scurry through the slave cabin grounds one night and followed him. He squatted behind a cart and watched Horace crouch below Fredericka's window. Unable to hear what Horace said, William was convinced of some valuable information to be gleaned. He understood how to exist by treachery. He also knew his place in the pecking order and informed the White overseer, Jimmi Wheel.

Years before, Jimmi Wheel was conscripted by the British Royal Navy. His wits helped him make boatswain, tasked with maintaining discipline and order and doling out punishment. He was discharged from his ship, *Virtue*, after it was hulked as a prison ship, and he cast about in the

Americas before stumbling upon Grafton Plantation, a place that would appreciate a man of his talents and temperament.

On a tip from William, Jimmi caught Horace during one of his nighttime interludes, crouched below Fredericka's window. Creeping behind him, Jimmi whispered, "What you think you're doing, boy?"

Horace froze, his face welded to the wood of the cabin.

"I said, what you doing, boy?" Now in a loud and vicious growl, Jimmi's bark reverberated through the slave compound. The muggy night stretched tautly and still as a wire. Nothing stirred, but the dark listened. In the narrow crevices of rocks and thorny bushes, insects stopped scrabbling, and crickets stilled their nighttime serenades. The slaves hunkered in the shadows. The only rhythmic movement was the violent hammering of Horace's pulse against the wall. On the other side, Fredericka pressed toward him. Between crisis and catastrophe, there occurs an ephemeral moment when time slows and the fabric of heaven splits open. In that dimension, they alone existed, beyond fear and threat, their breath blending into one unspoken pledge.

The nightmare that followed is shared by the bonded and bound, when flesh and blood, body, and soul are possessed by those who honor nothing. During the somber night, Horace lay shackled to the barn floor. The next morning, Grafton made his appearance, flinging the barn door open, flooding the rough wooden room in glaring light. He walked over to Horace huddled next to his chains, and bent on one knee, his high leather boots creaking under his weight. "You sniffin' around my girl, Horace?"

Horace turned away and said nothing.

"Seems like we've been here before." Grafton said, spitting on the floor. "You in cuffs, playin' uppity nigger. Me, affordin' my God-given duty to correct the situation." Grafton slid closer. "Tell me, boy, did you touch her?"

Horace remained silent.

"See, you gonna get a lickken', no doubt about that. But, tell the truth now, I'll spare you some."

Horace did not speak.

"Maybe she'll change your mind." Grafton motioned to someone.

Jimmi Wheel stepped into the barn, clutching Fredericka by her hair, yanking her head back. The terrified girl made little murmuring sounds as if she'd been crying.

Horace felt his heart leap out of his chest. The sight of her tugged at all his protective instincts. "She had nothing to do with me. She never even spoke to me." Horace's eyes softened on Fredericka's face. Despite her terror, she returned his gaze with an acknowledgment shared only by lovers.

"That true, Fredericka?" Grafton asked, still eyeballing Horace.

"Never touched m-m-me," she said.

"Let her go." Grafton rose and turned to Jimmi, who released his grip on the girl. "We need to teach Horace here a lesson in manners. Give him twenty." With that, Grafton stormed out of the barn.

"N-n-n-no!" Fredericka grabbed Grafton by the hem of his linen vest.

He swirled around in one sweeping, fierce motion leading with his shoulder to the back of his hand. A movement almost graceful, had the full brunt of his fury not plowed into Fredericka's face. The force hurled her to the ground, her face splattered in blood. "I'm running out of patience with you, girl." He marched back to the house, stabbing the heels of his boots against the hard clay.

"No!" Horace roared. "She didn't do anything! Frederica!" He tore at his shackles, straining toward her.

The girl huddled on the ground, clutching at her face, spitting and coughing, blood pouring between her fingers. Unable to speak, she held her other hand up to Horace to warn him, assure him, keep him quiet.

Jimmi Wheel was more than happy to oblige Grafton's order. "See," Jimmi said, relishing the moment, walking around Horace and brandishing his whip. "This is what we're gonna do. We're gonna strip you naked and then lay you on the ground, face down. We gonna tie your ankles and arms to pegs and nail them pegs into the ground, stretchin' you tight as a tent so we get a nice, friendly bounce of the Cat on that pretty back o' yours."

He signaled to William and another Colored driver standing nearby. They dragged Horace across the dusty yard to the corral and followed Jimmi's orders.

Jimmi slapped the whip playfully in his hand and waltzed around the prostrated man. "Now, before we begin," Jimmi said, "let me introduce the Cat to you. It's called the cat-o'-nine-tails. See, it's made of braided jute, nice an' coarse, and nine tails on it. But my favorite part is these here knots lashed on each bottom." Jimmi fingered the whip as he spoke, caressing each strand of the lash.

"The knots open the flesh. But not nice and easy like. They make a good rip into the meat of the skin. Now, the way I like to do it is to slash down one side and then up the other. And then, I like to go across. That way, we get a pattern like, an' make sure we split open every square inch. That way, I can get right down to the bone. It's the only way I like to do it. It's gonna hurt. An' you gonna bleed, boy. Blood's gonna run like a river. Puddles of blood gonna soak the mud. We're gonna make a mess. We're gonna have ourselves a real benjo, ain't we, boys? We're gonna make some noise!" Jimmi relished a laugh with the two overseers.

He leaned over Horace's splayed body. "But here's the thing, boy. You ain't gonna die. You just gonna suffer somethin' fierce. 'Cause after the 'cat' is done with you, we gonna wash you down with brine. Hoo, boy, that's gonna burn like hell itself. But salt water's the best thing to heal the wounds fast, so's you can get back to workin' for the Master, like a good nigger."

Horace was panting from the rush of adrenaline. His body trembled violently, anticipating his anguish. Just before the first lash, he saw Fredericka—tears and blood streaming down her face. He managed to smile at her as she rushed away. And he closed his eyes.

Jonathan

⊙⊙⊙

That afternoon, Jonathan Redburn came home to New York for the summer, having finished his sophomore year at Princeton. He wore a new suit that spoke of a young man going places and carried a new look of confidence in his eyes. After a few minutes of pleasantries with his father, Jonathan asked the question his father dreaded.

"Where's Horace?"

"Gone. Months ago." Spencer avoided Jonathan's eyes and went to the bar to pour a drink.

"Gone? Gone where?"

"Just gone." Spencer slugged down a jigger of whiskey.

"What do you mean, just gone?"

"He's working somewhere else." Spencer shrugged.

"Somewhere else?"

Spencer took another slug of whiskey.

Jonathan strode to the bar, poured himself a measure and a half of eighty proof, and guzzled it down. He squeezed his eyes shut and wiped his mouth with his hand. "Tell me," he said, his hands on his hips.

Spencer snorted. "Okay, so you're a big man now, Johnny boy." He walked across the room to the parlor table, paused, and tapped a finger on the tabletop. The table where he lost

Horace. He sat down with a weary sigh. "Think you're ready for the truth?"

Jonathan's fist tightened around his glass.

"I sold him." Spencer drained his glass and grimaced as he swallowed the sour truth he could not own. The poker game. Horace in shackles

Jonathan let his father's words settle on his shoulders, unsure of their weight and meaning. He turned his puzzled expression toward his father. "You sold my brother?"

Spencer sensed his irreversible sin the instant he let the words fly. His only recourse now was to step into the vacuum of that significant loss and fill the void with self-righteousness. "He was never your brother. Look in the mirror! He's Black for Christ's sake!"

Jonathan drew a quick breath, inhaling the suffocating odor of stale cigars. *Who was this man?* He needed another drink to stop the fear that he, too, could be expendable.

"He was family," he said, gulping down his drink. "How could you?"

With no retreat now, Spencer's only course was to justify his violation. He stepped within inches of Jonathan's face. "Now you listen to me, you spoiled, ungrateful little shit. I've given you everything. After your mother died, I bought Horace for you. He may have been your friend, but he was a slave, and he will always be a slave. You have privileges and powers afforded you that Horace will never have, and the sooner you realize that, the better. What do you think Horace could do out in the free world? A literate Colored? You think he could go to school? Become a landowner? Own a hotel? You think he has a sliver of a chance out there on his own? They'd cut him to shreds. He's worthless in our world. He has no skills, no talents. He's not a carpenter, a farrier, or a wheelwright. As far as I'm concerned, education was wasted on him. He's better off where he is, with a routine, a purpose, a place where he fits in with others of his kind. He's served his purpose here, and now he's gone."

"I provided you with all of this." Spencer said, waving his hands above his head. "All of this is mine. And one day, it will be yours. But until then, what I do with my properties is my business. You understand me, boy?"

Jonathan shook his head and slammed down his glass. "Where is he?"

"I don't know."

"I'll never understand you, Father," he said, and stormed out of the room.

⚬⚬⚬

THE GRAFTON PLANTATION TOOK ON THE STILLNESS OF a charcoal landscape, a lifeless composition of misery. Black faces peered up from white rows of cotton with haunted eyes and tortured gazes. Rough hands stuffed with cotton stalled in midflight from boll to the basket. The hard sun glinted like glass off every leaf and blade of grass. Laundry hung like withered skins on clotheslines. A still-life, paused for the crack of the whip, the rip of flesh, and the gush of blood.

Fredericka ran to the Big House as the whip split the air and slashed across Horace's spine, sending up shock and pain, and a guttural cry.

"Masta' Grafton! Masta'!" Fredericka hollered at the house from the verandah steps. "I'll do it. I'll do it!"

The second lash sliced between Horace's shoulders.

Henrietta came to the balcony and peered down at the slave girl. "You'll do what?"

"I need to talk to the Masta'! Please, Missus, please, I need to talk to him." Her pleas spluttered through the taste of blood in her mouth that made her gag.

Grafton came up behind his wife and motioned for her to get inside. Henrietta huffed, picked up her skirt, and wound past her husband, holding her chin up as if all of this was beneath her.

A third lash ripped into Horace.

"And?" he said from his perch, swigging down a shot of brandy.

"Anything. Anything you want. But stop the whippin' on Horace. He didn't do nothin'. I swear. I'm tellin' you true." She wiped the blood from her nose, smearing it across her face.

"My, my, you must be tellin' the truth. You stopped s-s-s-stutterin'." Grafton took another swig from his glass. "So, you're invitin' me, then? By your own free will?"

A fourth lash tore a strip of flesh off the slave's back.

"Yessir. Yessir. I is. My own free will." Fredericka glanced back at the yard. "But stop the whippin'!"

A fifth lash.

The air hung heavy with the odor of gardenias and blood. Grafton lifted his gaze to one of his men. The sixth lash curled across Horace's ribs. Then stopped. And life on the plantation resumed.

HOURS LATER, ROUSED FROM AN AGONIZING FOG, Horace heard Jimmi say, "I declare, you're one lucky nigger."

Horace opened his eyes. He was lying on his stomach. Bloody rags dotted the floor around his cot. The very act of inhaling caused his wounded flesh to expand and split.

"Yessiree. One lucky nigger. Only six stripes. Must be nice hidin' behind your girlfriend's bloomers." Jimmi poked Horace's back with the monkey's fist, the twine ball at the end of his whip handle. It burrowed into a bloody wound. Horace groaned. "But you ain't seen the last of my cat," Jimmi hissed through his black teeth. "I'm gonna get you, boy. We're going to finish the job. I'm gonna let you heal just a little, and then we'll go at it again and open up them lesions." He poked the bloody wounds again, and Horace grimaced. "A little bit at a time, that's my notion." He leaned over Horace, his foul breath swamping over the slave's head and purred, "Meow!"

Three weeks later, a letter arrived addressed to Jonathan Redburn, Skylark Hotel, New York City. It contained only two words in Latin, "*Adiuva me.*" Help me.

The Disguise

―――○◇◇○―――

ighteen months later, it would not have been notewor-
thy when a White man and his Negro body servant
entered Charleston's prestigious Devonshire Carriage
Hotel, except the White man was obviously in a bad way. A
sling cradled his right arm while his left hand leaned heavily on an ivory-handled cane. A muslin cloth wrapped close
about his face, suggesting a wound. Dark green glasses
guarded against the glare from the street and the curious
glances from the hotel's patrons. Despite his impairments,
he was well-attired in the day's fashion—a long dark cloak, a
white shirt beneath a smart waistcoat, and tall, heeled black
boots. He was attended by a large Negro, comparably vested
in a gray suit befitting a prosperous merchant's body servant.

Though the indisposed man limped as he crossed the
lobby, he held a certain aloofness, a high-headedness that
looked neither left nor right. It spoke of someone accustomed to finery, unmoved by the hotel's grand arches and
high columns, the gilded mirrors, or the artistry of the
wrought iron gates. This bearing of superiority did not stop
at the reception desk gleaming with Italian alabaster, where
he stood without a word, cool as the marble.

With artful hospitality, the clerk pretended nothing
was out of the ordinary and simply said, "Welcome to

the Devonshire. Mighty cold outside. Do you have a reservation?"

"We do, sir." The Black man spoke, careful to avert his eyes to the ground. "A room with full accommodations, sir."

"Certainly." The clerk gave a little cough and adjusted his bifocals. Without addressing the slave, he pushed the register toward his silent guest. "If you would just sign in, sir."

"He of delicate health, sir," the African said, "and hard a hearin'. He got bone pains of the hand. I speak for him. And write."

With overt delicacy, as if picking at a disagreeable food, the clerk fingered the register toward the manservant. "Very well, then." He took a hanky from his breast pocket and sniffed into it as the servant wrote with a practiced hand, *Mr. Basil Wallace*.

Checking the name, and satisfied with the protocol, the clerk presented a key with a perfunctory bow to the young man and slid the key to the servant. Turning to the White man, he produced a package and said, "Mr. Wallace, this arrived for you this morning, sir." He then handed the square box to the servant. "Your room is on the second floor, room twenty-two. Dinner service begins in an hour. If it would be more convenient, we could have it brought up to your room."

The imperious young man nodded and made his way up the staircase with some difficulty; his servant followed carrying their two bags, with the package tucked under his arm.

With the door locked safely behind them, the two new guests stared at the room.

"Lord have mercy!" the White man said.

The African dropped the bags and tore into the package given to them at the desk. Inside, a note and a leather pouch. The message simply read, "I will meet you at the dock in

New York. Good luck!" The servant emptied the bag on the bed—one hundred silver dollars. "Just as he promised," the servant said, carefully scooping up the coins and putting them back in the pouch.

The disabled man walked toward the four-poster bed and smoothed his hand up the spiraled wood frame, caressed the fine linens, and poked at the goose-feather pillows as if they might be startled and fly away. He sat gingerly on the bedside and gave a little bounce.

"It soft," he whispered, afraid to break the spell. He motioned to the African. "Try it."

The African sat next to him and bounced. "It's good," he said. "We're safe now."

The young man wriggled his right arm out of the sling and unwrapped the cloth from his face revealing a youthful face and a head full of short, cropped curls. The Negro helped him slip off his boots. Standing, the young man drew a small white envelope filled with seeds from his pants pocket and placed the packet on the side table. He unbuttoned his vest and his shirt and kicked out of his pantaloons. The freestanding mirror in the corner reflected not an impaired, arthritic man, but a striking, honey-skinned woman.

GRAFTON PLANTATION WAS UNDER SIEGE BY ITS ENRAGED owner. Frederick Grafton stood on the dirt floor in the middle of the tin shack that Horace had shared with ten others. Cold winter light slashed through the open door. The terrified slaves huddled on the rickety porch in the wind as Grafton's men pulled down shelves, tossed out the floor mattresses and shabby blankets, and rifled through the meager cups and bowls laid out on the fireplace's ash-filled hearth.

"Where did they go?" he roared at the slaves. "I'll hang you all up by the thumbs and lash you dead to the bone if I don't get an answer! Now, where did they go?"

"Boss," Jimmi said, tossing out a handful of rags that passed as clothes out in the mud, "You want the dogs? You got a lot of money on the run out there."

Grafton hollered back at Jimmi. "It's not about the money, dammit."

He stormed out to the porch and raised his whip to the first Black face he saw, slicing across the neck and cheek of a young boy. Blood spurted across Grafton's boot as the boy collapsed to the ground, his mother rushing to his side and kneeling over him.

A raw wind rustled the leafless branches of nearby trees, and a piece of paper fluttered along the ground where the mattresses had been thrown. It caught Grafton's eye as his arm hung in midair about to scourge the boy and now his mother. Instead, he strode over to the scrap and swept it up in his hand. A ticket stub for the steamer, *North Star*, in Charleston Harbor. Paid in full. Leaving the next day. He squinted at the signature, rubbing off the dust. The signature was clear. *Redburn!*

⤜∞⤛

HORACE WATCHED FREDERICKA SHAKE OFF HER DISGUISE like a caterpillar slipping from its cocoon, revealing her true incarnation. She stood naked in the middle of room twenty-two in the Devonshire Hotel, staring at her reflection in the cheval glass, all her terrors discarded in the garments on the floor.

"This is me, Horace," she said. "All of me." She stood in a shaft of sunlight glinting through the large window.

Horace stared back at her in the mirror. They held each other's gaze without speaking as a thousand words flew silently between them like sonnets not yet written. She turned to him, unashamed, but radiant in the afternoon light, and reached for him. She slid her hand into his.

Horace was transfixed. Her hand, so little nesting in his palm, a wren-of-a-thing, yet pulsing with uncommon strength and purpose. Curls spilled over her eyes as she unbuttoned his vest and helped tug off his shirt. She acquainted her fingers with the scars on his back as if each wound had a name. How baffling, how wonderful the angel-soft touch of her hands. How sweet the music roaming his senses in this uncommon hour on this uncommon day with this most uncommon girl. He closed his eyes and inhaled her. She smelled of lemons and leather. He could hear the beat of horses outside the window keeping pace with his galloping heart.

Fredericka could not name what she wanted, never having tasted the forbidden waters of personal desire. Neither wants nor needs were familiar companions in her young life. But she could feel something new—happiness and deeper—something that must be love.

And pleasure found them both.

Later that afternoon, still holding her in his arms, Horace whispered, "Frederick Grafton..."

She touched his face. "Shhh now, Horace. You be my first love."

"And you be mine," he said.

He pulled the satin bed cover about them both. "Tomorrow we take a carriage to the harbor, get on that steamer, and sail to New York. On to freedom. Our friend will meet us there."

"*Libertas*. I remember. From the book you be readin' behind the cabin."

"Jonathan's Latin book. Hid it inside my shirt just before Grafton hauled me out of the hotel."

"I asked the word for 'freedom.'" Fredericka's voice was as soft as the night.

"And I said *Libertas*."

"*Libertas*. It sound like prayin'. Made me love you. But," she said, "what is it, really?"

Horace said, "Freedom means nobody owns you. You own you. You even own time."

Fredericka leaned up on her elbow. "Own time?" She scratched her head, sizing up the idea.

Horace laughed. "That's right. Sleep and wake up whenever we want. Be masters of our own days and nights—the overseers of our own lives. We can want things. And have things. Nobody is going to whip us or hurt us or sell us. We can walk down a street and turn this way or that, just because we want to."

"I want to eat meat every day," she said.

"And I want to build something that belongs to us," Horace said.

"Want to find my mamma."

"Maybe someday we can find her. Me? I want to be somebody, make a difference," Horace said, getting more eager with every thought. "I want to teach you to read and write. I want to teach reading and writing to every slave, to every little Colored child. It's the way out. It's the way for Colored folks to learn suffering is something they can leave behind. It's not their lot. There's a world beyond the whip, starvation, and the White master. And I'm going to teach them."

"Ain't you gonna give them more misery? Like you said before, knowin' 'bout things they can't have? Maken' 'em mad?"

"'Ain't' isn't a word." Horace lifted her chin. "But I've changed my mind about knowing things and getting mad.

Anger is a good thing, Fred. Knowing what you can have. Angry 'cause you don't have. Having nothing makes you want. And wanting makes you get."

"There you go with them big ideas again. I wanna learn to read an' write, like you." She rolled over and kissed him on the cheek.

"I'll teach you. Starting with the word ain't, which isn't a word, but begins with the letter 'a.'" They both laughed.

Fredericka snuggled closer to Horace. "Tell me again 'bout the home we gonna have."

"It's going to be a nice house. Safe and warm. Plenty of wood in the winter and cool shade in the summer."

"And the garden. And me and you and Mamma all livin' together."

"The best garden in the whole world—with cabbages and carrots and beans. And you're going to plant all your seeds. We'll have flowers everywhere. We'll have plenty of food. We never gonna be hungry." He kissed the back of her head.

"And Masta' Grafton…"

"He's not your Master anymore. We're clear of him."

Fredericka searched Horace's face. "I have somethin' I wanna tell you." She hesitated.

Just then, a knock at the door. Fredericka clenched at the cover and drew in a sharp breath. Horace put a finger to his lips and crept to the door.

Another knock.

"Who there?" Horace said, putting on his best slave-talk through the door.

"Dinner, sir," came the muffled response.

"Leave it at the door, if you please," Horace said. "My Master sleepin'."

When he thought it safe, Horace quickly opened the door and slid the tray of food inside. The aromas filled the room. Their spirits lifted at the sight of roasted guinea fowl, currant jelly, minced ham dressing, raisin cake, and an apple. The starving runaways ate like royalty.

At the end of the meal, Horace took the apple and cut it, handing half to Fredericka and said, "The first fruit of our journey together."

She bit into the sweet flesh and smiled. "Taste like cold honey."

Horace took a bite, and pinched the apple's black shiny pellets from his lips and held them out to her. "Seeds for your collection."

Fredericka placed them in the palm of her hand. "We grows an orchard one day." She took a blue serviette from the dinner tray and folded the seeds into the cloth, tying it with a tight knot.

"One day. I promise." He gave her a long kiss. "You wanted to tell me something?"

Fredericka frowned back a dark thought and replaced it with a smile. "I tell you later."

They fell asleep to the clip-clopping of horses as the world of slave masters passed under their window.

But dreams doomed Fredericka's sleep. *A cough in the night. Water, thrashing, frothing, lungs burning. A cradled embrace. A shadow moves. The man at the door. The man in the bed. Water flooding the room!*

"Fred, hush, Fred, it's all right now. It's Horace. You're okay now, hush, hush, pretty baby." He stroked his warm hands over her hair.

"Water," she murmured and fell back into a restless sleep again.

Horace kept vigil for the rest of the night, his arms locked around Fredericka, but his head reeled, remembering their escape. He had hefted Fredericka, bundled inside a sack of cotton, onto a wagon loaded with dozens of other bundles bound for market. He cut the horse's rein, distracting the driver, who sought out another harness, while he hitched himself to the undercarriage by belts and hooks. How they escaped in broad daylight, as the cotton wagon rambled away from the plantation. The throbbing of his heart when the wagon stopped, and the driver relieved himself in the woods. He remembered wriggling out of his braces and jumping on the wagon bed. Which bundle was Fredericka? He whispered her name, but she didn't answer. He poked at the piles but kept watching the woods for the driver. "Fredericka! Where are you?"

The driver was coming back. A bundle moved. He grabbed it, hoisted it over the side, flung it over his shoulder and ran to the opposite side of the woods just as the driver mounted his box, took up the reins, and drove away.

Horace remembered the rare feeling of happiness when he opened the burlap bag, and Fredericka gasped for air, her hair and eyes and mouth speckled by cotton as if a flecked butterfly were emerging from her cocoon. Their disguises were bundled alongside her. Then they were running. The pounding fear of a posse on horseback, or worse, dogs that could chase them down and rip them apart. They sought refuge at the Quaker's house, and the abolitionist took them in his carriage to the hotel. And now, clinging to each other on the verge of freedom.

But his thought wandered to the genuine probability they could be caught at any moment. The cruelest hoax would be to lose his God-given time just as the seconds ran out. Betrayed by his own skin. If only men were turned inside out, and their only color was the color of blood. Horace felt his heart tighten thinking of what the morning would bring at Charleston Harbor.

The SS North Star

⎯⎯∞⎯⎯

The Edgefield Advertiser: April 3, 1843—$2,500 REWARD.
—Ran away from the subscriber, on the 3rd of April, two
Negro slaves, Horace and Fredericka. He is nineteen years
old, six feet high, copper-colored complexion with high
forehead and cheekbones, broad and square shoulders,
stands and walks very erect, though quite a sluggard in
action. He reads and writes. The Negress is sixteen, a
quadroon of very pale complexion, five feet five inches
high, with curly, shoulder-length dark hair and green eyes.
These slaves are mine, flesh and bone. I am to believe they
are seeking transport to a free State and to Canada. I will
give the reward of above to any person who will arrest
and confine them so I can get them. F. Grafton Plantation,
Beaufort County, South Carolina.

Dawn slashed a blade of light across the city of
Charleston. Horace sat at the writing table in the
hotel room, counting out their money while Fredericka donned her disguise. For months they had planned
and saved for this time. Every penny scraped from selling
cabbages, beans, and chickens from Horace's small garden
plot went into this dream. Fredericka altered their disguises from the Master's old suits. She pilfered discarded

garments from the Big House, created shirts and a cravat, and salvaged two pairs of boots from the local coroner's office. Reinforced with the package of silver coins sent to them at the reception desk, they had enough to purchase an escape route using first-class accommodations where the man-hunters wouldn't dream of looking.

Horace glanced out the window. "Carriage waiting. Time to go."

Fredericka pulled on her pants, boots, and vest, fixed her cravat, and tucked her wrapper of magnolia seeds and the blue serviette with Horace's apple seeds back into her pocket. She had slipped her arm into the sling and reached for her hat when Horace noticed something wrong.

"Fred, it's the wrong arm." He strode across the floor, his eyes wide and alert. He turned the sling around and gently pulled her right arm into the sling. "We gotta be careful, Fred. Folks will notice."

Fred sucked in her breath. "Sorry. Won't happen again."

They left the hotel the same way they arrived, silently, audaciously, walking into the lobby. Horace paid for the room and, with a shy nod, escorted the young planter out of the hotel and into the street to the waiting carriage, pulled by two black horses. Horace spoke briefly to the driver, who tipped his head ever-so-slightly in acknowledgment.

"All's fixed up, just like we planned." Horace slid beside her in the carriage. "Our Quaker friend is taking us to the harbor."

Passing in front of the hotel, the carriage turned onto a side street and toward an outdoor market. Raucous voices rose from the mart where a large crowd had gathered. Some White children stood on crates to get a better look as younger children chased each other through the crowd. A group of White women dressed in furs and bonnets greeted each other with smiles and chatter. Barrel-chested men puffed on cigars and stood around open stoves against the April chill. A big-bellied man cracked a joke, and coarse laughter erupted into the air. To one unfamiliar with Charleston, it could have been a country Christmas fair or a public square filled with jugglers and pantomimes. But a closer look would prove one wrong.

Upon large wooden blocks stood a Black man, woman, and child. All three were naked and shackled with heavy iron collars attached to a chain bolted to the floor. The woman clutched at the boy who clung to her leg. The man stood empty of spirit, caved in, as though his heart had been scooped out. More than a dozen chained and naked slaves stood shivering behind the riser, awaiting their turn at the auction block. A slave trader stood nearby directing a shackled man to grease up the others from a bucket of pork fat, an attempt to make their wounded frames appear glossy and strong.

The auctioneer, dressed smartly in a high, stovepipe hat and cinched waistcoat, prodded the woman and child with his cane. "Two generations of strong African stock. Good teeth, strong bones. Sold together or separately," he hollered. "And the boy don't eat much!" The crowd roared with laughter.

As their carriage rolled by, a bystander would have only noticed a slave and a bandaged White man inside, undistracted by the spectacle that drew the crowd to the street. But a closer inspection would have disclosed the bound man's eyes scanned the auctioneer's offerings, searching each face, hoping and dreading in equal amounts to see a familiar mother's face.

Charleston Harbor was a buzz of activity. Carriages and horses choked the streets. Sailors and longshoremen, mostly Black, hustled past with bushels of dried fruits, casks of whiskey, barrels of goods, and bundles of ropes and sacks. Hundreds of people flanked the dock in a chaotic scene of cargo, crew, and passengers. Vendors huddled over their wares in the cold, selling shirts, shoes, and hats, teas, and bushels of rice. The air was a stew of dead fish, steamy manure, and smoke from the chimneys and shops. Passengers alighted from their carriages with bags and trunks and clamored up the loading ramps onto the ships tied to the docks. Horace clutched the tickets tightly in his fist as the carriage pulled into the harbor.

Fredericka grabbed his hand. "Horace, what if…"

"We'll be all right, just like we planned. Let's find our cabin on the boat. We're almost there." He gave her hand a squeeze. "*Libertas.*"

The SS *North Star* was set to sail. The boilers steamed impatiently as the final passengers and crew made their way to their respective cabins and stations. The harbor bustled with ships under sail, steamers, and cargo. Seamen shouted orders, passengers called for porters and said their goodbyes to friends and relatives, as crates of cotton and rice were hoisted and hauled to the main deck. With all the commotion, no one noticed Horace and Fredericka making their way up the gangway through a crowded passageway to a small, damp stateroom that smelled of mold and tobacco. There were two berths pressed against the wall and a small porthole with a view of the harbor.

Inside, Fredericka shook off her disguise, unwrapping the bandage around her face and yanking her arm from the sling. "Horace, I'm skeery."

"Me too." He studied the activity out the porthole. "But we've done it now. No going back."

Fredericka shook her head vigorously. "I will die first."

"If it comes to that…"

"I die with you," Fredericka said, her voice barely above a whisper.

The steamer began to move. Observing their departure through the porthole, Horace breathed a sigh of relief as the shoreline faded to a distance, and the ship coursed slowly out of the harbor. Beyond his scope of that round vision were two men, a stocky man in a suit with high leather boots and a gangly man with a whip hanging from his belt. They were running along the wharf, cussing and motioning at the steamer, and were the last to scurry up the gangway moments before the crew pulled it up, and the ship sailed away from the dock.

The Waterfront

⚉

T he Port of New York reigned supreme as the entire country's distribution center, running more passengers and cargo through her harbor than all other ports combined. Cotton was king, and trade between the Southern states, New York, and Europe had formed a "cotton triangle" of business routes. Southern tobacco farmers and cotton growers shipped their goods from Baltimore and New Orleans to New York's busy port as ships carried manufactured goods from the Northern states back to the Southeast. Exports traveled across the Atlantic from New York to Europe as imported goods returned to the port for distribution throughout the country. This was a free state. An excellent place to get lost.

The *North Star* was a clamor of activity as the steamer entered the Port of New York. Waking up to the noise, Horace peeked outside their cabin door to see passengers hauling bags and babies, lining up to disembark. He closed the door and sprang to the porthole. Clipper ships, barges, schooners, brigs, sloops, steamers, and fishing boats all plied the waters of New York Harbor.

"We're here." Horace's face glowed with joy. "We're free."

"Free?" Fredericka tried to digest the word.

"We made it, Fred." He lifted her up off her feet. She wrapped her arms around his neck and pressed her lips to his cheek.

As they gathered their belongings, Fredericka held up the towel she used to disguise her face. "Does I still need this?"

"It's best we leave the way we came. You best put it on."

"But why? We be free of him, now. He don't even know we here."

"Don't take the chance, Fred. Put it on."

Fredericka sat on the berth. "If we free, I want to feel free." She stuffed the towel in the bag.

"They still have man hunters here, Fred, who don't care about the law. They can snatch us, drag us back. Put it on. Just till we get off the boat."

"All right then. But then, no more."

The couple left the cabin the same way they arrived: as a young wealthy White man bandaged across his face, dark green glasses, his right arm in a sling, leaning heavily on an ivory-handled cane, joined by his African personal assistant. They merged into the slow line of passengers waiting to disembark and climbed the stairs to the main deck. They were struck by a blast of cold April wind and a world beyond their imagination.

The teeming waterfront was a dizzying canvas of colors, odors, and sounds. A dusting of snow powdered the untrammeled edges of the wharf. The fragrances of spices, teas, coffee, and fish mingled in the salty air. Hundreds of ships crammed the docks; their masts with lines and cables reached toward the cold, blue sky like a forest of bare trees.

People pushed and shoved their way forward in the line, eager to meet friends waiting on the wharf, separating Horace from Fredericka on the deck.

Fredericka had never seen such a jumble of humanity and paused at the top of the gangway to take it all in. Someone jostled her from behind, trying to get around with their bags and knocked her cane to the floorboards. As she bent to retrieve it, her glasses slipped off her face and fell under foot of an impatient passenger. She stood up and yanked her arm out of the sling in a vain attempt to repair the trampled spectacles as people continued to shove past her. Frustrated, she pulled the muslin off her face.

Meanwhile, Horace was seven people deep behind her, caught in the mob of passengers. He scanned the crowd ahead for her, and as he did so, someone else caught his eye. A sight so familiar that at first glance, he almost dismissed it as a hallucination—Grafton on the wharf, and Jimmi Wheel standing next to him. They were studying passengers coming off the ship! Just then, they pointed up the gangway. Horace followed their gaze. They were aiming at Fredericka, who had just thrown off her disguise.

"No! Fred, don't!" Horace cried out, but too late. Grafton and Jimmi started up the ramp, pushing against the stream of passengers coming down, as Horace peeled away at the crowd behind her.

Fredericka felt a grip on her arm. Horace tugged her toward him. "Run! They found us!"

She looked over her shoulder as Horace pulled her away from the gangway, and for an instant, she made eye contact with Grafton. He fixed on her and hesitated halfway up the ramp, winded, catching his breath. He shouted, "Stop her!" and continued climbing against the descending crowd.

Hand-in-hand, Horace and Fredericka worked their way across the deck through the mob of crewmen and passengers, stepping over ropes and skirting around crates and barrels of cargo, coming to a stop at the railing, aft of the ship.

They peered into the water. "No," Fredericka whimpered, backing away.

"We have no choice." Horace tugged her back to the railing.

She shook her head. "But, I don't like water. I c-can't swim," she stuttered, and weighed back on her heels, but Horace kept a firm grip on her hand.

"Listen, Fredericka, we don't have time for this. You've got to trust me. Do you trust me?"

She nodded yes, but her terrified eyes were riveted on the thing she feared the most.

Horace grabbed a life ring hanging on the rail and slung it over his shoulder.

"We're going to jump..."

"But I'm skeery of water..."

He yanked at her hand. "Listen to me. This is our only chance. Take a deep breath. On the count of three, we jump. You'll go under, but I'm going to be there with you. I saved you before, and by the good Lord's hand, I'll do it again. You gotta trust me."

Fredericka stared at him. "You brought me back!" In that instant, she remembered the first time she saw him. She was floating somewhere above. She saw the copper-colored man kneeling on Henrietta's floor. The one who forced her to breathe.

"I've got you," Horace said, holding out his hand.

On trembling legs, she stepped over the railing with him. "I have somethin' to tell you," she said as they stood on the edge overlooking the water.

"Save it for later. We're going to make it. Look at me. A deep breath. On the count of three. One, two..."

"Horace," Fredericka cried, "I..."

"Three!" Horace leapt off the edge and pulled Fredericka with him, plunging them both into the icy waters of the East River.

White with Frost

∞∞∞

Grafton tore through the crowd on the main deck. "That way!" he signaled Jimmi to go around to the ship's fore as he scrambled aft, elbowing his way past crewmen and cargo. He reached the railing and looked down at the water. Nothing. They had to still be on the ship, and he would rip it apart until he found them.

When Fredericka hit the water, the impact slammed the air out of her lungs, and she plummeted into darkness, spewing clouds of bubbles as she sank. Despite kicking and clutching, with nothing tangible to cling to, air would not come, only gagging and lungs filled with pain. Her body began to relax, and her arms waved above her head like seaweed reaching for the sun. This drifting, weightless space had befriended her before. No pain, no fear. *How pretty the bubbles, like puffs of silver!*

Above her, Horace exploded out of the water wheezing and coughing. He seized the life ring bobbing next to him. The frigid water made his skin burn and fired his senses. He churned in circles, searching for Fredericka and ducked under to see her fingertips disappearing below. Inhaling a mighty breath, he dove for her fingers, quickly receding from him.

Fredericka felt a tug from above. She glanced slowly up to see Horace grasping her hand, kicking and jerking them to the surface, his face contorted with effort. She watched the murky depths slip away beneath her and light haloed overhead. Blasting through the surface, they gasped for the oxygen that stabbed their lungs and choked on the saltwater tearing at their throats. The sting of the freezing water cramped and numbed their limbs. Horace found the buoy and draped Fredericka's arms across it, and together they clung to the floating device, wheezing and sputtering. Fredericka shivered violently in the icy estuary. Horace felt his limbs stiffening, and he couldn't feel his feet.

Meanwhile, the tide had turned. The gentle lapping of the East River had become a strong current pulling them around the *North Star's* helm toward a bordering pier where a large sailing vessel had docked, dangling a heaving line. Still clinging to the buoy and Fredericka, Horace locked onto the rope and used it to swing them around to the narrow partition between the pier and the ship.

The ship chucked and creaked in the tide, the side-boards rhythmically jamming the space to the pier, tossing the couple under the dock. Horace released the rope and reached for one of the dock's pilings, thick with ice and slippery. His fingers were numb, but he succeeded in finding a tenuous hold on a cross brace with his one free hand while still holding on to the buoy and Fredericka. The tips of her hair had turned white with frost, and her body trembled violently.

Another wake and the ship lifted slightly and pitched its tonnage against the hawsers, heaving toward the pier. Horace lost his grip. The wake's momentum hurtled them toward the wharf bordering the street. Once again, Horace reached for a crossbar. This time he held fast. From this vantage point, under the pier, he spotted a wide ledge used as a catwalk for the dock. He let go of the buoy and hand over hand, from one crossbar to another, made his way to the ledge. Wrenching himself from the water, Horace reached for Fredericka and hauled her up.

They collapsed on the catwalk panting and shivering.

"My seeds…" Fredericka fumbled in her pocket and clutched at the blue serviette holding her apple seeds then curled into a shivering fetal position. Her eyes were closed, and her lips had turned blue, ice crystals fringed her wet hair.

"We've got to get out of these wet clothes." Horace struggled to his feet, eyeing a service ladder leading up to the street. "I'll be back, Fred. Hang on."

Upon the street, Horace ran into a traffic jam. A gridlock of horse-drawn carriages clogged the road, and further down, a ruckus of arguments and shouting. A swarm of humanity maneuvered through the congestion. Bowsprits of the docked ships pierced the street like a low unfinished roof. Vendors huddled in their booths with fresh oysters piled nearby in snow-mounded boxes as longshoremen hauled cargo off the ships. Tethered ropes and pulleys guided freight that swung precariously in the air.

Women fussed with babies bundled in blankets. Men shouldered baskets of potatoes and fish. Passageways were blocked by crates and barrels forcing passengers to drag trunks and suitcases through the street's grimy slush. Across the way, a hoard of people waved at a ship pulling away from the dock. Black stevedores loaded barrels of sugar and rice onto waiting barges. A handful of men were warping a square-rigger in from the river. Pushing the horizontal bars on a capstan around in a circle, evertightening a stout line attached to the ship, they winched the vessel closer to its berth. In this cacophony, no one noticed a freezing, wet Black man darting in and out of the throng's activity.

Desperate to find dry clothing, Horace spotted an empty carriage stuck in the snarl of traffic—bags and luggage piled inside. The driver and passenger argued next to the horse, who reared his head up and down as if he too had an opinion. Horace opened the carriage door and riffled through the bags. He snatched the one stuffed with clothing, snagged a wool coat crumpled on the seat, and quickly made his way back under the wharf to Fredericka.

She was delirious with cold, her hands and feet blue and cramped. Horace tore off her wet clothing and rubbed her frozen arms and legs and wrapped her in the dry pants, shirt, and a wool jacket from the bag. He stripped off his shirt and donned the coat. They would have to make do with their freezing leather boots and shoes.

A few minutes later, two men appeared on the wharf—a young White man and his Black companion, moving painfully through the crowd. Their destination, the Skylark Hotel.

⸺⸺✸⸺⸺

On the steamer, the slave hunters continued to tear through the cabins, searching the cargo, and interrogating the crew until the Captain finally put a stop to it. "You've been on this ship long enough," he said, "and if you haven't found them by now, they ain't here. Get off my ship!"

Standing on the wharf, Grafton was still defiant. "They've gotta be here." He glanced up and down the clamor of the street. "I can smell 'em."

A cold wind blew across the river as pedestrians hunkered under their collars and furs and scurried down New

York's chaotic Street of Ships. Horses snorted puffy clouds into the frosty air, trailing steamy mounds of manure behind them. Grafton signaled to Jimmi, who was trudging back and forth under the bowsprits of the ships hovered halfway across the street.

"C'mon, Wheel." Grafton began running through the crowded waterfront. "I know where they're going."

A Matter of Conjecture

⤸⤸⤸

N
ew York's Skylark Hotel was in a festive mood. It was Easter week, and fashionable couples strutted arm-in-arm through the massive entrance defined by two immense marble columns. Women wore colorful tiered gowns of lace and satin, their heads crowned by bonnets festooned with ribbons and feathers. The gentlemen looked crisp in their long coats, top hats, and polished walking sticks. Guests filtered through the massive gilt archway to the grand dining room where rich crimson curtains draped sixteen-foot windows. Pink and white roses populated heavy Italian vases, and white linen tablecloths offered the clientele a regal experience in the art of seeing and being seen. Echoing through the hotel, a live orchestra played waltzes in the ballroom.

Grafton couldn't care less. He and his scruffy companion took no delight in the delicacies of the elite. The planter had one thing on his mind. "I demand to see Spencer Redburn. At once!" He slammed his fist on the reception desk. "Tell him Frederick Grafton is here! And I want my goddamned property back that he stole from me!"

Startled guests gathered at a distance, disapproving of the burly man's uncouth behavior and his lanky, rough-hewn associate. The desk clerk excused himself and quickly ran up the red-carpeted staircase, disappearing around a corner.

The crowd of onlookers grew, and Jimmi flicked out his whip, forcing them back, "Watcha lookin' at, Yanks? You want some o' this?"

A woman gasped, and a gentleman next to her said, "Here, here, that's totally uncalled for."

Just as Jimmi was about to take the dandy on, Redburn appeared at the top of the stairs. "Call off your man, Grafton."

"Back down, Jimmi." Grafton cut through the crowd, taking a wide-legged stance at the bottom of the stairs.

The orchestra stopped playing, and hundreds of people poked out of doorways and around columns, clogging the hallways to catch a glimpse of the unfolding drama.

"What's the meaning of this, Grafton?" Redburn asked, still standing at the top of the stairs. "I find myself at a disadvantage here."

"You know bloody well why I'm here! You stole my property, and I want 'em back!"

"Them? Who? What are you talking about?" Redburn took two steps down. "Come up to my office, and we can discuss this like gentlemen."

Grafton spit on the marble floor. "You ain't no gentleman. You're a thief!"

The onlookers gasped at the man's accusation. Another shouted out, "Someone call the constables!"

Grafton fumbled under his coat. A man yelled, "He's gotta gun!" The horrified crowd jerked back several feet en masse like a single wary organism, cautious but curious.

Redburn put up his hands, "Now wait just a minute, Grafton, I didn't take anything of yours."

The gun trembled in Grafton's hand. "They're my slaves. My Fredericka. And Horace, I won him fair and square. I have the ticket stub, right here, signed in your name for the steamer they took off on." He held up the ticket in his other hand. "Now, turn them over or by God, I'll shoot you for the crook you are!"

A gasp shuddered through the onlookers. Redburn descended two more steps. "Let me see that ticket."

"Let me see my properties!"

What happened next is a matter of conjecture. Some witnesses said Redburn took another step down, his heel missed the landing, and slipped, he grappled for the banister, and fell forward onto Grafton causing the pistol to fire. Others said Redburn charged at the man, grabbing at the gun, and Grafton fired in self-defense. Yet others claimed Grafton shot the unarmed man in cold blood. What was not debatable was that blood ran thick on the white marble floor.

Grafton swung around the lobby, wild-eyed, waving the pistol in his hand. The horrified spectators scrambled away, ducking and screaming. Jimmi grabbed him by the arm. "Boss, best we get outta here." Grafton simply nodded. They bolted out a side door and into the street, passing Jonathan Redburn and the constables as they entered the building around the corner.

Exploding through the front entrance and leading an entourage of constables, Jonathan raced to his father's side. "Someone get a doctor!" he shouted and cradled his father's head.

Spencer Redburn gazed up at his son. "Jonathan."

"The doctor's coming, Father," the young man said, struggling to hold back tears.

"Horace…"

"I know all about it, Father; don't try to talk."

"You knew?" In his failing moment, with the light fading from his eyes, a look of disbelief and despair swept across Spencer's face. A lone drop of blood trickled from the side of his mouth, and on his last breath, he clutched his son's arm. "It was you?"

Meanwhile, Horace and Fredericka had made their way into the hotel through the service entrance to the kitchen. Cook, Horace's childhood mentor, was still at her post baking bread on a long wooden table.

Cook thought she'd seen a ghost. "Lord 'a mercy, child what you doin' here? And who that with you?"

Horace quickly explained their situation. They helped Fredericka to a high back wooden chair and tugged off her boots. Her feet were blue. He ripped his feet out of his own wet shoes and sat exhausted on the floor. Cook went into high gear. She wrapped warm towels around their feet, threw blankets over them, and gave them hot tea and pork knuckle soup.

While they ate, she foraged through storage closets and came back with dry clothing for them both. "It ain't much," she said, "but these should get you by. Clothes for a lady. And one of your old outfits that I've been savin'," she said to Horace. "Lord a' mercy, this be a day to end all days."

Cook sat at the kitchen table as they changed into the dry clothes. "Master Redburn a dyin' and now you's showin' up here half dead…"

Horace looked surprised. "Master Redburn?"

"He be shot dead, thas' what," Cook said, wiping tears with the corner of her apron.

Horace leapt to his feet. "Master Redburn?" He shook Cook's shoulders, "Which one?"

"Master Spencer," Cook blurted out, her heavy chest pulsing with sobs. "Just before yous showed up. Shot dead on the stairs!"

Fredericka gasped and put a hand to her mouth.

"Where's Jonathan, Cook?" Horace was already halfway to the door.

"He be with da' constables in da lobby, I expect," Cook said.

Horace bolted out of the kitchen and ran up the back stairs to the foyer. A low murmur permeated the massive hall as a scattering of guests, police, and hotel workers clustered in small groups. Near the staircase, a body lay covered by a white sheet stained with a blotch of red. Horace spied Jonathan sitting on one of steps swigging a bottle of whiskey. He walked around Spencer Redburn's remains and sat down next to Jonathan.

"I'm so sorry," Horace said softly.

"Not your fault." Jonathan's eyes were red and raw. "Just waiting for the body wagon, now. Fredericka?"

"She's safe. With me. What happened?"

"Your old friend, Frederick Grafton. Shot him."

"Grafton?" Horace glanced nervously about the room.

"He thought it was father who bought the ticket to the steamer." Jonathan took another lick from the bottle.

"Dear Lord! He was at the pier…" A hard knot tightened in Horace's stomach. Jonathan offered a swig from the bottle to Horace, who shook his head.

"I waited for you," Jonathan said, now slurring his words. "When you didn't get off the ship, figured you didn't make it. And a traffic jam on the wharf. By the time I got to the hotel, constables already coming up the street." He took another drink.

Horace put his arm around Jonathan's shoulders. "We must have arrived at the hotel about the same time. I'm so sorry…"

"I killed him, Horace," Jonathan sobbed. "I bought you that ticket. And now he's dead."

Horace shook his head, "Then we're both to blame. He was a good man. Like a father to me." He swallowed hard on those words.

Jonathan staggered to his feet, clinging to Horace's shoulders. "You'll always be a free man. I can do it now.

You'll have papers. I'll take you to Buffalo. If Grafton is still around, you're not safe."

Jonathan wobbled down the stairs to the lobby floor, stood over his father's shrouded body, took another slug of whiskey.

"I'm grateful, Jonathan. You've done your best for us. You answered my letter for help. You sent us the money at the hotel. Bought the steamer tickets for us. And now you have your hands full with all of…this." Horace nodded toward Spencer's body. "We can manage. As you said, I'm a free man. And we can outrun Grafton, if the constables don't get him first."

"Sic semper tyrannis," Jonathan said, nodding, and finished the bottle.

"Thus always to tyrants," Horace said.

The Erie Canal

—⚬⚬⚬—

The journey from New York to Buffalo on the Erie Canal took nine days. A cold and blustery ride, but for Horace and Fredericka, their birth canal to freedom. They spent daylight hours on top of the barge, drifting past churches and small towns dotting the landscape, enjoying the sights and sounds of early spring along the meadows and marshes. Fredericka didn't mind this windless, waveless, almost motionless waterway. She loved watching the horses and mules tugging the boat along the banks and wondered if they had enough water and were getting tired.

Horace marveled at the locks and the engineering of hydro-mechanics. "It says here in this paper," he noted with the enthusiasm of a boy with a new train set, "this is the second-largest canal in the world, three hundred sixty-three miles, but only four feet deep. This is a big ditch!"

"There be a bigger one?" Fredericka couldn't imagine it.

"Someplace in China. But, look, it took over five thousand Irish Catholics to build this canal. A lot of them died of swamp fever."

"Swamp fever?" Fredericka craned her neck over the side, feeling queasy.

Just then, the captain hollered, "Low bridge!" Up ahead, at a horses' pace, a wooden bridge slowly approached, barely the height of the barge. The passengers sprawled on their stomachs like felled trees as the bridge passed over their backs with only inches of clearance to spare.

Back on her feet, Fredericka put a hand to her stomach. "I don't feel so good." She hurried to the barge's side and vomited. "That swamp fever," she said, but she knew it wasn't malaria.

———⌘———

Horace and Fredericka made their way to Buffalo on the windy northeastern shore of Lake Erie to a modest hotel bordering the lake. With Jonathan's references, they obtained employment with room and board. Horace was a hotel custodian, and Fredericka worked as a maid. They slept in the basement with thirteen other hotel staff members, mostly Africans, their bunks partitioned off by curtains. Their cubicle contained a clapboard bed pressed against the wall with a mattress made of old clothes and distressed towels thrown out from the laundry room. For refugees, this was a sanctuary, a respite from months of fatigue and anxiety. A quiet nest they would need shortly.

———⌘———

Three months had passed since the murder and the runaways' escape through the canal. The cold spring dissolved into a humid, New York summer. Frederick Grafton scoured New York City as much as an obsessed man on the run could. With the police on his tail, he spent his first week hunkered down in a cheap hotel near the wharf, sending Jimmi packing back to the plantation for more money. Jimmi Wheel's orders included telling Henrietta her husband would be delayed returning due to unforeseen business opportunities in Nova Scotia. All this was in the hope of leading any police inquiries on a wild-goose chase and a cold trail and giving Grafton time to find Fredericka and Horace. He would deal with the police later. After all, this was a matter of self-defense and a man's right to his property. He had Jimmi as a witness on his behalf.

Jimmi returned with the cash, himself wanted as an accomplice to the demise of Spencer Redburn. Both men kept their heads down but their eyes open for anyone who might know the whereabouts of Grafton's two runaways.

Though Grafton would not admit it, this obsession was no longer about lost property, and it had become more than just personal. It was about love. The kind of love that turns itself inside out, twisted and unrecognizable, becoming the antithesis of itself—hatred fueled by retaliation. He would settle the score. And she would pay.

Grafton continued to send letters to Henrietta through a Nova Scotia post office, falsely reassuring her of his Canadian prospects. With no evidence of the police on his tail in the city, he became more comfortable with the notion that he got away with murder. Grafton began roaming the side streets in broad daylight, working his way through the barrios and Negro sections of town, including Sandy Ground, a well-known stop for the Underground Railroad. He intimidated dozens of former runaways and threatened and bribed freedmen for information on his two runaways, but his leads only led to dead ends.

But Grafton was not deterred. He made a habit of reading what he called the "Detestable *New York-Daily Tribune*." He hated it; not only was it a publication owned by Horace Greeley, a name that served to prod him regularly of his purpose and pursuit, but because it campaigned so blatantly against slavery. Within its pages, he calculated the routes taken by runaway properties, scoffed at abolitionist editorials, and ridiculed its support for women's suffrage. One day, however, a headline jumped off the page at him, *National Negro Convention to Convene in Buffalo for the Purpose of Considering Their Moral and Political Condition as American Citizens.* Grafton slammed the paper shut. "That's gotta be it!" he shouted out loud, startling Jimmi, who slumbered on his cot.

"Where else would you suppose a readin' and writin' nigger with an attitude would be headin'? To a place with others just like him, that's where! He's goin' to the god-damned nigger convention!" He spit on the floor. "Get your ass up, Wheel!" Grafton ordered. "We're going to Buffalo!"

The National Convention of Colored Citizens was gearing up for a showdown. Up to seventy delegates from a dozen states were expected to attend. At issue was how to change society's view of slavery and show an organized front to the world that African Americans were determined to be free, either through peace or rebellion.

Standing in the marketplace, Horace stopped to hear a Black preacher who was standing on a crate, addressing a small assembly. "The Black man is organizing," he extolled the crowd. "The Liberty Party is going to change the politics in this country from within. The Negro will have what he has been so long denied, the power to change the course of history, and under the Good Lord's grace, end slavery forever!" The crowd of mostly Black men and a few White abolitionists applauded while some passed out convention leaflets.

But others were not so fond of a long drawn-out peace process. One man lashed out at the preacher. "I say we fight back! We ain't goin' nowhere fast enough while our brothers and sisters and mothers are dyin' by the hands of slave masters. I say take up arms! Resist the White man!" There came another round of yays and a spattering of clapping hands in support.

Horace joined a group of men in the back of the crowd who seemed as excited as he was. They convened to a coffeehouse and sat for hours, discussing the future of slavery and the African's role in society. For every question Horace had, there were a dozen opinions leading to more questions. But one thing was sure: for the first time in his life, Horace believed he saw a future and a role he could play in that future.

Horace came home energized, telling Fredericka, "It's happening everywhere. Negros are meeting, getting involved. Frederick Douglass will be here next week for the convention. I could meet him. Help with a newspaper, organizing, and help others crossing the Niagara to Canada. We'll be part of it all, Fred!"

Fredericka turned away from him.

"What's wrong?"

"You can't." Her voice was sobering against his unbridled enthusiasm.

"But it's about freedom. We've always said, *libertas*..."

"I's haven' a baby."

Fredericka's words stumbled him back as if he were startled by a rush of birds. "Baby? We're havin' a baby? My God, that's wonderful! How? I mean, I know how, but, when? Why didn't you tell me?"

"Uh-huh. Winter, I's thinkin'. I tried tellin' you, but..." Her words were lost over the joy in Horace's voice.

"But this is wonderful news! Fred, I couldn't be happier. We'll need a cot. I'll build one. And we should think about his name…Maybe you should sit." He walked her over to their bed and eased her down as if she would break.

"Or her," Fredericka said, obliging his care and sitting. Then turning serious, "You can't do this abolition thing, Horace. Not now. It dangerous. I's gonna need you here."

"But Africans from all over are involved, Fred. It's not dangerous, it's what we always wanted."

He told her about his discussions that afternoon and how a decade of work had organized Black and White abolitionists. He spoke excitedly of the Northern free Blacks who had established a Negro Convention Movement, signifying for the first time, a Black activist network. "Black leaders are organizing all over, and I'm as qualified as any Black man to help the protest against slavery." But his words only produced more fear in Fredericka.

"I'm skeery, Horace. You be found by Masta' Grafton. You be arrested. They take you away. Promise you say no to this bad idea in your head," she begged, "for the baby."

It was a trade-off Horace was willing to make. Maybe next year, he thought. But for now, he would focus his attentions on Fredericka and the baby. He promised he would not participate in the convention, but didn't promise he wouldn't watch the parade of delegates walk into the meeting hall.

Meanwhile, Grafton and Wheel had arrived in Buffalo, a burgeoning city rapidly growing with the influx of the railroads, the canal, and lake shipping commerce. Newcomers were pouring in, and the town was a bustle of opportunity with people flooding the ranks of job seekers, businessmen, and entrepreneurs. Grafton was under no delusion that he could find solid leads to his slaves in this honeycombed environment, and instead, fixed himself on the convention.

If Horace was anywhere, he thought, he would be here. And Fredericka would be close by.

At nine in the morning, the two slave hunters stood at the corner of Washington and Seneca, across from the Public Hall. The area was crowded with onlookers, pedestrians, and dozens of horse-drawn carriages.

"This ain't right," Jimmi Wheel complained. "We got nothin' here. Maybe we should be thinkin' 'bout going back to the plantation." He slipped his whip out, slapped it against his thigh, bored with the interminable search, and hoped his boss felt the same way.

"Shut your bone box!" Grafton said, browsing across the Black faces congregating near the hall. "There's no going back until I have them."

Horace, meanwhile, had ambled up the opposite side of the street a block from the hall, stopping under the shade of a small tree. Up ahead, he saw a circus of activity: carriages blocking the road; and men, women, and children scurrying back and forth; curious onlookers like himself pausing to watch the scene; and reporters with notepads chasing after delegates. A little girl stood amidst the throng selling blueberries from a small basket. A group of young boys pushed and shoved each other to get a better view of the assembly in the street. Horace immersed himself in the scene, enjoying the hour's excitement, but experiencing a pang of frustration for not participating in this historic moment. But he would keep his promise to Fredericka.

Just then, one of the boys threw a firecracker into the street under one of the carriage horses. The terrified horse bolted. It swerved around a corner, throwing the driver into the street. Inside the carriage, a woman screamed. The runaway horse bowled through the crowd in front of the hall at full speed, careening into the little girl. Blueberries and blood spattered the street. The loose reins flapped against the carriage as the wild-eyed horse hurtled straight toward Horace and the tree. The carriage clipped the tree and flipped on its side, stalling the horse's rampage, pinning the passenger underneath.

Horace quickly grabbed onto a loose rein, anchoring it around the tree trunk, yanking the horse around, breaking his bit. The startled animal reared and shook his head, blowing and snorting, and bleeding at the mouth, sweat frothing his coat. Horace calmed the animal with a soft, "whoa boy, whoa," and stroked the horse's neck as people ran to help raise the carriage off the unconscious passenger.

There were calls for a medical wagon. Some people assisted the injured in the crowd, some patted Horace on the back. Some called him a hero. Others nodded their approval and spoke of the Black man's courage and presence of mind.

And amid the disaster, an elated Grafton spied his prey.

He elbowed Jimmi. "There he is! It's the pinch of the game now, my boy!" Grafton hawked a wad of masticated tobacco on the ground, fisted the pistol under his coat, and stepped into the street. He dodged past the commotion surrounding the dead girl, blueberries squishing under his boots, his eyes riveted on Horace. Grafton came up behind the unsuspecting African and cocked the pistol still concealed in his coat.

Just then, a hard slap came down on Grafton's shoulder, spinning him around.

"Frederick Grafton," a tall, imposing man in buckskin said, and before he could react, Grafton was wrenched into handcuffs. Then taking aim at Wheel with his pistol, the man said, "Name's Edward Honey. There's a bounty on you two. I'm taking you in for the murder of Spencer Redburn."

As Grafton was shuffled away, he caught sight of Horace's back, melting into the crowd. The runaway slave never saw him.

The runaway horse gave Horace an immediate profile as a hero in the Negro community and a "good boy" in the White world. Word of his heroics nibbled at him from the outside world, where he had promised Fredericka he would not actively participate. Still, without seeking his place in abolitionists' social context, he found himself more and more involved in that world.

It started with the occasional runaway seeking him out for food from the hotel kitchen. Then came the sporadic request for shelter, and Horace obliged by making room in the basement where he and the other Colored staff resided. He held reading classes in the basement at night, and soon the requests for shelter and learning became more frequent. In the way one slips into a routine with no real intention, Horace and Fredericka had become a gateway for the Underground.

Go West

⌘

In the cold and damp of January, Fredericka gave birth to a son, Isaiah. Horace wept as he held him in his arms, the baby's brightness radiating across his face, lighting up the room. It seemed as though their joy knew no bounds.

By midsummer, a letter arrived, postmarked New York City, New York:

JULY 17, 1844

Dear Horace,
Thank you for your recent letter. I congratulate you both on the birth of your son.

I have news of my own that will be of interest to you. Frederick Grafton and Jimmi Wheel have been arrested and found guilty of manslaughter, not murder, in the death of my father. I suspect bribery goes a long way with police and witnesses. The scalawags will be out of prison in October, but I hope we never hear from them again.

On another note, I expect to see you in person soon. I say this deliberately and with a high degree of anticipation. I plan on marrying. Her name is Emily. After settling Father's estate and putting legal matters and holdings in order, we are moving West. Emily will sail around the Horn to San Francisco Bay while I take supplies by wagon from St. Joseph, Missouri. We will meet up in Yerba Buena for the wedding.

They say there is an excellent opportunity in the West, and I have expectations of starting a loan office and perhaps even a hotel. It would be my utmost wish if you and Fredericka would accompany me if you are up for such a trek.

I propose we plan on meeting in St. Louis next spring and take the trip by wagon in the next year. I look forward to your decision and further correspondence.
Your friend and brother,
Jonathan

The letter invoked another arousal of emotions in Horace: excitement, inspiration, and a strong need to do something about it. West did not mean just a direction on a compass. West meant purpose, hope, and a new beginning, and now, a way to get there. With Jonathan...

He tried convincing Fredericka of the idea. "This boy should not grow up here, Fred, not like this. Not in this godforsaken cold and windy place. This child could be the master of his own fate. In his own world."

But Fredericka wasn't buying it. "Horace, what you sayin'? Where you think he's growin' up?" Fredericka chuckled as she cradled the baby. "This is home. We got food and work, and roof over our head. We be safe here."

"Fred, listen." Horace bent to his knees and looked up at Fredericka and the child. "This is no life, barely getting by, living in a basement with no light and bad air. No privacy."

He turned his head, nodding to the dozen others sharing cubicles with cots and bunk beds. "Hidin' runaways like us only makes us more likely to being found out. We could leave. Go West."

"What you mean by West?" Fredericka turned her head from the baby and gazed down at Horace, trying to gather his meaning.

"A way out, Fred. In his letter, Jonathan said we could go with him to California. I could work in a store. I hear talk there's land for everyone. Remember when we said we'd have a place of our own, with a garden…I reckon we could have a farm."

"A farm? Sakes alive, we have a baby now." Fredericka shook her head as if trying to shake a bad taste from her mouth. "Baby Isaiah not movin' from this place, for some wild notion. We have jobs. We stayin' right here where we safe."

But Horace tightened around that wild notion, and the idea of going West would not wither away. He did not discuss the subject out loud, but the seed grew quietly within him, taking root in his imagination: their own land, their own farm, making a stake in their own future. With time, he thought, in another year, Fredericka might warm to the idea.

And so Fredericka indulged Isaiah in her love, strolling with her radiant boy along the lakeshore only a block from the hotel. She kept watch over him in his basket while she cleaned the hotel rooms. Horace resolved to dream of moving West during his daily routine of mopping floors and maintenance jobs. At the end of every day, he made way to his nightly vigil, gazing out over the lake from the hotel's rooftop.

He loved the view of the night sky and the moon's silvery reflection in the water, but most of all, he loved sharing the stars with Fredericka. "See there, the four stars that make the corner of the cup? Follow the two stars on one side, and it always points to the North Star." He drew her fingers to the sky. "We're always safe following that star."

Fredericka rested her head on his shoulder. "What's that one, there," she said, pointing. "The bright one."

"Venus. The goddess of beauty and love. Your star." He touched his finger to her cheek. "I can see it sparkling in your eyes, beautiful as you!"

"Oh Horace, I ain't beautiful, is I?"

"And courageous and strong."

"You make me laugh, now. I ain't strong, and I ain't courageous without you."

"You don't see what I see. You just don't know it yet."

And so they were content for a time under their canopy of stars, but the winds in Buffalo were about to shift, and any settlement of mind was about to dissolve in the coming tempest.

The Cat

———— ✺ ————

L ake Erie had long been known for its violent nature. Cleaved by ice, not once, but three times, establishing boundaries and identities with each glacial insult. Eventually, it became an angry, lacerated wound. Native Americans who lived along its southern shore named it *Erige*, the Cat, and for good reason: the Cat was capricious, its unpredictability dangerous, its tantrums of thunder and lightning, spectacular. Due to its shallow depth, in summer it ran bathtub warm, and in winter, it was the first lake to freeze. Bordering Canada to the north, Michigan to the west, and New York on the east, it poured most of its fill through the Niagara River and eventually spilled over Niagara Falls. More than two hundred miles long and fifty-seven miles wide at best, the Cat was a narrow, shallow grave for those who showed it no respect.

Wind and water were natural companions to Buffalo, a city situated on the lake's sharp northeast corner. Buffalo had seen the Erie's fury and endured its temperaments. Until midnight on Saturday, October 18, 1844.

It began as a zephyr. A playful wisp of air that tousled hair and made children frolic in the park. It came from no discernible direction, just here and there, tossing scraps of paper in its path, whipping up confetti from the street and resting it a few feet away. For hours, the windy flurries became a steady breeze, enough to knock off a hat and have it tumble down the lane. In Buffalo, the wind was common around Lake Erie, and no one paid much mind to it, even when the breeze became a long, cold draft, pulling out of the southeast, but this was different. The wind was blowing from the north. By the second day, the gale had strengthened, bullying pedestrians, shoving horses against their loads, shrieking through the city, howling across the lake. By the evening of the third day, it had become an unrelenting fury with hurricane-force winds plowing across the long funnel of the great narrow lake like the hand of God scooping out the sea, piling the water of Lake Erie to its southern end, draining the northern shore to a sandy bay.

Such is the nature of the seiche, a violent collision of oscillating waves set up by a single-minded wind. The seiche begins when the wind stops. And once released, this massive build-up of water rebounds to the other side with the force of ten thousand locomotives. The collision creates a backlash of ferocious waves slamming into each other, boiling craters of water pumping up and down, punching and counterpunching, with no forward motion, nowhere for the energy to go, only a severe agitation of nature hell-bent on destruction.

But it was about to get worse. On this particular night, the wind did not stop. It shifted. To the opposite direction. With the same ferocity that bulldozed the torrent to one end of the lake, the wind unleashed the surge with all its kinetic weight and energy but added propulsion to it. The seiche was set in motion. The full force and volume of Lake Erie raced back to its receded edge, pushed by a cyclonic wind gone mad. A twenty-two-foot surge of water had a dead aim on Buffalo, asleep in the storm's bull's-eye. Only one man saw it coming.

The Seiche

Frederick Grafton had smoldered in jail for fourteen months. The best deal money could buy for killing a man, but it irked him that Fredericka and Horace got away. But not for long. Grafton hired the same son-of-a-bitch who chased him down, the bounty hunter Edward Honey, whose allegiance came with a price, regardless of who paid it. For a thousand dollars down and another thousand promised when the plantation owner got out of jail, it made for a decent bit of work on Honey's part. The bounty hunter had snooped around and found a line on the runaways. Now, October. Grafton had been released and had just arrived back in Buffalo as the wind picked up.

The wind hammered the city all day, even driving Horace from his regular visit to the rooftop, hunkering him down early with the others in the basement. He usually enjoyed his moments under the dark sky with no ceiling to limit his dreams and the vast lake brimming with unfulfilled potential. Where he felt most alive, where anything was possible. But this night was not one for dreaming.

Just before midnight, the gale's ferocity aroused him with a discordant high-pitched whine accompanied by a rumbling undertone, not thunder, but something else.

Isaiah began to cry, and Fredericka, already awake and terrified by the wind, walked the cold floor, trying to comfort the infant. Movement in the dark basement and frightened whispers made it apparent the other staff bedded there were also frightened by the noise.

Horace wanted to see it for himself. He jerked on his pants and shirt. "I'll be right back, Fred." He slipped on his boots.

"Where you goin', Horace? You not goin' out there! You not leavin' me and the baby! Whatcha wanna go out there for?" Fredericka's panic sounded as strained as the wind.

"Hush now, I just want to see what's going on out there. Want to make sure the doors are latched and the windows closed. Don't want the hotel to think I didn't do my nightly rounds. Don't you worry none. I'll be back. I promise." He paused to caress the head of his infant son and kissed Fredericka.

Horace bounded up five flights of steps to the fifth floor, taking two steps at a time. At the top landing, he flung open the door and crossed the hallway's length to another door that accessed a secured flight of steps to the roof. The entrance to the roof wouldn't move, held tight by the full force of the gale. He pounded at it, but it would not budge.

BACK IN THE BASEMENT, FREDERICKA ROCKED ISAIAH INCESsantly to comfort herself as well as to calm the baby. The gas lamps hanging on the cellar's corners cast shadows against the wall, eerily illuminating and then obscuring the frightened faces of the others huddled in their cots and sitting against the walls. Their whispers floated on the wind's howl as if their voices might rouse the devil's ear. But the devil was already there. Fredericka caught sight of him in the dim light.

HORACE MADE A RUN AT THE ROOFTOP DOOR. IT TOOK the full running weight of his body to force it open. Stepping out onto the roof, the screaming, sharp, horizontal blast rocked him back. The door slammed shut behind him. He grasped the four-foot-high railing along the roof's ledge and peered into the darkness.

FREDERICKA GAVE OUT A SHARP CRY. GRAFTON WAS creeping around the cots with Jimmi Wheel, who was holding a lamp. They scrutinized the maids' dark faces, the waiters, porters, and runaways gazing back at them. Grafton heard Fredericka and whirled toward her. His shadowy figure grew larger in the dusky light with each step until he loomed over her completely. Jimmi stood beside him, grinning. Fredericka shuddered at the triumph glowing in Grafton's eyes as he hovered over her and the child. "I have you now, you fuckin' little cherry," he sneered, "and your bastard!"

HORACE SCANNED THE MENACING VOID. MINGLED IN the cold and shrieking wind, there arose such an unearthly moan the air's substance seemed to incarnate into something concrete and grotesque. He could see nothing at all. In the depths of the horrific howling, was it possible, he thought, the faint clanging of a bell? And then, a vibration. Slight at first. The railing shivered under his fist. Now thunder, but not thunder. More like…grinding. What then occurred was a vision so out of context as not to be believed.

FREDERICKA FELT SOMETHING UNFAMILIAR GALVANIZE within her, a protective sensibility, a defensive edge, unafraid and defiant. She stood and faced him with the baby in her arms. "You thinkin' you have me?" The command in her voice caught Grafton by surprise. He took a slight change in his stance. Her voice rang out against the storm, pounding the bricks and mortar. "You don't have me. You nary had me, and this chil' you callin' a bastard? He your son! You his daddy, and his granddaddy! But you will never have us!"

ON THE ROOF, HORACE WATCHED IN HORROR AS SOMEthing grew high above him. A monstrous sight evolved out of the unearthly black maelstrom. A wall appeared. Towering above him. It moved upon him, gaining definition out of the dark as it closed in. Horace heard the insane clanging of a bell, louder, louder, the scream of men, and a bellicose blast of a ship's horn that split the night. The 250-ton paddle steamer, SS *Tinder*, borne on the surge of Lake Erie, careened into the building, ripping the hotel in half.

THE BASEMENT EXPLODED. THE *TINDER*'S BOW AND thousands of tons of water smashed through the cellar. Jimmi Wheel clawed against the immense and seething waves, but the overseer's whip caught on an iron rail pinning him into the deep. Frederick Grafton felt the ship's prow strike his breastbone. He was plowed up into the violent swell and hurled into a watery vortex of splintered timbers and shattered bricks as the ship's beam ground him into the second story stairwell of the hotel. The last thing he saw before the tsunami swallowed him in the hellish black water was the fire in Fredericka's eyes.

⊗⊗⊗

HORACE WAS IN THE AIR. THE SHIP'S IMPACT, THE WIND'S power, and the wave's onslaught hurled him into the abyss. He somersaulted through the monstrous dark, an insubstantial being of weightless proportions, a section of railing still gripped in his hand. His back slammed into the water. A rib cracked inside his chest. Breath came short and painful. The thrust heaved him violently against the side of a large, floating object. The railing still clutched in his hand jammed into something and held him against the sea's pressing tumult, giving him time to clamber up the lurching structure and clear it. He held fast through the night listening to the hiss of the flood, and the screams and cries for help rising out of the void, adding his own wailing voice to the misery, "Fredericka! Fredericka!"

Husherbye

⬥⬥⬥

That night hundreds of ships, barges, fishing boats, and canal boats were swept into the city by the seiche. No one had seen the lake disappear. No one had heard the wind shift. The fourteen-foot sea wall was no match for the twenty-two-foot seiche. Known only as a legend of ancient American peoples now made incarnate, the seiche pushed miles of hurricane-force, wind-driven water over the wall, ripping through the south pier and surging into Buffalo, engulfing everything in its path.

Screams pierced the night as the cold swirling waters rose. The furious sea pushed by the relentless wind flooded the city's lower districts, drowning people in their beds, rocking cabins off their foundations, sweeping away entire homes upon its swift and violent surge.

Passenger ships at the mercy of this invisible fury were tossed about like toys. The steamship *Louis* broke her shaft in the crashing oscillating waves that swept four passengers into the black night. The 318-ton *Robert Fulton* lifted like a feather and landed on the beach, throwing three passengers overboard. The *Julia Palmer*, held fast with anchors, rolled and pitched with three hundred passengers on board in Buffalo Bay. In a desperate attempt for rescue several days later, the frantic passengers sent a horse out upon the water. It swam to shore, with a note for help attached to its mane.

When the ship hit the hotel, Fredericka was caught in a huge wall of water and hundreds of tons of wood and iron exploding around her. The cataclysm tore the baby from her arms and embroiled them both in the flood's swirling, suffocating cauldron. A piece of wood slashed her face. She was upside down when she smashed into a floorboard jutting out from the hotel's main level. Her dress caught on the board as the surge swept past her, twirling her upright like a pinwheel above the water. The water shoved her across the room that used to be the basement and stuffed her into a tight corner on the stairwell's broken middle step. Her muted screams were unheeded in the seething, hissing waves rolling over her, and her arms flailed in the water, searching frantically in the dark for her baby.

And then, in what seemed an impossibility, she touched something soft bobbing next to her. Isaiah. She pulled his little body toward her and held him above the torrent. "Baby!" she screamed. The child managed a whimper and a cough. Fredericka hoisted the child on her shoulders as the water continued to rise, closing around her neck. She prodded her foot along the rung and found a footing on the next step up on the stairwell. Now, one foot higher, the water was chest deep. She went for the next step up, the water at her waist. But further attempts to climb higher were fruitless. The rest of the staircase was gone. She was trapped. Standing alone in the dark, the cold water rising, Fredericka began to sing Isaiah a lullaby. "Mammy's baby, go ter sleep / husherbye, husherbye, my honey…"

───── ◦◦◦ ─────

AS DAWN BROKE OUT ACROSS THE CITY, IT EXPOSED AN unrecognizable swath of destruction. Wrecked schooners with damaged hulls littered the port. Hundreds of boats of all sizes were oddly perched along streets, pressed up against buildings, laid about like dead whales upon the shore. Whole city sections lay in ruins. Bare foundations where buildings once stood were covered in water, mud, and rubble.

Entire homes were whisked away like so many tumbleweeds, some found on their sides, some miles from their neighborhoods, crushed against each other. Half-clothed people slogged through the water and floating rubble in a daze, passing dead bodies tangled in the debris.

Makeshift tenders with rescue personnel floated through the devastation, freeing people from their attics and rooftops, pulling them through windows. Splintered glass, signs, broken buggies, a dead dog, pieces of clothing, papers, cups, and twisted fences were gnarled together in the brown waters. Somewhere a child was crying. A man shouting.

Horace slid back into the cold October flood. He had to find Fredericka and the baby. The water was waist high, though no longer rising. He felt the tug of a slight current as the water, spent of its deranged passions, began a slow drift back to the sanity of the lake. The wind had eased slightly, but it still gusted across the city. Horace barely noticed the shivering cold, or his cracked ribs and bruised legs, as he plowed through the murky waters toward the lakefront and the hotel.

What he saw took his breath away. The hotel had been sheared in half. The rafters' broken beams poked out like lifeless limbs, windows were broken and dark, and the brick siding rose like a narrow chimney bearing up one side of the building. Around the corner, the building's entire side was gone; bricks were torn from their mortar down to the first floor. The staircase was exposed but still appeared intact to the basement. Horace called out in an agonizing voice, "Fred! Fredericka!" but the only reply was the sound of creaking wood and scraping metal jostled by the wind. Here the water was almost six feet deep, reaching his neck. Half swimming, half wading, he made his way to the stairwell, partially obfuscated by the shattered wall.

He saw a foot floating in the rubble. His heart raced with fear. He pulled at it, and a body bobbed to the surface. Jimmi Wheel, gray and ghoulish, stared back at him from the murky water, an expression of disbelief frozen into his lifeless face. Horace let out a shout and fell back, horrified. What was going on? Wind, water, ships and broken buildings. What *was* this? And what was Wheel doing here?

Horace felt off-balance. He was dizzy and light-headed. He swirled around in the water. Confusion pressed in on him. Why was he in the water? Just then, as if a feather on a breeze, could it be he heard singing? Even in this madness, he felt compelled to follow the sound.

He waded around to the stairwell. And then he saw her, Fredericka pinned in by debris, chest-high in water. On her shoulders she bore Isaiah, her fingers clinging to his little hands. The boy's head rested gently upon hers. The stairwell above her destroyed. She was shivering uncontrollably. Her lips had turned blue and her eyes were unfocused. He called her name, but she continued to whisper her song, *husherbye, husherbye, husherbye*, shaking in the cold black water, holding Isaiah up.

A streak of adrenalin jolted Horace to his senses. He frantically pulled past floating debris, wood panels, tree limbs, a chair, a partially submerged mattress, a large dresser, and a broken rafter still hinged somewhere above. He called to her, "Fredericka, I'm coming. Hold on," as he tore away at the debris pinning her to the stairwell.

When he reached her, he tried lifting the baby off her shoulders, but Fredericka held fast to Isaiah's hands, shaking her head. "Husherbye not your baby / Husherbye not your baby."

"It's Horace," he whispered. "Give me the baby."

"Husherbye Masta's baby, husherbye Masta''s baby…"

"Fred, we don't have time for this! Give me the baby!"

"Not your baby. Husherbye Masta's baby…"

Horace began to panic. The water was numbing cold. They could die here. What was she doing? What was she saying? "Give me the baby!" His voice more urgent now.

"Not your baby." She shivered. "Husherbye Masta' Grafton's baby."

A shot of anguish tore through Horace. *"Grafton?"* He could hardly choke the man's name out. His brain was on fire. He was in such a state of alarm; he couldn't identify the pain. No time for pain. He had to save Fredericka and the boy. In a calm and steady voice, he said, "Fred, Isaiah is ours, he will always be ours. Give our son to me, now."

Recognition flickered across her eyes, and Fredericka twitched her hands free from the child's fingers. Horace raised him up and into his arms. The baby was limp. Between the wind and the water, Isaiah had frozen to death during the night on Fredericka's brave shoulders.

Spasms of grief welled up within him, mixed with horror and anxiety and exhaustion until he almost lost himself. He wept bitterly as he looked over at Fredericka singing the lullaby again with her arms shaking in the air, still holding the absent form of her dead son. Standing in the godforsaken flood waters of Lake Erie, he cradled the infant's lifeless body in one arm and wrapped his other arm around Fredericka's waist, coaxing her toward him. "Fred, come on now, I've got you," he said, tears spilling down his face. He pulled her from the step and hitched her onto his hip, her feet not reaching the bottom, and he waded the baby and his wife through the water to higher ground.

Working their way to the city's north end where the water had receded, they stumbled through mud and rubble, and horrific scenes of death and destruction: a dead horse still attached to its overturned carriage, a body dangling from a tree, splintered glass in the mud, piles of fragmented wood where a building once stood, a young girl dead on the ground with a rod driven through her chest.

Mud-covered people combed through destroyed buildings, looking for survivors. A makeshift morgue had been set up with the unidentified bodies of men, women, and children lined up like rag dolls waiting for someone to claim them. A seaman stood stone still, gazing down at his family rumpled on the ground. His wife had tied their three children to her waist with an improvised rope to keep them safe, and they all drowned together. Further down at the courthouse, bodies were displayed in windows, and grief-stricken wails riddled the air each time a loved one was identified.

Fredericka did not react to any of it. She simply followed where Horace led, holding onto his hand, singing "Husherbye." As for Horace, he wrestled with life and death, joy and grief in equal measure—cradling his lifeless son and clinging to Fredericka. Like thousands of others, they stumbled through the city, seeking a survivor's camp for shelter, food, and warm clothing. It would take another day before he could let Isaiah go.

Half Now, Half Later

———⊗⊗⊗———

Henrietta Grafton was in a fine pucker. For over a year, she had been in charge of running the plantation. With only a few cursory letters from her husband, she was expected to manage the slaves, the cotton, and the house. Too much. This was not what she bargained for, all this work. That's what slaves were for. Why did she have to tell the overseers how many slaves to sell and which ones to buy? How was she supposed to know how much cotton to pick and how to negotiate the market price? Unacceptable. So hot and perspiring. This was man's work, and she was getting the short end of the stick, and she was right huffy about it. She was so mad at Frederick Grafton, she had a hankering to wring his neck.

Besides, where was Frederick now? First, he goes running off after two no-account slaves and then dashes off to Nova-god-forsaken-Scotia and sends letters describing what he calls "business matters in Canada." Next thing you know, he's arrested for murder and then in jail for months on end for manslaughter. Then off he goes again to Buffalo, all possessed like, with a single letter stating his imminent return with those two niggers.

Well, that was a coon's age ago, and not one word. In walks this Edward Honey, looking savage as a meat ax, drinking her tea, and wanting the other half of the money he says Frederick promised him. What was a woman supposed to do?

Henrietta could hardly contain herself with all the frustrations she had amounted. Still, she walked back to the parlor, having collected herself somewhat, and addressed the bounty hunter. "So explain it to me again," she droned. "What did Frederick promise you?"

"Half now and half later." Honey nudged the brim of his hat up with his thumb to get a better look at the woman. "He paid me one thousand dollars to find his maroons and promised $1,000 when he got out of jail."

Edward Honey had been man-catching for almost two decades and had acquired the reputation of a man who catches what he seeks. His prowess at investigating and trapping the runaway slave or the unlawful citizen was legendary, as was his vigor with the ladies.

Henrietta poured him another cup of tea. The man smelled of buckskin, a bittersweet aroma that made her skin tingle. She fought against the delirious imagination he might taste like a salted caramel apple. As the huntsman's wild scent rustled her skirts, she found herself admiring his long sideburns that swelled into a full, clipped beard and a mustache that crested over his lip like a mudslide. A big man, over six feet tall in stovepipe boots, he had centurion features—a chiseled nose and a broad temple one might call handsome.

"And did you find them?" She blurted out the question at full volume as if her own voice might quell her lusty imagination.

Honey gave her a greasy smile. "I did. I found 'em and told him where they were. Now I want my money."

Danuta Pfeiffer

"Do you take sugar?"

"I do." He tipped his teacup toward Henrietta and nosed the air for a whiff of her. The tang of uncooked meat and parlor velvet clung to her the way rat piss cleaves to cotton, a scent not unpleasing to his nature.

She slipped a teaspoon of sugar in his cup and stirred it for him. "I haven't seen nor heard a word from Frederick," she said with a sigh. "I'm just a poor woman who seems to have been abandoned." She stopped stirring, licked the teaspoon, and smiled when Honey's eyes lit up. Then she drove the utensil into the sugar bowl with the resolve of a knife into a carcass.

Honey looked at his cup, the picture of the teaspoon against her tongue still swimming in his head. He slurped the tea down in one satisfying draught. "I can see you are a woman needing to be avenged."

Henrietta tugged a hanky from her skirt, dabbed a false tear, and took a seat on the chesterfield next to the bounty hunter. "Any Christian man would understand my plight, wouldn't he?"

Honey removed his hat. A bear-greased curl, the size of a small sidewinder, dangled from his forehead. I'm Mormon myself, ma'am, but I feel for your predicament, I really do."

Henrietta leaned over and touched his knee. "A Mormon, you say? Do you have many wives, if I may be so bold?"

"Not yet, ma'am. But I'm always on the lookout to help those in distress like yourself." A devilish smile slid across his lips. She was a church-bell, alright, a bit too talkative for his liking, but that could be overlooked for the right reason.

"What if I asked your help to find my husband?"

"And if he's not to be found? Beggin' your pardon, ma'am, but sometimes a man absquatulates for reasons unknown."

"I can't imagine why he'd do that and leave this whole plantation to little ole me," she whined. "It's hard enough running a household, much less an entire estate without a man's help."

"It's a big job for a little lady, I can see that." Honey placed his teacup on the end table. "Dear lady, how can we help each other?"

Henrietta's voice turned steely. "Find the buck nigger and mulatto whore, and you can keep them both, sell them, shoot them, whatever you want. The bounty was two thousand five hundred dollars, so they're valuable enough to satisfy my husband's promissory note and then some. Plus, another $500 bonus to find Frederick." Then changing her tone to a snivel, "Just find out what happened to him. A woman needs to move on."

Honey's brows formed a threshold of storm clouds over the dark wet stones of his eyes. "Well, now, we just might have a deal. For I am a bitter foe to rogues, ma'am. And if your husband has run into foul play, or something else, I am bound to find him. We could start with the five hundred dollars."

"Call me, Henrietta."

Touching her hand that was touching his knee, Honey replied, "Let's say, half now, half later?"

Rebuild a City

───⊗∞⊗───

December in Buffalo was brutal. Fredericka huddled in a makeshift hovel assembled from piles of debris on the outskirts of town. Horace had rummaged through timbers and bricks, salvaging enough for a foundation and floorboards. Overhead, he fixed a tin roof laid upon walls of logs and insulated gaps with bits of clothing and straw. Two discarded chairs and a framed bed raised off the floor completed the shed.

He was hammering a door to the shack, hindered by the rusted hinges that wouldn't give. He threw the hammer on the ground in frustration. *This was freedom, nothing but death and destruction.* The mud was as cold and hard as his sense of defeat. The daylight hours were short, the temperature dropped, and the earth tilted away from the sun. Prospects were more muck and mold. Even as a slave, wagered, and owned, Horace had never felt so helpless. At least the plantation had some semblance of place—for what it was worth—a little food in his stomach, a hearth to sit by at night with those who suffered with him.

But this "freedom" rang hollow and dangerous. Runaways smuggled through the Underground brought more and more manhunters to the city. They were snagged for their bounties and disappeared overnight. It could happen to them too.

Intrepid volunteers boated runaways to Canada, but it didn't mean freedom if the hunters chased them down across the border. At least working and living at the hotel on the lakefront offered a place to live in the shadows where they could keep their heads down and their profiles low. But now, he and Fredericka were exposed and trapped, living in a drafty shed with no clear prospects in sight for a Colored man.

Horace turned to look at Fredericka sitting in the chair by the door frame, staring out at nothing. She seldom spoke, padded after him like a kitten, ate when encouraged, slept when told. She followed him everywhere, untethered by emotions, comforted only by her instinct to trust him. His heart ached for her, for them both, but there was no way out.

Until there is a way out. Even hardship must obey the laws of nature and bend to the will of time. Just as receding tides defy their ebb and advance again by the tug of the moon, upon the last drop of human endurance, there is a refilling that comes with the tug of opportunity. But in the seconds before that cup is filled, in that solitary space, humans either flounder or rally.

It is so effortless to fold into emptiness, to collapse into despair. Giving up takes no more effort than a final breath, a last embrace of disappointment, a bitter acquiescence to life's betrayals. Having surrendered, the eyes close, the heart succumbs, the tide has missed the moon, and one has missed it all.

So when an Irishman hollered at Horace, "Hey, you there, nigger," Horace felt himself withdraw, turned his back, and did not answer. But once again, the man shouted, "Nigger! You build this yeself?"

Horace rankled under the address and shook off his stupor long enough to reply, "I beg your pardon?"

"I beg yer pardon, he says." The man mocked him. "Well now, ain't ye a high-falootin' boy!" He laughed. "I'm askin' if ye built this shack by yerself. Mighty fine work for a nigger. Building from scraps if ye did."

Horace didn't answer.

The man spit a brown, sloppy wad of tobacco onto the frozen ground. "I'm askin' if you want work, boy, work. I've got work cleaning up, rebuilding. I'll give ye room and board for a day's labor."

Indignation pulled Horace to his feet. "I am not your nigger. And I am not a boy. I'm a man. And I have a name. It's Horace Redburn." Defiance heated his chest and ran up the side of his face. "You want to hire me? You pay me a man's wages, plus room and board with heat for my wife and me."

The man was taken aback, and then, with some admiration, said, "Damnation, you're an ornery Black cuss. I ain't nary heard a darkie talk in such a manner. Fine, then, but if you work for me, don't let yer attitude get the better of ye. Got it?"

Horace gave a nod.

"As fer the missus," McGraw chucked her a look and spit on the ground. "She White?"

Horace shook his head, no.

"She looks White. 'Tis agin' the laws of nature mixin' the races."

"I assure you, sir, my wife is not White. She is mulatto."

"Mulatto, ye say? You mean she has White in 'er?" He spit again, looked away, and after a pause, "Right, then, she can work in the boardin' house. Fer that I'll give ye room 'n' board. Name's Checker McGraw." And with the pitch of his chin indicating a scrabbly crew assembled on the street, he said, "The rest of the buffers, yonder. Thirty cents a day for Colored work. Best I kin' do."

"Forty-five," Horace countered as McGraw started to turn away.

McGraw spit through his teeth, "Key-rist! But you're a Gombeen! Forty or I'm done bargainin' with a darkie."

Horace nodded. "It's a deal."

Under the tutelage of Checker McGraw, Horace helped rebuild Buffalo. McGraw was an Irishman who had helped build the Erie Canal, and he found much work in the devastated city to keep a force of men well engaged. Horace learned the art of hammer and saw, measuring and framing, roofing, and in doing so, began to rebuild a life he and Fredericka had lost.

The boarding house was a ramshackle three-story building in the First Ward District of Buffalo, one of few buildings in the area that survived the seiche. Horace and Fredericka occupied the Negro section above the saloon in a small, unheated room the size of a stall. Horace hauled up the bed he had salvaged, the mattress stuffed with straw. Boxes and crates made for shelving on one side of the room for an ewer, basin, and an oil lamp. A raggedy throw rug on the floor and a small three-drawer dresser completed their abode.

A small window opened above the privy located five feet from the building. With no proper stench-trap, the noxious effluvia ill-afforded any fresh air to the room. Below, the saloon and dining area rang out with the blare and battles of tanked-up sailors, longshoremen, and canal workers. Fresh water was drawn daily from a well on a nearby street corner. And soap had long ago lost the challenge against the floors and walls saturated with the sour odors of smoke, urine, and unwashed men.

But Horace and Fredericka were grateful for it all.

Fredericka had little time to adjust to her new setting or to fully recover from the loss of Isaiah. She was quickly put to work by Checker McGraw's wife, Caitlin, who informed her new domestic that St. Catherine, her namesake, instilled the sacrifice of hard work as God's way of leading the poor from evil consequences. Since Blacks placed just below Irish Catholics on the social scale, Caitlin took satisfaction in lording it over someone below her rank. She worked Fredericka hard emptying chamber pots and wastewater, carrying coal for the saloon stove, cooking, serving food, cleaning, fetching water, and washing bed linens and clothing.

It was Mistress Henrietta all over again, but Fredericka was as dormant as the seeds she used to carry in her pocket. Still speechless from her trauma, she adapted to her plight with a sense of urgency, as if she could block remembrance with physical effort, as if the strain of muscles could overcome a broken heart. Merely nodding and pointing through the day satisfied her isolation and created a fortress against feeling. At night, she collapsed upon her bed with Horace and slept exhausted without dreaming. She continued in her love for him but with a vague passion only her skin remembered—his touch a curious respite beyond the need for words.

But life was about to change for them yet again.

It Takes a Bullet

⸺⸺ ∞∞∞ ⸺⸺

E dward Honey pursued his interest back in Buffalo. Amid the tumult and displacement of much of its citizenry, his skill was restricted to nothing short of an amateur sleuth, stopping men on the street, bribing whores, and hanging out in taverns hoping for a break. No one gave him the time of day. It seemed everyone was looking for someone, and few cared to invest time or resources on two runaway slaves from a Southern cotton plantation.

Honey returned to the Grafton Plantation to report to Henrietta on his dismal findings: the facts of the flood, his suspicion that Frederick Grafton and his sidekick Jimmi Wheel may have been among the unidentified dead and buried, along with the two runaways. But without any evidence, his findings were inconclusive. Nevertheless, he stayed as a plantation guest and took in the comforts he found there.

It gnawed at him that none of his prospects in Buffalo could be found. Honey had the nose of a hound, and he sniffed around the idea that one, maybe two of them could disappear, but all four? This hound was not easily pulled off the scent, and he resolved to get back to Buffalo, but he would wait out the winter and invest his time in the remuneration of a wealthy, grief-stricken potential widow.

By the following spring, he needed some distance from Henrietta. Her money was good, and the sex wasn't bad, but he couldn't stand the woman. So he thinned out her crop of slaves, generally women and children, pocketed the money, kept the men in the fields, and hightailed it back to the city on Lake Erie with the promise of findings. He had to get back to doing what he loved, man-hunting.

⸺⸙⸺

Buffalo was humming with activity. Spring was in the air, and construction work was on the rise. Horace had been working longer and longer hours, and he could feel his weariness catch up to him as he climbed the boarding house staircase and walked down the hall. The room was dark when he unlocked the door. He found Fredericka curled up in the corner, tears streaking down her cheeks. He bolted to her side. "Fred, what happened?"

All she could do was shudder and point to the door.

"Did someone come in? Did someone hurt you?" Panic rose in his voice.

She nodded.

"Who was it? What happened? Tell me!" When she couldn't answer, he pleaded, "Fred, for God's sake, talk to me!" The sound of raucous laughter and the out-of-tune piano from the saloon downstairs filled their room. Horace fumbled around for matches and lit their small oil lamp. The shadows danced on the wall and flickered across Fredericka's face. Horace dipped a cloth into the water bowl and wiped a spot of blood from her lip.

She wanted to tell him about the sailors in the hall. How one of them pinned her to the wall, and the other one drove his hand up her skirt. How she tried to scream, but no sound came out. She wanted to tell him they called her a pretty nigger and how they stripped off her undergarments. One of the men already had his pants undone, but when he came close, she managed a swift kick to his groin. While the man screamed in pain, she bit the other man's hand holding her to the wall. This gave her time to find a small paring knife in the pocket of her apron. A few thrusts of the blade in the air gave her time to back down the hall, into the room, and lock the door. She wrapped herself into the corner of the room, hoping they wouldn't try to come after her and knock down the door. Horace had come home just minutes later. The sailors had already gone.

But her words did not come. Instead, Horace read in her eyes, the fright, the flash of anger, and the pain. The knife still held trembling in her hand. He took the knife and placed it on the side table next to them. "Who was it?"

She pointed downstairs and held up two fingers.

"Two men? From downstairs?"

She nodded.

"Did they come in the room?"

She shook her head.

"Dammnit, Fred! I should never have left you alone in this pigsty! It's all my fault!"

She shook her head and put her fingers to his mouth, imploring him to stop. Still sitting on the floor, he wet the cloth with the tip of his tongue and caressed the tears from her face.

"We've got to get out of here, Fred. I'm not leaving you alone anymore. I promise we'll find a way out of here. In the meantime, stay put. Don't go out."

She shook her head and twisted her hand up as if to say, "What do you expect me to do?" She slapped her fist in the palm of her hand—defiant. She would not cower.

"Okay, okay. I know. But promise me you'll stay clear of the saloon. Don't go anywhere alone if you can help it. Promise me?"

She nodded.

"And I promise you. We will not live like this for long. I'm saving up a little money. We could go to St. Louis and meet Jonathan there…" His voice trailed off. He was resolved to come up with a plan for St. Louis, but the timing never seemed right with Fredericka's condition and their lack of money, but a plan would be forced on him.

BUFFALO HAD REBUILT FROM ITS LOSSES IN THE FLOOD, and the town awoke to its prosperity, invigorated and bustling. It didn't take long for Edward Honey to track down the Negro population and render the whereabouts of a Colored man with his White-looking wife. Horace was working on a framing job with McGraw when Honey showed up. The bounty hunter was rolling tobacco and leaning against a two-by-for. He licked the paper, stuck the cigarette in his mouth, and swiped a match against his belt buckle.

"You Checker McGraw?" Honey lit the cigarette and blew a wisp of smoke with a casualness that spelled trouble.

"The same." McGraw held up a board toward Horace, who was standing on a ladder above him.

"Hear you gotta boy workin' for you, name of Horace. Tall, lanky-like, tanned color. Kinda looks like the nigger on the ladder."

"What ye want to know fer?" McGraw put the board down.

"Owner wants her property back. Belongs to a plantation in South Carolina."

Horace felt a jolt in his chest. He called out from the top of the twelve-foot ladder, "Mister McGraw?"

McGraw put a hand up, stopping him while staring down Edward Honey. "Ye may have noticed, this ain't South Carolina. 'Tis a free state, and I ain't nary heard of a man named Horace."

"Is that right?" Honey tossed the cigarette on the ground. "Well, I've come to take the nigger back, just the same. There's a bounty on his head, and I have a warrant for his arrest." He pulled out a paper from his jacket and handed it to McGraw. "Now, get down off that ladder, boy."

"Wait a minute," McGraw said, quickly reading through the document. "This here is a warrant from South Carolina. You got no rights here. He stays with me."

Honey pulled a six-shooter from his belt. "I guess you don't understand. I'm not askin' you, I'm tellin' you, the nigger comes with me." He wiggled the gun at Horace. "Come on down, boy. Game's over."

Horace took a step down. And just as he took another step, he leaped from the ladder, falling to the ground but not before shoving the ladder toward Honey, toppling him over. Honey's gun went off. The bullet struck Horace in the shoulder. He grabbed at his wound and struggled to his feet. Honey lay under the ladder, unconscious. McGraw stood between them.

"Run, man, run! I'll hold him off as long as I can," McGraw said.

Horace was in shock. He wanted to know if he killed the man. He wanted to thank McGraw. His arm hurt. All he could say was, "But…"

"Go!" McGraw knelt next to Honey. "He's okay, lad, now go!"

When Horace burst into the boarding house, Fredericka knew something was wrong. Her green eyes lit up with fear when she saw the bloodstain on his shirt.

"We gotta go, Fred." Horace tugged her arm, and Fredericka dropped the pail of ashes she was carrying. "Now!"

They ran through the boarding house and out the back door, past the privy, crossing through alleys, ducking around buildings, and winding their way through the narrow, windy streets to the docks. Foundries and factories lined the harbor. Mechanic shops were working overtime, and a brawl had broken out in front of one of the taverns. The fugitives went unnoticed, wriggling between barrels of sugar, crates of wheat, and hiding behind nets filled with cargo. Horace's shirt was now soaked with blood. He was breathing hard.

Fredericka tore a strip off her skirt and bandaged his arm. "Need…doctor," she said. She looked pale, and distress played across her eyes.

Horace managed a smile. "So it takes a bullet to get you talking to me again? I'll have to remember that." He touched his arm and winced. "I knew you'd come back," he whispered, and then more urgently, "We gotta get out of town."

She shook her head, no.

"Listen to me, Fred, we've been found out. One of Grafton's men—a bounty hunter. We spent months helping rebuild this city, Fred, but we're rebuilding the past. People, they don't care about the law or people like us. Runaways disappear every day. It's not safe. Jonathan's been writing to us about going to St. Louis. We could go West with him. I need you. Can you help me, help us?" Horace leveled his gaze on her in the fading light. "Can you do it, Fred? Can you? 'Cause we ain't going back." He was sweating now and panting with pain.

With every anxious breath from Horace, Fredericka felt her panic subside. A sea of calm flooded through her as warm as love. Horace needed her. Somewhere between her head and her gut, she found a trove of strength, a power yet unfamiliar but within reach. That accessibility squared her shoulders and softened her eyes as though she were looking at a summer sky. A surge of confidence lifted her to her feet. "Ain't…isn't a word," she said. Pulling Horace up, she whispered, "Let's go."

They blended into the dark waterfront. The harbor was infested with lake vessels and steamboats. Although night had settled over the city, the port was busy with longshoremen, crates, nets, and merchandise. Apples, poultry, potatoes, and pigs lined the pier in a jumble of boxes and barrels. Despite the hour, passengers had lined up for embarkation on a steamer bound for a port in Detroit and journeys west. Nobody took notice of two Negroes boarding the steamer while clutching a crate of green beans.

⸺⧼⧽⸺

EDWARD HONEY WOKE UP WITH A GOD-AWFUL HEADACHE. The blurry visage of a man hovered over him. "Where am I?"

The blurred face responded, "You're in McGraw's Boarding House in Buffalo, New York. I'm Doc Musgrove. You've had a pretty good bump to the head."

Honey tried to lift up.

"No, you don't," Musgrove said and gently pushed him back down. "You won't be going anywhere for a while. Do you know your name?"

"Honey. Ed Honey." He grimaced and put his hand to his head.

"You'll be okay, but it's gonna hurt for a while." The doctor packed a few items into a satchel on the bedside.

"What happened?" Honey winced.

Another voice from somewhere in the room said, "Ladder. Hit ye in the head."

The doctor added, "You have a commotion of the brain, probably a fractured skull. Just need time to rest up. Yer lucky." He got up, shook hands with a man in the corner, and left the room.

"Who 'er you?" Honey rasped, addressing the man in the corner.

The man came closer to the bed. "I'm McGraw. This is my place. You came to me lookin' fer Horace."

"Where is he?" Honey tried rising up and then eased his aching head back on the pillow.

"The darky's gone. Sorry 'bout the bump to ye head, but yer welcome to his room for as long as ye need."

"His room?" Honey shot a glance about as if he could catch sight of his fugitive.

"Aye. 'Tis the last room in me boarding house. Figured I owed you a place for the knock on the head, at least till you get back on yer feet. I'll see ye get some supper." McGraw turned and left.

Edward Honey was not a man to take defeat lying down. Henrietta's bounty for the slaves had slipped his grasp, but he would get it back. Besides, getting bettered by a nigger was no good for a man of his reputation. A fractured skull? Honey didn't give a rat's ass about that, except his headache was fierce, and seeing double wouldn't help him aim a gun, and the damned ringing in his ears disturbed his peace of mind. But this was nothing compared to what he would inflict on that sonofabitch nigger when he got his hands on him.

He struggled up from the bed and swung his feet to the floor. His head felt like it was going to rip off his shoulders. He blinked his eyes, trying to focus. The room wasn't much to look at: the bed, a rag of a rug on the floor, a side table with an oil lamp, and a small, three drawer dresser. Honey wobbled to his feet and went to the dresser. Holding the top for balance, he tugged on the first drawer. It contained two shirts, a calico dress, a pencil, and a scrap of paper with the alphabet scrawled on it. The second drawer held some more clothes and a few candles. The third drawer had a book in Latin and a bundle of letters from the Skylark Hotel in New York City.

St. Louis

∞

G old was just over the horizon, a time soon to come when no forfeit would be too dear for the pursuit of nuggets gleaming in the sun. For now, however, the precious lure was the promise of new land, new life free of disease, and an escape from the harsh landscape of poverty. It seemed no one could resist this gilded covenant: severe sacrifice for a promissory note.

Seduced by this unequal transaction, a massive wave of fortune hunters, adventurers, immigrants, farmers, entrepreneurs, and dreamers flowed in from every corner of the world. They were drawn to the idea of free land and endless bounty from the earth. Some would make their way across the seas, leaving behind famine and despair to embark on a new world filled with the bread of opportunity.

Some facing bankruptcies, depression, and unemployment bade farewell to home and hearth, hoping for a fresh start. Others turned a few good games of poker and faro to their advantage, gambling on an uncertain future, parlaying their way to the last horizon of comfort and civilization, St. Louis, Missouri. Situated at the crossroads of opportunity, this was the gateway to auriferous dreams. Three years before Sutter's Mill and the discovery of precious stones in a pan, new life in the West carried a glimmering promise of wild freedom, and the land rush had already begun.

Spring arrived early in St. Louis that year. Or maybe it just seemed early with so much hustle and bustle in the streets. The pace was quicker, the talk slicker, cash flowed as fast as the booze. Everything was in motion. A wild sea of anticipation. Throngs of merchants, bullwhackers, gamblers, clergymen, politicians and farmers, Indians and Mexicans, fur traders, and outlaws filled the streets with the dazed look of an unquenched appetite.

Hotels were overcrowded, blacksmiths were overworked, saddlers and gunsmiths worked feverishly to provide equipment for the arduous journeys to California, Oregon, and Santa Fe. The air hung heavy with the odor of horses, mules, and oxen and the cacophony of wagons and whips and the holler of men. Everyone was eager to participate in the torrent, make their mark, plow their own destiny, whatever it took, and whatever the cost.

Horace stepped into this social intoxication a sober man, his sensibilities calculated in equal measure of fear and fate but not so weighted on either side to divert his focus West. He stood at the entrance of Joseph Murphy's wagonyard. Wood, wheels, and workmen occupied the vast yard smelling of sawdust and pitch, and ringing with the sounds of hammers and saws, and smiths pounding iron. The buzz of activity energized the air.

Horace removed his hat, addressing the wagon builder. "The name's Horace Redburn," he said above the clamor. "I'm looking for work." He fiddled with his hat in his hands, but his muscular body bristled with confidence. Fredericka stood beside him, her gingham dress tied back with a bustle, curly hair lapping her shoulders, her honey complexion aglow.

Joseph Murphy was a busy man. He stood at his workbench, sawing a longboard. The Irishman glanced at Horace and then back to his work. "Got no time, boy." He picked up the slat, blew off the dust, eyed the edge, and set it back on the bench. He gave out a sigh and scanned his shop, his hands on his hips.

Horace handed him a tool resting nearby. "You'll be needing a smoothing plane, Mr. Murphy."

Murphy looked surprised. He paused for a moment staring at Horace, and then pushed the plane back toward him. "Go ahead, then," he ventured and crossed his arms.

Horace jumped at the chance. He stroked the plank's rough-hewn side, bent over it, and eyed the line. He took the plane in his large, steady hands and whisked it along the wood, peeling the fibers to a smooth, straight edge.

"Now size it," Murphy said, unmoved by the demonstration.

Horace made a quick check of the adze, mallets, axes, and chisels hanging on hooks along the wall. He grabbed a rule and deftly measured the plank. "Ten feet by four inches, sir." Horace gripped the rule as though his life depended on it.

"Type of wood?" Murphy asked.

"Ash."

"What about ash?"

"It's strong." Horace met Murphy's duel head-on, taking to the Irishman's drill, anxious to make an impression, but careful not to show the White man a sense of pride.

Murphy uncrossed his arms. "What'd you say your name was?"

"Horace, sir. From Buffalo. Worked for Checker McGraw."

"You know McGraw?"

"Yessir." Horace lowered his head and fiddled with his cap.

"Good man, McGraw." Murphy considered the Negro before him.

Overhearing the conversation, Murphy's accountant, Charles LaBoutain, strode up alongside Murphy. From Horace's downcast perspective, he noticed LaBoutain's shoes first—shiny, long, and black. The bookkeeper's feet extended into peg-thin legs and narrow hips pinned in by a no-nonsense waistcoat. His angular frame tapered up to stiff shoulders upon which teetered a gooseneck and a sharp Adam's apple that bobbed when he spoke.

Fredericka felt an instant dislike to the man and stepped in closer behind Horace.

"If I may, sir," LaBoutain addressed his boss. "May I make a few inquiries to this man's status?" A Puritanical pinched nose loomed over a long face and a chin severe enough to pierce wood.

Murphy shrugged. "Be my guest."

"You hired out?" The bookkeeper snipped at Horace.

"Sir?" Horace felt his chest tighten, his pulse begin to race.

"Hired out. From your owner." LaBoutain's voice dripped with derision.

"No. No, sir. My wife and I, we are emancipated." Horace lied. Aware his challenge to a White man's contempt could land them in trouble, Horace shrunk back and placed the rule he held in his hand back on the wall.

LaBoutain pressed on. "So you're self-purchased? Or man-umitted? Got a freedom license? Folks 'round here don't cotton to free darkies with no license from the State of Missouri."

Horace tried to swallow, but his throat had gone dry. "Yessir," he faltered, thinking maybe he and Fredericka should make a run for it. "I have a license somewhere about…"

Just then, Fredericka came from behind Horace, touched his arm, and avoiding eye contact, addressed the accountant as though talking to her boots. "We have it. Back in the boardin' house, with our things." Horace held his breath and gazed at Murphy for his verdict.

Murphy waved them both off. "Enough. Ye can start tomorrow. Daybreak."

LaBoutain pressed him."But, sir, his papers…"

"I need all the good help I kin get!" Murphy blasted back at the bookkeeper. "You know it as well as anybody. I can't keep up with the orders as it 'tis." The accountant glowered at Horace, turned on his heel, and huffed off.

"Thank you, Mr. Murphy, sir, you won't be disappointed," Horace said, taking Fredericka's arm.

"Best not be," Murphy mumbled as he returned to sanding his wood and back to the business of building wagons.

Out of sight of the wagonyard, Horace lifted Fredericka off her feet and kissed her. "We're going to make it, girl!" he cheered. "We're going to make it!"

EMILY MANHEIM WAS THE SIXTH DAUGHTER OF A NEW York City tailor. A broad-minded girl, she wanted more from life than the endless toil of her mother and sisters: cooking, washing, sewing, and cleaning after a household of children. She dreamed of independence and escapades, store-bought clothes, and pretty bonnets. So when she met Jonathan Redburn during a fitting for a suit at her father's shop, it was fate and fortune. They kept company frequently, meeting for dinner, carriage rides in the countryside, and picnics in the park until their courtship led to significance. Jonathan Redburn was in love. Emily Manheim felt the same way. When he proposed marriage—she proposed a wedding in California.

The tide of opportunity had swept the country toward an aggressive pursuit of the West and the promise of new beginnings, and Emily envisioned her own manifest destiny in the allure of California. Jonathan was infatuated by the girl and her extraordinary dream, as much for her hunger beyond the constraints of a suffocating society he loathed, as by the girl herself. Ill-suited to the boredom of business, each passing day filled Jonathan with Emily's inspiration for a life out West.

Their future was set. Emily would board a ship for the journey around Cape Horn in South America and north to Yerba Buena in California, soon to be renamed San Francisco. The voyage was advertised to take upward of four months or more. Onboard, she would carry some furnishings for their new home. Meanwhile, Jonathan would travel West by wagon train, driving oxen, mules, and cattle for their stake in the frontier.

The day before her departure, as they ambled through the park, she handed him a velvet box. "A small remembrance," she said, twirling her parasol. Inside, a locket on a silver chain, and inside the locket, her tiny portrait. It rendered her likeness with dark ringlets framing a long face, bright, determined eyes, and heart-shaped lips. She was wearing the bonnet he bought her, trimmed in roses and ribbons. He removed his top hat, swept the chain over his head, and clutched the locket. "I will keep it with me always," he promised.

The fate of dreamers—Horace, Fredericka, and Jonathan— converged in St. Louis. The ongoing correspondence between Jonathan and Horace spurred the resolve for their westward migration. One sought adventure and love, the other, freedom and independence. The hopes of each unable to survive without the other and the call of the West afforded their opportunity. There was no going back from hope.

A Toast to Love

———— ∞∞∞ ————

Joseph Murphy's wagon yard was a noisy cacophony of saws, ladders, timbers, poles, hammers, wheelwrights, blacksmiths, and men either buying or building wagons. The wagon builder couldn't make prairie schooners fast enough, the demand by far outpacing the supply. Joseph Murphy had meticulous standards. For quality and craftsmanship, the Irishman's wagon building company was considered one of the best, and in 1845, St. Louis was the world's capital for wagons.

Earlier that spring, hundreds of Murphy's red, white, and blue farm wagons sparkled with fresh paint and spotless white canvases in a large field behind his shop. Each was a promise of a shiny future. By summer, the inventory of wagons had vanished, and the demand to provide the next spring's supply pressed everyone into overtime.

June was hot and humid in the city, and Horace was fighting a losing battle against the sweat trickling from his brow and burning his eyes. He was lying on his back, tarring the seams on a new wagon bed, when someone gave him a swift kick to his thigh. Horace shot up from under the wagon. "What the hell?" He flashed a smile of recognition. "Jonathan!" he cried.

"Hells' bells, I hardly recognized you smothered in sawdust," Jonathan said, grabbing Horace's shoulders and staring at him. "And your arms—beefier than I remember. You look strong as an ox!"

"Strong enough to take you on any day!" Horace whooped.

To the workers' astonishment, Horace and Jonathan embraced with great bear hugs, each slapping the other on the back. The two friends took another look at each other and, with a laugh, embraced again.

"When'd you get in town?" Horace wiped his hands on a rag. "I was expecting you next month."

"Last night. Couldn't wait a minute longer. Good to see you, my friend. It's been too long." Jonathan's eyes were bright and alive and filled with expectation.

"Almost two years," Horace said, sighing.

"Seems longer." Jonathan's voice fell for a moment.

Horace took his leather apron off and hung it on a hook. "Shift's nearly over. Hope you don't have any plans for dinner. Fredericka will love to see you. She's a seamstress now. We have room in the boarding house."

"I'm starved." Jonathan slapped Horace on the back as they left the workshop.

Dinner later that night was a joyous affair among the three friends. Though the room Horace and Fredericka shared was small, the flicker of oil lamps and candles warmed the walls, and the bottles of wine Jonathan brought made it a festive occasion. "A sparkling Catawba, all the way from Cincinnati," Jonathan boasted as he uncorked the first bottle.

"Jonathan," Fredericka asked, "is it true you teach Horace Latin?"

Jonathan burst into laughter. "No, my lovely woman, the other way around. He taught me! Horace was always reading books—he was the one who should have gone off to school. I pissed it away on wine and women."

"What you mean?" Fredericka's face gleamed in the candlelit room.

"I was always chasing the ladies," Jonathan said, and then becoming serious, "until Emily, that is. You'd love her. Here's her portrait. A locket she gave me." He slipped it from around his neck and passed her picture around. "She's bright and funny, and my God, fearless! California was her idea." He slipped the chain back around his neck. "She'll sail around the Horn, taking supplies, money, and whatnot. By the time I get there next fall with supplies, we'll have our digs all set up. We're getting married there. Horace will be best man, won't you Horace? And we'll travel West together, right?"

"I'd be honored to be your best man, sire." Horace gave a little bow of his head. "And traveling together would be a great adventure."

"You not goin' anywhere without me." Fredericka picked up a spoon and waved it in the air. "Besides, who's gonna do all the cookin' and washin'?"

"Jonathan, of course!" Horace roared, and the three friends shared another laugh around the table.

Jonathan poured more wine. "We'll need supplies, horses, mules, cattle, oxen, wagons, and a crew to get us there. I hardly know where to begin." He took a sip from his glass. "We need rifles and ammunition, and I can't even shoot a gun!" He laughed. "We can buy the wagons here and steamboat up the Missouri with 'em. Load up in St. Joe. I hear we can buy most of our supplies there and catch a wagon train by next April, May at the latest. There's a lot to do in the next nine months."

As they settled around the warmth of the dinner table, Horace became quiet, peering at Fredericka with an odd look on his face, his hands clasped in front of him, his eyes sparkling with what could have been tears, except for the glow on his face. "Fredericka," he spoke softly, and both Jonathan and Fred had to lean in to hear him. "We haven't made it official, really. I mean, we know we belong together, but we've never, you know, had the ceremony. Signed the papers..." He drifted off and closely watched her face.

"You sayin' what I think you sayin?" Her shy gaze behind her bangs of curly hair made his heart beat faster.

"We've been here talking about Jonathan and Emily getting married in California. How about you and me getting married?"

"You mean, for real?"

Horace jumped up and came around to her side of the table. "For real. Let's get married. We could find a preacher... here in St. Louis..."

"Why, that's a top idea!" Jonathan sprang up and poured another round of wine.

"No," she said, taking Horace aback for a moment. "Let's get married next year, on the wagon train, after the baby is born."

Horace blinked at Fredericka as if he didn't understand the words. "Baby?"

Fredericka nodded.

"We're havin' a baby?" Horace could barely speak above a whisper. "Oh, Fred!" he said with a sigh. "This is wonderful news!" He kissed her gently and caressed her cheek with the back of his fingertips.

"I want to marry you on this wagon train, where we is free. On free ground. I want us to marry in true freedom. I want our baby to be born free. Then we gets married. Where we not havin' to look behind our backs for the hunters to take us in the night and sell us down the river. Celebrate our new life with the baby. With Jonathan."

"All right then." Horace lifted her up from her chair. "You got yourself a deal, lady." He kissed her again, and setting her down turned to Jonathan, "And you'll be *my* best man?"

Jonathan shook his hand. "Congratulations to both of you. And it would be my honor. Here's to love!" He toasted, and they drank to the hope of it all.

To Build a Wagon

⌾⌾⌾

Joseph Murphy sat at a workbench sanding a wheel hub, stroking it for texture, blowing off the dust, and eyeing it for evenness when Horace walked up to him.

"Mr. Murphy, sir, I'd like to ask a favor."

Without looking up, Murphy said, "What is it?"

"I'd like to build my own wagon, sir."

Murphy raised an eyebrow, paused momentarily, and returned his gaze back to the wood. "What makes ye think ye can?" he asked, puffing at the sawdust collecting on the heavy wooden nucleus that would spin a wagon two thousand miles across the wilderness.

"I don't, at least not all of it, not yet." Horace tumbled out his ideas in a broad, unbroken thought. "But I've learned some here already, and I'm willing to learn more. I'll buy my own materials, if I could use the shop at night, after my shift? You see, sir, Fredericka and I, well, we're thinking of moving to California next spring, and I'd like to have a wagon I build with my own hands. For Fred and the baby."

"Ye just said a mouthful there, Horace," Murphy said, pushing away from the hub and drilling his eyes into Horace. "Buildin' a wagon. Havin' a baby. Travelin' West." He lifted his pipe from the bench, stuffed it with tobacco from a pouch in his apron, lit it, puffed on it, and studied Horace.

"You know why I'm filing the hub, Horace?" He tapped the massive wooden block with his pipe.

Horace shook his head, no.

"Because my wheelwrights didn't make the correct indentation for the spokes. I had to file the face of each mortise to hold the shoulders of the spoke when they make contact with the hub. Ye see the hub is everything." Murphy's eyes sparkled with intensity. "Made of osage orange and oak. It's dense and durable. Same for the spokes and the felloes. Feel the wood, Horace." Horace placed his hands around the hub as Murphy continued. "The hubs are the centerpieces connecting everything to everything else. Do you get my meanin', lad?"

"Yessir. The hubs have to be strong enough to support the spokes."

Murphy looked pleased. "But those hubs have to go through hell first. They're boiled in oil, dry-seasoned for years for the fibers to toughen and tighten. They've got to bear out the weather and the wear. And those spokes, they ain't spokes, Horace. They're rays of power flarin' out to the rims, supportin' the felloes capped with tight iron tires."

Horace grew entranced with the impassioned lesson. "Yessir. Those iron tires have to be four inches wide and half an inch thick."

"Unless I'm building a freight wagon, and then the tires could be eight inches wide. And you know why?"

"To hold the weight?"

"To hold the weight and prowl the mud. The wider, the better." Murphy put his pipe down, getting more and more animated. "It's all connected, don't you see?" He strode over to a partially constructed wagon, pointing and bending around the structure, enthralled by the beauty of it all. "The reach is connected to the two-axle assemblies, the hounds latch the rear axle to the reach, and the front axle to the tongue, and the bolsters shoulder the wagon bed. Wheels hold the axles, the axles hold the wheels, a counter-pressure of parts holdin' the wagon steady. Do ye foller me, lad?" He rested his hands on his hips.

Horace nodded and took up the fevered explanation, pointing at the wheels. "And the back wheels are bigger than the front wheels, making for a better turn radius."

"But the wood always comes first." Murphy wagged his finger and repeated, "The wood must come first. Hickory for the axles, 'cause it's hard and wiry." He made a fist. "And ash, for the sideboards because it's strong. Y'see, Horace, it's all about diversity. Different kinds a' wood have different strengths for various tasks. Ye need multiple species to give flexibility and balance to the whole, to make it strong. Use only one wood, and the wagon'll fall apart." He sat back down, reaching again for his pipe.

"I think I understand." Horace was thoughtful for a moment. "Where does all the different wood come from, sir?"

"Call me Joseph." Murphy clutched the pipe between his teeth. "As fer where I get me wood, that's fer me to know. I have me particular forests growin' in different regions and certain lumber procurers who grow and dry just what I want. As fer the buildin' of the wagon, what part ye gonna build first?"

"The box, Mister, uh, I mean, Joseph. I've been building those boxes all summer." Now Horace was pacing, getting more and more excited about his project.

"Right ye are, Horace. And the dimensions?"

"Well now, I'd set up one large board for the bottom, twelve feet long, four feet wide. Then I'd bolt two planks to the long sides of that board."

"They be the sideboards," Murphy batted back.

"Right." Horace could almost see his wagon coming together, plank by plank. "These sideboards would be about two or three feet high. Then tar the gaps." He nodded at Murphy for agreement. He felt encouraged and motivated for the first time since he was a boy, growing up with Jonathan, a feeling as splendid and new as the vision of his wagon.

Murphy waved his pipe at Horace. "Then, ye get a narrow beam the same length as the Yankee bed to support the wheels. Strong enough to support the box's weight and all yer freight and belongin's. You'll need two four-foot beams bolted perpendicular to the underside of each end of the long main beam. And do you know why, Horace?" Murphy was enjoying this game.

"For the brace. To attach a triangular brace to the underside of each end of the four-foot beams."

Murphy lit his pipe again and eyed Horace. "But it must be sized for the axle. The axle must fit through it and be able to move freely. And the wooden triangle, make sure it points downward. And then what comes next, Laddy?" he asked with a sly smile.

"Then comes the axle?" Horace volleyed back.

"Right. The axle goes through each pair of braces. And then come the wheels to the end of each axle. And ye don't bother tryin' to build yer own wheels. Ye get 'em from the wheelwright. It's just common sense, man. Ye see?"

"Why not make my own wheels? I could learn..."

"Listen to me, lad, unless you plan on spendin' a lifetime learning the art of wheel makin', just get 'em from someone who has. The wheel is the heart of yer wagon. The spokes are the veins carryin' powers to the rims. It's all about connections. The joints and mortises must be exact so when you pound in the spoke, not even air can pass through. It's tight, as tight as any earthly bond, and then it's clad in iron. Now there's the ticket," he said.

Signaling to Horace with his pipe, Murphy rose and walked over to a foundry cauldron burning red with hot coals, searing the surrounding air with intense heat. Murphy tapped the stem of his pipe on a wheel newly mounted with an iron tire lying on a nearby bench and said, "Yer lookin' at pressure. Thousands of pounds of shrinking iron over the rim is forcing the spokes into the hub for the final strength. Invisible to the naked eye, but the wheel is nothin' without that shrinking force inside the heart." He tapped his chest with his pipe. "You get that, Horace?"

"Yessir, I mean, yes, Joseph." Horace's heart raced. How often had he called upon that shrinking force, how grateful he was for the pressures that made him strong. Connecting the raw pieces of his life together, he could build a future with Fredericka, an iron-clad bond for her, for him, and for a family. He felt like he could explode with anticipation, his fingers twitching for the labor ahead, building a wagon for Fredericka, for love.

"Now listen, lad, there's more," Murphy said. "Ye need to attach two more short beams to the top of the long main beam."

"The wheelbase?"

"Right ye are. These two beams measure the same as the beams supportin' the axles. This is where it gets a wee bit tricky. Ye attach 'em a little in from the axle beams, bolted on their long sides to give a wee bit o' height above yer wheelbase. Then you can bolt the Yankee bed to the beams." Murphy puffed on his pipe.

"And the tongue, Joseph?"

"No troubles there. Ye get a long wooden pole that attaches to the front of the wheelbase, then use yer singletree and double-tree to hold the tongue in place so it can move up and down.

The singletree is about as long as the axles and sits below the tongue. Then you take the doubletree about the length of the crosspieces above the wheels. That one sits on top of the tongue. Then it's a matter of makin' the yoke. Are ye keen on that lad?"

"Yessir. It's a short pole attached perpendicular to the top front end of the long tongue. For the harness. To attach it to the yoke."

"There you have it then." Murphy stood. "It's pretty simple, really." He waved his pipe, dismissing all impediments to the task. The two men grinned at one another and at the accomplishment of a wagon built to the imagination.

During this conversation, Murphy's accountant, Charles LaBoutain, approached him and stood stoically by the wagon builder's side awaiting Murphy's acknowledgment. The thin man cradled a ledger book. His sleeves were rolled up, thick spectacles bridged low over his nose, his lips tight as a wire.

LaBoutain knew how to wait. He'd been waiting all his life. To Charles LaBoutain's mind, immigrants seemed to spread across Missouri like mildew, bringing poverty, disease, and filth. And still, he had to wait, for his own fortune to strike, his status to grow, to make his mark. It didn't help that his boss had coddled up to a nigger with no credence given to his own expert advice to check for papers. The bookkeeper thought he could be a partner in this shop if he waited long enough. But wait was all he did. Murphy gave him no respect, and the bile began to soak his tongue with bitterness.

Murphy relit the bowl of tobacco in his pipe and continued, "So, if ye want to truly learn, I'll teach ye, Horace."

"Yessir. Thank you, Mr. Murphy," Horace replied, and then reacting to Murphy's raised index finger, chuckled and said, "I mean, Joseph, thank you, sir."

LaBoutain feigned a cough. "Mr. Murphy, we have business matters to discuss." He looked down the narrow shaft of his nose at Horace and sniffed. "Privately."

Ignoring the accountant, Murphy waved his pipe at Horace. "I like you, Horace. Yer a fast learner, a good worker, and I trust ye." He gave a wink at Horace and raised his voice, "Not like some of the louts 'round here who don't give a tinker's damn and would sell their own mother if they think they could get a few drinks and a game of faro off 'er." He glanced at three scruffy men sitting on a bench nearby, who looked up at him and scowled.

"I'd rather sell me own mother than work with a nigger," muttered one of the men, Benny Stark, a sour-looking man with a dark, unshaven face. His two compatriots at the bench nodded in agreement. LaBoutain, still awaiting Murphy's acknowledgment, turned to Stark and the men and snickered in agreement.

"What's that ye say?" Murphy roared.

"Nothin', sir," Stark said.

"Best be nothin' boy, or ye'll not work here another day."

Stark lowered his head like a disciplined dog and, with clenched teeth, pretended to do measurements on the bench table.

"All right, Charley," Murphy said and sighed, rising from his bench, "what is it?" The two men walked off, leaving Horace flushed with the prospect of building something of his own. He decided to keep the project a secret from Fredericka. This was going to be a surprise, her gift.

During the ensuing months, under his mentor's guidance, Horace built his wagon, learning about connections and counter pressures, braces, axles, and beams. By winter, he had bolted and tarred his twelve-by four-foot wagon bed and sideboards, waterproofing the seams against the onslaught of the arduous journey that was sure to come.

By spring, Horace had painted the sideboards deep blue, the wheels red, and oiled the exposed wood to a deep, gleaming bronze.

With the wagon assembled, he crowned it with the cover, using thin beams for the bows: five arched strips of hickory, soaked for pliability and bent into shape to the sides of the wagon bed. Across the bows, he stretched the ten-ounce heavy cotton duck cover waterproofed with linseed oil.

For a week, he sewed the drawstrings into the canvas hems, front and back, to allow the bonnet to close against the night and the elements that may come during the day. He thought how Fredericka's delicate fingers could have done a better job of hemming the cloth, but this project was his secret, her gift. He looped a fine rope through grommets along the edges and tightly snugged the canvas to the bows.

He dangled a bucket of tar and tallow from the rear axle—as much a balm of faith for a smooth journey as a lubricant for the wheels. A long tongue of oak in front of his wagon attached to a short perpendicular pole for the yoke. This final piece would connect the beasts who would pull it and the man who would drive it.

Finally, the day came when Horace took a step back. With his hands raised, he was ready for a missed lynchpin, a loose hook, or an untarred gap. He studied his creation with an unerring eye. Approaching reverence, he walked around the wagon, running his fingers across her sideboards, taking a sure grip of a spoke, stroking the iron molded to the rims, patting the box. Each part was a friend, every board familiar, each touch a blessing.

When his hands reached the sideboard above the left rear wheel, he caught hold of an idea. One last thing left to do. Rummaging through the toolshed, he found a chisel and a mallet. Back at the sideboard, he carved out two small letters, blew off the dust, and brushed it with his fingertips. Placing the tools back on a bench, he untied his leather apron and dropped it to the sawdust floor.

That evening, he brought Fredericka to the shop, promising a surprise. The yard was dark and quiet. Most of the crew left for the night except for Charles LaBoutain, who had come to the yard to gather payroll chits, and Benny Stark, who had found himself a cozy dark corner with a bottle of whiskey. Neither of whom was seen by Horace. Holding her hand tightly, Horace led Fredericka through the shop to a small area in the back. The light from their lard-oil lamps ricocheted through the dusky building, glinting off tools hooked to the walls and glancing across the ceiling's open beams. There, in the back, a wagon stood shimmering in the lamplight, casting shadows dancing on the wall behind it.

"It's ours," Horace said, stopping. "I built it myself."

"Ours?" Fredericka's hand nested on her burgeoning stomach and their unborn child. The warm, nutty scent of flaxseed oil, the sweet aroma of fresh-cut wood, and the tang of new paint flooded her senses.

"Ours," Horace said in the crepuscular light.

"Go on. You can touch it." He placed his hand on hers and laid their hands against the carriage.

"These boards? Smoothed by the plane with my own hands. And see the wheels, they'll take us to the promised land. Only have to build the seat now."

Fredericka ran her fingers across the spokes. "Rays of the sun," she said.

Lurking behind a pile of wood, away from the couple's lamp, LaBoutain watched and listened.

"And see here," Horace gently pulled her to the left rear sideboard. "Look," he said, "You've been studying your letters. Can you read these?"

Fredericka touched the two small letters carved into the wood, and read them aloud,

"H. F. It's you an' me," she said. "Horace and Fredericka."

LaBoutain raised an eyebrow, and a slow smirk creased his face. *I've got you now.* He pulled back into the shadows, nearly tripping over Stark and his bottle, stirring him from his drunken stupor. LaBoutain put his fingers to his lips to quiet the roused man and pointed slowly toward Horace and Fredericka. Stark rolled over from his slumped position against the wall onto his hands and knees and tried to focus on LaBoutain's attention.

"Well, I'll be fucked." Stark shook the fog from his head and squinting his eyes said, "The nigger has a White whore."

At that same moment, Horace and Fredericka were bathing under the wagon's warm glow. All the world's turbulence and troubles vanished. Soon, the time would come when these singular forces of nature: wood, metal, man, and beast would come together. They would be connected to a coach with red wheels, blue sideboards, and a bright white canvas to cross a continent, to settle scores, and to build a new world. But for a price.

THE SHOP YARD WAS HUMMING WITH ACTIVITY THE NEXT morning when Horace arrived. He paid little attention to the workers bent over their tables and benches and saws. He barely noticed no one looked up or caught his eye. He didn't hear the snickers behind his back or when the entire shop fell silent when he grabbed his apron and turned to his wagon. He didn't even notice his guts had been ripped out.

The bright white cover had been slashed from front to back, and red paint spattered over the gash like a wound. Three wheels were bashed in, the spokes broken and splintered. One wheel stripped off entirely left the lopsided wagon lying on its axle. Crippled. And dripping in red letters across the green sideboards, the word *NIGGER*!

Horace dropped his apron to the floor. He stood before his beloved wagon the way a man stands at a funeral for a friend: hollowed out, too weak to hold his head up, shoulders drawn down as if pelted by rain, arms dangling and useless to the situation.

A sound behind him abbreviated his mourning, a rustle of boots, a shift in the air. He pivoted slowly around on his left heel, the air felt thick and heavy. He raised his eyes to see Benny Stark's slimy grin and a dozen other men holding bats and blocks of wood and iron pokers.

"Missouri don't set store to niggers parlaying with White women," Stark snarled.

"What?" Horace could barely speak.

"We're talkin' about one uppity nigger who thinks he's better than Whites, that's what." Stark walked up to Horace and put a large wood spoke under Horace's chin. Horace refused to move and glared back at him.

"You lookin' me in the eye, boy?" Stark's face was so close Horace felt the spittle on his breath.

"I am not a boy." Horace pushed his chin down on the spoke in defiance of Stark's threat. "I am a free…"

A mighty slam against his shoulders came from a man behind him, and Horace was on the ground.

Stark walked around the groaning man. "You cavortin' with White women, Horace? You rapin' White women?" Stark kicked him in the ribs with the toe of his hobnail boot.

Horace let out a howl and curled into a ball. "I don't know what you're talking about," he wheezed, desperate to breathe against the pain in his chest.

Another man appeared from the crowd, his brown pant legs drooping over his boots. "Niggers ain't supposed to read," Pant Legs jeered and whacked a heavy chain across Horace's heaving chest. Horace screamed in pain.

"Niggers supposed to know their place," another man in oversized overalls came down on Horace's legs with a two-by-four. A bone cracked and splintered in his leg. A kick to the groin. The pain excruciating, sent long streaks of blinding white light into his brain. And the blood felt warm as it soaked the floor.

The last thing Horace remembered was the sound of a club colliding with his skull.

The Grand Adventure

⸺ ⌘ ⸺

A cold February wind blew off New York harbor when Jonathan kissed Emily goodbye at the foot of the gangway to the 125-foot Yankee trading vessel *Brooklyn*. "I should be going with you. It isn't safe," he said in a moment of regret.

"Don't be silly," Emily said, adjusting his cravat. "It's going to be an adventure, and I'm going to make the most of it. Just think, I'll be making history sailing halfway around the world to California, crossing the equator twice! Besides, there's a hundred children onboard, some of them only knee-high to a bumblebee. They wouldn't be going if it wasn't safe, would they?" She gave a coy, reassuring smile.

Jonathan glanced up at the gangway and the stream of passengers embarking the ship. She had a point. Seventy men, sixty-eight women, and one hundred children, mostly Mormons, had chartered this vessel for the journey to the West Coast of the Americas. He had managed to secure passage for Emily as one of the twelve non-church members. There would be no swilling of whiskey and drunk louts to fight off. And the ship was well stocked with provisions.

"I suppose," he gave in. "You're as safe as you could get with a bunch of Latter-day Saints. Just don't go marryin' one of them."

She poked her finger on his chest. "Just remember it's a journey of the heart." She slowly traced an outline of a heart on his cloak. "I leave New York, swing wide into the Atlantic, and then south the full length of South America. We sail around the tip of the heart, that's the Horn, and swing north, clear on up to the Pacific Islands, and then swoop into San Francisco Bay. And meet you in Yerba Buena!" She gazed up at him. "My heart will be complete when I see you again. I'll think of you every day."

"And I'll keep you close." Jonathan tugged at the locket around his neck.

They embraced with a kiss to last for months through their new journeys meant to culminate in an unknown land.

Emily's cheeks were rosy pink as she pulled away, turned, and headed up the gangway. Clutching her bonnet in the wind, she stopped and gazed up at the ship and then down to Jonathan on the dock. "Isn't it all so thrilling?" she cried, flush with excitement.

He thought how much he loved her. How beautiful she looked. How much he would miss her. How tiny she looked on the deck, waving back. "I'll see you in September," Jonathan hollered as the *Brooklyn* slowly pushed out of the harbor. He watched the white sails billow with air until the three-masted ship became a speck on the water and soon seemed to merge with the clouds on the horizon and disappear.

They Broke It

———— ⌾ ————

Fredericka crept into bed. *It's late.* Horace hadn't come home yet. She smiled—he must still be working on the wagon. He wanted to install a brake and lever and get a good strong spring for the carriage seat. *But he should be home soon*, she consoled herself—home—what a strange idea. The boarding house here in St. Louis was not much better than the one they had left in such a hurry back in Buffalo. Still, it was home. Their own bed, a safe place for just the two of them. Fredericka felt the kick of a little foot and caressed her round, ripe belly. *Just the two of them, but not for much longer.* A great tenderness spilled over her like warm honey. She had never felt so free, so happy, so complete, feelings all so new to her, as new as the life she carried. As new as the life they were about to embark upon.

She soon fell asleep and dreamed of flying through skies of deep blue with fluffy clouds buoying her up, clouds that became a canvas roof. She twirled around in her dream and saw Horace, his burnished face, dark, delicious freckles, and red, tear-filled eyes. *Tears? Why was he crying?* In an instant, Fredericka bolted awake, shivering.

She sensed something wrong. The room smelled different. Not the happy, warm glow of bliss. Something else. She couldn't shake it. She swung heavily out of bed and stood. The wood underfoot felt cold and uneven beneath her feet. The shawl she pulled around her shoulders did not cut the chill in her bones. Their little room was shadowy. She reached for a match and lit the lamp. The light flickered against the wall. Nearly dawn, and Horace still hadn't come home. A streak of panic shot through her. She tugged on her boots, clutched at a coat hanging on a peg, and raced out the door.

A gusty blast of winter shocked her lungs as she stepped outside. The weak, gray light of dawn seemed to lack the strength to fight off the night's dusky remnants. Shadows smudged the walls and puddled in the corners of the alley leading to the wagon yard. The icy street crunched under her boots.

Making her way to the front of the yard, she tried the warehouse door. Locked. The morning crew hadn't arrived yet. She banged on the door with the flat of her hand in case someone, Horace, may still be inside. No reply. She hiked around to the back of the building. Heavy with child and becoming more anxious by the moment, she paused, panting for air.

That's when she saw the wagon. It had been hauled from the yard and dumped on its side in a heap of discarded timber fragments, split woods and iron pieces. Then, she spied Horace sprawled on the ground next to the trash pile. Blood clotted his hair and stuck in a crusty patch to his face. His eyes were bruised and swollen shut. His lips bulging and cut. A blood-soaked gash sliced across his forehead. His left leg was twisted in an unnatural angle.

She rushed to his side. "Horace!"

Horace gasped and waved his arm in the air, clutching for her. Fredericka grabbed his hand. "I's here. I's here."

In a rasping voice, he managed, "The wagon. They broke it."

March to Zion

———— ⬡⬡⬡ ————

Illinois was no place for Mormons. Hostilities rose against the religious sect for marginalizing themselves from secular society, for their growing political power, their claims of divine favor, and eventually their practice of polygamy. In neighboring Missouri, anger spilled over to violence, encouraged by Governor Lilburn Boggs, who issued Missouri Executive Order 44 to exterminate all Mormons from that state. For the Latter-day Saints, time to move. The Exodus was on.

Henrietta didn't want to go. Why put herself out in a frigid winter to travel to some godforsaken outpost when it was perfectly warm and sensible to stay put in Buffalo? Henrietta had followed Edward Honey to the windy city, giving over the plantation's care to an overseer, and hoped for a new beginning with this man.

"But, Eddie," she argued, slicked up in a modern purple and red frock, "taking a wagon train West on some wild-goose chase in the snow? Are you crazy?"

"Look, Retta," he said, stuffing his bags with a few personal belongings, "my people are on the move. They'll be heading out soon. They need scouts. And I have reason to believe your properties are on the move West as well. I can scout for the Saints and track the niggers at the same time.

It's my God-given duty, and by God, I'm going. You stay put, and I'll let you know when I catch up to the runaways. Remember, we had a deal. If I catch 'em, they're mine."

Edward Honey always got his man—be it coon or criminal—and he wasn't about to let his reputation slip. He had Horace Redburn in his crosshairs. During the past few months, from the information gleaned in the letters he found in the dresser between Jonathan and Horace, Honey had a lead on the slaves and new information that could deliver more than their price at the auction block. The objective was not only the capture of runaways, but his success would push his reputation into a whole new sphere. And he'd be damned if he was going to tell Henrietta his plans. Besides, the woman had dogged him all the way from South Carolina. He needed to get away.

Henrietta felt like she had fallen off a cliff, and her gut hadn't caught up to the rest of her. She felt like she was grappling the air for something to cling to, something to keep her from her own lonely abyss. Honey was slipping away. She grabbed his arm with both hands. "Eddie," her voice hovering on alarm. "I know you need to get on with things. But I'm going with you, I am, of course. And I can help you. I can pay our way. Please, Eddie, take me with you."

Honey shook his head. "Retta, you may have a pocket full of rocks, but money won't get you across the Plains. It's a nasty business. You're not cut out for it. And I'm not cut out for bein' a nursemaid to no woman." He pulled his pistol from the top of the little dresser by the bed and eyed the barrel. "Needs cleaning," he muttered, rummaging through his satchel for his kit.

"Listen, Eddie." Henrietta was becoming fretful with every breath. "I have a trunk load of gold eagles stored up. And I will allow I am a lady of no uncertain breeding, but just the same, I'm not scared of an owl." At the top of her voice she cranked out, "And you have no idea what I can or cannot sustain. I'll give you the money, but I am going with you!"

Honey's lips curled into a crooked smile as he eyed down the barrel of his pistol. He got her just where he wanted her. And her trunk load of gold eagles.

That February, Henrietta got what she wanted, but not what she imagined: a tramp of one thousand three hundred miles with a band of religious refugees led by a fanatic called Brigham Young, destined for Zion in some "Great Basin." It was supposed to be easy—a matter of weeks. But nothing in that Midwest winter was easy. It was bitterly cold. Colder than anything she had ever known.

Edward Honey had signed them up for this great crusade out of duty. But it was never her duty. She hated the 5:00 a.m. bugle call for the wagons in the morning and trudging through knee-deep snow with no shelter from the blizzards raging against them. Henrietta had nothing in common with these so-called Saints and their prayers, syrupy faith and friendliness, and god-awful intent to keep going despite the frostbite to feet and fingers.

One evening, two weeks into the journey, Henrietta had crawled into their wagon for another shivering night when she awoke to the terrifying screams of a woman. She yanked herself up, joining several others who had been aroused and ran toward the screams. What she saw made her skin crawl. The wagon "doctor," a pig farmer from Vermont, held the bloody, severed foot of Sarah Parker. "Frostbite," he said. He shook his head and threw the foot in the cinders of a dying fire pit. "Got to gangrene. Had to take it. She'd a' died otherwise," he said, wrapping Sarah's stump in a rag quickly soaking it to crimson red. The woman's pathetic groans mingled with the whispered prayers of her family through the night. They buried Sarah Parker the next morning along with the remains of her charred left foot.

Days turned into weeks, and the graves became more frequent. Snow turned to rain. Henrietta hated the mud, the pushing of the wagons sinking axle-deep in the mire, slogging through the relentless storms, and tripping over the rocky beds of icy rivers in frozen feet. And for what? To make two stinkin' miles a day. When the supplies dwindled, she even hated that she was grateful for the rationed gruel of flour and water. Her hands were cracked, her face was blistered and burned from frost and wind, her legs cramped, her boots shredded, and what little was left of her clothing was tattered and torn. She was hungry, tired, and fiercely cold.

She hadn't wanted any of this, and worst of all—she was going it alone. Edward hadn't returned yet. He had her money. "Scouting," he called it. "Looking for provisions," he said. That was fifteen weeks ago. The wagon train hadn't even made it out of Iowa Territory yet. They were supposed to be in this Great Basin by now. Henrietta was beginning to panic.

Honey was relieved. He had dumped Henrietta on the Mormon train with no intention of meeting back with her, setting off instead with Henrietta's stake, not for provisions but for St. Louis and the hunt for Horace Redburn. He wasn't much of a Saint, after all.

To Rescue a Wagon

⎯⎯⎯ ∘⧳∘ ⎯⎯⎯

Horace could hardly breathe. "Doc say you got broke ribs. Broke leg. In a splint. Broke head. But you be okay." Fredericka tried to sound encouraging, wiping a wet cloth over Horace's lips and rinsing it in a basin next to the bed.

Horace winced. "The wagon…" His hand pressed against the sharp pain in his chest.

Fredericka changed the bandage on his head. "It be all right now," she tried to assure him. "Old man in the street with a wheelbarrow. Hauled you home. Doc say you lucky to be alive."

"Doctor? We can't afford a doctor." Horace lifted his head for a sip of water from a cup she brought to his lips.

Fredericka smiled. "The Doc that lives downstairs. He the one who takes too much to the blackstrap. I tell him I fix him some hot corn-pone with chitlins if he come help you."

Horace shook his head. "That quack? He's a drunk."

"Now, you hush. That quack fix you up, thas what." Fredericka tried to sound indignant, but she felt relieved Horace was alert enough to talk.

"How long have I been like this?" He reached for his face, touching the bandage.

"Four days. I swear, you sleepin' like a dead man." Fredericka's hair fell in her tired face. "I declare, Horace, I was so skeery."

"The wagon. Where's the wagon?" Pain shot through his chest with every breath.

"Still back of the yard. But, I can help fix it," she said, pretending to be cheerful.

"Fix it?" Horace wheezed. "How you going to fix it?" He tried sitting up but started coughing. As he groaned in pain, Fred lightly pushed him back to his pillow.

"I got me some canvas, and I'm to stitchin' a new cover for starters." She tugged a bundled oil cover from the corner. "See here? I do it just like you." She held the canvas toward Horace, who groaned again.

"You can't fix a whole wagon, Fred."

"What 'bout Jonathan? Maybe he can help…"

She didn't finish the thought when Horace shot back, "He's done enough. It's no use. We tried. You were right. We outta' settle down. Baby and all. Crazy dream, going West…" He coughed and groaned in pain again.

Fredericka grew worried by his despair and wiped his face again with deliberation. "Horace, no. Now, you talkin' crazy. You's sick. Thas all. When you get to feelin' better, why thas when you see things better too. I made us a pot of hog and hominy and even baked you a johnnycake for when you get to feelin' better."

"Not hungry." Horace winced and closed his eyes, trying to contain the agony of breathing and the throbbing of his leg.

"You just rest up now." She pulled the covers over him. "Everything's gonna be all right." She had never seen him like this, vulnerable and as damaged as the wagon. He was always the one reassuring her. The strong one. But there he was now, all broken up, inside and out. She couldn't watch her man go down, not like this, not without a fight. Up to her to do something.

The next morning, after seeing to Horace, Fredericka slipped outside the boarding house. A heavy cushion of snow had settled over St. Louis during the night, muffling the city's noises. She picked her way past mounds of dung steaming in the snow that trailed behind the carriages and heavy horses padding along the street and made her way to the wagon yard.

The wagon still lay on its side by the trash heap like a giant dead bug, the left rear wheel resembling a jumble of broken bones. Snow had piled along its sideboards, and a corner of the ripped canvas flapped in the wind. It just couldn't lie there, untended, unloved. She dusted off the snow from the rear of the wagon and lay her fingers on the etched letters H.F. With the edge of her shawl, she slapped the snow from the smashed spokes and tried to wrench one free from the rim. It wouldn't budge. She stood in the snow, helplessly staring at the wagon. *Stupid girl. Can't do it by myself.* Clearly, she would need help, lots of help.

Fredericka pushed open the giant warehouse's front door and walked into the clamorous yard. As she stood there, the din diminished as several dozen men raised their heads from their work, taking notice of a woman wrapped in a gray shawl standing in the sawdust.

"I come for help," she said with an unwavering voice.

The men looked at each other, hesitating in the unfamiliar circumstance of a very pregnant fair-skinned woman glaring at them.

"I am Horace's wife." Her voice carried through the yard. "Some you men beat him. Wrecked his wagon. Hurt him bad. Got what you wanted. Now I want help fixin' it."

"Well, I'll be damned. She's a White-lookin' nigger!" Benny Stark stood and shot a wad of tobacco from the side of his mouth to the floor. He took a hammer from his bench and walked toward her.

"We don't cotton to niggers here. Ain't that right, boys?" He threw the question over his shoulder to the white and hardened faces behind him. The men slowly rose from their benches. The tension in the room grew.

Fredericka sensed this was a bad idea. "I wanna talk to Mr. Murphy," she called out, "or a boss man."

Stark strode closer to her, slapping the hammer in his palm, a shit-eating grin on his face, spittle running down his chin. "You're plum outta' luck." Stark crept closer to her. "Boss man Murphy's back East. Been gone a month. LaBoutain's in the other building yonder. Nobody's here. Ain't that right, boys?" The men snickered, gathering behind him.

"Guess your boy Horace ain't learned his lesson, sends his wife to fight his battles." The gang closed in around Fredericka. Her eyes darted from one to another. Her heart pounded against her chest, her breathing came short and shallow. *What had she gotten herself into?* One of the men made a swipe at her with a wheel spoke, and the mob laughed when she shrieked.

"What's say we find out just how Black you are under all them clothes." Stark hawked a gob of masticated tobacco at Fredericka.

"No. No. No." Fredericka backed into the wall behind her, leaving nowhere to run.

Stark lunged at her, stripping her shawl and blouse off her shoulders. The savagery of the attack made her scream, and she pulled her arms to her face. The men whooped and laughed. Another man tore her skirt and ripped it away— more cheers from the mob. Fredericka kicked and screamed again. Then, as one man held her against the wall, another took a knife and cut her undergarments off as the crowd jeered louder. Stripped naked against the wall, she was fully exposed, her bare breasts heaving over her pregnant belly. For a moment, the men fell back to look at their handiwork.

Face-to-face with terror, Fredericka's mind flashed to another terror she had known before. Frederick Grafton, the silhouette in the shadows, the outline of a monster in the dark. In that fear, she found peace in her mind's eye of sky and summer clouds. She called upon that transcendence now. She did not cry out, nor did she fight.

Instead, she closed her eyes and imagined a roaring blue sky and flying on the wings of a bird, tracing the trail of her sanctuary through the clouds. She felt the rushing wind as she flew toward heaven's gate. Before the threatening mob, she held herself aloft, palms up, her arms outstretched, regal and free of menace or fear.

The men were silent, as if stunned by the sight of a naked goddess heavy with child, some shocked at their own barbaric instincts, some humiliated by their weakness to defy the pack, and others with no conscience at all.

"Get her!" Stark's voice shattered the moment. No one moved. "C'mon men, get her!" Benny Stark turned to the quiet throng of men. "What's the matter with you? She's ours for the takin'!" Still, no one made a move toward Fredericka. Some turned away. "Well, if you ain't got the nerve to fuck this Colored pussy, I'll have a go at her myself!" Stark moved toward Fredericka, who remained motionless before him, her eyes closed, her arms still raised to the heavens.

"No, me first," came a voice. A large, rough-looking man in a leather apron stepped forward. He held an iron poker in his hand. "Hey now, Big Jim," Stark said, chuckling. "That's more like it." Stark wiped his nose with the back of his hand and spit a wad. "Go ahead, Big Jim, you first."

Big Jim stood between Stark and Fredericka, towering over them both. "No. You take me on first, then her." Big Jim was big. At six feet, ten inches tall, a lifetime of muscle-hammering ironwork made him a formidable giant. He didn't talk much, didn't have to. No one ever crossed Big Jim.

"What?" Stark stared up at the man.

"Like I said."

Stark didn't like where this was going. "What? Look, I mean, she's just a nigger." He pointed at Fredericka. "A Colored whore, just standin' there, waitin' for the takin.'" He wiped his nose again with his sleeve, seeking support from the men. Big Jim didn't speak another word.

"I mean, what are you all waitin' for?" Stark hollered. When no one answered, it was clear he had no support, and he sure as hell wasn't going to take on Big Jim. "Alright, you goddamn cowards, alright," Stark snarled, picking up his coat from the floor. "What the fuck. I was just playin.' Can't a guy have a little fun?" He pushed his way through the silent horde and went back to his bench. The others followed suit and quietly assumed their workstations.

Big Jim picked up Fredericka's clothing and held them toward her. "Get dressed," he said in a low, booming voice, "and best get on outta here."

Fredericka blinked, half-dazed, lightheaded as though coming off a cloud. She steadied herself, gave a slight nod at the big man, took her garments from his hand, and slowly dressed. The men in the yard averted their eyes. Without a word, she opened the large wooden door, stepped into a freezing wind, and closed the door behind her.

The falling snow had buried the narrow street leading away from the warehouse, leaving hers the only tracks in the white drifts. Fredericka barely noticed the storm. Instead, as the trauma in the wagon yard wore off, she felt pangs of humiliation and defeat. How would she tell Horace? *I fixed nothin' 'cept nearly getting myself and the baby killed.*

She had walked about a hundred yards when it happened: a gush of warm water ran down her legs and into her boots. Then the first contraction hit. She grabbed her stomach and doubled over in the snow. The baby was coming.

⦵

AT THE BOARDING HOUSE, THE ROOM WAS COLD AND DARK when Horace awoke in pain. "Fredericka!" He strained his voice, but she did not answer. The incessant throbbing in his leg and the sharp, stabbing in his chest were unbearable. He was thirsty. He called for her again, but again, no response. He tried getting up. No use. The effort exhausted him.

He thought he heard something—a rapping at the door. "Fred?" he panted. "Fred? That you?"

The door cracked open, allowing light from the dingy hall to seep across the floor. He saw a figure in the doorway. "Thank God," Horace wheezed. "I was beginning to worry…"

The figure came closer. Horace couldn't make out the details. He tried to focus. "Fred?"

"My, my, my," came the response. "Seems like you're all wrapped up. It's been a long time coming, boy."

The bandage over Horace's head only afforded vision in his left eye. His brain wasn't working right. The figure stood against the light. "Who are you?" he whispered.

The figure bent over him so close he could smell the onions and tobacco on the intruder's breath. "You're headin' to the auction block, boy. The name's Edward Honey."

The Atlantic

———⟨∞∞∞⟩———

The same day Henrietta left Nauvoo, Illinois, with the company of Latter-day Saints on a journey to the Great Salt Lake, Emily sailed out of New York Harbor on *Brooklyn*'s inaugural voyage with 226 Mormons bound for California.

Emily's zeal for this adventure was not dashed when she went below deck to the living quarters to discover her bed was a bunk bolted to the floor next to dozens of other bunks running along the portside. Nor was she dismayed she couldn't stand upright and could only walk hunched over due to the low ceiling. She wasn't disheartened by the backless benches attached to the long narrow table that was to be their dining area. She didn't even mind the dim light and the cramped conditions or only two privies onboard. But her enthusiasm waned when the ship encountered its first storm in the Atlantic.

The sky had turned black. Gale force winds and high waves rolled the ship down one crest and up another, some waves broke across the bow and flooded the upper deck with the ferocity of a swift-running river. The passengers, almost half of them children, held tight down below. The women and children were lashed to their bunks. Due to the fire hazard, the oil lamps were extinguished, and to prevent the ship from taking on water, the crew latched down the vents, which were the only other source of light. The passengers were in a dark, sealed compartment with little air, shrieking with each pitch and roll, some getting pummeled by unsecured baggage, others trying to dart the heavy barrels loosed from their ties by discerning the sounds of the back and forth crashing. Some passengers held onto the table and benches, and some sat on the floor, clutching a stay line. The storm pressed on for three days and three nights.

Emily felt dizzy. She needed air. She began to sweat, hunched over, holding onto the post of her bunk. Her face felt clammy. A dull headache formed, and uncontrolled saliva dribbled down her chin. The vomiting began seconds later, unrelenting vomiting. Down her dress, on her feet, the floor. She couldn't help herself. She couldn't let go of the bunk, she couldn't see, but she could feel her guts twisting in her throat. For the next two days and two nights, screams and shrieks rose up in the roiling sea mingled with the odors of puke and piss as the passengers retched and heaved and soiled themselves in the dark, airless hold of the middle deck.

During this terrible gale, Captain Edward Richardson made his way down to the passenger deck with a grim announcement. "Ladies and gentlemen, this is the worst gale I have ever encountered, and I fear to tell you I am not certain of our survival. I suggest you prepare to meet your Maker." Instead of finding the Souls in distress, they began to sing and pray against the storm's fury and roar. One mother of four, harnessed next to Emily's bunk, declared, "We were sent to California, and we shall get there!"

———⊙⊰⊱⊙———

BY THE DAWN OF THE THIRD DAY, THE STORM HAD SUB-sided. The crew opened the hatch and ventured down the ladder into the hold, wearing rags over faces to open the vents. The overwhelming stench made some of the men gag. When the light cracked through the vents and the oil lamps were lit, the full extent of the storm's devastation became visible. Men, women, and children lay on the floor soaking in vomit and feces, many unconscious, dehydrated, or injured. A baby cried in a dark corner. A woman with blood dripping from her head lay groaning. Some managed to stumble to their feet and helped the others up the ladder. Others called out for water.

After the crew assisted the passengers above deck, Captain Richardson, a stickler for cleanliness, assigned two of the healthiest men to clean the living quarters. The men were given long sticks and rags to scrape the length of the soiled deck and pails of seawater to wash it down. A crewman later steamed a concoction of vinegar and chlorine to sweeten the air. This chore would be repeated every two days and rotated through the adult population during the voyage.

When several of the passengers complained of their circumstances, Captain Richardson addressed the entire group that evening. "Ladies and Gentlemen, that was rough, but I'm tellin' you this, from what I hear tell of captains that found themselves in these seas, we'll be battlin' a dozen more of these tempests before we're done, maybe harder, fiercer, and more punishin' than this storm what we just come through. Prepare for the worst."

And he was right, a series of storms battered the *Brooklyn* clear to the coast of Africa before she turned south for the most challenging part of the voyage around Cape Horn.

During that first storm, Emily had found herself clinging to her bunk tied with her petticoat as a last-minute appeal to her self-preservation. She had one thought ringing through her mind, *Only three days in, and this was already a very long adventure.*

<hr />

THE SKYLARK HAD ONLY FILLED HALF ITS ROOMS, AND the feeling of emptiness engulfed Jonathan. This was the low period in New York for the hotel when winter kept most people from traveling. More than that, he missed his father who filled the hotel with his personal magnetism, sense of style, and the lavish parties. And he missed Emily. He envisioned her sunning herself on the deck, bundled in a blanket, watching the ocean and the sky, rocking to sleep each night under the stars. He wouldn't admit it out loud, but in some small way, he had hoped to make the voyage with her, a far more comfortable passage than the one he had chosen for himself. But he had promised Horace and Fredericka they would travel together. He was going to be the best man at their wedding. Plans were underway.

Jonathan's office was already cleared of his personal items, and an interim manager had been hired and trained weeks before. The place was in good hands. He strolled through the hallways one last time, drinking in his father's voice, visiting the sites where he and Horace played hide-and-seek, where they sat with their tutors, where they rolled apples down the hall. Happy times. He had left many times before, for school, for reasons outside his control, but this going was different. It was his decision this time, and a longing he hadn't experienced before, nostalgia, a sad knowing that upon his return next time, it wouldn't be like coming home. It would never be home again.

The following day, his luggage sent ahead, Jonathan boarded a train. Horace would be waiting, and the trip of a lifetime lay ahead.

The Uncles

Huddled in the snow in the wagon yard's back alley, Fredericka felt another paralyzing contraction. The pain took her breath away, but within seconds, it had subsided enough for her to call out for help. Still, no one came. Another shot of pain, and again she cried for help. Again, no one heard her.

The snow was falling heavily now out of a bulging white sky that seemed to press down upon her. Oddly, she noticed some other part of herself stood aside, disentangled from her distress. An unemotional self, an observer more than a participant, who saw everything, who absorbed her circumstances with an odd curiosity as if the spinning of the world slowed to a crawl. The Other thought how the snowflakes rained down like long strings of pearls, like Mistress Grafton's, how the pearls dusted her wrap, settling gently on her eyelashes. *Pearl dust*, the Other thought.

Slamming her from this reverie, another pain wracked her body, squeezing her spine as though it might snap from the pressure. She was panting now, the pain coming in short, quick bursts. She tried lifting her head and clawed at her clothing. The baby was coming. Red blotches stained the snow beneath her. "Help," she screamed. "Help!"

No use, the Other mused, *She would have her baby in the snow, the warm, steamy baby would quickly cool, freeze, lose consciousness, and sleep forever. It would be painless. They would drift away together...*

Just then, she felt a shudder and arms under her head and legs. She opened her eyes. Instead of falling pearls, she saw a man's rugged face, his mustache drooped over his lip, concern across his brow, the smell of leather and oil rising up from his apron. Big Jim!

With Fredericka in his arms, Big Jim lumbered back to the wagon yard. The jostling brought on another sharp contraction and another shriek of pain.

"Clear la table!" Big Jim hollered as he blasted into the yard.

The men bolted from their benches and stared at the huge man cradling a girl in his arms, the same girl they abused, the girl that shamed them into submission.

"Clear la table, goddamnit! She's havin' her baby!"

One of the men quickly swiped tools and woodchips from a large wooden table and tugged his cap off, unsure of what to do next. Big Jim gently laid Fredericka on the table. She was panting hard now, grimacing with the effort of labor. The men surrounded her, their faces and scruffy beards gazing down upon her like white porcelain plates. Wham! Another forceful contraction hit. She let out a yell. "Horace!" she screamed.

"Someone get Horace," a pale-faced carpenter yelled.

"Hey, we don't know anything about babies," Benny Stark said. "We should let the nigger take care of her own self. This ain't none of our business." He spit on the ground, the brown drool running down his shaggy beard. "I say we leave her to her own kind."

The last thing Stark was aware of was an enormous thud against the side of his head, a flash of light, and then everything went dark. Big Jim stood above him, a two-by-four board held high in his massive hands.

"*Un otre?*" he growled.

The other men shook their heads.

"*Apportez de l'eau!* Water!" Big Jim shouted, turning back to Fredericka and rolling up his sleeves.

"And a curtain for Christ's sake," Scamper Finely, a skinny wheelwright hollered as he pulled a canvas tarp across the floor and rigged it across an overhead timber.

"Get Horace," Big Jim said.

Half a dozen men bolted out of the wagon yard, relieved at having something they could do, leaving the others to fumble with the duties of midwives. Led by Sam Buchanan, a tight-muscled Irishman, the posse wound through the backstreets and plowed through ankle-deep snow coming upon the boardinghouse where Fredericka and Horace lived. As they rounded the corner to the building, two men stumbled from the door. Buchanan's first reaction was that the two men were drunks, falling over one another.

Stepping closer, Buchanan noticed one man's head was bandaged, his left leg dragging beside him. The larger man had him tied by the neck with a rope, and the bandaged man appeared to be struggling to breathe. It was Horace. Buchanan couldn't help but feel complicit in the scene unfolding on the boardinghouse steps. He was part of the mob that attacked the Black man a week earlier. His lunge with a board broke Horace's leg.

"Let's get him, lads," Buchanan whispered to the group hunkered down by the side of the building.

"Now wait a minute," cautioned Marty Canton. "I'm not pickin' no fight over a darkie. What if the motherfucker has a pistol? I'm not getting shot over no nigger."

Buchanan turned to the hesitant men. "Jesus, Mary, and Joseph! It's a fight, boys. Who's gonna go back and tell Big Jim Horace got away? I say we go!" A splotch of spittle blew out of his mouth and burned a brown hole in the snow. He rubbed his hands, partly against the cold but mostly in anticipation of a good brawl.

As Edward Honey dragged Horace off the entrance's last step, Buchanan was already on the bounty hunter and knuckle-punched him in the face. Surprised by the attack, Honey fell backward in the snow, jerking the rope and yanking Horace off his feet and on top of him. Screaming in pain, Horace rolled to one side, clutching at his ribs, his splint-held leg sticking awkwardly at his side.

Honey staggered to his feet, blood gushing from his nose. He wrangled for the pistol in his belt. "Get the gun!" Buchanan hollered as three men tackled the dazed bounty hunter to the ground. One man held him down as another pummeled him into oblivion. Bloodied and unconscious, Edward Honey soaked the snow red. The six-man posse hoisted Horace, groaning in pain, to their shoulders, and trundled him through the snowy back streets of St. Louis.

"Where are you taking me? Put me down!" Horace groaned through the jostling.

"Hang tight, Horace. Got someone waitin' for ya," Buchanan said, grinning under his cap.

The wagon yard was quiet. Workers gathered outside the drawn curtain, keeping their own counsel, whispering to one another, or merely pacing.

"*Madam, aidez-vous?*" Big Jim's voice was velvety soft as he asked permission to help the distraught woman. Fredericka nodded, sweat trickled down her neck. As tender as a kitten, Big Jim gently disrobed her under the cover of her shawl. Another jolt of pain and Fredericka gave out a cry.

"*L'enfant vient*! Baby comes," Big Jim called out to her.

"Should she be pushin' or something," a short, portly man inquired, holding a kettle of hot water outside the quickly rigged privacy cubicle.

"Shut up," another quipped. "Let Big Jim handle this."

"I hear tell he had kids. In Canada. Married an Indian. They got kilt. That's why he's in Missouri. Lost the entire bunch to marauders," said another.

While the men shuffled around and gossiped, from inside the contrived shelter, Big Jim called for a blanket, "*La couverture!*" Then another mighty cry from Fredericka. Some wrung their hands, and others took their hats off. Then a second, different voice, a baby's.

"*C'est une fille*! A girl!" Big Jim emerged from behind the curtain, bare-chested, cradling an infant squiggling in his shirt.

The men erupted in cheers, proud as uncles. "Yay!" they shouted, shaking hands, and patting each other on the back, acknowledging each other with something between joy and relief, a reprieve of shame.

"This calls for a drink!" a woodworker hollered, producing a whiskey bottle to everyone's delight.

Big Jim laid the infant in Fredericka's arms. "*Une beaux fille*. Beautiful girl," he whispered.

Fredericka shifted her eyes from Big Jim to the baby. A warm glow flooded Fredericka's face as she held the tiny fingers of her newborn and stroked the soft down of the baby's head.

"Whatcha gonna call her?" Scamper Finely, the wheelwright asked, poking his head around the curtain.

"Bo," Fredericka said and smiled. "I'm gonna call her Beautiful."

⊶⊷

Joseph Murphy was satisfied with his trip back East. It had been a month of bargaining for timber, hiring experienced ironworkers, and contracting a new architect to expand his yard. Business was good. Wagons were a growing demand. He had done many such trips in the past, leaving the daily responsibilities to Charles LaBoutain and his managers. He felt confident everything in the yard was under control, until now.

LaBoutain was huddled over his books when Murphy entered the cluttered and claustrophobic office. He didn't look up when Murphy entered the room and slid behind his desk piled high with papers, invoices, contracts, and payroll reports waiting for his return. Usually, his accountant was an incessant, self-indulgent chatterbox who always sniffed the air for places where he could assert his authority or opinion. Quiet was not one of his strong suits. Something was up.

"Think I'll take a look around." Murphy pushed back from his desk. When LaBoutain didn't respond, Murphy stopped at the office door and said, "Come with me, Charley."

"Yessir." LaBoutain jerked his pencil-sharp nose up from his accounting books.

In the yard, Murphy was not prepared for what he heard, or rather, what he didn't hear. Not a hammer or a saw. Not the hubbub of a busy shop. Not the clamor of men shouting or cussing. Just. Silence.

He shoved the side door open to the yard to see a dozen or so men huddled together, their backs to the workbenches. Some were sitting against the wall, others passing around a bottle, and most curious of all, these hard-drinking, raucous, vulgar men were whispering.

"What gives here?" Murphy barked. The laborers sprawled against the walls, jumped to their feet, and others placed their caps back on their heads, some tried to hide the booze behind their backs. "Why aren't you men workin'?" When no one answered, he bellowed, "Well? Are ye all deaf?"

"Shhh," Max Cartwright, a small delicate man who dwarfed his overalls, murmured as he stepped forward. "Bo's nappin', sir."

"Napping...?" Before Murphy could finish his statement, the men cleared a path to the center of their attention; in the shop's corner, a mattress, and a makeshift bedroom lay a woman cradling an infant. A curtain partially draped around the bed and lying in a cot next to her, Horace, with bandages patching his body.

"What the hell?" Murphy put his hands on his hips. "What's going on here?"

Nobody spoke. The baby whimpered.

He turned to LaBoutain. "Charley, what the blazes...?"

Charles LaBoutain wrung his long scrawny fingers. "Well sir, if you will remember, I warned you about hiring niggers. They're nothin' but trouble, I said. And, well, you see a bunch of the boys, they..."

"They helped me," Horace interrupted, "when the wagon tipped over on me."

The men glanced nervously at one another, but still, no one spoke. Murphy spit on the floor. "Ye say the wagon tipped over on ye?" He wasn't buying it.

"Yessir." Horace's voice was stronger now. "Wagon rolled over me. I must have had a loose bolt or something."

"Murphy sized up the men crowded around the little family in the corner. He spit again. One man scratched his head, another shuffled the dust with his foot. No one made eye contact.

"A loose bolt." Murphy pursed his lips. "And the wagon just somehow tipped over. That's what yer tellin' me. That right, lads?"

The men muttered an unconvincing agreement.

"And the wagon would be where?"

"Out back," Smitty Green, a lumberman offered, cocking his head over his shoulder.

Murphy strode to the backlot. No one followed him. When he returned moments later, his face burned red with rage. Wagons were precious, and the precision and craftsmanship of each vehicle in his shop was a matter of intense pride, maybe even love. To Murphy, a crippled wagon was a broken heart, but on the range, it meant the difference between life and death. He was no sentimental fool. He eyed the men, one by one, and then said in a seething undertone just above a whisper. "Fix it. Now. Get Horace and his wife and babe home. And LaBoutain, get off my property."

⌘

EDWARD HONEY WOKE UP IN A POOL OF BLOOD IN THE snow with a screaming headache and a broken nose. He managed to pull himself together enough to stumble into a tavern, slump into a chair, and slug down a whiskey shot. Things weren't going well. The slave, Horace Redburn, had eluded him yet again. He would settle the score once and for all. He would have retribution.

Supplies

⊶⊷

By the time Jonathan arrived in St. Louis, Horace was up on crutches, and Fredericka and Bo were back at the boardinghouse.

"Jesus!" What happened to you? I leave for a few months and come back to find you have a baby and looks like you took a bashing to boot," he said, trying not to sound too concerned.

"Her name is Bo," Fred said, lifting the child to Jonathan's open arms.

"She's beautiful!" He cradled the baby, cooing at her. "Hey there, I'm your Uncle Johnny."

He handed the baby back to Fredericka and stared at Horace. "What the blazes happened to you? You still up for the journey? You look a bit damaged there, brother."

"I fell. I'll be fine."

"Sure you did." Jonathan could feel his pulse quicken. "Who did this? Tell me."

"Leave it," Horace waved him off. "There's nothing you can do."

Jonathan stood up, shoved his hands in his pocket, and scowled at Horace. "Leave it? You get yourself half killed, and you want me to leave it? I can help find the bastards who did this and get the law on their tail."

Horace gritted his teeth and slammed his hand on the table, jolting the baby awake. Ignoring the infant who began to cry in Fredericka's arms, Horace shouted, "Look, Jonathan, the law isn't going to help me. I'm a Black man in Missouri. The law here says the color of my skin makes me an incompetent witness against a White man. So what you gonna do with that? Huh? What you gonna do?"

Fredericka, startled by Horace's outrage, tried to calm him and the baby. "Horace, now don't get yersef all wrathy. Get Bo all stirred up and all." She bounced Bo in her arms until the baby stopped fussing.

"Sorry, Fred, Jonathan, it's just that I'm not even allowed to be an educated man here. Negroes aren't supposed to learn to read or write, by the same law you say is supposed to protect me. They say literacy could lead to rebellion. It's not right. It's not human, but there you have it." He lumbered back into a chair, defeated. His leg throbbed, and his head ached, and his ribs reminded him not to take a deep breath.

Jonathan pulled up a chair next to Horace. "I'm sorry, Horace," he said, and then brightening up. "What say we have a drink?" He went to the corner of the room and retrieved a bottle from a leather satchel. "Authentic French brandy, my friends! Bring some cups!"

Fredericka brought two tin cups to the table, and Jonathan poured a healthy serving in each. "Here's to forgetting the past." He raised his cup and gulped the brandy down.

"To the past," Horace said, taking a sip, "and never forgetting."

Jonathan poured himself another tumbler. "Let's say we make a list of what we need to get us the hell out of Missouri." He smiled and put out his hand.

Horace shook his hand. "Okay, brother."

"So, time to think about stocking up the wagons. And just to be clear, you built your wagon, so I'm paying for supplies and the teams. No argument."

Horace eyed Jonathan and nodded. "You sure? 'Cause we can't do it without you, Johnny."

"Sure as I'm sitting here. What'll we need to get us to California?"

"Keep it light," Horace said, as Jonathan took a pencil to paper he pulled from his jacket. "No more than two thousand pounds to a wagon. They say it's too hard on the oxen pulling more than that."

"Oxen? Not horses?"

"Horses eat grain, and can't take the heavy loads. Oxen will eat anything on the trail. They're slow but steady. We'll need six oxen at least, four to pull, and two spares. But first, we'll have to haul the wagon up the Missouri on a steamer to Independence. Get oxen and supplies there. Shoe the oxen, last-minute repairs. Then rendezvous with a wagon train."

Jonathan was scribbling furiously. "How'd you know all this?" he asked, looking up from his notepaper.

Horace chuckled. "I work in a wagon yard, city boy." He realized how much he missed his old friend.

Fredericka came to the table, rocking Bo in her arms. "We'll need pounds of shorts."

Jonathan looked confused. "The whole bran flour, not the superfine?"

Fredericka gave a chuckle. "If you be buyin', but I like my shorts, the whole bran makes for good johnnycakes and such. And we need hardtack, bacon, sugar, coffee, dried fruit, salt, and pepper. And don't forget the saleratus for bakin'."

"Saleratus?"

"You know," she said and laughed, "baking soda. You don't do much cookin', do you?"

"Shorts and saleratus it is," Jonathan said. "I can taste the biscuits already. And whiskey!"

Fredericka continued with her list, ignoring his comment. "A cast-iron skillet, Dutch oven, coffee pot, plates and cups, knives, forks, you know."

Horace pitched in. "Don't forget matches, canteens, water bucket."

"Soap!" Fredericka added, at least thirty pounds and candles."

"Why not just bring oil instead?" Jonathan asked.

"Too heavy. Candles are better," Horace said, stretching his leg on a chair.

Fredericka added, "Clothes too. Woolsack coats, oilskin coats. I be needin' a couple of cotton dresses, and yous need some wool pantaloons, buckskins, lots of cotton shirts, flannel shirts, socks, boots, hats, a sunbonnet, baby clothes, and a sewin' kit." She cooed at the baby.

Horace winced, trying to adjust his broken leg to a more comfortable position. "Let's not forget tools to repair the wagon: a shovel, hatchet, augers, gimlet, hammer, a hoe, plow, whetstone, oxbows, axles, kingbolts, oh, and ox shoes, some extra spokes, ropes, chains, and maybe an extra wagon tongue. A couple of saddles, harnesses."

Jonathan kept writing, and said, "Slow down, slow down, you're talking faster than I can write. Okay. There now." He looked up and poked the pencil's butt end to his chin. "How much flour are you thinking we need?"

Horace looked up at him. "They say at least two hundred pounds. Each."

Jonathan gave out a low whistle.

Horace continued, "But they say we'll also need about one hundred pounds of salt pork and a barrel of brine to keep it in. About twelve pounds of coffee, twelve pounds of sugar. Each. That's not all. We'll need about fifty pounds of rice, two bushels of beans, two bushels of dried fruit, maybe some cornmeal…"

"And a butter churn," Fredericka said.

Jonathan looked up from his list. "What about pistols? They say there's Indians." All three stared at each other.

"Don't know about pistols and such," Horace said. "Against the law for a Negro to have a gun. Slave or no slave, they just see a Black man, and I'm a dead man. Besides, haven't heard much about Indian troubles. Most likely, we'd need it to ward off White men and other scalawags, present company excepted."

"Hell-fire," Jonathan chortled. "I've never held a gun. Thought about it once, when father…but they say we need some protection. And we should have powder, lead, and shot for hunting, right? And how about a cast-iron stove?"

Horace roared with laughter. "Too heavy! Look, we're already close to our weight limit with what we have."

"Yes, but I promised Emily I'd bring her grandmother's china set and her mother's spinning wheel and several trunks…" Jonathan said.

Horace shook his head. "Can't do it. We still haven't made room for two hundred pounds of lard or the vinegar and molasses."

"And the cow," Fredericka prompted. When she mentioned the bovine, both men shot out simultaneously, "The cow?"

"For milk. For the baby. For makin' butter. We need a cow."

Jonathan stopped writing again. "I think we'll need another wagon. And I don't want you to worry about anything. I'm paying for everything!" He stood up on his shaky brandy-boozed legs. "Nature is calling. Show me the door!"

While Jonathan relieved himself in the alley, Fredericka sat in a rocking chair, nursing Bo, and said, "Man makes a lot of promises when he drinks."

"If we can't trust Jonathan, we can't trust anybody," Horace replied.

The Big Muddy

⊂∞∞⊃

The Missouri River was a dangerous sidewinder with swift, unpredictable currents. Relentless flooding devoured its banks of rocks, soil, and timber, eroding old boundaries, constantly changing course, disgorging its belly of sediment and flotsam, and forming new sand bars. Sometimes the river concealed its treacherous digestion just beneath its murky surface with cottonwood snags piercing the surface like a dead man's hand, tearing the bottom out of a boat. The Big Muddy was also a byway to the great frontier, the defining, though meandering, line between civilization and the Wild West. The river floated the dreams of thousands of adventure seekers, gamblers, miners, fur traders, trappers, and immigrants from St. Louis to the last outpost of civilization, Independence, Missouri.

Even from the riverbank, Horace thought the steamboat, *Lulu Simone*, looked jam-packed. It's three decks were stacked upon each other like a tiered cake, each tier slightly smaller and narrower than the deck below. Each seemed to bulge with cargo and humanity. The lower deck was stacked with cords of wood to fuel the furnaces that would drive the boilers and the boat's substantial side wheels up the Missouri. Barrels of sugar, flour, and whiskey were loaded higher than a man's head. Horses, cows, pigs, and crates of live chickens were interspersed between bales of hay, timbers, furniture, trunks, carriages, heaps of new saddles, boxes, and ropes, and tools of every variation. The upper deck carried the wagons.

Horace could see his Murphy on the deck's outer rim; its blue boards and red wheels seemed to sparkle in the spring air. He had to smile. Thanks to Joseph Murphy, the wagon had been rebuilt by the same thugs who nearly destroyed them both. Now he and the wagon were both restored, bones and boards renewed. The second wagon Jonathan needed would be purchased in Independence, along with supplies, oxen, and Fredericka's cow.

Horace glanced at Fredericka standing next to him, rocking Bo in her arms, babbling and cooing at the infant. She glowed with a baby back in her arms. Bo was three months old, her mother's beauty already shining through. He nodded to Jonathan, standing next to her. Jonathan nodded back and gave a broad smile. He was practically jumping out of his suit, twitching with excitement, absorbing every moment. They stood on the riverbank, swarmed by a frenzy of passengers, mules and horses, luggage, cargo, and grim-faced Black crew members.

After the cargo was brought onboard and secured, the ticket master blasted a whistle, and the passengers were allowed to board. Horace, Jonathan, and Fredericka embarked across wide wooden planks from the riverbank to the boat deck. Holding little Bo, Fredericka, careful of her step along the plank, gently touched down on the deck. The ticket master tore off the ticket stubs and pointed Horace and Fredericka to his left. "Lower deck, to the left, make way, make it quick," he ordered, and then he reached for Jonathan's ticket. "Top deck, sir, to the right. You are in the Connecticut State Room C, across from the dining room and parlor."

Jonathan said, "Just a minute, there's been some kind of mistake. My friends and I are supposed to have indoor quarters."

The ticket master, whose beard held the cornmeal residue of the man's previous meal, seemed startled at the inquiry. "Begging yer pardon, sir, but niggers don't go top deck. Top deck staterooms are reserved for gentlemen like yourself. Your, uh, friends, they're in steerage with the rest of the mudsills, you know, half-breeds, savages, immigrants, the working class, you know." Cornmeal Beard continued to snap tickets and direct passengers.

"But, I paid for…"

Before Jonathan could finish, Horace put a hand on his shoulder and interrupted, "It's okay, Johnny, we'll be fine."

Jonathan stared at the lower deck crawling with a motley assemblage of Indians, Mexicans, Chinamen, Negros, deckhands, hunters, fur traders, trappers, and somber-looking riflemen of questionable characters. A gambler sat on a bale of hay ready to deal a game. Immigrants with families and dozens of children rigged spaces along the filthy floorboards with coats and blankets. They wedged between bales of hay and sacks of grain for the long and arduous journey up the river. The stench of manure and sweat wafted through the swarm of livestock and humanity"

"But, you're outside!" Jonathan objected. "The baby, Fredericka, you can't…"

"Yes, we can," Fredericka said. "Seen worse. Don't make a fuss now. You go on."

"Well, I'll come and check on you. Sure you'll be alright?" The two ex-slaves nodded and melted into the crowd as Jonathan made his way up the staircase to the place for "gentlemen."

Horace had found a place to hunker down near a cord of wood. High enough to keep the sun off Fred and the baby and out of the wind. The boilers were going day and night, and smoke from the stacks often choked the air when the boat slowed around sandbars and crept around treacherous snags. The river was a ribbon of chocolate-brown water with churning eddies, muddy banks, scruffy islands, and dense forest-laden shores.

"It's beautiful!" Fredericka said, watching the riverbank roll by. "All those trees and birds. And look at all them flowers. I be gettin' some seeds when we get to Independence." She closed her eyes and welcomed the misty wind and water as the boat steamed up the river.

It had been a relatively mild ride on the first day until the weather changed. A cold drizzle settled in through the night, and Horace huddled with his wife and baby on the wet wooden deck until he conceived an idea. Rigging some logs from the woodpile overhead, he created a lean-to covered with a thin blanket and fashioned a raft of short wood timbers and planks held together by hemp ropes to keep them above the wet deck. Despite his efforts, the continuous drizzle chilled them to the bone as they tried desperately to keep Bo warm and dry.

Meanwhile, a few feet above them on the enclosed Top Deck, Jonathan finished dining at a table set with linen, candles, and whiskey. Three fellow passengers joined him at the table: Hank Lowe, a big, bloated, round-faced man who constantly chewed on an unlit cigar in the corner of his mouth; Sam Crittenden, a brooding sort, with a full beard, wearing a shabby wool suit that had seen better days; and Cuthbert "Cuddy" Ogden, the brash son of a wagon master. Cuddy frequently tugged at his crotch as if his britches were too tight.

Jonathan regaled the trio with his dreams of starting up a business in California with his father's inheritance, how he planned on marrying his beautiful Emily in Yerba Buena, and his intention of purchasing supplies for two wagons in Independence. Eager to impress his dining companions and warmed by liquor, Jonathan failed to see the glint of avarice in his table companions.

"Excuse me, friends." Jonathan rose somewhat wobbly from the table with a hot plate of beefsteak and potatoes for Horace and Fredericka. "I have companions below in need of nourishment."

Before Jonathan had moved a step, Cuddy Ogden yanked out a deck of cards from his inside pocket. "You game for a hand or two to pass the time?" He spit on the floor with a grin.

"Me? No," Jonathan said, laughing. "I don't play."

"I'm in," Crittenden said, pocketing his watch. "Come now, my man," addressing Jonathan, "why not join us?"

"I'm in," Hank Lowe said, lighting up another cigar. "Whiskey all around!" he called to the waiter.

"Well, gentlemen," Jonathan replied, "if you're talking whiskey, I may be inclined to join you in a drink, but I'm not much of a gambling man."

"You still in your breeches, huh?" Cuddy mocked, scratching his crotch. "Gotta learn sometime. I've seen lotsa fellas victimized by shecoonery 'cause they didn't know how to play. It behooves you to learn, like me. Shit, I been playin' poker since I was head tall to a rat's ass." Cuddy spat on the slimy floor and continued to shuffle the cards, with a grin so broad the tar from his tobacco dribbled down his chin.

Crittenden said, "C'mon son, play with the big boys. Or you still wettin' the bed at night?"

The men laughed. Jonathan felt his face flush with embarrassment. He was not a boy any longer. He was a businessman now who owned a New York hotel. He was getting married.

He bristled at the contempt of these men who mocked him how his father ridiculed him for wanting to be a man. He was not a child. He would not be treated like one. "I'm in," he said, downing a glass of whiskey as the warm plate of food turned cold, and the rain continued to fall.

<hr />

THE *LULU SIMONE* WAS CHARGING FULL STEAM AHEAD against the oncoming current, but rainclouds had obscured the moon, and the long night was dark when the ship hit a sandbar. The first sound was a scraping like the muted friction of a man's whiskers rebelling against a shave. Then followed by a harsher grating as the steamer and all its cargo, containers, and contingent of passengers lurched to a stop. Screams went up from the lower deck as two barrels of whiskey toppled from their mounts and rolled their crushing contents across the deck over a hapless man in its path. They smashed into a crate of windows and mirrors, sending shattered glass into the air. Horses panicked and pulled at their harnesses, whinnying and stomping in their open paddocks.

Horace, Fredericka, and Bo were asleep against a load of stacked wood. The lean-to was affixed in such a way as to hold off the careening lumber above, but the kinetic force slammed Fredericka and the baby forward against an unforgiving mound of stiff, thick ropes. Fredericka tumbled on her side, the baby careened out of her arms and rolled onto the floorboards crying.

Horace hit a support beam, knocking him unconscious. Minutes passed. From a faraway place, Horace could hear people yelling and then Fredericka's voice. He blinked his eyes, his head hurt. Everything was dark and blurry. He listened to her voice again. The haze lifted. "Fred?" he called. "Fred?" He shook his head and wiped his eyes.

"No!" he heard her scream.

"Fred!" His voice was urgent, as he scrambled toward her on his hands and knees. Reaching her, he stood rocking on unsteady legs. When he finally managed to focus, he was shocked by the sight of her. Fredericka had struggled to her feet, heaving the baby up with her. She had hoisted Bo over her head and straddled the infant on her shoulders, clutching the baby's arms with her hands like another time not so long ago in a flood, trying to save Isaiah.

Fredericka would not lose Isaiah again. Her heart pounded against her chest with the anticipation of water, surging, suffocating swells of water. Fear so bitter she couldn't breathe. But she could scream, "No!" She screamed, "No!" She screamed, "No!" She screamed, "No!"

Horace grasped the baby off her shoulders. "Fred, I'm here. We're okay." He searched the baby for signs of harm. "Baby's okay," he said.

Fredericka stared at him. "Water coming."

"No, no flood," he said softly. "No water. See? Bo's okay."

He touched her face. "You're bleeding. I'll find some bandages. Can you take Bo and stay here?" He guided her to sit on a nearby crate.

She quietly nodded and wrapped her arms around the baby. "No flood," she said. "No water."

Over the toppled cargo, he spied an oil lamp that had turned over, and a fire burst into life along the tongue of the spent fuel. Horace leaped over the jumble of loose cargo, tugged off his shirt, slapped at the fire, and extinguished it. Panting with the exertion, he surveyed the scene before him. Some men tried to quiet the mules and horses protesting against their harnesses. Chickens, spooked from their overturned cages, nervously flapped around the deck.

People rushed to and fro and checked on each other. Some men heaved a carriage back up on its wheels; a group had formed around a dead man crushed by the loose barrel. Deckhands hollered orders as the smokestacks continued to belch black smoke into the dawning sky. In the dim light of dawn, Horace could see his wagon, a bright and beckoning beacon, still intact. He couldn't help but smile.

Just then he heard the bark of a man behind him. "You. Boy. Get your ass down there with the others and dig this boat out." Horace turned to see the snarling man wearing a faded blue uniform that had long ago seen its prime and a blue hat outlined with a tarnished gold braid. Horace glanced down at the sandbar. Half a dozen slaves loaned out for crew duty were standing knee-deep in water, shoveling sand out from under the hull. It seemed to Horace a defeating exercise as the sand continuously shifted back with the oncoming current.

"I'm a free man," Horace replied to the Faded Uniform. "I'm no slave."

"Look, boy, I don't give a rat's ass who you think you are." The officer pulled a pistol from his belt and pointed it at Horace. "You take that there shovel, get down there, and dig! Or so help me I'll blow a hole through that black head of yours!" The Faded Uniform kicked a shovel toward Horace.

Horace stood motionless for several seconds, debating his pride against the pistol. Cursing under his breath, he picked up the shovel and lowered himself down the rope ladder, descending knee-deep into the cold and muddy water with six other Black men. The task was hopeless as one of the rented slaves, Micah Higgins, complained with a nod up at the stranded craft. "White man got no sense. Havin' us shovel sand in da' water. It jus' run right back at us. Make no sense."

"Where you from?" Horace asked as the silt and sand drizzled off the scoop of his tool.

Micah answered without looking up from the sandbar. "I's from Mississippi. Loaned out to work this here ship. Gonna make me some freedom coin. Gonna buy me outta here one day." He stopped digging and stared at Horace. "Can I ask you somethin'?" The rain had subsided, and the moonlight glistened through the clouds just enough to glance off Micah's shiny, coal-dark face. The other men paused from their labors, silent participants to the conversation.

"Sure." Horace plunged the shovel in the sand and leaned against the handle.

"How do it feel? Bein' free."

Horace glanced around at the men around him. He recognized the weariness behind the eyes, the drooping shoulders, and the concaved chests; he was all too familiar with the symptoms of those who suffer the evisceration of hope.

"Who's free?" Horace clutched again at his shovel. "I'm down here diggin' with you all. Free or not, we all gotta keep diggin.'" He drove the spade into the sandbar and tossed the silt over his shoulder. Micah gave a snort, and the rest of the men thrust their shovels into the mud, slinging the muck away bit by bit as it seeped back in.

Along the upper deck, most passengers slept through the grounding in their stateroom beds, awakened only by the stillness of the boat and men's shouting. As for the late-night gamblers, Jonathan had been hurled across the poker table, scattering the chips and cards to the floor. The three other players tumbled alongside him, clinging to the cards in their hands.

"What the blazes?" Jonathan rose to his feet and tugged on his waistcoat, sweeping back his hair from his forehead, vaguely aware of a numbing sensation across his brow from the booze.

The other men from the table wrestled to their feet in an ungainly fashion, all trying to discern the cause of the abrupt interruption to their game. "It appears we have stopped," Crittenden said, brushing off cigar ashes from his sleeve with the cards still in his hand, following the others to the outside deck.

Hank Lowe pulled on his cigar as he gazed below at the confusion on the cargo deck. "Looks as if they have it all under control. What do you say we finish the hand?"

"I gotta go." Jonathan scanned the crowd below. "Got friends down there."

"Not so fast," Lowe said. "I'm still holding my cards." He flashed a nod at the other two men, Crittenden and Cuddy. "Gentlemen? Your cards?" Each held up their cards, still gripped in their hands.

Jonathan rocked on his heels, dizzy from the midnight shots of whiskey. He shook his head vigorously, trying to clear his thinking. "I don't have my cards. I dropped them in the fall."

Crittenden shook his head, "Defaulted, then?"

"No." Jonathan steadied himself on the table. "I just dropped them in the fall."

"I'd say the pot goes to the best remaining hands," Lowe said.

"But, you have all my money on the table!" Jonathan said.

Crittenden chuckled. "Like I said, you gotta learn to play with the big dogs, isn't that right, gentlemen?" The other players stood together, grinning at Jonathan.

"That's the rules," Hank Lowe said, shrugging. "Your money's forfeited. That is, of course, unless you have something else to bring to the table?"

"I could send for money from New York," Jonathan said, wobbling on his feet. "It will take time of course..." His words trailed off in the realization that time wasn't on his side. The wagon trains would be leaving, the season for immigrating was short, and his lost cash was stacked high on the poker table. He swallowed hard, as hard as the thought that now hammered his brain.

Horace would never have to know. It would be just a bet to get his cash back, money for the supplies and oxen. He still had to buy his own wagon. Horace and Fredericka would understand. Maybe even approve.

His thoughts ricocheted from friendship to desperation. "I've got a wagon. On the boat. It's worth at least two hundred dollars."

As the sun rose on the Missouri that morning, the turbid river had excavated sufficient mud and debris, freeing the steamer from the sandbar despite the long night of hopeless shoveling by the slave labor and one bitter free Black man. The *Lulu Simone* resumed her northern course upriver, but the damage had been done.

The Horn

⎯⎯⎯∞⎯⎯⎯

E mily was sure she was dying. The *Brooklyn* had been at sea for four weeks, half the time battling brutal winds and tumultuous waves that continuously swamped the deck. The passengers were forced to endure the dark and airless hold below deck for days on end, with only a few days of respite above deck between the storms.

Below, with the vents closed against the waves, and the hatch locked down for weeks, with no sense of day or night in this unrelenting hell, she had lost all sense of time and space. Her only stability was the post she clung to when she could no longer endure her soiled bunk. Her feet were awash in feces sloshing the floor, and she was suffocating in the thick, sticky air that smelled of urine, rotting onions, and vomit.

The dark held an undercurrent of torment, mingling the muffled sounds of agony with the prayers and songs of the faithful. These were not her prayers, and these were not her songs. If she were not dying, she thought, then she was indeed going mad, if not from the putrid hold, then from thirst and hunger. If she were not dying, then she wanted to die. She wanted the torment to end so very much that she began to find comfort in repeating the whispered prayers of her traveling companions.

Danuta Pfeiffer

After what seemed an eternity, the ship's rocking subsided, and the stormy seas quieted. Emily noticed the clanging and chaos ebbing until the only sounds were the muted sufferings of her fellow passengers in the dark. Someone above yanked the hatch open, and the hot white flash of daylight burned her eyes. Passengers scrambled toward the steps of the hold, some crying, others holding up their arms like sun-starved flowers. Men, women, and children stumbled up the wooden stairs and fell on the deck topside, gasping for the sweet air as sailors passed around water.

A weathered sailor with a scruffy beard offered Emily a dipper of water from a bucket. Shaking and dehydrated from seasickness, Emily was barely able to grasp the ladle and put the cup to her parched lips.

She wiped her mouth with the back of her hand. "Thank you kindly, sir." She leaned back against the sideboard.

The sailor laughed, exposing a wide gap where his front teeth used to be. "I ain't a gentleman, lass, ye don't call me, sir. They calls me Toothless."

"They call me Emily." Her voice was weak. "It's so hot... Where are we?"

Toothless scratched his sweat-stained armpit. "Ye get used to the heat after a time. Storms blew us clear across the ocean to near Africa. Cape Verde islands. But nows we be sailin' the trades south. Should be crossin' the equator any time."

"The Equator?" Emily struggled to her feet, balancing on Toothless's arm. "I've never seen the equator before."

She peered over the portside, scanning the vast ocean as if to locate the demarcation line. Searching vainly for something solid and firm, all she saw was endless dark blue water. "Silly me," she chided herself. "I thought I would feel different going from one hemisphere to another. Change somehow, you know, from the top of the world to the upside-down world, but all I feel is sick and dirty." She pulled back from the railing and slid back to the deck floor.

Toothless gave her another ladle of water. "You be Mormon?" he asked in a low voice.

She shook her head, no.

"Well, if sick's what ye be feelin', I have a tincture to make ye feel a bit chirkier." He paused, waiting for her response.

"What is it?"

He glanced over his shoulder and whispered in her ear. "These Mormons don't know a good thing when they sees it. All them rules and regulations. It's laudanum, m'lady. Just a tinge of opium mixed with a little liquor. I kin get it to you cheap."

"Sakes alive! I never! Maybe I'll feel better by the time we get to California. It shouldn't be long now, right?"

Toothless shook his head. "California, ye say? Got months to go before California, lass."

"Months?" How would she endure months more in the middle deck, unable to stand upright under the low ceiling? How could she possibly manage to live cramped in eight feet of space between passengers? And if that were not impossible enough, how to bear the smell of the two cows and forty pigs mingled with the odor of crated chickens and the puke and the decay of dead varmints that even the rats couldn't tolerate? How would she manage the constant wave of nausea that overwhelmed her?

"But I can't!" She gripped the sailor's arm. "I have to get off this ship!"

Toothless patted her hand still wrenched around his arm. "Now listen, m'lady, everybody here is in the same boat, if ye get my meanin'. Like I said, I kin git ye somethin' when you be needin' it. You jist ask for old Toothless." He stood up and worked his ladles of water down the row to the others.

Emily looked around her. Over two hundred passengers crammed around her, shoulder to slouched shoulder on the deck. Makeshift shade cloths did little to alleviate the unbearable heat and oppressive humidity. Her stomach cramped again. The hot oak deck scorched her skin. Too weak to move, she felt warm vomit drizzle down her chest.

Two days passed. The lifeless sails slapped against the masts in a sad rebuke of the windless sky. Emily hadn't moved from her spot on the deck. She was neither awake nor asleep but had fallen in and out of a sickening torpor. Her appearance was that of a rotting peach, blotched and scorched by the sun, lacking the turgidity of form, melting from the inside out.

In her stupor, she heard a loud cry rise up from one of the passengers. The three-month-old son of Joseph Nichols had died. During that mournful day, his parents wrapped the infant in a cloth, and after prayers and hymns, cast his little body into the sea. It would only be a week later when fifty-nine-year-old Elias Ensign would join baby Nichols at the bottom of the ocean.

The *Brooklyn* languished in the doldrums two more days, and Emily's condition continued to deteriorate. Some less-impaired passengers offered her dried bread. Others gave her tonics of castor oil, but her stomach cramps persisted, her thirst endured, and the heat and nausea drew her one step closer to death each day. Toward this end, Emily finally accepted the potion from Toothless, and the laudanum did its work. The pain subsided. The cramping stopped. Her nausea eased, and finally, Emily slept.

On the morning of the fifth day, the ship's sails began to flutter. Then, inhaling the wind, the sails billowed. The desperate contingent on the *Brooklyn* felt their hope renewed. Cheers went up as the prow hissed and sliced through the waves, and the Saints broke into hymns of praise as the ship proceeded south to the turbulent waters around Cape Horn. But the singing soon stopped when the ship began to climb and fall in the bruising swells, swaying and lurching in the mountainous depths, and the *Brooklyn* became as liquid and formless as the sea.

In the weeks and months that followed, Emily relished in the remarkable concoction of alcohol and opium. She didn't care when varmints ate the cheese or the candles melted in the heat. She did not complain about using buckets for toilets or the lack of privacy. She became adept at drinking switchel, the stagnant water spiked with molasses and vinegar, by filtering the slime through her teeth. She was not concerned when the butter and lard went rancid or the weevils got into the flour, rice, and hard bread. She didn't mind the bug-infested beans, or the putrid meat, or the rats. She did not grieve when scarlet fever and consumption ravaged the passengers or when diarrhea and dehydration took the weak to their watery graves. When the ship stalled on a windless sea, she reveled in the stillness, and when the vessel fought the ice of Antarctica and the storms of the tropics, she found euphoria in the violence of nature.

All the while in her laudanum dreams, she imagined herself the heroine of her own marvelous adventure.

The Raw Deal

The *Lulu Simone* struggled against the current for another week, hitting snags and running aground, navigating around eddies and spontaneous islands of mud. She passed forested banks and treacherous shoals and forged through relentless cold rains to the mounting curses of passengers and crew. But grief had not yet hit Horace and Fredericka, who were comforted by their wagon rocking gently on the deck above them, cradling their dreams.

Fredericka and Horace had been sleeping with Bo against their makeshift bed of potato sacks when Fredericka awakened stiff and cold. She rose quietly, wrapping a shawl tightly about her shoulders, and moved softly past the sleeping passengers bundled on the deck's floorboards and stepped barefoot to the front of the boat. Standing in the gray morning light, watching the riverbank curve and narrow, she thought how the mist cradled between the trees like giant balls of cotton, each limb cupping a husk of fog. She thought of how far they had come from the plantations and pain, and wondered how far they had yet to go.

As the steamer took another turn, she spied a heron standing in the thick marsh, wading in a slow ballet along the shallows. Each wide step of its willowy legs precise, and long toes delicately plucking in and out of the water until it stood perfectly still, neck coiled. The heron gazed past its own reflection, divining the watery world below, ready to strike its prey with a viper's thrust. Fredericka was mesmerized by the bird's fierce concentration, and she felt her own bones, spine, and legs lock into the same stoic patience, her throat tight, her breath still, as the world passed through the bird's eye, life pausing into a single muted moment.

But the steamer's intrusion broke the stillness. The crane made a deep croaking sound, and his guttural call released the moment. Fredericka jolted from the trance, sweet air rushed her lungs, and she stared up in awe at the magnificent creature above her. The bird's head hunched into its shoulders, its legs trailed long and loose behind, wings fanned a slow beat against the gray sky. It circled her once, twice, and on the third go-round, the heron's fierce golden eyes shot a glance through her. In that augury gaze, Fredericka felt the loft of the air below her feathers, the wind combing her back. She was light and airy, and the day was bright, but the moment had passed. She was back on the boat, gazing up at the dusky shadow of a great bird gliding into a thicket of trees until it disappeared.

The bird animated a group of Indians huddled next to a pile of saddles and harnesses. They spoke in a quickened tongue, pointing at the creature, pointing at Fredericka, nodding and smiling among themselves. Curious, she approached one of the Indians, an elderly man with a regal posture whose eyes, she thought, were as penetrating as the bird's. "What does it mean?" she asked.

The Indian stared at her for a long moment before he spoke. "We are Kaw. People of Wind. People of Water. Heron is our water spirit. Heron comes to you. Heron is your animal spirit. You are the heron."

Danuta Pfeiffer

"I am the heron? But I'm scared of water."

The Indian spoke again. "Heron is water. Heron strong."

Fredericka shivered, an abrupt reminder of the cold and damp pressing against her.

Just then, Horace appeared by her side. "Everything okay?" He eyed the old man but addressed Fredericka. The Kaw Indian turned away and did not speak again, but Fredericka could not shake the bird's omen.

As the steamer continued to plow the Big Muddy, growing evidence of the great movement West began to reveal itself in the encampments of emigrants sheltered in tents and wagons inhabiting the open spaces along the riverbanks—voyagers destined to the great trek to the land of promise.

That evening, while eating a dinner of hard biscuits and dried fruit, Fredericka eyed Horace with a smile and said, "I got me some more seeds 'for we left."

"What kind?" Horace said, chewing his meager meal.

"I got me sunflowers," she said, pulling a wad of folded paper from her pocket. She unfolded the paper and spread the seeds with her fingers. "They's big and beautiful like you. Big ol' brown face looks happy. I'm gonna plant 'em with the corn in our garden. And see, I even write they's name on the paper, like you teach me—S-U-N-F-L-O-W-E-R."

"It's my favorite. You've learned fast. So proud of you."

"I write all my seed names, now." She tucked the seeds back in her pocket.

"You have a pile of seeds, that's for sure. You're soon going to run out of pockets," he said with a sigh.

"What's itchin' at you, Horace?" Fredericka already knew the answer.

"Jonathan. We haven't seen him since coming onboard."

"You think somethin' happened to him?" Fredericka lifted Bo from her nest of sackcloth and cradled her.

"I expected to see him by now. Was sure he'd show up down here, at least for a visit."

"Guess he's feeling so high and mighty in the White Folks Class. He's plum forgotten 'bout us down here." Fredericka tried to joke, but Horace wasn't laughing.

"Not like him…"

At sunset, the boat began to slow with a change in the sound of the steam engines. "Not another snag!" Horace stood to view the problem.

"Independence!" A crewman hollered. "Independence!"

At the sound of that call, the weary travelers who had been huddled in corners and bundled all across the deck floor shook off their blankets, coats, and rags as if shedding old skins and rushed to the railings where, with renewed vigor, they waved and hailed the strangers along the shore as if they were dear friends.

Here, on the verge of the wilderness, dozens of campfires glowed in the crepuscular light, illuminating the faces of men, women, and children crouched in a golden hue around the smoldering flames. A band of Mexicans wearing sombreros sat on a fallen log and watched the steamer dock. Four rough-looking men, played cards around a stump. A lone man stood against a tree, his long rifle lingering under his arm. Some grizzled long-haired men in buckskins and beards gazed up at the steamer in disgust; one spit on the ground and turned away. Horses, mules, and oxen were hitched around dozens of scattered wagons, and chickens squawked underfoot.

"This where we getting off?" Fredericka held Baby Bo close.

Before Horace could answer, the gangplank slapped into the mud, and deckhands were already leading the horses and mules off the steamer.

Horace looked up at his wagon, wondering if he should help with the harnesses holding it. Still, the tussle of unloading passengers, equipment, and baggage directed his attention to Fredericka and Bo. "Better get our bags. We'll meet Jonathan on the dock."

Hours passed. The air turned cold. Jonathan still hadn't come off the boat. The steamer had been disgorged of her passengers and most of the freight. Fredericka and Horace sat on their bags on the river's edge, staring at their wagon still onboard. While they waited, a small dog wandered by begging for handouts.

"What takin' so long?" Fredericka fed the mongrel crumbs from her bag.

Horace petted the dog but kept staring at the steamboat. "Don't know. Jonathan should be here by now."

Apparently, grateful for the food and the comfort of company, the mutt curled up next to them. Fredericka elbowed Horace. "We got us a friend," she said, chuckling, and then wrapped the baby with an extra blanket. "Gettin' cold. Need a fire." She glanced around, eyeing the fire pits of nearby emigrants.

Horace jumped to his feet. "Something's wrong." Alerted by the urgency in Horace's voice, the dog sprang to attention.

Just then, Horace noticed his wagon getting dislodged from its moorings on the deck. The crew then lowered it by bull and tackle to the first deck. Then two men pushed and pulled it across the plank.

"Thank the Good Lord!" Fredericka rocked the baby in her arms. Horace gave a sigh of relief and walked toward the two men with his wagon, Cuddy Ogden and Sam Crittenden. The dog following close behind.

"Thank you kindly." Horace removed his hat with false deference he had learned to give the White man in unfamiliar territory. "I can take it from here."

"What you say, boy?" Cuddy chewed his tobacco extravagantly and spit on the dog's head.

"My wagon, sir. I'm here to take my wagon." Horace felt his throat go dry.

"Your wagon?" Cuddy scoffed, scratching his crotch. "Hey Crittenden, this Black sonofabitch says this is his wagon!" Crittenden came from behind the wagon, his pudgy face red with the effort of pushing the cart. "What the fuck's he talkin' about?" the man puffed, leaning against the sideboard catching his breath.

Fredericka walked up close to Horace. "What's happenin', Horace?"

"Stay outta this, Fred. You and Bo go over there now and leave this be."

"I ain't leavin' you." Fredericka now rocked the baby up and down a little too vigorously.

Cuddy whistled for a third man in the distance who walked toward them, leading a pair of mules. He hiked his britches, stuck his thumbs in his belt, and sneered. "You gonna hitch them mules to my wagon, ain't you boy?"

"No," Horace shot out, a surge of panic coursing through him. "No, sir, I mean, this is my wagon. There's been some misunderstanding…"

"Didya hear this nigger?" Cuddy clawed at his crotch and spit. He walked up to Horace, inches close. Crittenden flanked Cuddy, legs spread apart, his fat bulk threatening. Behind him, Hank Lowe chewing on a stogie, pulled up with the mules.

Fredericka could only whisper, "Horace…"

Cuddy's attention cut to Fredericka. He stepped toward her. "Who have we here? A White woman and a nigger baby? Ain't that against the laws of nature or somethin', Crittenden?" Cuddy had a crooked smile on his face that made him look clownish and cruel.

"Sure is," Crittenden snarled. "Sure as hell is."

The little mongrel weaving around this tightening mob lifted its leg and peed down Cuddy's pants and into his boot. "What the…?" Cuddy yelled, jumping away from the dog.

Crittenden and Lowe laughed. Horace smirked. Cuddy was enraged. He tore the baby from Fredericka's arms. "You laughin' at me? Huh? You think this is funny?" Cuddy ran to the plank between the steamboat and the bank. He dangled Bo by her legs upside down over the water. "Is this funny?"

Bo was shrieking. Cuddy laughed, his mouth wide and dark as he dipped the baby up and down closer and closer to the water.

Horace bolted to the plank with Fredericka pushing behind him, pleading, "Give me my baby!"

Horace reached for the infant. "Now you give that child, here," he said, trying to remain calm.

"My baby! My baby!" Fredericka screamed.

A crowd gathered on the bank watching the scene, but no one seemed to have the stomach to intervene.

Cuddy's eyes were bulging and wide, pumping the baby up and down, hollering, "Tell me this is funny!"

Fredericka screaming. Horace arching his arms to the baby. Crittenden and Lowe agitated, ready to fight or ready to run, licking their lips, anticipating the outcome the way tigers anticipate meat. The horrified spectators on the bank were paralyzed by the drama.

Then a gunshot followed by a cloak of silence, broken only by the screams of the baby and her mother. Then a command, "Stop it, Cuddy. Give the child back. Now!"

All eyes darted toward the sound of the shot. The shooter was a man in a dark hat holding a rifle in the air.

Cuddy blinked as though coming back to his senses. "But Pa…" he said, "we's just havin' a bit of fun…"

The crowd murmured, "It's Alexander Ogden, the wagon master, the kid's father."

"Do it. Now!"

Cuddy stepped off the plank, and Horace snatched the baby from him. He handed the terrified child to Fredericka, who cried, "Baby, baby, my baby!" They examined the child to see if she was injured and tried to calm the infant. Fredericka sobbed, holding the baby in her trembling arms.

The man slung his rifle over his left shoulder, turned, and walked back into the dark encampment.

The drama over, the crowd dispersed. Cuddy's two accomplices stood nearby, their hands in their pockets, gazing at their feet. As Cuddy stepped off the plank, the little mongrel had the misfortune to wander underfoot. In the act of pure rage and frustration, Cuddy thrust his boot into the poor dog's ribs. The animal yelped in pain. As the dog lay panting and groaning, Cuddy kicked it again with another merciless lunge of his boot. The strike hurled the little mutt into the river where, after a few seconds of pawing at the water, its little nose sank and disappeared in the coffee-colored river.

Cuddy turned to Horace and grinned as if his cruelty had satisfied a deep need. "Now get your Black ass over to them mules and hitch up my wagon."

Horace glared at him. "You threaten my child and now think you're taking my wagon? This wagon belongs to me."

His heart slammed into his chest, his fists curled at his sides, his mind racing, the baby still crying.

Where's Jonathan? Just then, Horace saw him. Weaving down the plank. Disheveled. A bottle in his hand. His waistcoat open, his shirt unbuttoned, his speech as sloppy as his manner. Nevertheless, Horace felt relieved at the sight of him.

"There," he said. "That's Jonathan Redburn. He'll vouch for me."

Cuddy grinned and spit in the mud. "Hey, Redburn," he hollered at the drunken man. "This here nigger says this is his wagon. I say I won it fair and square." He spit again. "And all the contents in it. Ain't that right?"

Jonathan pointed his bottle-held hand at Horace. "Thas my man!" he slurred, and staggered toward him. "Thas my man, Horace, my brother!" He took a long swig from the bottle before stumbling into Horace, who tried to hold him up.

"Johnny, what's going on?" Horace tried to keep Jonathan on his feet. "Who are these men? Tell them that's my wagon."

Jonathan wobbled against Horace. "Is true, isn't it, Horace? You're my brother." He patted Horace on the chest and slid down the bewildered man's arms and into the mud, where he sat in an ungainly fashion holding his whiskey bottle in his lap. "I saved your life, didn't I? Didn't I? Got my father killed. Thas what I did."

Horace crouched beside him. "What are they doing with my wagon, Johnny?"

"Lost it, Horace. Played it out and lost it, thas what."

Horace felt the blood drain from his face. He grabbed Jonathan by his jacket. "But it wasn't yours to lose, Johnny."

Jonathan brushed Horace's hands away and snorted. "I tol' 'em it was mine. Who's gonna take a nigger's word over mine, huh?" Jonathan took another slurp from his bottle.

Horace stared at him. His hands still in midair from Jonathan's swipe. He swallowed hard. "Johnny, you don't mean that."

Jonathan flashed his bloodshot eyes at Horace. "You always thought you were smarter an' me with your Latin bullshit and readin' fuckin' Shakespeare. Impressin' people. Well, you don't impress me, no sir. You're no better an' me. You're the slave. I'm the goddamned Master. Mr. High an' Mighty, you're nuthin' without me."

"Johnny, you don't know what you're saying..."

"My father's dead 'cause of you, Horace." Then, raising his bottle as if in a toast, he railed, "I traded his life for your Black ass...so you owe me...thas what...it's jus' a God-damned wagon...Goddamnit...An' besides, who's gonna believe a slave?"

Horace's heart bashed against his chest like a wild bird thrashing in its cage. "If you felt like that, then why all this, huh? Why all the letters and the big dreams to go West?"

"'Cause I needed your muscle. Your protection. You're big. You know shit, thas why."

"And you hate me for it? That doesn't make any sense!"

"I don't have to justify myself to you...or anybody." Drool slid down Jonathan's chin. "And I certainly don't have to jus-tify myself to my father. You took care of that, didn't you?"

Fredericka, becoming more and more alarmed at this exchange called out, "Jonathan, you be all liquored up. You don't know what you're sayin'."

Horace reached his hand up to stop her. He searched his friend's face to make sense out of the words that cut him in half. But there was no sense to be found. There never was. There never would be. Spencer Redburn was never his father. And Jonathan was never his brother. They had no ties to him in blood or color, but more cutting, there existed no bond to him in their souls.

"Horace?" Fredericka's voice and tear-streaked face and the cry of his baby daughter drove home another reality. Horace rose heavily to his feet, bearing the unsupportable burden that Spencer and Jonathan had both gambled with his life. He had wagered everything on them. But he had always been disposable, a possession, a thing to them. A slave. He owned nothing, was nothing, belonged to no one. All that he had or ever could have would never be his.

All he could feel was an upwelling cry for mercy.

———⊗⊗⊗———

The bounty hunter, Edward Honey, was playing out all his options. Two runaway slaves weren't hard to track this side of the Canadian line heading West. He knew they were on the move, but so was he. A good nose for inquiries and a sketch of his targets linked Honey to St. Louis and Murphy's Wagons. From there, an easy task to find the embittered and self-righteous accountant, Charles LaBoutain, who strung out his tale of suspicions regarding Horace and Fredericka, the woman with a tainted color, too dark to be White, and her baby.

But the "Uncles" were not so accommodating. When queried, each worker in the wagon yard gave a different rendition of the story. One said Horace and Fredericka took off for Mexico. Another scratched his head, saying he thought he saw them loading up for Canada. Yet another recollected Fredericka had persuaded Horace to take her and the child back to Buffalo. But the more they failed in their collective recollections, the more convinced Honey was that the runaways were bound for a place not mentioned—St. Joseph and wagons to the West. His gut was partial to this hunch.

Honey was going to Independence, where the wagon trains were assembling in St. Joseph.

The Contract

⊶⊷

F orgiveness comes with the price of forgetting. Horace couldn't shake Jonathan's drunken slurs: *A nigger's word, runaway, father's dead 'cause of you, I traded his life for your Black ass, slave.* Color could never be forgotten between them. Horace had crossed a threshold from trust to doubt, and from love to loathing. Spencer Redburn's wager on his life was not an aberration. Like father, like son—they both saw him as a commodity, an article of trade, an unregrettable loss.

"It's over, Johnny," Horace said. "We're making our own way."

Jonathan's eyes burned from lack of sleep and a hangover. "I had the best intentions. You gotta know that, Horace. They got me drunk. They played me. It's not my fault!" He threw the empty bourbon bottle aside and struggled to his feet, wavering on shaky legs. "What about San Francisco? And Emily? I thought we were in this together, huh, Horace? Huh? We will still have my wagon!" Jonathan flapped his arms like a weak fledgling.

Horace turned and walked away as Jonathan called out to him again, "We can all use my wagon, huh? I can't drive the wagon alone. Horace!"

When Horace didn't turn around, Jonathan wailed, "Horace. Goddamnit, Horace, it's just a goddamned wagon!"

Horace didn't turn around.

"Alright, go on then. You go on then! See how far you get without me. I'm your ticket, boy! I'll go without you then! Don't you walk away from me! Horace! I'll make it up to you! I promise! Horace!"

On their own, Horace and Fredericka wandered along the riverbank before Horace shuffled to a stop and sat down on the bank. "I don't know what I was thinking. Taking you and the baby on this wild chase. Must have been outta my mind. What's the point?"

Seeing Horace lose hope frightened Fredericka. It frightened her as much as the dark and muddy water rushing past the bank. What could she say that would ease his mind and stop her own fear? Just then, a movement on the opposite bank and a heron lifted into the air. She remembered the Kaw Native's words, "Heron is strong."

She wasn't strong, but she was tired of being frightened, tired of being hungry, and tired of the White man's threats. Cuddy's attack on her daughter set something hard in her mind. Instead of being shattered, the shocking incident emboldened her. If Horace had lost hope, she would defy it.

She squared up to him and looked him straight in the eye. "I ain't sittin' by this riverbank waitin' to die. We gonna keep movin' till we can't move no more." She stood up.

"Look, Fred, we don't have shit. No money, no wagon, and no help. Cuddy even took the damn cow!"

"No help? You mean no Jonathan. You don't need nobody, Horace. Now you looky here. That wagon is part of you." She pointed at the carriage disappearing in the distance. "The canvas, the wood, the wheels—thas your skin, your muscle, your legs. That carriage is your heart. You gonna give it up without a fight? Those White men took it an' we gonna foller. And one day, we gonna get it back." She yanked the damp hem of her cotton skirt around, hefted a bag in one hand, tucked Bo under her arm, and proceeded to walk toward the encampment vowing, "We've come this far, I ain't goin' back now."

Horace shook his head. "Damn, you're a stubborn woman," he said, rising to his feet, but he knew she was right.

Dragging their bags and following a distance behind Cuddy and the wagon, they joined the multitude of travelers on the outskirts of Independence. Here, a thousand emigrants had converged, and hundreds more were making the trek daily, joining in the chaotic activity of organizing caravans, arguing over leaders, bartering, holding meetings, drawing up rules and regulations, and swapping stories and rumors of the wilderness ahead. Whole families congregated around makeshift camps. Small children chased underfoot, their stored-up energy yet to be spilled upon the prairies. The smell of bacon, beans, and coffee in the air seemed to console the fears ahead.

"We can do this, Horace," Fredericka said. "We can work our way through it. We done worse." Fredericka sat on her bag and nursed Bo, her eyes darting around the disorganized assembly. Above the rabble's noise, she recognized a man's voice and rose to see him.

Alexander Ogden, the man with the shotgun who stopped Cuddy, stood on the box of an open wagon addressing a gathering around him. Stationed just behind him, she spied Ogden's son. Cuddy stood with Crittenden and Lowe, chewing and hawking tobacco, elbowing each other in some secret joke. Cuddy leaned against Horace's wagon with the same crazy grin on his face that he wore when he held her baby over the water, kicked the dog, and forced Horace to mount up the mules. Fredericka gritted her teeth against his garish look but kept her head down as she and Horace moved toward the crowd to hear the speaker.

Ogden wore a squat, stovepipe hat with a wide brim that clung to his head like a black kettle top. The trimmed hedge of a beard, wiry and white, rounded down from his chops to his chin, a stark frame for his gaunt clean-shaven face and his sunken cheeks smudged dark by years of dirt and deprivation. His clothing was drab and gray—wool trousers tucked into high leather boots, a linen shirt under a wool vest—except for the bright red bandana tied tightly around his neck.

His stature, though of average height, was elevated by his stentorian voice as he rallied the crowd: "I pledge to you, as your Wagon Master, I will drive this caravan under the laws of the Lord. I will not abide by profane language, drunkenness, or cheating while gambling. I will not abide cruelty to animals or any other thing incompatible with the conduct of gentlemen."

He made a slight adjustment to the rifle he cradled in his arm as if it were an extra limb. "We do not fight. We do not kill. I am the final word, judge, jury, and executioner. Anyone who murders will be hanged. Anyone who fights will be detached and left behind. We will pause on the Sabbath to rest the animals and give us time to meditate on the Lord's goodnesss." Ogden's eyes burned with the sheen of polished mirrors, eyes that spoke not of the familiarity with beauty nor the exploits of adventure, but of shock and wildness, a modern Moses who had witnessed God's face in a fire.

Someone from the crowd shouted, "How many miles do we travel in a day?"

"I expect ten to fifteen miles a day, depending on the weather and trail conditions. Rise at four, cattle yoked by seven, and travel about six miles by ten in the morning. Rest, cook, and eat. Then in two hours, load up for the second drive of the day for about four miles. We'll camp during the hottest part of the day and give the cattle a rest, let them take to a water hole to cool off. If conditions improve, load up for the evening drive for another two to four miles and get into the evening camp by about sunset. This should get us into the Oregon territory by September."

Someone gave a low whistle, and another murmured, "That's five months from now."

"That's right," Ogden said. "I expect each wagon to have sufficient grease for your pails, as a failure to grease will ruin the boxes. At least once a week, grease the hook of each ox train, the goose-neck of the tongue, and the rings in the yoke staples. And when we get to water, sit your wheels in the shallows and let the wood soak up to fit snug against the rims. Wood dries out on the prairie. A broken wheel on the trail will only lose us time."

Another man yelled from the rapt gathering crowd, "What about Injuns?"

"I assure you, the Natives make no problems for the wagon trains. If need be, we can trade goods with them. All due respect will be given to any person we meet on the trail, whether Indians, Whites, Mexicans, or Blacks, as difficulties often occur when we abuse and insult inoffensive people. Self-respect and friendship must occur between all people for the well-being of this adventure. I stand firm on this."

"I have horses. Will there be enough grassland to feed them?" a man asked.

"I don't recommend horses to be pulling your wagon," Ogden said. "They may be fast, but they're not strong enough to pull two thousand pounds for two thousand miles, and they require too much feed. Horses are for scouts. If you don't have four oxen for your wagon and a spare, you're not in my caravan."

"What about supplies?" another asked. "Will we come upon some relief out there to re-supply if we run out of food?" A few people nodded in agreement; that was a good question.

"We could resupply at Fort Laramie, but that's a gamble," Ogden replied. "You are required to carry all foodstuffs from the start. If you don't have two hundred pounds of flour, one-hundred-fifty pounds of bacon, ten pounds of coffee, twenty pounds of sugar, and ten pounds of salt for each person in your wagon, turn around. You're not in my caravan."

"And one more thing," Ogden called out. "This is no joy ride. We have two thousand head of cattle we're driving to Oregon with the wagons. This is a long, hard journey. For the next five months, bullwhackers, women, and children— everyone walks except the sick, the old, and the very young. No other exceptions. We leave on the morrow, Monday, April twentieth, at daybreak." He climbed off his wagon, and people surrounded him with questions and petitions to sign up for his convoy.

A tangible sense of excitement rose from the dispersing crowd; one man laughed. "I hear Oregon's a pioneer's paradise. Why, they got fat pigs running around already cooked with knives and forks sticking in them so you can cut off a slice whenever you're hungry!"

Another said, "Oregon cannot be outdone in wheat, oats, rye, apples, peaches, or fat and healthy babies!"

And another said, "They're giving away three hundred and twenty acres to every man!"

The enthusiasm was not lost on Horace and Fredericka. "Oregon sounds nice," Fredericka whispered.

"Ogden sounds like a fair man, despite his son," Horace answered, sounding more optimistic. "If we can, we should go with his wagons. Maybe I could find some work to pay our way."

"I could service out to wash clothes and cook. There's plenty of families who could use the help," Fredericka said.

Horace rested his hand on her shoulder. "Just stay away from Cuddy."

He scanned the scene of pioneers and wagons around them. The camp activity had become more intense by the hour as people finalized their preparations for the long journey. Some signed up with wagon trains, while others, like birds busy with their nests, finished loading their rigs with beans, salted pork, dried fruit, coffee, vinegar, salt, sugar, plows, rocking chairs, chamber pots, feather beds, quilts, and fiddles. Horace figured if he could introduce himself to some of them who could use more muscle, they might let him and Fredericka tag along. He spied one man who struggled to load a piano into his wagon, but the bulky instrument, listing to one side against the back of the wagon, was not cooperating.

"Can I give you a hand?" Horace asked.

The emigrant was a short, middle-aged man with a long mustache and balding gray hair that draped his head and ears like a raccoon pelt. His wife, younger by some years, stood nearby, holding a fringed white parasol. She wore a pretty white bonnet with yellow roses embroidered around the edges, and a matching yellow dress overlaid with a white apron. The young woman was heavy with child and she watched Horace with suspicion.

"Much obliged." The man dusted off his hands. "'Tis heavier than it looks."

Eyeing the piano, Horace said, "It may be too heavy for the wagon, if you don't mind me saying, sir."

"That was my wife's mother's. She insisted," the emigrant said somewhat apologetically. With a great deal of effort, the two men shoved the piano into the wagon box already piled high with books, water kegs, clothing, a cast-iron skillet, a standing mirror, and a butter churn.

"Thank you kindly." The man wiped his sweaty brow with a hanky.

"I'd be willing to offer my services to you and your wife if you are needing an extra hand. My wife yonder could help with…"

Before Horace could finish, the pregnant woman jeered loudly," We don't need no niggers hangin' on."

The man with the raccoon hair shrugged. "My wife says no."

It was getting late, and Horace felt the urgency of the day. The wagons were rounding up in groups that would be leaving by daybreak. He had no time to lose. He ran around countless prairie schooner enclosures, clumped like puffy clouds on the flat terrain, entreating anyone for work on the journey in exchange for food and a place by the fire at night. He was rebuffed at every turn.

Sunday, April 19, 1846, and the night was cold. Horace found Fredericka and Bo huddled next to a small fire she scraped together with twigs and tumbleweeds. He squatted beside her and rubbed his hands against the warm flames. "No luck," he said. They spread out a blanket, and tucked in together with the baby. They fell into an uneasy slumber watching the flames flicker and die.

JUST BEFORE DAYBREAK, A DIN AROSE FROM THE ENCAMP-ment. Men were shouting orders. Tin dishes clanged over early morning fires as the sun rose. Horace sprang to his feet. Two thousand cattle and several hundred horses had been herded toward the encampment, some yoked to their respective wagons, and the rest wrangled behind the caravan in a giant herd. Teams of oxen stomped and reared as the mule skinners and emigrants hawed and whooped to keep them in line for their yokes. A boy led a cow to the back of a wagon where his mother waited to milk it. A man tried to herd several loose chickens into their pens, and children scampered around their anxious mothers. With breakfast quickly consumed, tents were struck and loaded.

The tension was tangible in the teamsters' and mule skinners' shouting commands. Sounds and smells rose in the dust with the morning sun—the braying mules' stubbornness, the oxen grunting, and the emigrants hollering and arguing over their place in line. Slowly, chaos gave way to order. Sixty wagons were organized into fifteen divisions of four wagons to each platoon. Women and children had taken their places, some in the wagons, most standing.

Drivers took to their reins. Outriders on horseback stilled their mounts. All waited for the signal that would change their lives, their world, and the face of a nation. For an instant, nothing moved. The pioneers had paused upon a threshold between the past and the future. Were there regrets? Did some ache for what they were leaving behind? Did some wonder, *Do I really want to do this?* Was the risk worth the gain? How many felt the churn of dread, or felt the cramp of fear? Who didn't have a pang of raw emotion? Did some hunger for the challenge ahead? Or gaze from this precipice and wonder, *Is it too late to turn back?* In the stillness of that anticipation, the clear notes of a bugle rang out, and in one mighty surge, the river of expectation burst forth as the flood of pioneers began.

From the margin of this giant field, Fredericka watched Horace, running now from wagon to wagon, beseeching the drivers, hollering against the day's raw nerves, "Please, sir, do you need another hand?" Forty wagons passed him by in a slow march spewing him in the dust as twenty other wagons and the herd of cattle plodded behind them.

Then, just as one thought that chaos had given birth to order, there arose commotion and confusion, and the movement of this giant, segmented organism ended abruptly. Oxen snorted to a standstill. Men shouted "whoa!" to their teams, and the rattling of pots and pans came to a halt. No one could see the trouble beyond the wagon before them.

Horace raced ahead on foot, breathing hard; sweat poured down in white streaks from his dusty face, his open shirt held together only by his faded suspenders. He came upon the source of the problem: a wagon had shifted its load and lay on its side, holding up the entire wagon train. The four-oxen team had tangled in their yokes and were down kicking furiously, crying "me-wah, me-wah!" A man with a whip was beating the beasts in some twisted enticement to force the animals up.

The sight of the whip made Horace cringe, and before he could think, he ripped it away from the man's hands. "No, sir." He was out of breath from the run. "No, sir, that isn't the way."

The emigrant, Eddy Knight, a shoemaker from Alabama, shouted back, "Whatcha' think yer doin', boy?"

A man on horseback galloped to the scene. Ogden, the wagon master. "What's going on, Mr. Knight?"

"This nigger's interfering with my wagon. He took my whip…"

"Mr. Ogden, sir," Horace said, breathing hard, "we gotta release the yokes before they can get up. Whippin' won't do any good. Then unload the wagon." He pointed to the exposed undercarriage. "And see here, the bolster came loose on the wagon's back end. Made it unstable. Shifted the weight. That's why it went down, but I can fix it, sir."

Ogden swung around on his horse, impatient with the delay, and addressed the sullen emigrant. "I'll tell you this once, Mr. Knight. You do not whip your animals. You address every man with respect even if he be Black. I will not hesitate to take you off my train. Is that understood?" It was impossible to dodge the piercing gaze from Ogden's eyes. Knight nodded in submission.

"As for you, what's your name?" Ogden's horse whirled around, stabbing at the ground impatiently.

"Horace Redburn, sir. At your service." He was still panting from the effort, his healing ribs from the beating in St. Louis stabbed at his chest.

"You can fix this wagon?"

"Yessir! I used to build wagons for Joseph Murphy in St. Louis. I could use a job on your wagon train, me and the missus, sir. If you would have us."

"Fix it. I'll hire you on as a bullwhacker, $25 a month. You keep these wagons moving, help with the cattle. You and your missus welcome to bed and board back behind the chuck wagon." Ogden dashed off.

Now, Horace and Fredericka joined the farmers, clerks, schoolteachers, and trappers, the adventurers, the scoundrels and gamblers, Mexicans, missionaries, bankers, and shopkeepers, the blacksmiths, builders, the reluctant women and rambunctious children, the innocent and the brave. All were bound for the unknown. None knew of the hazards that lie ahead, the treacherous rivers, the forbidding mountains, the prairie's endless dust and dangers. These perils would not diminish the heroics of seeking a better life in the fertile valleys of paradise. The arrogance and confidence of their Manifest Destiny would drive them to the Pacific. Some would perish, and some would survive their dreams. On that first day, a free man's cry rose up from the caravan, "Farewell to America!"

The Last Train Out

———⬦⬦⬦———

Jonathan was at a loss. He didn't know how to handle oxen or harnesses or fix things. He was just a city boy. He never figured to make the trip across the continent without Horace to help him. He didn't even know how to cook; he was relying on Fredericka for that. And he faced other problems: he lost most of his money in the poker game. He would have to write back to New York for more. It would take at least a month before he could purchase his wagon, oxen, last-minute supplies, and hire a couple of teamsters to help the drive. To add to his anxiety, he was running out of time; the travel window was short, and most wagon trains had already left. And Emily was waiting for him in California. What he really needed was a drink to clear his head.

———⬦⬦⬦———

THREE WEEKS LATER, AS JONATHAN SAT IN A TAVERN moping over a whiskey, nine wagons pulled into Independence. Thirty-two men, women, and children from this small company entered the town searching for supplies. Jonathan's ears perked up when one of the pioneers came into the tavern, asking if there were any more wagon trains for the overland trip.

Jonathan ambled up to the man at the bar. "Excuse me, but are you still planning on heading out this late?" he asked.

"Yep," the man said, "leaving tomorrow."

"But they all left weeks ago. Sorry, I don't mean to be rude, the name's Jonathan Redburn, from New York."

"James Reed, from Illinois. Traveling with my wife, Margaret, her mother, and the children. And ten other families." The man had a broad forehead giving the impression of a long face. A full, dark beard covered his narrow chin. "We'll be leaving with or without joining a train."

"But they say wagons leaving now won't make the distance before winter."

Reed put his hand on Redburn's shoulder and leaned in, piercing Jonathan with his deep-set eyes. "There's a shortcut. Bought the map in Chicago."

He produced the pamphlet from his jacket, *The Emigrants' Guide to Oregon and California*, by Landsford W. Hastings. "Says there's a new shortcut across the Great Basin. It'll save us three hundred fifty to four hundred miles on easy terrain over the mountains. We'll beat everyone to California," Reed said.

Jonathan was intrigued and followed Reed out to the street. He was astonished at Reed's contingent of wagons, cattle, and horses. Of particular interest was a curious two-story wagon pulled by eight oxen. "What is it?" Jonathan asked.

Reed jammed his hands into his pockets and rocked back on his heels. "That, my good man, is a house on wheels."

Reed's twelve-year-old daughter, Virginia, came skipping up behind her father and said, "I call it my Prairie Palace."

"Had it built special," Reed said. "With a built-in iron stove, spring cushioned seats, sleeping bunks for the kids, even a feather bed for my mother-in-law. She's poorly.

Consumption. Can hardly walk. But she didn't want to be left behind. She has a couple of servants, so she'll be fine. Yessir, I want to make my family as comfortable as possible for this trip. Even managed to pack in some fine wine from Europe!"

"All this must have cost a fortune," Jonathan said.

"Spared no expense. Made my fortune in lead mining back in Illinois. That's where I met George and Jacob and the other families."

"Why, this is remarkable!" Jonathan tapped his fingers on his lips and then blurted, "Could you use another traveler? I need to get to Yerba Buena; my fiancé is waiting for me there. I've got a wagon but no oxen. I own a hotel in New York, perhaps you've heard of it? The Skylark? No? Well, in any case, my money's not come through yet. I could write you a promissory note for my oxen and supplies."

Reed surveyed the disheveled Jonathan, his soiled suit, unshaven stubble, the smell of whiskey on his breath. "We won't bring someone along who can't pull their own weight."

"I have documents ascertaining my credentials. And I assure you, I can pull my own weight." Jonathan tugged at his jacket and felt his face flush with embarrassment.

Reed thought a moment. "You might be able to join up, if the other families and the Donner party agree."

<hr />

JONATHAN AND THE DONNER-REED WAGONS LEFT INDEpendence on May 12 for what they hoped was a four-month easy trek to California.

The first morning out, they were met with a horrific thunderstorm. Lightning bolts fractured the black clouds for hours, and thunder blasted over them until their bones ached. The rain shot at them in fierce, lateral, wind-driven waves, stinging their eyes, and panicking the cattle.

Margaret Reed, who suffered from severe migraines, sheltered in the two-story wagon with pillows around her head, trying to keep the thunder at bay. "Make it stop!" she screamed, as her four children and seventy-year-old mother, Sarah, huddled around her like frightened chicks. They threw their arms over their heads with each pounding as though bombs had gone off.

The twelve children of the George and Jacob Donner families scrambled for cover under blankets, shrieking at every thunderous roll. When the storm lifted, they were swamped, stuck in mud, and soaking wet. Two horses had stampeded away. The damp and the cold aggravated Sarah's condition, and she couldn't stop coughing.

They made fewer than ten miles that day.

An inauspicious beginning.

A Matter of Numbers

⸻

E mily set foot on the pier in San Francisco Bay a different girl. Her ringlets had long lost their curl, her porcelain skin was blotchy and blistered, and the budding girlish frame had become gaunt, her clothing shabby. She craved laudanum.

That tincture of opium had eased the endless ocean voyage discomforts. This was not the laudanum of Paracelsus, with crushed pearls, musk, and amber, but a bitter, brown substance containing all of the comforts of opium, morphine, and codeine.

Toothless, the sailor who had supplied her with that Byzantine drug, and several other dock workers hauled her luggage and household supplies to the waterfront. Lining the wharf were her trunks of linens and laces, chests of dishes and dresses, boxes of hats, a chest of drawers, a standing mirror, a bed frame and mattress, blankets, kitchen utensils, enough to build a nest. Initiating caution and feeling all the wiser for it, she collected her jewelry from a small box. She deposited the items into her dress pocket, along with the bank notes Jonathan gave her. This act did not go unnoticed by the sailor.

Emily surveyed the marina and opposing hillsides. "Where are all the houses?" she asked.

"Town's got plenty of tents and such, shanties, adobes and the like," Toothless offered.

"But, where are the hotels?"

"Ain't no hotels for the likes of ladies such as yerself."

"Where are all the people?"

"People, Ma'am? Town's got near four hundred souls. Mostly men. You be a sight for sore eyes in these parts." Spittle of tobacco leaked from the side of his mouth.

"But this is not what I expected. Where will I sleep and eat? Where shall I store my things? My fiancé will be here in three months. I'm supposed to find a place to set up house. This isn't right!"

This was supposed to be the adventure of a lifetime for Emily, a girl of seventeen for whom everything was an adventure. To say this was a disappointment was to put it mildly. This was disillusionment, the collapse of a dream shrouded in fear. A shudder ran through her.

Toothless noticed her shiver. "'Spect you be needin' more help with your 'condition.' Feel less troubled," he said with a wide, gummy grin.

She needed to feel untroubled and listless. She wanted to wake to a world of predictability where Jonathan would be waiting, where there were houses, not tents, hotels, not outhouses, and people, lots and lots of people, not a dingy cluster of nomads and Natives and Mormons and sailors. She wanted to be where ladies wore pretty frocks, and where manure was shoveled from the streets. She wanted the scent of perfume, not the odors of leather and piss, and music from grand ballrooms, not the creaking of ships and the screech of seagulls. She imagined New York, not this new San Francisco, where life was a matter of numbers, and men outnumbered women seventy to one.

"Yes, yes. I certainly could use more of your substance," Emily said and nodded to Toothless.

"I can tell you where to find all the laudanum yer heart desires, but, you know, old Toothless, he needs a little something in his pocket, if ye get my meanin.'"

"Of course, yes, I see." Emily reached into her pocket, drawing out a small ring. "This belonged to my Aunt Clara."

"'Tis fine." He closed his fist around the shiny object. "Now, if yer a mind to, there's a Chinaman, name of Ho Ling, yonder, over that sandy ridge. The place has a buffalo skull on the door. Tell him Toothless sent yer."

"What about my things?"

"I will care for them, missus, till ye return."

Emily climbed the ridge and down the other side in search of Ho Ling's opium den. Not so much a den as a dark shed the size of a four-horse stable lit by two lanterns. The hut was lined with bunk beds filled with men slumped over pillows and curled under blankets. Some were smoking with their eyes closed. Ho Ling was a short, bald-headed man, except for a lengthy dark pigtail that traveled down his back. He wore a tunic that measured to his knees over wide cotton pants.

"Toothless sent me," she said, wondering if the China-man understood her because he neither blinked nor spoke.

Ho Ling led her to a bunk and put out his hand. Emily fumbled for a small silver brooch from her pocket. Ho Ling inspected it and left, returning moments later with a long opium pipe and an oil lamp. He adjusted the tube over the light and motioned for her to lie down to position herself to the pipe. Then he withdrew to the corner of the shed.

Emily inhaled the vaporized drug, the sweet savor filling her lungs, her head, and her dreams. She loved the euphoria, that pleasant dulling sensation and cloudy discernment that blurred the sharp realities distressing to someone of her expectations. Everything had seemed so perfect, falling in love with Jonathan, the son of a New York hotel owner, planning a rendezvous and wedding in California. She sailing from New York; he traveling by wagon train with supplies. She loved ringlets and ribbons, and he had aspirations. The perfect plan.

However, plans run into random events that change their course, forming unpredictable outcomes. In Emily's opium daze, visions of her six-month voyage swirled through her brain. The twenty-four thousand endless miles of sea, flashes of tropical storms, and the icy Antarctic, foul water, stifling doldrums, vomit, and varmints, and death shrouds, all flowed in and out of her mind in a drowsy fog.

Several hours later, she awoke. New patrons had filled the bunk beds around her. She slipped out of the shack and made a groggy return to the pier to retrieve her luggage and trunks and to find a place to stay.

It will come to no one's surprise to learn that everything was gone.

Wolves

———⚬⚭⚬———

Fredericka was bewildered by the wagons and horses, the noise and the dust, and clung tightly to Bo. The first day on the trail was filled with enthusiasm by the pioneers, but the excitement hadn't caught up with Fredericka. Horace had been outfitted with a mule by one of Ogden's men and put to work with cattle, but she walked all day behind the line of wagons carrying the baby.

That night, her first concern was where to sit, where to settle, and where to sleep. With no wagon of their own, they were at the mercy of the wagon master's company of bull-whackers, drovers, scouts, and their families for a sheltering spot. This wasn't a new feeling, this sense of being adrift in a sea of White suspicion and the hunched shoulders that spurned her approach. She had long grown accustomed to being dismembered, piece by piece, by a society that never invited her into their fold.

She stood in the center of the encampment feeling overcome by the sight of Horace's wagon, theirs but not theirs, their first possession, their home, so close but out of reach. She longed for its shade and the sweet linseed smell of its canvas. She wanted to tuck Bo into her baby blanket and fold the child into that safe haven. Instead, she stood under the glare of strangers greedily coveting their own meagerness.

Cuddy's defiance made matters worse. He sat on the tongue of Horace's wagon, eating their provisions off dishes she had procured. He seemed to relish in her distress and flashed her a lizardry grin. Her focus was drawn not to her dress that he yanked from the wagon bed to wipe his mouth, or the way he clawed at his crotch, or spit on the ground. She only saw his eyes, adrift in milky white globes—greedy, unmoored eyes that would never fasten to kindness.

Cuddy faked a yawn. With an exaggerated stretch of his arms feigning weariness, he climbed onto the cozy corn husk and Spanish moss mattress she made, wrapping himself under the covers where she and Horace were supposed to find relief.

Fredericka was hungry and tired and felt her knees buckle. A touch on her shoulder and she turned to a gaunt-faced woman who addressed her in an unusually high-pitched voice. "You are welcomed to join us," she said, pointing to her clan of seven children around a campfire. "I'm Mrs. Sarah Bidwell. My husband is Mr. Robert Bidwell, but I just call him Jacob. He's a wrangler. Used to be we were farmers, but the farm went bust in the depression a few years ago. So now he helps with the cattle and all and oftentimes cannot help me with the camping. It would be of great assistance to have another set of hands unpacking the wagon and pitching the tents and such. The children help gather the buffalo chips and weeds for the fire, but with the cooking and washing, well, I'd be grateful for the help and the company."

Sarah's squeaky, child-like voice was in stark contrast to her face. Though in her early thirties, she had the road-weary look of a woman twice her age. Her complexion bore the same prairie drab gray as her dress, and her vacant eyes spoke of someone who knows misfortune yet walks irresistibly toward it.

Danuta Pfeiffer

For the first time in days, Fredericka felt her breathing ease as she followed Sarah to her campfire, where a pot of pork stew bubbled in a large iron cauldron. The aroma of hot food aroused her hunger and clawed at her stomach.

Sarah stirred the pot and said, "Jacob got us this bacon in St. Louis, but I swear the children love mush and milk more. Could be the sugar I add to it." With a signal from his mother, one of the boys got up and offered his stool to Fredericka. Although she was still cautious of the thin, White woman, a wave of gratitude swept over her, relieved to have a place to sit. She eyed the children, ranging in age from about three to fourteen.

Sarah pointed to the eldest child first and counting them down said, "This here's Rebecca. She's the oldest, pretty as a picture and a good helper with the other children. And then Miriam, she's the quiet one, always thinking; then the rascals, Tommy and Jasper. Tommy never learned to talk, but he makes up for it with mischief."

"I lost my baby tooth!" Jasper said, grinning a big gummy smile with his front tooth missing.

Sarah pointed to the girls. "This is Seneca, she loves her rag doll, and this is little Snippit. We call her Snippit since she's only three years old and the youngest. Now you get on and get yer Mamma some more fire makin's," she said, scattering all but Snippit from the campfire.

Fredericka thought how Sarah's voice sounded as if it squeaked through reeds of grass, and how desperately the woman needed conversation, as if all her words had been bottled up waiting to spill out.

"Coming here was not my choice," Sarah said, poking at the fire with a stick. "But my husband leads us by the will of God and the 'Oregon Fever.'" Sarah smiled for the first time.

"He says there's a valley with soil rich beyond comparison and where there is hardly any rain, save for the dew heavy enough to compensate. Jacob says it's the Garden of Eden where clover grows as high as your chin. We're gonna start ourselves up a farm."

She sighed and then in her bird-like chirp said, "Why, look at my manners, I've done all the talkin'," and I didn't even get your name? Where you headin'?"

"I'm Fredericka." She nodded to the bundle in her arms, "and this here's Bo. We were goin' to California," she said, and then for the first time, she realized that with Jonathan out of the picture, their destination was not that secure. "I guess we go where this wagon train goes now. Oregon, I reckon.' Horace and me, we need to consider it."

Sarah shook her head and stared into the fire. Swatting a strand of hair from her face, she said, "Jacob and me, we don't consider things much. He says God made women to be the handmaidens of their husbands. Women being the weaker vessel and all. Jacob says men get themselves perplexed and soured out in the world so that women can stay home to prepare our maternal instincts for affection and to soothe their vexed temperaments."

Sarah paused and then said, "He gets soured with the drink most nights." Shaking off her reflection as quickly as it came, she forced a laugh. "But I don't mind, of course. Jacob says the Bible teaches women to be submissive to their husbands so that the word of God may not be discredited. Jacob and me, we don't talk much. Jacob says I do enough talkin' for the both of us. Says I am better off just acceptin' his authority as being my husband and all."

"I don't know 'bout all that." Fredericka unbuttoned the top of her plaid calico dress and began nursing Bo. "All's I

Danuta Pfeiffer

know is Horace and me want to be the owners of our own days and nights. Horace says one day we can even own time."

"Own time? That would be nice." Sarah sighed, rising from her stool and chirping for her children who flocked around the campfire hungry for their pork stew. The children eagerly attended to their meal, slurping the casserole with the voraciousness given to those who had just walked fifteen miles over a dusty prairie.

Fredericka was dizzy with hunger, and the warm, salty food sparked a ravenous appetite that felt unquenchable, but she left half her bowl untouched. She slid the dish behind her dress on the ground, thinking if the generosity of these strangers should fall short, at least Horace would have something for his stomach.

Just after sunset, Horace appeared near the wagons. He spied Fredericka and Bo near the campfire and made his way slowly toward her. Fredericka quickly poured him some coffee and greeted him with a smile. Horace was parched and dusty and could barely lick his lips. He guzzled the coffee and wiped his mouth with his shirt sleeve. Fredericka introduced him to Sarah, pointing out the children who were playing nearby. Sarah kept her eyes to the ground and simply said, "Pleased to meet you," and quickly walked to the creek with a load of dirty clothing.

"Where's the mister?" Horace scanned the scene, feeling uncertain about the accommodation.

"Sarah says he works with the cattle. Have something to eat." She handed him her half-plate of stew. He no sooner gulped down a couple of spoonsful when Jacob came into the camp and approached the campfire. Horace froze. He knew the look all too well, the red, swollen eyes, the staggering posture, the stink of whiskey, a toxic mix when dealing with White men.

"Who you?" Jacob slurred. "What you doin' near my fire? Eatin' my food? Takin' comfort with my wife?" He yelled, "Sarah, get your ass over here!"

Horace bolted up, dropping his plate on the ground. Fredericka rushed to his side. "No sir, Mr. Bidwell. This here's my husband, Horace… "

"You're no-good Colored trash!" he roared back. "What the hell is goin' on 'round here? Sarah!"

Startled by the shouting, a small cluster of people rose from their campsites and huddled on the periphery to watch. Sarah ran up from the creek. She looked pale and frightened, and the children cowered behind her. "Jacob," she peeped. "Jacob…"

"What these blackies doin' here?" He wobbled toward Sarah. Coming up close to her, he took her by the neck with both hands and snarled, "You let them darkies eat our food and stain our table? Did he mess with you? Huh? Did he touch you?"

Jacob's grip tightened around Sarah's throat, and tears streamed down her face as though he were squeezing water from a rag. Unable to breathe, and her eyes bulging, she could only flap her hands against his chest. The eldest girl, Rebecca, tore at his arm. "No, Daddy, no!"

Jacob took a swipe at her with one hand, and the girl went down. The other children began to cry. Horace took three quick steps toward Jacob. He wanted to break the man's fingers and jerk him off the woman's throat and thrash his drunken ass to an inch of his life. Horace felt the muscles in his arms tighten, and his breath come short and hot. He envisioned the bloody pulp of a man at his feet, begging for mercy—a kindness he would deny. He wanted to make the man bleed and feel the pain his White privilege granted him over the lives of others less fortunate, or weaker, or the wrong color. He wanted justice. He wanted to punish all the Jonathans and Spencers and Graftons in the world for their cruelty and avarice. For cutting him like a dead branch from the family tree. He wanted to take Jimmi Wheel's whip and lash them all to the bone. He tasted the raw meat of resentment against all men who had power. He wanted to tear the man's head off.

Instead, Horace heard himself say, "I'm a bullwhacker. Work for Mister Ogden, like you. My wife is Fredericka."

Jacob's watery eyes darted from Horace to Sarah.

"Like you said, we're just worthless Black folks. We're not worth making you irate." Horace's heart was pounding, and his hands shaking with every self-effacing word.

"The wagon master might make you quit the train if you hurt her. Best let her go, now," Horace said.

Jacob didn't move. Sarah's eyes fluttered and closed.

The crowd of emigrants had grown larger, watching the scene play out. No one spoke. No one moved.

"I'm begging you, sir," Horace said, flicking his eyes over the crowd of White onlookers, praying someone else would step in, all too aware of the precarious situation of a Black man begging for the life of a White woman. He was caught up in it now with no way out but to continue.

"You want to beg? Get on your knees, boy!" Jacob snarled, enjoying the moment. "And swear you're a worthless piece of shit."

Horace slipped to the ground. "Let her go, sir."

"Say it!"

"I am a worthless piece of shit."

"Louder!"

"I'm a worthless piece of shit! Now you let her go!"

And with that, Jacob released the choke hold on his wife. His hands ached from the effort. He was just tired.

He watched her with indifference as Sarah fell to her knees, coughing and sputtering, clutching at her throat. Fredericka and several other women ran to her as Jacob weaved his way back to the campfire, where he would soon pass out, snoring loudly from his drunken stupor.

Horace, kneeling in the middle of the camp, struggled for composure. He looked up at the porcelain White faces peering at him as though he were an odd insect. No one had come to his aid. He was the spectacle, the Black man on his knees. Nobody. Humiliated to save a White woman from her own husband.

A flood of shame and anger swept over him as he slowly rose to his feet. While the crowd dispersed, he collected Fredericka and Bo and laid their sparse bedding outside the wagon circle. There, in the moonless night, he found some comfort in the level-playing field of the dark.

But sleep would not come to Horace. He felt hammered down like a nail. Life had always been about power, a force residing outside good and evil, just and unjust, moral and immoral. Power carried no values except what men did with it. Men like Jonathan. Like Cuddy. And Jacob. The White badge of authority lied to him. Bought and sold him. Abused him. Betrayed him. He was lower than a lice-infested wife-beater. He scoffed at the irony—angry for admitting the truth—he was worthless. Horace ate the bit of food Fredericka stowed away from Sarah's campfire, but all he tasted was bitterness.

THE TREK WAS IN ITS EARLY STAGES, AND THE PIONEERS were still full of bluster and hope, the cattle fed and healthy. The prairie beckoned to the horizon with grasses and wild blossoms swelling into waves of greens and browns, grays, and yellows as far as the eye could see. Fredericka reveled in the world of flowers, collecting lacy yarrow and white pussytoes, and drawing pictures of the delicate pink prairie smoke.

At one stop, they camped by the Big Blue, a small tributary of the Kansas River. A sparkling spring gushed from a ledge of rocks rising ten feet from the bank, filling the basin with a clear, cold pool of water. Fredericka stole a few precious minutes to lie down in a beckoning tuft of green grass by the water's edge. She listened to a chorus of insects fill the sultry afternoon air, no one song overpowering another. Frogs kept the beat, and the insects filled the background, while the crickets carried the melody. The earth was warm beneath her back, and she felt like the little girl who dreamed of flying beneath the magnolia trees at the plantation.

Here was the world of natural things, where every flower had its own place, each creature its own song. This was the world she belonged to, the natural world, where color thrived, where she could find her own place and sing her own song and be made whole.

Fredericka especially loved the evenings at camp. She didn't mind the routine of unloading the wagons, setting up the tents, or building a fire. Sarah showed her how to bake bread and prairie pancakes from unbolted flour. "Trick is in the sifting," Sarah said, "to remove the impurities."

Fredericka learned to cook bacon, and biscuits, and corn-meal soup, prairie style. She loved the children's joyful noise as they played Leapfrog and London Bridge, thinking how their laughter and shrieks of delight sounded like so many happy bells—a riotous sound so rare to the ear of one denied such simple childhood pleasures. Music filled the evenings as one man played the fiddle, another a harmonica, and someone else a banjo. Jacob could be found passed out with a jug of foul-smelling liquor most evenings, while Horace and Fredericka managed to dance a turn or two as the whole camp enjoyed the longer-lasting sunsets of late spring,

Horace and Fredericka had settled into an uneasy truce with Cuddy and Jacob; the peace made easier by Cuddy's absence scouting for water holes and Jacob's work with the cattle. They found a painful comfort in the knowledge that their stolen wagon was part of Ogden's convoy. However, Cuddy found every opportunity to spite them with it, forbidding them to sleep in or under it while taking personal satisfaction in flaunting the items he found in the wagon—Fredericka's utensils, cups, and bedding; Horace's clothing, tools, and supplies.

Fredericka had quickly applied herself to help with Sarah, steering clear of Jacob, helping with the mess wagon, and taking in occasional washing when water made itself available. Under this arrangement, food was plentiful, and the couple was allowed to take shelter from the night beneath one of Ogden's supply wagons.

The wagon master had turned over a mule to Horace for his work with the random obstinate oxen or wayward wagon, but Horace had to learn the lesson of mules the hard way. No sooner had he put the animal in a harness, the mule objected, reared up, busted its straps, and bolted off. It took Horace all day on foot to find the animal that had finally wandered back to the herd at the end of the train. After several failed attempts at controlling the animal, and to the great entertainment of the outriders, he was given a horse instead. While not familiar to mounts of any kind, Horace was quick to accustom himself to the saddle as much to avoid the pain of derision as getting bucked off the horse.

The wagon train had traversed the prairies for eight sunny and uneventful days when the extraordinary forces of nature and geography conspired against them. Trapped between the jagged Rocky Mountains to the west, the Gulf of Mexico to the south, and the Canadian Prairies to the north, the flatlands were an expressway for violent weather.

Four o'clock in the afternoon, a fast-moving current of air cleared over the Rockies and went awry. It dipped into a low-lying trough of air. Winds in the upper atmosphere pulled the air up from the surface, causing a vast low-pressure system across the Plains that acted like an empty bowl. Unimpeded by natural barriers, hot moisture rushed in from the south and collided with cold air pouring in from the north. The Rockies blocked any release. The impact exploded over the prairies and triggered a monster.

At first, the sky appeared calm and billowy with white clouds that seemed to merge with the horizon. The unstable air was not to be placated by a dainty cream puff sky. Instead, the tranquility gave way to agitation, and the clouds swirled above each other, fighting for dominance, creating billows of dark cliffs and ridges in the sky.

The darkening embankment descended. A long black ledge of clouds scraped the earth, obscuring the late afternoon sun. The heavens thickened, and churned, and beat the soft tissue of daylight into a battered and bruised false night. The wind shrieked, kicking up debris and dust, and the prairie grasses flapped to a frenzy in the tempest. From the cold north and the hot south, the atmospheres were tinged with the odors of ice and fire as they smashed into each other. Lightning slashed the sky and struck the earth, disgorging giant plumes of dirt and flashes of flame. Thunder blasted the air without mercy. Again, lightning sliced through the clouds, its twisted, wiry tentacles electrifying and terrifying, again and again. The relentless, punishing rage of the prairie storm began.

Then the rains let loose. Not the pitter-patter of rain-drops, but the painful sting of sharp, hard-pelting rain, torrents of rain, blinding, wind-driven, roaring rain that shelled the ground with such force that each drop shattered and splintered back into the air. The thunder pummeled the air overhead, shuddering the bones of man and beast.

Outriders shouted orders to round up the wagons into their divisions. The wild-eyed oxen and horses yanked on their harnesses and yokes. Some broke loose and bolted away. The terrified cattle behind the wagon train bawled and bumped into one another, seeking refuge from the thunder's fusillade.

Just then, an eerie spectacle of electricity filled the air. It began with a flash of lightning that splintered, forking against the sky, spawning chains of charged electric tentacles that turned into blue lightning hitting the ground and rolling across the prairie in great balls of phosphorous. The air contained the sweet, sharp smell of sulfur as the electricity crept along the ground, manifesting in the horse's ears, the brims of the wrangler's hats, and the tips of the cattle horns.

"Foxfire! A wrangler yelled, warning of the electrical phenomena but startling the agitated cattle that swarmed like a singular beast rushing into an instant panic.

Fredericka huddled with Sarah under her wagon with the children. Bo cried next to her in a soggy blanket. Thick, cold, sticky mud clung to Fredericka's elbows and knees and soaked through her cotton dress as the rains pelted down and puddled around them. She felt the stampede before she saw it, at first thinking it was the pounding of her heart in the mud. She heard men scream, "Ride for the lead! Get 'em into a mill!" as a roaring rampage of hooves rumbled past her face. The frantic animals careened into a nearby wagon, turning it over, crushing two children and their parents. Sarah's wagon vibrated as the cattle thundered past.

Through the thunder and sky-splitting lightning and torrential rain, the wranglers whipped their horses into a hellish race to get ahead of the stampede. Horace was mounted along the charge's outer edge in this wild fray when he saw Jacob take the lead at the front of the herd, heading them off, turning them into a mill—running the cattle into themselves. The frightened herd swerved to the left of Jacob, rounding into the swirl. Horace, still a novice at wrangling, copied the other men whooping and hawing at the herd, maneuvering them into the mill.

As another bolt of lightning struck the ground, Horace saw Jacob's horse tumble, snapping his foreleg in a prairie dog hole. The horse plowed headfirst into the ground. Jacob catapulted into the air, over the horse. Horace hesitated, *Should I rescue the son-of-a-bitch or let him walk back to camp?*

Just then, another sharp strike of lightning followed by an explosive crack of thunder shocked the frantic herd. Disoriented, the cattle swerved again, charging directly toward the downed man. Horace galloped toward Jacob to get between him and the stampede, but he was too late. The terrified cattle swallowed Jacob underfoot. The wranglers eventually spun the herd into itself, and the milling soon settled the animals down, but not before their hooves had torn Jacob's body apart.

When the storm abated, Alexander Ogden directed Horace and several other men to dig graves. Only nine days in and the wagon train had seen five fatalities. Under the rain clouds, they buried John and Mary Hastings and their twin daughters, Elizabeth and Eliza, and Jacob Bidwell.

Fredericka stood at Jacob's gravesite with Sarah and her children. Sarah stared numbly at the fresh bank of dirt. No one made a speech on his behalf, nor offered words of remorse. Tommy and Jasper ran back to the wagon and began playing Cowboys and Indians. Seneca waved her doll at the grave. "Bye-bye, bye-bye, Daddy!" she said. Rebecca stared at the grave for a few seconds and marched off ahead of the others.

"We're burnin' daylight," Ogden said at the gravesites. "What with the storm and all, it'll take another four hours sloggin' in this mud to make Pappan's Ferry." Ogden donned his hat, mounted his horse, and yelled for the wagon train to reassemble and move. Horace looked down at Jacob Bidwell's grave, searching for his own emotions. Did he feel remorse? Could he have saved him? Was there any sense of guilt for hesitating to help the man? Horace knew the answer. He swung the shovel over his shoulder, leaving the heel print of his boot on the grave's mound.

They made camp later that night near the Kaw River's south bank, a narrow river, with high waters and a swift current brought on by the rains. Fredericka stood on the bank watching the water etch into the mud. The Kaw. The old Native who talked about the heron. Her totem. "Heron is strong." A shiver played across her shoulders. She didn't feel strong, and she still hated water.

Early the next morning, Ogden assembled the drovers and bullwhackers to the ferry. Two ferries would be employed. Horace thought how risky the ferries looked, simple flatbeds with a bullnose flap at the front, ostensibly to keep something from rolling forward into the river. Each raft was guided by a rope tied to a tree on each side of the embankment. The ferry owners, three brothers of French-Canadian descent, were in a heated discussion with the wagon master. Etienne, one of the brothers, slapped the back of his hand, insisting on a fee of one dollar per wagon transfer, while Ogden argued that the price was too high and his men would be doing most of the work. In the end, the ferrymen prevailed. Fees were collected, and the wagons lined up for the transport.

The difficulty became apparent when each wagon had to be hauled close to the raft before unhitching the oxen. The drovers and bullwhackers then had to push each wagon onto the rafts, complete with their loads in one unifying bout of human strength. The oxen, horses, and all two-thousand head of cattle would have to swim across. Men, women, and children would ride the wagons across on the rafts guided by two Kaw Natives who tugged them across with long poles. The reverse process would then have to take place on the opposite bank—the wagons had to be pushed off the rafts, and with great effort, up a muddy embankment where the oxen would be re-yoked, making way for the next wagon coming in. A huge undertaking requiring all the men to push, and shove, lift and carry all sixty wagons, twice.

The process did not go off without mishap. The first wagon was loaded, but the wagon tottered and capsized, sending its entire load and passengers screaming into the waters. They had neglected to strap down the wheels. Fortunately, the family of four was quickly rescued and hauled out with ropes with no loss of life. No one made that mistake again.

The crossing took all day. The weary emigrants made camp on the north bank while Horace and the other men drove thousands of cattle across the frigid river, herding them nearby. It took some time for Fredericka to locate and milk Sarah's cow and to help set camp for the night. She helped Sarah unload the wagon, set up tents, have the children gather wood, and build a fire while Sarah cooked up dinner.

"It's been a long day." Sarah gave a weary smile and turned to Fredericka. "We could use a little treat. You know how to make a pudding?"

"I can learn prairie cookin." Fredericka sat on a log next to the kids.

She watched Sarah blend molasses and milk together, a half-cup each. She added half-a-cup of butter, a dash of baking soda and salt, and mixed it in a tin bowl. To this, she added two cups of flour, half-a cup at a time, and producing a tin of raisins, added a handful of these. She spread the thick and chunky dough into a deep bread pan and placed it in a large kettle of boiling water that sat atop a mound of pebbles gathered at the river's edge.

"Make sure the water only boils up halfway to the sides of the cake pan," Sarah said, covering the pan. "There now." She dusted her hands with satisfaction. "We let that steam up for a bit, and we have ourselves some good molasses pudding!" Fredericka and the children licked their lips in anticipation of such a treat, slurping their cornmeal mush, eyeing the pudding for dessert.

Horace stumbled in an hour later. He slugged down hot coffee and gobbled the food. "Ogden tells us we still have to cross the Red Vermillion, Black Vermillion, and the Big Blue Rivers before even reaching the Platte," he said and collapsed with exhaustion under Sarah's wagon.

They had traveled for ten days and made eighty-one miles. They had 2,089 miles to go.

THE WAGON TRAIN SLOGGED ON, AND THE DIFFICULTIES grew. Horace could barely keep up with repairs to broken axles, joints, and wheels, and heaving wagons out of muddy ravines. At one steep riverbank, the wagons had to be unloaded, and the pioneers put to work tarring the wagon beds' joints and seams to resist leaks and the ravages of the crossing. The wagons were then tied to ropes, and each lowered down the banks to float across the river. Supplies and loads were strapped to makeshift rafts and carried by mules and horses through the swift current. The oxen had already forded the river, and Ogden ordered them herded to the top of the bank. There, the teams were harnessed again to the wagon beds that had floated across and were waiting at the bottom of the bank. The oxen pulled the wagons, inch by inch to the top, while men, women, and children pushed from below.

Rain pursued them across the prairie. Fredericka watched distant black-bellied clouds release curtains of rain that rushed over them as the air filled with the cold smell of iron and celery. Finally making camp by the shallow banks of the Platte was a sad and soggy affair. While Horace and the other men unyoked the oxen and corralled them inside the circle of wagons, Sarah, Fredericka, and the children set up tents on the cold and muddy ground. Fredericka's wet dress clamped to her skin, chilling her to the bone, her fingers stiff with cold. The children were soaking wet. Sarah's sodden bonnet dripped damp rivulets to her shoulders. Snippit couldn't stop coughing and had developed a fever. The buffalo chips and kindling were as wet and dreary as everyone's mood, and fire that night was impossible. "At least we have the cow," Sarah said, motioning to the beast tethered to the wagon's rear. The travelers had to make do with a cold supper of mash and milk.

Sarah was inconsolable sitting on the axel-tree, wrapped in a damp shawl, shivering in her sopping calico dress. "Whatever will become of me and my babies? How will we live? What will we do?" she sobbed.

Fredericka took Sarah's hand and was shocked at how thin and frail, how lifeless it felt, how Sarah seemed to exist on the edge, almost without a pulse. Fredericka felt a foreboding she could not shake, even while trying to reassure the woman. "You best without that man," she said, trying to rub some sense of life back into Sarah's fingers. "You can live. You can do. Jacob can't hurt you now."

Sarah would not be consoled. "You think a woman has any chance in this world alone, with children to feed and no man?" Her once chirpy voice had been reduced to a whisper. "Jacob wasn't much, I'll give you that, but now I have nothing. We're the same, you and me. We have no choices. No future. No say in this world. We're just…women."

"But you have everythin'," Fredericka said. "You is White!" Even as she spoke those words, she could not escape feeling Sarah's decaying sense of hope.

Just then, a scream erupted in the camp. One man grabbed a gun from the back of his wagon. The emigrants clustered around a miserable site. A rigid arm stuck out of a shallow grave in the mud. The fingers had formed a frozen claw as if the departed had tried to scratch their way back to life. Flesh had been stripped to the knuckles.

Ogden made a brief appearance. "Wolves. They dig up the dead. Let it be a lesson. If you must bury your dead, bury 'em deep," he said.

The rain had soaked the wagons, leaving the bedding and supplies damp, the musty odors nauseating with little time or opportunity to dry out the saturated tents and bedclothes. Snippit coughed all night, and her fever grew worse by the hour. The little thing died before breakfast. They buried the child on the outskirts of the campground, marking the crude little cross with her pink bonnet.

"Bury my poor Snippit deep, so no wolf gets her," Sarah cried. And the wagons pushed on.

The Platte River was notoriously wide and shallow, measuring four feet deep by half a mile wide. Swollen by the rains, the mud was thick and treacherous, the ever-changing shallows hiding gravel and quicksand.

After a debate with the wranglers and emigrants, whether to unhitch the oxen and wheels, float the boxes across, or hitch twelve pairs of oxen to each wagon and escort them one by one, Ogden made the decision that it would take too much time either way. He ordered the wagons to cross, in a line, one by one. A costly decision.

The first wagon stalled in the middle of the river, stuck in the mud. The second wagon behind it also stopped. Amid the whooping and hollering bullwhackers, the oxen began to bawl, confused, and panicked by the commotion of men and mud. In the traffic jam, the ox team in the first wagon became unyoked. The team behind, rearing and fretful, threw the chains over their heads in the wrong direction. Now both wagon teams were in disarray. The first wagon began to sink in the quicksand, while the second wagon, pulled to the side by the panicking beasts, turned over.

Amid the screams and hollering and bawling, both wagons lost their cargos, tins of food, clothing and bedding, tools, saddles, gunpowder, rifles, pots, and pans scattered upon the waters. Men, women, and children riding in the wagons were tossed into the water. One man managed to slog to the sandbars and onto the other side. Two children disappeared under the water. The two mis-chained oxen in the upset second wagon drowned. The first wagon disappeared, leaving only the hooded canvas flapping upon the water as its oxen plodded safely to the opposite bank.

This chaos gave rise to the alternate plan of escorting each wagon with twelve pairs of oxen. To keep their water-weight light, the men stripped off their clothing, save for their shirts and hats. Some men rode horses, while others stood in the water and cussed and bullied, and whipped the big brutes back and forth across the river, escorting each wagon separately.

Horace was on horseback, up to his thighs in water, calling "Yee-haw! Yee-haw!" when one wagon tilted perilously in the water and got stuck holding the balding emigrant with the pregnant young wife. She sat screaming in the wagon's seat, clutching her white parasol, now a grimy tatter, while her other hand clung to the sideboard. The piano she had insisted upon loading had shifted, tore through the canvas, and dangled over the water. The wagon tottered against the rain-ravaged river pushing one way, and the oxen yanking another.

Before Horace could reach them, the wagon overturned casting the woman into the water, her skirts blooming about her like an open flower. The parasol, like a fallen petal, floated downriver. The young wife flailed and screamed as the water gushed around her. She gripped the overturned wagon's flapping canvas just as the piano let loose and slipped over her, plunging her under its ivory and ebony keys. Horace reached the wagon in time to release the oxen and fish her sputtering husband to a sandbank, but his young wife was gone.

Fredericka watched the procession in horror. Each wagon wavering dangerously in the engorged river, the wheels sinking into the muddy bottom, the emigrants walking up to their waists, holding their babies, shoes, and boots in their arms. Some tumbling in the water, struggling back to their feet, wranglers rushing to help on their horses. Horace was yelling and prodding the oxen ahead. When Fredericka's time to cross came at the rear of the caravan, she froze. She stood at the lapping water's edge, shaking her head, refusing to face the inevitable. Sarah and the children had gone ahead, the smaller children in the wagon. Sarah had begun to wade behind her wagon when she turned to see Fredericka paralyzed at the river's edge. Sarah turned back and reached out her hand. "You can," she said. "You told me so, yourself."

Fredericka reached for Sarah's hand, cradling Bo in her left arm. Horace was far ahead, waving and hollering at the oxen. She had to do this. She took a deep breath, closed and then opened her eyes, and together with Sarah, waded into the river. The water crept up to Fredericka's knees and then her waist. With every step, fear squeezed the air out of her.

Her throat was closing, her breathing shallow, and her heart racing. The water was cold and menacing. The thick mud sucked at her bare feet. The rain-gorged river threatened to topple her, but she kept on. The water reached her chest. She knew this feeling, the snarl of water suffocating her in a bucket, the crush of water against her lungs in the harbor, the seiche in Buffalo, the delirious fear. Losing Isaiah. Just as she thought she could bear it no longer, the waters ebbed down from her chest, and with each step grew shallow, and she reached the bank with Sarah.

She turned and faced the river, scanning the gray shallows and beige sandbars, the smooth pebbles reassuring beneath her feet. The river did not look so fearsome after all. For the first time in her life, she felt what could only be described as triumph. She would befriend these muddy crossings. She was stronger than streams and braver than mud, baptized by that which she feared.

It took the entire day to get all the remaining wagons to the river's other side. The travelers were cold and exhausted. The bedding and clothing from the relentless storms were still clammy and damp. They were forced to make camp without making a single mile that day. The emigrants built large fires from scraps of wood and sagebrush, unloading all the sopping contents from their wagons and laying them out in an attempt to dry.

The following day was the Sabbath, and Ogden was resolute. There would be no traveling on the Lord's Day. Between the storm, the river crossings, and the Sabbath, they had lost four precious days. The wagon train would take the time to dry out, but Ogden was determined to make up for it. "We'll travel ten hours," he proclaimed before Sunday service. "Up an hour earlier and camp an hour later. Be ready for it."

That Sunday, Sarah's health had deteriorated. Frail and feeble, the distress of losing Jacob and Snippit drained whatever strength she had left. She woke up with a sore throat. Her body ached. By noon she had a fever and began coughing up mucus. By the time the caravan moved again, she was so ill she had to ride in the wagon, but the box's rocking and bouncing did not help her rest. By the third day, she developed a dry, hacking cough, but she felt a bit better and managed to help with the children and cook a few meals.

The wagon train had been following the Platte for days, crossing muddy gouges in the trail, marshes, and sandpits. Slow going. Wagons continued to get stuck in the swampy catches. Horace could not count the number of times he dug out wheels trapped in gulches or unloaded wagons and gathered brush for wheel friction, urging the reluctant oxen with blows and oaths to motivate the beasts forward.

Camping alongside the banks of the Platte did not furnish much relief. "This water ain't fit to wash the children's clothes. Can't drink it," Fredericka moaned one evening by the campfire. "There's a cup of water for every bucket of mud."

"I hear some ladies putting cornmeal in the water," Sarah said between fits of coughing.

"Well, if it works, maybe Horace won't have to chew his coffee!" Fredericka said.

Just then, a distant howl echoed across the prairie. "Wolves," Sarah said with a shudder. "Horrible wolves. They've been following us for days." The words sent her into a coughing frenzy, and Fredericka rushed to her with clean rags to sop up her bloody spittle.

"Don't let them get me," Sarah gasped. "Promise me, you won't let them get me."

A few days later, Sarah woke up with a fever again. This time she was so weak she was unable to walk and was back in the wagon. Her chest ached. The pneumonia virus had spread to her lungs. Her persistent coughing shredded her lungs and produced a bloody mucus. Chills rattled her body. By noon, when the caravan stopped for the midday break, the pernicious virus had infiltrated her blood system, ransacking her body. Her heart raced. She had trouble breathing. By evening, she was delirious, murmuring, "My children! My poor children," as she lay dying.

Horace dug Sarah's grave by the trailside. The children stood with Fredericka, grim and quiet. "Dig it deep." Fredericka mourned over her friend. "So the wolves don't get her."

In five weeks, the Bidwell family lost one child and both parents to the prairie. Ogden placed the children in the care of Horace and Fredericka. "'Tis a shame," he said. "We will arrange for the children's disposition at Fort Laramie. Until then, they and their wagon are in your care."

The children stood around their mother's grave, staring at the ground in disbelief, as though Sarah would jump up from the earth and wipe her hands on her apron and squeak out "Time for dinner!" As the minutes passed, their disbelief dissolved into a glaze of emptiness.

Fredericka understood that vacant stare, helplessness, and despair from the loss of a mother. She thought of Annie, her own mother, lost somewhere in the cruel White world, sold like a mule. She remembered the wheels rattling on the gravel, her own strangled voice, and the terrified look in her mother's eyes. Words could never restore that loss. She remembered how badly she needed the comfort of human touch. A privation left wanting in her. Fredericka stepped toward Rebecca and reached for the girl's hand. "I can help, if you let me." Rebecca, still staring at the grave, took her hand.

Fredericka said, "Let's gather the young 'uns. We'll be movin' soon."

The wagon train pushed on across the prairie that stretched out in a boundless ocean of green, undulating grasses. Their journey took them across a landscape pockmarked with the discarded antlers of elk and the white-washed skulls of buffalo. And the night was filled with the distant serenade of wolves.

Honey's Obsession

T he docks in St. Louis were bustling with activity.
Steamers belched up and down the Missouri with
cargo, and passengers, and one Edward Honey. He
had boarded the *Doria* bound for Independence. Gazing
into the coffee-colored water, he recalled the letters he
found in Horace's room back in Buffalo and felt confident of
the runaways' intentions to join a wagon train. He tracked
their movements to the *Lulu Simone*, learning they had
boarded just three weeks earlier. It wouldn't be long now,
he thought, to hog-tie them and sell them. He could smell
victory the way a hawk smells a gopher.

A smile crept over his lips. He was glad to be rid of
Henrietta's company. The Mormons would take care of her,
he was sure of it. He had left her in the company of others
with a horse and small cart. He wasn't heartless. She'd be
fine, he told himself.

By the time Honey reached Independence, all the caravans had already left for the journey West. Most latecomers
would have to wait it out for another year. Although June
had closed the opportunity for the inexperienced traveler,
Edward Honey was the exception. He traveled light with a
horse and two pack mules. His guns were loaded, and he
took off for the Oregon Trail.

HENRIETTA STILL CLUNG TO THE HOPE THAT HONEY would appear over the vast horizon. She wanted to quit, to go home to South Carolina. She wanted tea brought to her on the verandah and to feel the cool shade of magnolia trees. She wanted a bath, clean clothes, and servants. What was she doing in the middle of this godforsaken place with no food, scarce water, and no man? How the hell did this happen? She had run out of options. Forward was the only choice now—forward to the goddamned promised land.

For weeks, Henrietta kept pushing the cart, long after the horse died, following the Mormons. The cart was part of her now. She breathed with every rotation of the wheel and felt her heartbeat over every rock. She leaned upon it, took cover under it, and began to converse with the rim's rickety clatter. Every stone was an effort, every gravely pit a grave. The Mormon travelers seemed to be disappearing daily. Those who still remained had no strength to bury the dead adequately, sparing only sagebrush, a few rocks, and some woeful prayers before pushing on. Eventually, even they disappeared, reluctantly wandering ahead while she perched on a boulder. Despite the Mormon's entreaties, prayers, pleas, and implorations, Henrietta had refused to budge another inch.

She had come to the end. With each agonizing mile, her cart had grown heavier. She could do no more. She adjusted the rawhide strips and the tattered wool fragments sticking to her blistered and bloody feet. She felt woozy in the relentless sun and dizzy with a constant buzz ringing in her ears.

Henrietta eyed the cart and the small oak chest containing her few belongings. Though only the size of a breadbasket, its leather straps with shining buttons and silver buckles, once a prideful possession, now loomed large and menacing, a demanding, ungrateful passenger, mocking her efforts, oblivious to her pain, torturing her life. The sun burned down on her head. Thirst and hunger gnawed at her body. She hated the chest; she hated it's punishing revolting existence, it's fat and lazy position of privilege, perched in her cart as if it had earned its place, as if it deserved to ride at her expense.

She leaped to her feet, disregarding pain and exhaustion, and with the last vestige of her might, she roared at the sun, and screamed at the cart, and screamed at the chest. Planting her hands upon it, she bellowed, "Be damned with you!" and dashed it upon the boulders. Then kneeling, smashed it with a rock. With anguish spent and bloodied hands, she sobbed dry tears amidst her possessions strewn in the sand.

The sun set over the plains in glorious hues of orange and blues and slowly turned the clouds to the color of blood before plunging behind the horizon. Henrietta knew she was dying. This was her sepulcher, adorned by stars scattering the night sky like the dust of diamonds. In this heavenly vault, even the wolves were silent. The running thought in her wizened, dehydrated brain repeated over and over again, "Fuck you, Edward Honey."

Ahusaka

⸺⊶⊰❀⊱⊷⸺

F redericka swiped a stray curl out of her face and tucked
it in her bonnet. Caring for six children was daunting.
At least with Sarah, the family was almost manageable,
but now with their mother dead, it seemed impossible. It was
the end of another cold and drizzly day following the river,
crossing silty streams, creeping along from one mud hole to
another. Here the Plains were bare of trees, and the grasses
were short and sparse.

Fresh water continued to be a problem as Fredericka
lamented, "It's bad to ford, ain't no fish, too dirty to wash, and
too thick to drink." With Horace called upon to lift wagons out
of the muck and chase down strays, she had to learn to master
the wagon and oxen on her own and soon had found her ability
to whistle and whip and cajole the team as good as any man.

The cold rain and the day's monotonous plodding put
everyone in a bad mood. At the campsite that evening, Fredericka employed the children to unyoke the six oxen, unload
the wagon, and set up their tents in the mud. She sent Rebecca
to milk the cow while she rummaged for the cornmeal in the
wagon. With no dry kindling, there would be no warm fire
again tonight and another dinner of cornmeal mush. The
Bidwell children huddled wet and miserable along the axel-tree
like turtles on a log, slurping their sad dinner in the waning light.

Fredericka was reminded how the beat of their spoons scraping across tin plates sounded like the rhythms coming out of the slave quarters on a Sunday at the plantation. She could almost hear the slaves banging on pots and kettles, slapping their hands and thighs to ancient tempos, and the raw bursts of laughter bubbling up from their tortured souls. This night on the prairie seemed to draw out the shrill songs of crickets and the croaking of a thousand frogs from the marshes. She thought how the distant coyotes joined in music, and the whole dark night was filled with the harmony of life, happy, she thought, in the simple joy of being alive.

Fredericka hefted Bo to one hip. "Listen, children. You hear them songs from the crickets and frogs? You hear the beat?" She took Miriam's plate and knocked at it with a spoon. "C'mon now, Tommy, what do you hear?"

Tommy thumped his plate, and Jasper banged his spoon on a cup. Seneca waved her doll in the air. The children were laughing and banging out a rhythm with the critters in the night.

While the children beat out their chorus, Fredericka settled down on an overturned bucket to nurse Bo when she saw a form emerge from the darkness beyond the camp. At first, she thought, Horace. As she rose to greet him, she noticed the man was wearing three tall feathers in his hair. He was barefoot and held a bag in his hands.

"*Indians!*" she gasped, afraid to move. The children stopped their drumming and dropped their plates.

"Miss Fredericka…" Rebecca's voice trembled.

The Native stopped walking. Then nodded at Fredericka, motioning her to approach him.

"Shhh," Fredericka whispered to the children over her shoulder. "He's not gonna hurt us."

"But…" stammered Rebecca, "it's an Indian…"

Fredericka rose slowly and handed the baby to Rebecca. "Gonna be all right. You just sit tight now," she said.

Fredericka turned toward the Native. She had never seen an Indian on the plains before, although she had heard stories of their aggressive nature and violent dispositions. But then, she'd been around the White world long enough to figure the Indians couldn't be worse. She eyed the camp's perimeter. Horace was not anywhere around. She wasn't about to call out for him and startle the Indian. The nearest help was a wagon parked fifty paces away, an infinite distance when facing a savage in the dark.

The Indian motioned for her again. She took several steps toward him. His features became more apparent to her now. His hair hung in braids halfway down his chest. He wore buckskin trousers. A leather pouch, shaped like a sling, wrapped around his bare chest. He was a young man, with a long, broad nose and shining, direct eyes.

As she approached, he held out the bag. He nodded at her again. She nodded back. Feeling more confident, Fredericka took three more steps toward him and took the bag from his hand, locking her eyes on his. He nodded again. She opened the deerskin bag and gasped.

Inside was a bouquet of edible wild plants: black mustard, buttercups, chickweed, dandelion and elderberry, evening primrose and milkweed, wild rose, chokecherry, and watercress. Fredericka had been drawing plants, drying them in the sun, and saving seeds all her life. She recognized some of them and others were new to her. This was such a prize! And beneath this bounty, wrapped in burlap, a hunk of meat.

"Tatonka," the young Native said, noticing her puzzled expression, "Buffalo." He pointed at the meat.

"I don't understand," Fredericka said. "For me?"

The Native nodded, putting his fingers to his mouth. "Food," she said, smiling. "Yes, yes, I understand."

He clasped his fingers together.

"You want to trade!" Pointing to the campsite, she said, "Yes, please, come. Come. Sit with us."

The Native hesitated and surveilled the camp.

"It's all right. Come."

The Native approached the camp, cautious as a cat, checking his surroundings, looking over his shoulder. Despite the mud, he lowered himself to the ground, next to the children, and crossed his legs. The children could only stare, hardly breathing, barely moving, their jaws slack in astonishment.

Still standing, Fredericka said, "These are the children," stating the obvious, unsure how to proceed. Pointing to her chest, she said, "I am Fredericka." Pointing back at him, "You?"

"Ahusaka." He flapped his arms and pointed to the sky.

"Ahusaka," she repeated. "You mean, bird?" She pointed at the sky.

He shook his head, no, and tapped his shoulders and flapped again. "Ah, you mean wings? Like wings to fly?" She flapped her arms.

Ahusaka smiled for the first time.

"Children, this is Ahusaka," Fredericka said. "His name means *wings*. Now, tell him your names."

One by one, the children chimed in their names, Rebecca, Miriam and five-year-old Seneca piping up, "Since Snippit died, I'm the baby of the family now."

Jasper called out his name and said, "And this here's Tommy, but he doesn't talk, so I talk for him. And I'm getting new teeth!" Jasper showed Ahusaka the nub of his new front tooth.

Ahusaka nodded at Rebecca, and she blushed and looked away, pretending not to be fascinated by the remarkable stranger.

Fredericka rummaged through the Bidwell wagon and pulled out a shirt, and a hat belonging to Jacob. He wouldn't be needing these anymore, she thought. She handed the young Native the goods.

Ahusaka stood, removed his sling, and put the shirt on. He patted his chest and smiled.

"Now the hat!" Jasper said, handing it to him.

Ahusaka took the long feathers from his hair and carefully placed the hat on his head, nodding with satisfaction. "Tom-ee," he said and handed the feathers to the silent young boy. Then from the sling, the Native pulled out dried twigs, pine needles, and buffalo chips and two stones. He piled the kindling, struck the rocks together, causing a spark, and blew on the smoke until a small fire crackled in the mud. The children clapped their hands with glee.

"Thank you for the fire," Fredericka said.

Ahusaka gave a short tilt of his head to Fredericka, turned, and, as quickly as he had appeared, walked back into the night.

"Well, I'll be!" Fredericka exclaimed. "You see, children, people are jus' people all over the world. It don't matter the color of their skin. We's all the same deep down. We jus' need to give everyone a chance, thas all."

Just then, a gunshot split the night air.

The Gallows

⸙

Horace had finished piloting the last wagon into the circle and was helping corral the cattle and oxen when the shot rang out. A sentry shooting at marauding wolves again, Horace figured.

Fifteen more minutes passed since the gunshot. Horace rode the train's perimeter, and when he spied the single small campfire and recognized the Bidwell wagon, he had to smile. Fredericka was full of surprises, building a fire in this muddy wasteland. No sooner had he dismounted from his horse, Fredericka ran up to him. She was out of breath and clutched his shirt. "It's Cuddy," she said. "He shot Ahusaka!"

"What? Who's...?

"An Indian. A friend. You gotta help him!" Fredericka pulled at his shirt. "Help him!"

"Okay, alright, alright, show me." Horace followed her as they pushed their way through a crowd to a grisly scene.

Three wagons had been pulled together, their long wooden tongues used to support the yokes of oxen, had been disassembled, lifted, and tied into a tripod. A noose dangled from the gallows. On the ground lay the bloody body of a man, his features distorted and grotesque from a brutal beating, his limbs hogtied behind him.

Cuddy Ogden stood above the unconscious Ahusaka,

waving his rifle above his head like a man with a trophy hunt. "We here got ourselves an Injun!" Cuddy shouted, "A real dangerous Redskin!" Cuddy hopped into a mocking dance around the Native.

Some in the crowd laughed and egged him on. "Yeah, that's it, Cuddy! Show 'em who's boss!"

Fueled by the mob and whipped into a frenzy, his face wild and raw, Cuddy threw down his rifle, drew a knife from his belt, and sawed-off Ahusaka's braids. Waving them in the air, he shouted. "I got me an Injun souvenir!"

More jeers and laughter from the crowd, but this time for more blood. "Scalp him! Scalp him!"

Cuddy knelt next to the man and lifted back Ahusaka's bloated, bloody face, his knife drawn to the man's forehead.

"That's enough!" Horace barked from the crowd, pushing his way to the front. "That's enough, Cuddy!"

Cuddy looked up, sweat and grime dripping from his face, the knife poised at the Native's scalp. The unconscious man groaned. Cuddy dropped Ahusaka's head to the ground and stood up. "Who you talkin' to, Nigger?" He twirled his knife in his fingers. The crowd seemed agitated, excited, shuffling their attention between dramas.

Horace swallowed hard. Before he could speak, Fredericka came from behind him. "That Indian did no harm to no one. He was unarmed. He brought us food and…"

"So, we got us two nigger Injun-lovers here!" Cuddy snickered. Some in the crowd strained for a better view, some chuckled at Cuddy's taunt. The air was tight and tense and as sharp as the knife in Cuddy's hand.

"Wagon Master rules say we can't shoot or kill an unarmed man." Horace pointed to Ahusaka. Several in the crowd nodded in agreement.

"I'm in charge here," Cuddy hollered. "When my father's out scouting, I'm Wagon Master. I'm makin' the rules now. This is an Injun, a dangerous savage. You want to let him go so he can come back to rape your women and strangle your young 'uns? I say we hang this Redskin fucker!"

Curiosity gave way to an expression of fear and survival, defense at any cost, and the mob's passions were inflamed. United by their primal natures, these simple pioneers, farmers, bankers and bookkeepers, teachers and preachers, wives, and mothers lost their singularity. They became one irrational surge of energy, domesticated dogs forming a feral pack of predators on the hunt for a lamb. Men and women alike threw their fists in the air, demanding blood.

The mob cheered, "Rapist! Murderer! Savage! Take him to the rope!" They dragged the comatose Native to the gallows.

"No!" Fredericka screamed.

"Stop!" Horace rushed toward Ahusaka.

"Hold 'em back!" Cuddy commanded as hands and arms appeared restraining Fredericka and Horace.

"Hang him!" Cuddy ordered. The mob roared approval.

"No!" Fredericka screamed, wrestling against her captors.

"You'll pay for this, Cuddy!" Horace yelled.

The men pulled Ahusaka up from the ground, his arms and legs still tied behind him, and slipped the noose around his neck, making it tight. Then they let him go. He jerked three times and then stopped. Ahusaka's wings took flight.

Their appetite abated, the crowd went quiet as the Native's bound torso swung from the gallows. The only sound was the creaking of the wood. Some women clutched at their mouths, forbidding the inevitable regret that would come. Others buried their children's heads in their skirts in a vain attempt to hide them from the monstrous scene. One man removed his hat and wiped his face hoping to rouse a different dream. The shackles of arms and hands holding Horace and Fredericka slipped away. The rabid mob dissipated into individual units of guilt, the frenzy for blood sputtering into unspoken shame.

"Whatsa matter with y'all?" Cuddy called out to the dwindling crowd. "He deserved it! We all know it…" But his voice fell on a dead night. He spit on the ground and hiked his britches. "You all gonna thank me, one day," he grumbled as he skulked off.

Fredericka stood before the lifeless body of Ahusaka and wept. She had seen this kind of work before, grown up with it all her life. Her acquaintance with cruelty did not dull its pain. She had lost a friend, not to an accident or other unforeseen calamity, but to another kind of sickness, the invisible kind, buried and waiting for an excuse to claw its way out.

Horace and two other men, took Ahusaka's body down and laid it on the ground, cutting the straps binding his arms and legs. Only then, Horace recognized one of the wagons used for the gallows—the red wheels and the blue sideboards and the letters H.F. carved into the left rear sideboard of his wagon. His heart sank for the misery of it.

They covered Ahusaka's body in burlap and laid him in a cart to be buried the next morning.

—◦◦◦◦—

THE 4:00 A.M. CALL CAME EARLY. THE SENTRIES FIRED off their rifles, alerting the travelers to a new day. Just as they began to mill about, making another cold meal without fires, breaking down their mud-strewn tents, and packing their wagons, a bugle call went out and over the prairie. A bugle usually meant time to move forward, but it was still early, the oxen hadn't been yoked yet, and the cattle were still corralled. Another bugle blast and three hundred and forty people slowly emerged from their morning tasks and followed the sound, assembling at the gallows.

Ogden Nash stood in the light of dawn upon the cart bearing the young Indian's body. The gallows loomed behind him. For long minutes, he stood there, towering above the pioneers, glaring at them from under his stovepipe hat. His white beard wrapped about his chin and chest like a magistrate's collar. His rifle was slung over his arm, his stance rooted in authority, solid and impenetrable.

"I'm only going to ask this once," he said, casting an eye over the crowd. "What happened here?" Ogden Nash was the law, the judge, and the jury. The dead Ahusaka, the plaintiff. Justice demanded a defendant. One could almost hear the mud sucking at the boots of the assembly, seeping into their souls. In the distance, a horse snorted, an ox bawled, a cow bellowed for milking. The court was in session.

Horace and Fredericka stood back with the children. Fredericka took half a step and made a move to speak when Horace clutched her arm and shook his head. "Not yet. Let it play out."

"I will not ask again." Ogden hefted his rifle up and into the crook of his elbow. "We will stay here, in this very spot, barred from our destiny, burning daylight, burning days or weeks if need be, until this price is paid. Paradise in Oregon will not come to those who disobey the laws of God." He skimmed the reluctant crowd, probing for one hesitant expression, for one set of eyes deliberately avoiding his, and his gaze rested upon his son.

Cuddy stood alone on the crowd's edge, in a swath of isolation as if bathed in repellent. He was looking down, biting his nails.

"Cuddy?" Ogden called out, a question in his voice.

All eyes turned toward Cuddy in voiceless accusation.

"Cuddy." This time it was not a question.

"Pa," Cuddy said, tugging at his pants, and pointing at the cart in a nervous gesture, "Pa, it was an Injun. A savage. Ask the niggers, they took him in! I defended this wagon train against the son-of-a-bitch. That's what I did. Them niggers put us all in jeopardy!" He spit and wiped his mouth with the back of his hand, then stood with his hands on his hips, expecting some sort of gratitude.

"Horace? Fredericka? What's the story?" Ogden called over his shoulder, not taking his eyes off his son.

"Now." Horace nudged his wife. "Tell it like it is."

"It's true!" Fredericka called out. "The Native came to our camp. He heard the children playing music. He offered us food. We traded some of Jacob's old clothes. His name was Ahusaka. He was unarmed. He didn't hurt nobody."

"Who shot him?"

"Well, I did, Pa," Cuddy scoffed. "No tellin' what that savage coulda' done."

"You did more than that," Fredericka said. "You beat him near to death, tied him like a pig, and then hanged him. We tried to stop him, but a bunch of these good folks here held us back and let him do it."

Murmurs went up from the crowd. A shadow creased some faces, but no one attested to their culpability, feeling guilt but not speaking to it, hiding their blame to fester into torment—their sentence set.

"Does she speak true?" Ogden called out. "Was this man unarmed?"

"We didn't see no weapon," one man in the assembly said, with others nodding in agreement.

"Why'd you shoot him, Cuddy? Why'd you hang him?" Ogden asked.

Cuddy gave a nervous laugh. His shoulders twitched and his eyes darted about for some kind of reassurance. "'Cause he was an Injun, Pa! He was gonna come after us. Maybe take some scalps. Maybe rape our women. I saved us! Ask anybody!"

"Did he attack anyone? Did he threaten anyone?" Ogden barked. "If there be witness to such acts, speak up now!"

The assembly shuffled uneasily about, but no one spoke.

Ogden dropped his rifle back over his arm, pointing it to the ground and spoke in a low, slow voice. "I left you in charge, Cuddy. You knew the rules," he said. "Shooting an unarmed man is akin to murder."

"But Pa…" He clawed at himself as if he were about to shed his skin and another lifeform struggled to emerge.

Ogden paused and breathed a deep, long sigh. Pulling his hand to his face, he wiped away any threat of emotion. He had set the ground rules, the law was there for everyone, even his son. He spoke the heavy verdict, "Cuddy Nash, you have been found guilty of murder." A collective gasp rose from the pioneers.

Then Ogden delivered the sentence: "By the laws designated by God and man, you must face the consequences. By sunrise, you are to be hanged by the neck until you are dead and buried in an unmarked grave. Take him to the gallows."

Two of Ogden's men approached Cuddy and tied his hands behind his back. "No! Pa! No!" Cuddy cried. "It's not my fault! It's the niggers! They let him in! They're to blame!" His legs failing him, they dragged Cuddy through the mud to the gallows. They propped him up on a wooden stool and hitched the noose around his neck.

"You gonna take a nigger's word over me, your own son! Pa! It's not my fault! It was an Injun! A savage! I'm your son! Pa!" Cuddy's bladder let loose, and his pants darkened with the stink of fear as he tried to bargain his way out.

"I'm glad your mother isn't alive to see what you've come to, boy," Ogden said. "You've always been a bad seed. May the Lord have mercy on your soul."

Ogden mounted his horse. "It's your wagon again, Horace. When this is over, get it out of my sight."

Nodding to his drovers, Ogden said, "You know what to do," and he rode away as the sun rose over the prairie.

He Smelled Him

⸙

The wagon train wasn't hard to follow. The trail was rutted, deep, and fresh as a heap of steaming shit. Edward Honey had simply to follow the graves, the occasional carcass of a dead ox, and the discarded possessions of overstuffed wagons: a grandfather clock, a chest of drawers, a cast-iron stove, a vase, broken porcelain dishes, mirrors, books, a rocking chair.

Several days into his journey, a fierce prairie storm kicked up its heels, slicing the sky with lightning and rocking the air with thunder. The ferocious winds and the razor-sharp rain forced him to take sanctuary between the legs of a bloated mule decaying by the trailside. Honey held fast to his horse's reins, but the steed reared up in fright, tearing the reins from his hands, and peeled off into the open prairie. His two pack mules had dashed off minutes before.

When the storm subsided, Honey roused himself from the stinking carcass to survey his situation. He stood to see a rattlesnake slinking out from under the corpse, having found the same retreat from the storm. *A comrade*, Honey thought, watching the rattler slither away. With his horse and mules gone, along with his provisions, his only recourse was to hope to find his horse. He still had his pistol strapped to his waist, his rifle and enough ammo in his shoulder bag to repel any untoward situations. He shivered as the wet, cold drizzle invaded his clothes and stuck to his skin. He hoisted his rifle, turned west, and began to walk.

Four hours had passed since the storm, and Honey had not seen hide nor hair of his horse nor mules. The prairie stretched out in rolling hills of grass with no sign of a tree or even a bush, but Honey was convinced that the wagon trail he followed would lead to a campsite and possibly water. After another two hours, Honey viewed what looked like a green fringe along a distant crest. It looked like trees. Where there are trees, hopefully, there's water. He marched toward it. The ridge proved to be a cluster of bushes and scrabbly trees surrounding several pools of water.

Honey shouldered his rifle strap, scrambled down the embankment, and threw himself facedown in the thrushes, slurping at the water. His thirst quenched, he pulled up to see a shadow of dark tadpoles squirming out from under a rock he had displaced and a large green bullfrog staring him down from a nearby lily pad. *Frog legs*, he thought to himself, realizing the nag of his stomach. He took out his pistol, aiming it at the amphibian and took the shot. At the same instant, something stung the back of his neck. He slapped his neck and missed the shot. The frog leaped from his pad and plunked into the water.

Seconds later, Honey slapped at another sting on his neck, another on his cheek, his chin, as a swarm of blood-hungry mosquitoes rose up from the slime and the mud, clouding the air around him. He brushed at the swarm with his hat, slapping his skin and face and swinging his hands around his head. The relentless bloodsuckers dive-bombed him, stinging, slamming into his face, swarming in his ears and nose, humming over their feast. Honey let out a groan and lunged up the embankment, the swarm chasing after him. He tore uphill at branches and scrub and out to a clearing. He swiped his hat against his leg in disgust and anger, his face puffy and itchy. Frog legs would have to wait.

Honey hunkered down for the night, collecting scraps of brush and sparked a small fire with his knife and flint. The warmth was soothing, and the smoke was a deterrent against the pestilence of night.

A distant crack of thunder woke him early the next morning, not that he slept well on the sodden ground with his clothing still damp and clinging from the previous storm. Clouds clotted the sky in thick globs of gray, and a light drizzle soaked the air. He would push on, he was determined. If fate be his kind partner in this quest against nature, he figured he would doubtless succeed in catching up with two damned slaves. Despite the mosquitoes, he took a final drink by the pool's edge and followed the wagon trail once again.

Slow going in the mud. The rain didn't let up all day. Rivulets of water poured off the rim of Honey's hat, puddling on his shoulders, and streaming down his back. He pulled his collar up, trying to prevent the making of a new river inside his shirt. The lead-colored sky hung sluggishly along the horizon, promising a dreary end to another day. Hunger gnawed at him. As he plodded past a grave roughed up by animals, for the first time in his life, Edward Honey sensed a quaking in the pit of his stomach, the acrid taste of what could only be called fear.

The emotion was fleeting. In that ephemeral moment of doubt and uncertainty, a form appeared ahead, at first a dot of white against the wolf-gray clouds, but then becoming clearer. A wagon pulled up alongside the trail a mile or so ahead. Getting closer, his heart pounded with expectation. Eight oxen were yoked to the wagon, their heads hanging miserably down, as though statues in the mud. Approaching slowly, Honey called out, "Hello?" and when no response, he called again, "Hello!" Still nothing.

He glanced left and right and spied, a few yards from the wagon, a campfire, its ashes cold and soggy, long since drenched by rain. A kettle hung below a tripod of stakes, and a tin cup half-filled with cold coffee perched on a nearby rock. Still seeing no one, Honey grabbed the cup and gulped down the cold brew. He wiped his mouth and threw down the cup. An eerie silence enveloped the scene, save for the buzzing of flies. He moved toward the wagon as distant thunder once again grumbled in the sky.

He smelled him before he saw him. He saw the man's boots first, splayed on the ground behind the wagon. They were new boots, and though muddy, the leather uppers still burnished with hints of polish. The man himself had been dead for at least three days. Flies darted around a bloody foam that leaked from his nose and mouth, and a sulfurous odor rose up from the bloating cadaver. The body lay directly behind the wagon. An open bottle of whiskey was next to him on the ground. A rifle, its muzzle pointing outward, lie on the wagon bed.

Honey knew instantly what had happened. A common mistake made by greenhorns. The man, obviously traveling alone, had too much to drink. He must have sensed a need for his rifle, reached for it by the muzzle, it got hitched, sprung the lock, and discharged. The man killed himself by accident.

He rummaged through the wagon, grabbing a handful of dried apples and stale biscuits. The wagon had been outfitted well with plenty of food, blankets, supplies, and even several cases of fine Irish whiskey. He opened a bottle and took a couple of long swigs. Despite his hunger and thirst, his deductive skills were sharp as ever. He surmised that the dead man had been traveling alone, maybe left late, and was trying to catch up to a wagon train, or perhaps he was a Turn-Around. Honey guessed the situation to be the former, the wagon was still new, provisions hardly touched. No, this greenhorn was heading West.

Honey unyoked the oxen to let them feed on the grassy stubble and dug a grave. Yanking his kerchief around his nose and mouth to dispel the gagging odor, he dragged the body to an unmarked grave.

The Bloody Flux

Horace stood before his wagon in a bittersweet moment of conflicting emotions. He was warmed with joy in its return. His wagon, built with his hands, caressed with linseed oil and carved with their birthmarks. But now, an accomplice to murder and hanging, its pole used in the gallows. Still, he thought, it was justice, as if the wagon had rendered the sentence to its own theft. Consolation enough. Besides, now they had two wagons.

The drovers buried Cuddy next to his victim, Ahusaka.

The evidence of graves, rotting carcasses of buffalo, and dead oxen along the marshy Platte River was a grim reminder that the campsites had been well-used before. It had become difficult to find a spot to sleep and eat without sharing it with something dead. The shallow water was increasingly muddy and stinky, and Fredericka frequently found herself dumping out vermin swimming in the kettle.

The pioneers had resorted to digging their own water holes along the contaminated shore, hoping for a clean supply for bathing and washing. That was an unequal transaction, often producing more filth than they were parting with. Everyone showed signs of the bloody flux, with people dashing off to squat nearby to discharge their bowels. Women attempting some degree of privacy enlisted other women to veil them with their skirts, but more often than not, they had no time to procure the assistance.

They had been camping in sewers. Explosive bouts of diarrhea created more fecal contamination that seeped into the shallow streams and watering holes, dispatching cysts and parasites. Bacteria ulcerated and gouged the travelers' intestinal tracts, causing dehydration, fever, and thirst, causing more contamination. The ugly cycle of infection played out day after day until cramping and shitting became common and more unbearable.

Nine-year-old Tommy was the first child to be affected by the bloody flux. One family offered Fredericka castor oil to help mitigate the child's dysentery. Still, Tommy had lost so much fluid and salts that his malnourished and dehydrated body could not sustain itself. He died within four days. Six-year-old Jasper died next. Fredericka had been up with Jasper in the wagon all night, cleaning him, replacing the soiled linens, washing out his clothing in the muddy water, trying to get him to drink some milk, but the child died despite her efforts. In all, twelve children in the wagon train perished from dysentery that week.

Fredericka was beside herself with grief. "Poor little Jasper," she cried. "He will never grow his front teeth. And Tommy will never learn to speak a word."

Each day, Fredericka and Horace stood with the other mourning families by the graves. The trail was a veritable cemetery of children marked with mounded stones, some with crosses, some with their names scratched in the rocks, others bearing a toy soldier, a doll, a child's hat.

At Jasper's grave, Fredericka was devastated. "I promised Sarah." She was too weary and too sick herself to cry. "I let her down. At least he'll be in heaven with his mamma, now."

Sarah's remaining children, Rebecca, Miriam, and Seneca, showed no emotion. Their vacant eyes had seen too much suffering, and their short lives had experienced too much loss.

Horace put his arm around Fredericka. "It's not your fault. It's this godforsaken place."

"This is no place for people," Fredericka said, casting a worried look at her baby Bo in her arms, "No place for children."

The wagon train moved on, but the emigrants hadn't really experienced the ravage of disease until they passed a watering hole on a particularly sewage-infested bank on the Platte's south side. The dead lay in rows of a dozen or more, some only half-buried, legs and arms visible in the dirt, other graves exhumed by animals. Two dead buffalo and a dead cow lay putrefying in the stagnant water. Swarms of flies droned the air, the smell of sewage and death was overpowering. The travelers hurried past, holding scarves and hats to their faces and noses, not daring to stop for water or rest. But death followed them.

HENRY COKER WAS A BULLWHACKER, A ROUGH AND tumble sailor out of Portsmouth who desired a taste of adventure in the wild West. He contracted to work a one-way trip on the Oregon Trail. Whipping and cussing bulls came naturally to him, as natural as whiskey, women, and poker, with women being the least of his prospects. They were repulsed by his sweat-soaked rags and vermin-infested hair.

Coker, like the other bullwhackers, could be identified by his smell—reeking of animals, axle grease, sweat, urine, and tobacco juice. Fair to say, personal hygiene was not at the top of his list. He always had a pack of cards in his pocket, ready for a gamble at the day's end, but he carried something else as well, a bacteria lurking in his gut, the microbe, *Vibrio cholerae*. He'd been gulping water from one stagnant pool to another, never bothering to boil it. Coker thought he just had a bout of the flux, and the mule skinners and bullwhackers chided and teased him for having to squat so frequently.

Soon, the disease became persistent; he was puking and shitting by the minute. He became too weak to walk and rode in the back of a wagon, cramped by pain into a fetal position, relieving himself in explosive watery diarrhea. During the long, hot, and dusty morning, his heart pounded as he vomited and gagged. By midday, he had lost five gallons of body fluids. Coker was dead.

Ogden had seen this before: the blue tinge to the dead man's skin, the sunken eyes, the wrinkled hands, the vomiting, and diarrhea. Cholera. Ogden ordered a quick burial with the man's whip and the deck of cards. Fearing infection, he ordered Coker's few belongings and the stinking wagon to be burned. They moved on without stopping for food, afraid of contamination, but too late.

By supper that night, three of Coker's card-playing bullwhackers came down with severe symptoms and by dawn another two. All five died by dinnertime. By the end of the third day, the disease had ripped through the wagon train. Relentlessly, it ravaged the young and old, the weak and the strong alike, taking out the entire Steep family of five and fifteen other adults.

The emigrants lived in constant fear of dying. They tried to stem the disease by administering castor oil, rum, tincture of opium, and water mixed with pepper sauce, but the death toll continued to climb, day after day, affecting every family in every wagon. Forward motion had to be maintained, the window for traveling weather was short. Ogden ordered extra graves for those who still lived but were about to die. For some who were breathing but sure to pass, burial came before death, while others were cast aside the trail to wait out the Grim Reaper. This was not without humanity, as Ogden designated a Keeper to linger with the dying so they would not meet death alone as the wagon train mercilessly moved on. The Keepers always caught up soon enough. With little ceremony, few words, and no time to mourn, the wagon train trundled on as if chased by the devil himself.

A week later, they camped overnight north of the riverbed further into the prairie, looking for higher grasses to graze the cattle and oxen and cleaner spaces to set up tents. Fredericka's routine for the night was as tedious as the day. She unpacked the wagon and pulled out the two forked stakes and a rod for the campfire. She plunked the stakes into the ground and placed the rod into the forks. Wood was a luxury not to be found, but sagebrush and buffalo chips abounded, and she put this fuel in a small hole dug in the ground and sparked a fire. A kettle of water for coffee hung over the fire from the rod.

Fredericka proceeded to make pancakes from flour, water, and baking soda, but before she could get the dough in the skillet, it had become black with mosquitos that persecuted them day and night. Horace and the children were always hungry, and dead bugs in the dough were the least of their worries. She clamped an iron lid over the skillet and plunked it on the fire's coals. No one seemed to care that the smoky food always had the pungency of ashes, sagebrush, and the wild, skunky odor of buffalo chips, much less the ricey texture of dead skeeters.

Danuta Pfeiffer

Even the tiniest of tormenters could kill. One mosquito carrying a microscopic parasite could bring down a human. Somewhere along the trail earlier that week, young Rebecca didn't even feel the bite.

Rebecca awoke complaining of a headache. She managed to help load the wagon with Fredericka and saw to breakfast with Miriam and Seneca, but the headache grew worse, so she rode in the wagon. Riding brought little comfort with the wagon's rocking and jostling, bouncing and bumping over ruts and rocks. The constant barrage of clanging and banging pots and kettles, the continual shouting and jeering at the oxen, and the clanking of harnesses and chains made rest impossible.

By midday, Rebecca's condition worsened with a high fever, followed by bouts of severe shaking and chills. Her sweating, vomiting, and pain increased. Fredericka was frantic, and she sat in the wagon with the sick girl, keeping Rebecca warm, then swabbing her shivering, sweating body, and giving her sips of water. The two remaining children, Miriam and Seneca, walked alongside, Miriam holding baby Bo.

At camp that night, no one spoke of their fear. Fredericka stayed with Rebecca in the wagon while Horace set up camp and made the fire. Little Miriam helped with the beans and bacon for dinner while Rebecca's condition deteriorated as diarrhea, vomiting, and fever weakened her tired young body.

"Hush now, you gonna live, and we gonna have a nice little farm in Oregon." But Fredericka feared the girl was dying. Another child dead. Another grave. This cannot be! The child suffered so. There must be something, somewhere, anything she could do. A medicine, an herb. She squeezed her eyes closed and took a long, deep breath. Something Annie, her mother, told her years ago. Something about bird's-foot, how the women would talk of bird's-foot and used the seeds for sickness, to help give strength after whippings. She had collected that plant earlier in the spring and gathered its golden seeds in a tin. Under the bedding with her other seeds. Her heart raced with the thought of it. She searched her containers and found the one with the drawing of three small leaves, the tiny seeds rattling in the bottom.

Fredericka jumped out of the wagon and filled the tin with water.

"She dead?" Horace's mournful tone spoke of too much death and dying and digging. He stood. Miriam and Seneca gazed up with their sad little faces.

"Not yet." Fredericka held the tin with both hands as if it were a precious keepsake.

The next morning, Rebecca could no longer hold her head up, so weakened by the intermittent fevers and chills. Fredericka spooned the solution of water from the soaked seeds into the girl's mouth. She placed a cloth dipped in apple cider vinegar and water on Rebecca's forehead. And though the wagon train continued its noisy, painful, and bumpy trek, Rebecca's fever waned. By nightfall, she managed to eat a small bit of cornmeal mush, and by next daybreak, she was sitting up on her own, the fever gone. By week's end, Rebecca was up and walking again.

Malaria had been beaten. The cure did not go unnoticed by others in the wagon train, who began to suspect Fredericka's strange powers.

Cholera continued to take its toll. One child, ten-year-old Kitty Parker, wasn't afraid of death as much as she feared the wolves that howled every night and prowled around the campsite's boundary just out of reach of gunfire, digging up the dead and scattering the bones. "Bury me six feet deep, so the wolves don't eat me! And pile rocks on top!" she cried to her mother, Esther, as she lay dying. "And bury me with my hair comb. Promise me, Mamma, promise me!"

Kitty Parker died the next morning, just before the call to roll out. Esther was beside herself with grief and exhaustion. "My girl is lost!" she cried, tears running down her face through the dust of five hundred miles. "We are gonna bury her six feet, six feet!" She pointed to a spot on the trail, "Here."

The wagon train was about to move. Ogden wasn't keen to wait on burials and grave digging. Esther's husband, Hiram Parker, and two drovers dug a quick, four-foot pit. The drovers considered the grave to be deep enough and rushed off to their duties with the cattle, leaving Hiram to pull the body into the ditch, but Esther would have none of it.

"It has to be six feet!" she railed at the men walking away, her anguish welling up in her throat. "I promised her. If you can't do it, I'll dig it myself!" Before her poor husband could stop her, the bereaved woman climbed down in the grave and began clawing at the dirt with her bare hands.

Her shocked husband climbed into the narrow pit with her and pulled Esther out, promising to dig it six feet deep.

Esther stood at the gravesite and, upon spying Fredericka nearby, shouted, "Why is my girl dead while the nigger's Rebecca lives?"

Fredericka felt a stab of pain in her gut, that all-too-common White ploy of false accusation and inevitably, a price to be paid.

Horace felt it too and stood a little closer to her. "Don't mind her. She's full of grief. She doesn't know what she's saying."

Ogden was impatient. "What's the holdup? We need to roll!"

Hiram gave a slight wave of his hand, grabbed his shovel, and dug the grave to six feet. They buried Kitty with her hair comb in the middle of the rutted trail, where the wagon wheels passed over her, pressing down on the dirt, packing hard her grave against the night's predators.

Fear, doubt, and superstition gripped the travelers. What are we doing here? Why did we come? Can we turn back? Who will die next? Will I be buried alive? Will I die alone? What will become of my family? Who's to blame?

"The niggers brought this on us," one woman claimed.

"They came on the train last, brought us nothin' but sorrow," agreed another.

"It's Black Magic with demon powers," said another. "She healed Rebecca, but none of our folk get better."

Their rumblings grew.

Register Cliffs

———— ◦≋≋◦ ————

One would think that shared suffering of disease and death would be a great leveler, but instead, the emigrants searched for someone to blame.

Ellen Foster's five-year-old son, Gabriel, slipped out of the wagon and fell. The wheel rolled over his chest, severed his arm, and killed him. In the next wagon, Mary Clapper gave birth to her sixth child, a boy. A birth fraught with difficulty. Mary died several hours later, and the baby boy did not survive his mother. They buried all three near camp that evening and reinterred the bones of another child found strewn about and gnawed by the wolves.

The mosquitoes swarmed about the traveler's heads in great stinging clouds, and rattlesnakes coiled under the wagons and slithered into tents while they slept. One bite took Jonas Kellogg to his grave; another struck and killed an infant as she slept. The misery piled on. The water was thick as mud, washing impossible, and the mounting death toll from cholera created panic.

The emigrants' fears grew louder, until one evening, they convened a meeting insisting on new terms with the wagon master.

"We should divide the wagon train," one man called out. "We're running low on good water; people are sick and dyin' and slowin' us down. I say we leave the sick behind and carry on with those that are healthy."

"I say we leave the niggers behind, take their wagons," yelled another. "They've got two wagons and eight oxen, a cow, and a horse. Why should they have two wagons when most of us only have one?"

"We could use their oxen," hollered another.

"And the woman is a heathen!" screamed Esther Parker. "Why does her baby live, and others die?"

Alexander Ogden tried to settle the clamor. "We need every man, woman, and child. We're driving cattle, heavin' and repairin' wagons, fordin' rivers. We're not even halfway to Green River. That's forty days from here, and things will get even tougher."

"I won't eat nigger dust," said a man in the crowd.

"I say we leave 'em!" crowed another.

Horace and Fredericka stood near the gathering, Horace still holding a shovel in his hand from digging the last grave. He felt his face flush and his pulse quicken. "You men," he shouted, "I helped grease and tar your wagons. I herded your cattle and found your strays. I helped carry you across a dozen rivers. I buried your dead. I pulled you out of mud and pushed your wagons up hills. Fredericka has nursed your sick and taken in orphans. She washes your clothes. And you talk of witches and eating our dust?"

He thrust the shovel on the ground in disgust. "Then bury your own dead. As for my wagon, it belongs to me and mine, and I'll kill the man who tries to take it."

Fredericka felt the heat and despair rising from Horace, but said nothing.

"Now wait a minute, everyone. Now listen to me," Ogden said. "We are not dividing this train, and I'll hear no talk of killin', but if it brings peace, Horace, you and yours take the rear with your wagon but keep up. As for the Bidwell wagon, we'll use it up front to carry extra supplies out of Fort Laramie. Horace is still in my service. As for the rest of you, I'll be needing every man here to get us across this land. If anyone has a problem with that, you can leave this train now." He cocked his rifle and held it in the air.

The crowd stilled and then, like a torn tissue, thinned out and dissolved. Horace and Fredericka cleared out the Bidwell wagon and delivered it up to Ogden along with its oxen. Fredericka and Horace kept their own wagon, four oxen, and the cow. The next morning, they took their positions with the remaining three Bidwell children, Rebecca, Seneca, and Miriam, at the back of the train.

⎯⎯ ∞ ⎯⎯

THE WAGON TRAIN CROSSED THE SOUTH PLATTE RIVER and headed west, skirting the south side of the North Platte. Fredericka gazed upon the open grasslands of the high plains with awe. The world rolled into one sweeping, unending expanse that met the sky on all sides. The vast harsh, white light held a beauty where every creature and growing thing, big and small, had carved out space enough to grow. She could almost smell the sun in the dust and dead grasses as it blistered her lips and burned her eyes.

She reminded herself that suffering was the price of freedom. She prodded the oxen forward, sometimes riding the reins from the wagon, other times merely walking with the baby in her arms. The children trudged along, humorless, tired, filthy, occasionally taking turns riding in the wagon, but the heat was stifling under the canvas, and most of the time, they preferred to walk. The hard ground baked in the shadeless noonday sun with no escape. Up ahead, Horace herded the cattle kicking up billowing dust in great relentless clouds that made breathing behind the wagon train almost impossible. At camp each night, Horace rolled the wagon into little creek beds, soaked the wheels' dry wood back into their rims, and greased the axles. Miriam milked the cow while Fredericka unloaded the wagon, rounded up buffalo chips, made a fire, and baked biscuits.

Fredericka still found comfort in discovering new flowers: yarrow, white sage, the prairie onion, and the fragrant hyssop. Though she didn't know their names, she reveled in their simple beauty and found comfort in their endurance. Each evening, under the glow of sunset, she would draw these prairie splendors, tucking what seeds she could find in the pockets of her apron, and securing them in little packets of burlap and discarded tins she found among the items tossed along the route.

Flowers were sometimes easier to find than children. One morning, just as the wagon train was about to roll, Martha Gladstone lost her three-year-old boy, Nathan. He had simply wandered off without a sound. Ogden delayed the wagons for two hours while everyone searched for the child. They never found him. His frantic mother begged for more time, but her pleas could not stop the march forward. Her grief haunted the wagon train for days as she called and wailed for her child all night long, hoping in some small miraculous way, he would follow the sound of her voice and come back to her. In the end, Martha stopped talking altogether and never uttered another word.

Losing little Nathan to the Plains shook everyone, and Fredericka was determined to keep Sara's children close.

Miriam and Rebecca watched after Seneca and often helped with Bo, and Fredericka watched over them all.

No one was prepared for the challenge ahead, a steep incline obstructing their trail in the middle of the plain. Too long to go around, the emigrants would have to push over it, and push they did.

They had been climbing all day, the oxen straining at their chains, their shoulders jamming into the yokes hauling the wagons up the mercilessly steep ascent. Many families threw out more of their surplus belongings to lighten their loads, but the climb grew even more perilous. Wheels skidded over boulders and jammed into crevices. Men put their shoulders to the wagons from behind and climbed the rugged hillside until they eventually reached the top. The view of Ash Hollow and the North Platte River valley below took Fredericka's breath away. With trees, freshwater streams, pools of water, rolling green hills, and forage for the animals, a virtual paradise awaited them below.

But hell stood between them and the land of milk and honey, a treacherous, twenty-five-degree descent down Windlass Hill. The first wagon to attempt the descent rammed against the cautious plodding oxen, overturning, strewing goods and supplies along the hillside, killing one of the oxen. Another emigrant attempted to pull up on his brake, and when the wheels continued to skid, his son rammed a pole into the wheel, but instead of stopping, it splintered the spokes. The family watched their father hurl down the slope in the wagon and smash into pieces at the bottom of the ravine in a bloody, twisted mound of dead oxen and splintered wood. The dead emigrant was found with the reins still clutched in his hands.

Ogden ordered Horace and the other men to arrange a series of ropes and pulleys fastened to each wagon and tied to twelve oxen, then lower the carriages down the steep grade. Fredericka and the children stood nearby, watching the laborious task when the cattle behind them became unnerved by the racket of men shouting and the bawling of oxen. They began to stampede. Seneca and Rebecca were standing several yards beyond Fredericka's reach. The cattle bolted before she could save them. The herd drove over the children and over the hill. A bloody mass lumbered and slid and rolled down the other side, crashing into wagons and sweeping up the oxen into a frightened, gory swarm. The hill took five lives that day, the cost of paradise.

Fredericka did not remember the rest of the day. She could only see Seneca's little body mangled under a tree and Rebecca's checked gingham bonnet snagged on a bush fretting in the wind, as if her soul was not ready to let go. She did not hear Ogden's call to muster the remaining wagons and families. The lush valley and fresh spring water held no appeal, and the grassy meadow was not a sanctuary for the living but had become a boneyard for the dead.

Fredericka insisted on digging the children's graves herself next to a small clutch of wild jasmine. She tucked Seneca's rag doll next to her little body, "so she won't be lonely," and hung Rebecca's bonnet on a rough-hewn cross. She gathered yucca and wild roses, currant, and wild grape growing nearby and stuffed them away in the wagon.

Fredericka wept over their little graves. "I will plant these to remember you always." Turning to Miriam, forlorn and lost, Fredericka wrapped her arms about her. "Forgive me, child. I couldn't save Rebecca or sweet Seneca after all. They be out of danger now."

Later that night, Fredericka was quiet and listless. Horace had arranged bedding for them outside the tent next to the fire and tried to console her. "The stars are bright tonight. And you don't have to look up to see them."

"Don't…" she said. "I lost those babies. Couldn't save them."

"Not your fault, Fred. You can't be held responsible for every accident and lost soul."

"But Horace. Babies. I keep losin' babies."

"Not true. You have Bo and Miriam. And you have me."

"If anything ever happened to you…" Fredericka's voice had an edge of fear in it.

"You close your eyes. And you remember you are brave."

"No Horace. I'm not."

"Listen to me, listen." Horace pulled her toward him. "You remember who you are, that's what you do. Did I ever tell you, the whole sky is right here, in your eyes, scattered in your freckles? I see the Big Dipper, the North Star, Venus, the whole world, right here in you. Don't ever forget that."

Through the night, Fredericka watched the stars swirl above them and wondered which stars belonged to Rebecca and Seneca.

For the next two days, the pioneers made repairs, reconfigured their wagons, washed clothes in the cool ponds, and rested under the shade of cottonwood trees before moving across the wild plains.

Traveling for several more days, Fredericka saw a strange monument rising up from the earth, a massive tower of rock that looked like a mud castle. As they drew closer, she realized it was two formations. They paused near these towers at midday break.

"They call them Courthouse and Jail rocks," Horace said.

"Good thing we passing them by. Let's get our bellies full enough to run from the law," Fredericka said with a slight smile. "Miriam, let you and me whip up a batch of johnnycakes."

Horace was glad to see Fredericka's face light up for the first time in days.

Fredericka purchased an egg from Mildred Flackner's family. She beat the egg and added three-eighths cup of milk, one-half cup of water, one tablespoon of melted lard, one-half teaspoon of salt, one cup of cornmeal, one-half cup of flour and a tablespoon of sugar. She mixed it all together and dropped small batches on a hot skillet over the fire and browned them on both sides. She served them with a little dab of butter from the churn hanging on the back of the wagon.

"Here's to the cook," Horace said, kissing Fredericka on the cheek, "and to those glorious freckles." Maybe it was the sunshine, or the mysterious rocks, or the johnnycakes, but Horace had a feeling the earth was shining brighter.

Moving on, another formation, Chimney Rock, appeared in the distance, a slender spire rising over three hundred feet in the air, protruding out of a conical base and resembling a helmet with a spike on the top. The emigrants approached it for two days, but they never appeared any closer to it.

"Like this slog," Fredericka lamented, "our legs keep movin', but we don't seem to be gettin' anywhere."

Eventually, the wagon train reached Scotts Bluff, an eight-hundred-foot-high ridge with a natural saddle in the landscape leading to the pass. At camp that night, the wagons circled, and the campfires emanated a warm glow as the pioneers celebrated a landmark. They had made it a third of the way.

Later, in Fort Laramie, the wagon train resupplied their provisions of flour, bacon, jams, wheels, and tools. They reset tires, soaked wheels overnight, greased the axles, and spliced whiplashes. Horace and Fredericka marveled at the teepees and the Natives camped outside the fort. They mingled freely with the pioneers, trading goods and sharing campfires.

A day's push later, and the emigrants camped at Register Cliff on the banks of the Platte, where they could graze the livestock in lush pastures and take time to rest for the journey's most challenging part yet to come. Horace was mesmerized by the one-hundred-foot wall skimming the trail, not for the archaeology but for the humanity carved into it—hundreds of names chiseled into the sandstone. He walked along the vast ledger, stroking his fingers across the desert's guestbook. These were fellow travelers with sorrows and hopes, losses, and expectations. When everything seemed so perilous and tenuous, here was a sense of permanence etched into the rock's membrane. This wall was the reminder of souls, a sacred ground.

Horace could not hold back his urge to claim his place in history. He rushed to Fredericka. "Come," he said, taking her hand. She knew better than to argue or to ask with such insistence in his tone.

"Look." He gazed up at the massive register. "Names. Hundreds of them, maybe thousands."

"What does it mean?"

"It means they were here."

A settling hovered over them like shade from the sun as the enormity of the cliff's purpose made itself evident.

"I want to be here too," she said with the reverence of one soon to be baptized.

"We'll need the right tool." Horace bent to the ground, picking up rocky chunks, giving them a swift examination and dispensing each one until he grabbed a shard and hefted it into his hand measuring its weight and gravity. Satisfied, Horace surveyed the cliff face for space. "There!" He pointed to a chalky canvas just above their heads. They climbed up a crumbly ledge of sandy pebbles, and he offered Fredericka the stone chisel.

"You first," she said.

He took a prayerful breath, and gripping the chisel firmly in his hand, he etched his name into the sandstone's gritty flesh:

H O R A C E

He handed the tool to her. Beneath his name, she carved her own:

F R E D E R I C K A

They stepped down from the ledge and gazed up at their names emblazoned high on the rock, high enough for heaven to read, a document to their existence fused in stone.

"We were here." Horace felt a euphoria welling from deep within him, a sense that all the mountains he had climbed, all the rivers he had crossed, and all journeys he ventured belonged to him. The world was in him, and he belonged to it. The thing he had sought had been here all along, pulsing and forever his.

Horace felt the sun's last golden rays warm the back of his shoulders, warm like his love for Fredericka. He took her hand. "Fred…" In that unspoken moment, the touch of her strong, little hand overwhelmed him.

Fredericka searched his eyes for the words that were lost to him. "What is it, Horace?"

He pressed her fingers to his lips. "I promised you a long time ago…"

"What, Horace?"

He took a long breath and removed his hat. "We said we'd do this on the trail. I can think of no better place or time. Before the Lord and our names on this cliff, will you marry me?"

"Why, Horace!" She blinked back tears but didn't know why she was crying.

"Does that mean, yes?"

"You mean now? Here?"

"Right here. Right now."

How she loved his brassy face, his eyes, alive and insistent, full of expectation. Her pulse quickened, and her throat felt dry. She untied her bonnet and removed it. Tilting her head up to him, she said, "I will marry you, Horace. Before the Lord and our names on this cliff."

"I don't have a ring and we don't have a preacher." Horace swallowed hard and squared his shoulders. "But I have my name—if you'll take it."

She tilted her head slightly. "I don't need no ring, Horace. And no preacher. Your name is all I need. But…what name?"

A glimmer of a smile crossed his face. "Then, from this day on, you are my Fredericka, my brave girl, my wife." He reached up to the cliff one more time and below their signatures, carved their last name:

FREEMAN.

<hr>

THE MORNING BUGLE RALLIED THE EMIGRANTS OUT OF their tents at 4:00 a.m. Smokey campfires lit up the dark dawn as the men wrestled with yokes and oxen and saddled stubborn mules and horses. They ate a quick breakfast of bacon, beans, and coffee and packed up their wagons.

As the wagon train rolled out, Fredericka and Horace spread their wagon out half a mile to the side to eat less dust from the wagons in front. The plan worked. The move to the side relieved most of the powdery clouds from her eyes, and she was able to remove herself from the clattering noise and observe the fauna, gather seeds, view the sky, and think about Horace and their future together. *Mr. and Mrs. Freeman.* She felt a lightness in her step, and the rocks and shrubs took on a luster as if they shared her joy.

In this daydream, she sensed a slight change in the wind, a glimmer from the sun, and a silence in the air. She stopped walking. She glanced down to see a lizard at her feet, transfixed and still. Pointing northeast, a bit to her left and slightly behind where she stood. "What's goin' on little fella'?" Her gaze settled on the direction the creature faced, and she saw what looked like a boulder or a mound that appeared to move. Was it a trick of heat and sun, or had it moved? The protrusion moved again, an imperceptible shift. Shielding her eyes, she stared at it. A quarter-mile away or more, but yes, it moved. Was it a wolf? A deer? Fredericka called Miriam to jump in and turned the wagon toward the object.

Drawing the wagon closer, she saw a small cart. Probably some discarded piece of overloaded furniture from a previous wagon train, she thought. But then, something else. Yes, just in front, a pile of rags flapping in the wind. But no, not rags. Fredericka stopped the wagon and jumped down for a closer look. A body. A woman. Rumpled in the dirt. With no blood-soaked ground around the corpse, she hadn't been dead long enough for the wolves to take her. What was she doing out here, alone? She would have to bury her, to fetch a shovel. Just as she turned to the wagon, a scrawny hand shot up and clutched her skirt. Fredericka screamed, and she wrested her dress from the grisly clutch, shocked by seeing death come alive.

The specter of the corpse and the clawed hand nearly caused her heart to leap out of her chest. After a few moments to catch her breath, she gathered the courage to lean in for a closer look. The dead woman groaned and waved her hand. Fredericka knelt and swept the hair from the woman's face, caked in dirt, sunburnt, blotched, and blistered. A fly crawled across her cheek; her clothes were the same drab color as the sagebrush. The woman opened her mouth to speak, but no words came.

"Water! Miriam," Fredericka called. "Hurry!"

Miriam jumped from the wagon and ladled water from the side barrel and handed it to Fredericka. "Drink." Fredericka held the woman's head in her lap. "Drink."

A few sips, and the woman coughed and gagged, clutching at Fredericka's arm. "A little at a time." Fredericka dabbed the woman's scabbed and scalded lips with water. "You come right up out of your grave. Gave me a start, but you be all right now."

Fredericka and Miriam fashioned a bedroll crib and slid the woman to the wagon, hefting her inside.

"You sit back there with her," Fredericka instructed Miriam. "We gotta catch up with the others."

As Fredericka drove the oxen forward and rumbled along the patchy, dusty squalor of the prairie, she couldn't help think an impossible thought. *Do I know this woman?*

Put Her Back!

⎯⎯⎯◯◯◯⎯⎯⎯

L ater that day, at camp, Fredericka told Horace how
she found the woman, and they discussed what to
do about her. She was delirious, coming in and out
of consciousness and obviously needed care.

"It is not our place to care for the woman or make that
decision," Horace said and decided to ask the wagon master
if someone else in the company would be willing to take her.

"She bein' a White woman and all," Horace explained
to Ogden, "might be more comfortable if she were with
her own kind. Might not be too seemly to be riding in the
back of a wagon train with the likes of us," he added with
a slight edge to his voice.

"We don't have the resources to pick up strangers or
stragglers," Ogden said. "You found her. You keep her."

That evening, Fredericka went about the business of
caring for the distressed woman. She assembled a few rags,
a basin of warm water, and crawled into the wagon to bathe
her. At first, she dabbed at the bedraggled woman's face,
trying to avoid the sunburned scabs and swollen, cracked
lips, and slowly managed to scrub off layers of dirt from her
cheeks and chin, lifting dirt and dust from the woman's eyes.
With each stroke of cloth and brush of water, Fredericka
etched out the lines of her eyes, the arch of her brows, and

the curl of her lips as the woman's face became more visible. Shock turned to horror as the canvas of Henrietta Grafton came to life, and she opened her eyes.

"You!" Fredericka dropped the washcloth.

"You?" Henrietta's voice was hoarse.

The women stared at one another, each scrambling her gaze over the other's face, each staring at a ghost from their past. Fredericka's disbelief dissolved into memories and the smell of raw meat and blood, images of whips and water, rape and incest, shattered teacups, and her mother bought and sold. Fredericka's first instinct was to run. Run from the hounds and the men with hats and beards and rifles and chains. Run from the ragged, wretched, awful menace laid next to her lap, pretending to be weak and sparse of bone and will. At any moment, who will leap from her bed and devour her and take away all that she is and ever will be and make her again what she was—a slave.

Fredericka felt like she'd been shot. She stumbled from wagon and ran for Horace.

"She's here, Horace! It's her! The devil has come for us!" She clutched at Horace in a panic.

"Hush now, what are you saying woman?"

"It's Mistress Grafton, Horace. The devil herself. The woman I found. It's her, Horace. What we gonna do? We gotta put her back where she come from. Get her out of our wagon. She's gonna kill us, that's what!"

"Wait a minute. Wait a minute." Horace took her by the shoulders. "Settle down, now. Calm down. You saying the woman in the desert is Mrs. Grafton? From the plantation? Girl, that's impossible. Maybe she just looks like her..."

"Horace, I tell you it's her! You think I could forget that face? Go, see for yourself, but be careful!"

Fredericka stood rooted to the ground, afraid to move, and watched Horace stride to the rear of the wagon. He threw the flap back and stared into the bed. Fredericka watched his body stiffen. He stood for long moments, unmoving, his hat shielding his eyes. She couldn't tell what he was thinking or if he was speaking. Each second was an agony. An evil nightmare from the past had caught up to them. What to do? Where to hide? What would happen to the baby? These thoughts burned through her, unresolved, frantic, taunting until Horace turned back to her.

He was quiet and somber. "You're right," he said. "I wouldn't have believed it. But that's her, Henrietta Grafton!"

"What are we gonna do, Horace? She seen us now." She took Bo into her arms from Miriam. "I say we put 'er back."

"Put her back?" Horace removed his hat and wiped his brow with his sleeve.

"Yessir. Put her back where she come from. Let someone else find her."

"She'll die out there, Fredericka."

"Better she die out there than we die in here."

"We can't do that."

"Why can't we? Why can't we, Horace, huh? You think she would save us? You think she don't want us dead? Why should we save a mean, White devil who will bring us nothin' but bad?"

"Listen now, listen. I don't know how she got out here on the prairie, and I don't know how you found her. But Lord, what's done is done. You can't kill her any more than I can. Besides, who's gonna believe a delirious old woman you found half-dead on the prairie?"

"But Horace…what if she was comin' after us?

"No. We take her in. We do what's right. Whatever comes, we deal with later."

"Horace, she ain't nothin' but trouble!"

"Then, she's our trouble."

THE NEXT MORNING, A COLD WIND BLEW ACROSS THE plains, and the sky was gunmetal gray. Fredericka's fingers were stiff and cold as she wrapped Bo in a second blanket. She poked the campfire's embers with her other arm with sagebrush, tossed it in, and blew on the smoke until the flames spun up. She threw in some buffalo chips and boiled water for coffee.

"Looks like another storm." Horace stretched his back, feeling his bones creak. "You're not talking much."

"Huh-uh."

Horace put his arms on her shoulders and pulled a hair back from her face. "Don't let that woman in there get to you," he said, jerking his head toward the wagon.

"How do I do that?"

He pulled her close and held her in his arms and whispered, "Because you're good."

"Not that good."

Fredericka made coffee and fixed up biscuits dipped in bacon grease while Horace rounded up the oxen, yoked them to the wagon, and saddled and mounted his horse. Before riding off to tend to the cattle, he took the biscuits from her hands and asked, "You gonna be okay?"

She bit her inner lip and gave a faint nod. Another day of tending to young Miriam, baby Bo and now, Henrietta. Waiting until the travelers from the other wagons hurried off, she relieved herself in the communal ditch, carefully wrapping her long skirt about her for a semblance of privacy. She had avoided Henrietta until the very last moment, packing up the camp and loading the wagon around Henrietta's bedding without a word. The other wagons had filed out and began to move by the time Fredericka built up the courage to face her former mistress and climbed into the wagon with cold coffee and a dish of biscuits.

Neither woman spoke. Henrietta reached for the food, eyeing Fredericka suspiciously. She gobbled down the biscuits and slurped the coffee.

When the two women finally did converse, the practice of rank and privilege had not waned over the hundreds of miles of plains and prairies, as if neither knew another language.

"I want bacon with breakfast, next time." Henrietta smacked her lips with satisfaction and wiped her mouth with her hand.

"Yes, Ma'am." Fredericka averted her eyes, yet feeling somehow awkward with this renewed submission.

"You know I don't drink coffee." She gave a disdainful glance at her cup. "I prefer tea. Your Mammy was always a better house slave than you ever were."

That was the gut punch. The bile of the past flared up. Fredericka could taste the rot of her buried memories, stale and sour, unreconciled and unforgiven. And something else. Rage. She had never allowed its heat to surface and its power to betray her. Now she owned it, in all its unleashed and bitter glory, focused into one sharp, single objective, to rip the sneer off Henrietta's face.

She grabbed Henrietta's bony wrist, tugged her from the wagon, and wrangled her to the ground. Henrietta lashed out and punched Fredericka with her free arm, twisted around and bit her hand. Fredericka screamed and released her grip. Henrietta got to her hands and knees, panting, when Fredericka yanked her backward by her hair, dragging her across the ground. For a hundred yards, Fredericka heaved the Mistress of Grafton Plantation over the brush and burls of the plain, reducing the flailing woman to the flapping specter of a wounded crow.

Finally stopping, gasping for breath and towering over Henrietta, Fredericka trembled, not from fear, but from years of constrained justice and shielded emotions and the cruel leverage of race and abuse. All of this and more was about to let fly with the full force and fury of God himself. Fredericka reached for a butcher knife stowed in her apron and held it over Henrietta. The woman whimpered and put up her hands.

"I will tell you why you deserve to die." Fredericka's voice was as sharp as the blade in her hand. "You sold my mamma. And Masta' Grafton, your husband, he used me in unnatural ways whenever he took a liking to. He was my daddy, and I had his child, but I was jus' a child myself! By God's grace, my baby Isaiah died 'fore you could get your hands on him. You sent hunters after us. We run clear across this godforsaken country gettin' away from you, and here you come again. Well, you ain't comin' after us no more!"

"I didn't mean to!" The whites of Henrietta's eyes flashed with alarm in her dirt-encrusted face. "It's just the way it was! I'm a God-fearing woman! You can't blame me for that!"

"You call yourself God-fearin'? You think God would rip a mamma from her child? Where is she? Where is my mamma?" Fredericka's fist tightened over the knife.

"Sold. At the auction. I don't know anymore. I swear, you can't blame me for not knowing."

"I can! I can blame you. You think I can't blame you 'cause God said it? God lets girls be raped? God drowns little girls in a bucket of water? God makes you better than me 'cause you is White? You can whip the flesh off people because God says so? You can make slaves outta children? That's no God. That was you."

"It's in the Bible." Henrietta appealed her case and shifted the blame. "Jesus never said slavery was a sin. I just followed the Lord, that's all! You can't blame me for being Christian."

"I can blame you!" Fredericka leaned in low next to her and brought her face up close to the terrified woman. "'Cause you showed no mercy. And you enjoyed it."

Henrietta seemed to collapse from the inside out. Kneeling in the dirt, she hung her head and pleaded. "I'm not bad, Fredericka. I'm just a woman, like you, caught up in it all…"

"I ain't nothin' like you," Fredericka said. She stood and put the knife back in her apron. "I know who I am."

She turned and walked back to the wagon.

Henrietta crawled after her. "You're not leaving me here. You can't leave!"

Fredericka didn't turn around. She put the children in the back, sat in the bucket, took the reins, and pushed the oxen forward to catch up with the other wagons. As thunder rolled across the distant horizon and the sky turned a muddy green, Henrietta became a speck and vanished behind her.

The Tornado

⊷

alf an hour later, bruise-colored clouds blotted the sun, the wind stalled, and insects hushed their chatter. The prairie felt as tense as a wire. Fredericka pulled the oxen to a halt. Ahead, she saw the wagon train and watched a black wall of clouds massing overhead in frightening mounds and swirls. A stout breeze picked up as the storm grew closer. She turned and looked over her shoulder to where she left Henrietta. The wind rose stiff and dusty. Horace's words rang in her head, "Because you're good."

Damn that woman! She turned the wagon around.

She pushed the oxen hard, yelling and slapping the reins as they lumbered back across the prairie. The wind snared the canvas loose, and it slapped against the bows beating in time with the oxen's hooves. The pots and pans bashed and clanged in alarm against the gale that chased them.

"Yee-haw! Yee-haw!" Fredericka pressured the bewildered team hauling the wagon by fear as much as the insults of her reins. Debris stung the air, and lightning shocked the sky, and the space between heaven and earth became as black as a cauldron, but Fredericka pushed on.

Minutes later, she spotted the silhouette of Henrietta pressing against the wind, her garments wrapped her frame as tight as tar. Henrietta fell to her knees. Fredericka jumped from the wagon. The wind tore the bonnet from her head, held flapping on her back by the ties around her throat. She marched up to the prostrate woman and hollered above the driving wind and dust, "You are a mean, old devil, and you ain't worth savin'!" The wind whipped about the two women, but Fredericka stood her ground.

Henrietta shielded her face from the storm. "I'm sorry! I'm so sorry!"

"And you ain't better than me!" Fredericka's fury rode the wind as lightning sliced the sky.

Henrietta bobbed her head, her face blasted by the spitting dust.

The wind abated as tiny pellets of ice pinged the ground. "And you ugly too!"

The prostrate woman could only sob in agreement.

"And you gonna write us our freedom papers, or by God, you can rot in hell!"

Again, Henrietta nodded.

"And my mamma's too!"

Henrietta choked in agreement.

The pitter-patter around them became a volley of hard and heavy hail, stinging and cutting their arms and faces. Fredericka took Henrietta's hand and pulled her up.

As the storm let loose, they ran for the wagon. Fredericka grabbed the baby and helped Miriam out of the wagon bed, and together with Henrietta, they took shelter under the carriage. Hail, now large as stone, sharp as glass, and lethal as bullets rained down on them. The hail shredded the canvas and slashed the oxen who bawled and bled and yanked helplessly against their yokes.

Wind, lightning, and the pounding hail gave way to a distant roar, like a thunderous waterfall. The noise grew louder and more ominous. From her vantage point under the wagon, Fredericka watched the prairie grasses panic, twisting and flapping with such ferocity as if they were trying to wrench themselves from their roots and run. A long, dark cloud dropped from a tight-fisted cloud and touched the ground stirring the earth like a bowl of soup.

Henrietta turned to Fredericka. "It's the finger of God come to punish me!" She buried her head under her shawl.

Fredericka watched the storm with horrible fascination. The roaring seemed to swallow the whole world.

From under the shawl, Henrietta made pledges and promises and struck bargains with her Lord to be a better woman, though she was sure she was doomed.

Day turned to night. Stinging and slicing dust blasted the wagon and their clothing. Tugging at the wagon, the oxen wailed and bawled as the swirling debris grated the flesh from their bones. Bo fidgeted under Fredericka's arms, but she couldn't hear the child above the storm's blast. The wagon above them shuddered, and before Fredericka's bewildered eyes, the wheels lifted up and floated inches above the ground. *It must be God!*

She ducked her head down and clung to the baby. Seconds later, her body lost the sensation of gravity, and God held her in His hands. But God changed His mind and slammed her back to the ground. A rib snapped in her chest. Gasping for breath, her hands scrambled in the dirt for the baby. Bo was gone. The wagon floated back down. The wind toyed with the carriage as it rocked and swayed, and the wood groaned. Finally, the undulating blasts of wind and lightning became a dull and distant roar as the wagon stilled. The tempest passed, its fury reduced to a dusty whistle.

Fredericka scrambled out from under the wagon, holding her painful chest. She searched for Bo and winced each time she called the child's name.

Miriam and Henrietta stood dazed and traumatized, their clothing shredded to rags. Flecks of debris and grass had embedded their cheeks, giving their mottled faces the appearance of being pickled. Tucked under Henrietta's arm was Baby Bo, who sniffled and fussed.

"I got her," Henrietta said. "I grabbed the child before the wind got her."

Fredericka took the baby in her arms, and with shaking hands, examined the bundled child.

"She's all right. Bo's all right." Henrietta nodded, her grimy, cadaverous face lit only by a spark of hope in her eyes.

Fredericka nodded back.

Two of the four oxen were dead. One was impaled by the splintered tongue of the wagon. The others were down, kicking, bleeding and panting, tangled in the yokes, and the rigging.

"What will we do?" Miriam asked, limping on a swollen ankle.

"We can't travel with a broken tongue, and we can't move the dead oxen. The others are too tangled up to move. Henrietta, you ain't lookin' so good, and you can't walk. And we gotta baby. Alls we can do is wait." Fredericka's ribs ached with every breath. "Horace will find us. We got food and a rifle. We make camp."

That afternoon the air became hot and muggy. Clouds of mosquitoes appeared out of nowhere, blackened their faces and stung them relentlessly. They took cover under their shawls, and despite the heat, built a smoky fire to dispel the insects. Flies feasted on the oxen carcasses and tormented the injured beasts still bawling and bleating in the twisted gear. Fredericka made nervous glances to the horizon, hoping to see any sign of Horace. Her anxiety and regret growing with each passing hour.

Finally, in the distance, she spotted a man on a horse. "It's Horace!" she called to the others, waving her hand to the rider. "He's found us!" But as the figure grew closer, she stopped her hand in midair. Horace didn't ride an Appaloosa. The spotted horse and rider grew closer.

"Indians!" Henrietta ran to the wagon and pulled out the rifle.

"No!" Fredericka motioned to Henrietta. "Put it down! He won't hurt us."

The Native pulled up to the camp and surveyed the scene. His eyes landed on each of them, the wagon, and the oxen. The bedraggled women stood before him tense and alert. No one spoke. No one moved.

In one fluid motion, the Native threw his leg over the horse's head and slid down from the mount. He moved to the oxen puffing and heaving on their sides in their tangled chains and yokes. With swift efficiency, he drew a blade from his side and cut the constraining straps from the dead beasts and unlocked their collars. He retrieved a rope from his horse, tied it to the first carcass, pulled it aside, and repeated the task with the other dead animal, clearing the corpses from the riggings. The trapped animals struggled to their feet. He unhitched their yokes, and the oxen plodded to nearby brush and began to graze.

Fredericka, Henrietta, and Miriam glanced at each other with cautious smiles. The Native moved toward them and stood quietly without a word.

"Thank you." Fredericka wasn't sure what else to say.

The Native remained still. His youthful face did not show emotion, neither joy nor sorrow nor expectation.

He didn't smile, and yet he was not unsmiling. Fredericka understood that kind of constraint in the service to another, the unspoken expectation of gratitude, and the despair when it is withheld. She sprang to the wagon and pulled out one of Horace's calico shirts. The Native clutched the shirt and examined it. He slipped it over his head and shrugged his shoulders into the sleeves. He stood a moment longer, adjusting to his new apparel and satisfied with the transaction, he leaped on his horse and trotted off.

"Well, I'll be!" Henrietta sighed, sliding the rifle back in the wagon.

Hours later, as darkness closed in, their campfire was the only speck of light on the vast prairie. Through the pain in her chest, Fredericka had managed to cook a warm meal of mush and raisins.

Henrietta didn't eat. "I don't feel so good," she said, exhausted and more fragile than ever.

Fredericka leaned over to her and touched her forehead. "You have a fever. Go on, get some rest in the wagon."

Henrietta, not needing any encouragement, curled up in the wagon and fell into a deep sleep. After the meal, Miriam took to her tent. Fredericka sat on a pail by the fire, cradling Bo in her arms, waiting for Horace.

HORACE HAD BEEN PUSHING THE HASKELL WAGON OUT of a gulch when the tornado hit. When the hail began, he managed to unhitch the oxen and shelter with George and MaryAnn Haskell in the ditch under the box. As the funnel cloud tore near them, it shoved the wagon into the gulch just enough to entomb them. In that dark encasement, all they could hear was a wild roar, the blast of dust against the fibers of the wagon bed, and the ominous thuds of heavy objects as if they too demanded shelter from the storm. Throughout the ordeal, Horace held his palm against the wood praying for Fredericka and Bo, their images in the brutal tempest almost too much to bear.

After the clamor dissipated and the storm subsided, Horace and the Haskell's clawed themselves out from under the wagon. Horace pulled the couple free, one by one, each covered in dirt and debris. He swiped the dust from his hair and face and peered at his hands, chalky and bloody *like the hands of a dead man.* He shook his head and turned his thoughts to Fredericka. He had to find her.

Running through the wagon train, he was stunned by the destruction. The tornado had stampeded and killed cattle, scattered horses and cows, and wrecked wagons. Anxious families searched for missing children; others wandered about retrieving bits and pieces of belongings. He passed the wreckage of a wagon that had overturned crushing Charles and Maria Parsons. He passed Tom Monroe, who lay dead clutching his chest, and Grover Smyth weeping for his wife, Alicia, and their infant son, who both died due to the unfortunate timing of childbirth. Emigrants stumbled about dazed, wounded, disoriented, but Fredericka was not among them.

On the camp's border, he spotted his horse huddled with several other spooked mares. Mounting his horse, he swung around the grounds again and recognized Florence McGuire, whose husband had just died of cholera the day before. She was disheveled and aimless and holding a live chicken that flapped in her arms. When he asked about Fredericka, she merely pointed. East.

"But why…?"

But the woman meandered away.

Horace turned his horse around, and as the sun set in the West, he galloped in the opposite direction.

All things come together in time when human connections and resolve meet end to end. Neither Horace nor Fredericka sensed the shift in gravity or the unseasonable chill that tapped their shoulders like the fingers of a tailor during a fitting. Still, change and chance heralded an appointment with time.

Sage Wishes

‒‒⚬∞⚬‒‒

A buzzard glides the thermals above the prairie floor, sniffing the air for blood and decaying meat. When the time comes, and the air rises with the noxious fumes of death, it will spiral down to eat the dead.

It can wait.

Fredericka tossed a branch of sage into the fire. The savory aroma seemed to soothe the shattered air; the smoke brushed across the brilliant stars. *Sage for protection and for the permittin' of wishes* her mamma used to say, and Fredericka delivered her prayers for both. The herb flamed and sparked, infusing the night with its magical legacy.

Such is the way of wishes; they do not follow the logic of human desire. As the smoke billowed and the flames pierced the night like needlepoints, Fredericka felt a breath on the back of her neck. She pulled her shawl tighter and clutched Bo asleep in her arms. Out of the corner of her eye, she spied something move. She slowly turned her head. Inches from her cheek, a face glared at her.

Fredericka shrieked. Shot to her feet. Her ribs stabbed with pain. The face appeared disembodied, shadows flickered in the gullies of his cheeks and the furrows of his brow. Her pulse rammed into overdrive. She swayed backward and bumped into the wagon. The sturdy sensation of the wood against her spine took hold, and she stood fast.

The figure formed before her. A man in buckskin, with sharp, thin features and a curious ringlet of hair coiled above one eye. He was armed with a gun holstered about his waist.

"What do you want?" Her voice trembled.

He cocked his head to one side and looked at her with detached curiosity as if her torment amused him.

"Who are you?" She was becoming more horrified by each passing second.

He let out a sigh of boredom, and with an effort as languid as pissing on the prairie, he drew the pistol from his holster and pushed back his hat with the muzzle. "Name's Edward Honey." His voice was as soft as the hiss of a snake.

He pointed the gun at her with a careless swing of his wrist. "And you must be the fugitive mulatto, name of Fredericka."

"Who's in the tent?" Honey kicked it with his foot. "Come on out. Now."

Miriam poked her head out. "What's happening?" she asked, half-asleep and stumbling to her feet.

"Where is he?" Honey sounded tired.

"Who you mean?"

"Don't play games with me, girl. Where's your man? He hidin' in the wagon?" Holding the gun on Fredericka and Miriam, he signaled for Fredericka to step aside and peered inside the dark box. He saw a rumple of blankets. "Come on out." He waved his gun in a tight circle.

A moan rose from the wagon, but Henrietta didn't budge.

"Old woman. She's sick," Fredericka said. "Maybe got the cholera. You welcome to her."

Honey shot a nervous glance into the wagon again. Using his gun, he lifted the blanket and saw a woman's skirt and feet and quickly stepped away. "Where's the boy, Horace?"

When Fredericka didn't respond, Honey wrenched her to the ground by her arm, against the wagon wheel. Her ribs screamed with pain. The baby whined.

"Take the kid," he said, motioning to Miriam.

Honey strode to his horse, grabbed a rope, and tied Fredericka's arms to the spokes. He pulled off his neck bandana and gagged her with it.

Turning to Miriam, he said, "Got no quarrel with you. Go back inside the tent."

Squatting by the fire, he threw a branch into the flames. "He can't be far. We can wait."

HORACE RODE THROUGH THE NIGHT. THE MORNING SUN pierced the horizon and rose, blazing in a cloudless sky. He spied the outline of a wagon in the distance and raced toward it.

Jumping down from his horse, he called her name, "Fred?" No answer. He closed in to the smoldering campfire. *Where is everybody?*

He heard a muffled sound coming from the wagon. He took a step and saw Fredericka gagged and tied to the wheel. He leaped toward her. She mumbled through the gag. Tried to warn him with her eyes, but too late.

A gun clicked next to his ear. Horace froze.

"At last we meet," Honey growled. "Hands up."

Horace turned to face him, slowly lifting his arms. He cast an anxious glance back to Fredericka. "Let her go."

"Oh, I'm not letting her go. I just got her."

"If you hurt her, I'll…"

"You'll what? Jump off another ladder?" he said, snickering. "Nah, you're in no position to threaten me, boy. I got you now." Honey made a show of twirling the pistol around his fingers and then holstered the gun. "And you're not goin' anywhere without her and the kid."

He swaggered closer to the campfire. "Sit a while." He kicked a bucket over to Horace and placed himself on Fredericka's three-legged stool.

Horace sat on the overturned pail, riveted to Honey's every move. The bounty hunter feigned disinterest and riffled through his shirt for a pouch of tobacco and papers, offering Horace a greasy smile.

"You smoke, Horace?"

Horace didn't answer.

"No, I don't suppose you do. Niggers just pick tobacco, they don't smoke it, ain't that right?" He pulled out a paper in one hand and sprinkled the loose tobacco into it from the pouch. Taking his own sweet time, he rolled the paper, licked it, set the cigarette between his teeth, and lit it with the stub of a branch from the embers.

"Take me," Horace said. "Let her go."

"No, no boy, you don't get to bargain. Your chips are all played out. I got 'em all." He pulled on the cigarette, inhaled, and whistled out smoke through his pursed lips. "See, your problem is that you don't know your place, you and all them darkies. You think you can run and hide your Black ass? Pretend you're above the law? Or maybe you think you can just blend in?" He laughed to himself.

"You have no authority out here." Horace glared at him.

"I am all the authority out here." Honey let out a mean laugh and pulled a bottle of whiskey from his bedroll next to the stool.

"Drink, Horace? Nah, don't suppose you do that neither," he said, taking a swig. "Got this off some poor dead critter some ways back. Thought he could make it across this territory by himself. And he was White! Where you think you were going? Huh? California, Oregon Territory? You didn't have a chance." He took another long draft of the whiskey and wiped his mouth with his hand.

"I make my own chances."

"Not if I have anything to do with it." Honey took another drink. "You can't outrun me, outgun me, or outdrink me, any sooner you can catch a weasel asleep."

"What if I can?" Horace dared him, watching the bounty hunter's every twitch.

"You wanna try me, boy? I like games." Honey fondled his mustache, and his eyes grew to slits.

"You drop that pistol and take me on, man to man." Horace rose and kicked the pail aside with the heel of his boot. He took a wide stance, his arms dangled loose and ready at his sides.

Fredericka made a muffled groan behind her gag and shook her head.

"It'll be okay," Horace assured her, without taking his eyes off Honey.

Honey grinned and threw his cigarette down. He stood and unbuckled his belt and let it and the gun fall to the ground. "Come and get it."

Horace kicked the fire pit, sending ash and embers into Honey's face.

Honey stepped back, wiping his face. Horace hurled himself at the gunslinger. They both went down. Honey plunged his fingers into Horace's eyes. Horace groaned and toppled over. Honey crawled for his pistol, but Horace tore at the man's clothes and pulled him back. They rolled into the fire's cinders. Honey growled in pain, heaving Horace off him. Horace tumbled to the side, grabbed the bucket, and swung it against Honey's head just as the man came at him. Honey fell back. Horace grabbed the pistol just as the gunslinger pulled a knife from his boot and held it to Fredericka's throat. Both men were gasping for breath.

Honey snarled, "You run out of chances, boy. Throw down the gun."

Fredericka's eyes flashed at Horace, and she shook her head, *Don't do it.*

Horace offered the man a grim smile. "I make my own chances. Toss the knife."

"Now lookee here," Honey said. He licked the sweat dripping from his mustache. "We got us a standoff. What if I just cut her?"

"What if I just blow your foot off?"

"Fair 'nuff." Honey considered it for a bit. "Why don't you just toss the pistol, and I'll let her go.

"Why don't you just go to hell?" Horace said.

Honey grabbed Fredericka's hair and threw her head back, flashing the knife on her skin, "Let's see how far you want me to go." His knife drew a pinch of blood on her throat.

"Okay, okay," Horace said. "Just don't hurt her." He threw the pistol on the ground.

"Now, get over here." With his free hand, Honey yanked a set of handcuffs from his britches. "Cuff yourself to the wheel." When Horace hesitated, he shouted, "Do it!"

Horace shackled himself next to Fredericka. In that instant, Honey kicked him in the head. Horace slung over and passed out. Fredericka let out a muffled scream.

"Teach you to mess with me, boy," Honey sneered.

Just then, a voice came from behind the wagon. "Let 'em go, Eddie."

Honey froze before his two runaways. *What the hell? It couldn't possibly be...* "Henrietta?"

"One and the same," came the response.

He put his hands on his hips and shook his head, his back facing the unimaginable. All he could do was bow his head and chuckle.

"Hen-ri-et-ta." He emphasized each syllable, shaking off his disbelief. He turned and faced her. "How in the blazes...?"

She held a rifle pointed at him. Her hair hung greasy, long, and straggled, her clothing torn and faded to the color of mud, her face scabbed and blotchy, sunburned and blistered, and her eyes rimmed red as saffron. She looked like a rat, half-eaten. "You're lookin' fine as ever, darlin'." He shook his head, still not believing his eyes. "What in God's name are you doin' here?"

"Where you left me, you son-of-a-bitch."

He put up his hands in a gesture of peace and took a step toward her. "I admit it; I was gone longer than I planned. I was comin' back for you, darlin', right after I caught up to your runaways. That's why I'm here. To come lookin' for you."

"You left me out in the godforsaken desert to die!"

He took another step toward her. "You didn't die, did you? And here we are. Together. We can sell the niggers in Fort Laramie. Plenty of folks there be needin' a couple slaves. What do you say? Give me the gun."

"They're not yours to sell. They're mine."

"That wasn't our agreement, Retta. Remember, if I found them, I could keep 'em? Now, put down that rifle."

"You already made off with the rest of my stash. Toss your knife over."

"Now, Retta…" He took another step forward.

"Don't you 'Retta' me. I said, toss it!" She shook the rifle at him.

He paused to think about it. Henrietta looked mighty purposeful with that rifle. He plunked the knife in the ground as if it were a game.

Henrietta called Miriam from the tent, "Put the baby down and get the pistol."

Honey switched his eyes back and forth from the girl to Henrietta, calculating every move as she placed the baby in the wagon and picked up the pistol.

"But, we finally have 'em. Why would you want to let 'em go?" Honey's fingers twitched as he spoke, as if they carried on a different conversation.

"'Cause you never came back for me." She swung her head toward Fredericka. "But she did."

Honey took a step closer. "Damn Retta, there's no call to get wrathy over a simple misunderstandin'. We can be together. Go to California. Now, give me the gun." He reached his hand close enough to grab it.

She cocked the rifle and jammed it to her eye. "Back off."

His hand paused in midair.

"I don't give a fart for any of your pisspot promises. Now you let 'em go, or else."

Honey's eyes squinted into gashes under his brows, and his tone turned menacing. "Or else what? You gonna shoot me, Retta?" He coiled back. "You choosin' them coons over us?"

"There ain't no us, Eddie. I saw the hand of God come down in judgment on me. I promised to be a better woman, and he passed over me. I ain't about to tempt the Good Lord no more. But you, you're a prevaricator tried and true, and I…"

Honey struck. In a single thrust he sprang at Henrietta and ripped the rifle from her hands. A backhanded blow against her face spun her onto the ground. The force tore the hat from his head.

Honey was breathing hard. He spit on the ground and retrieved his hat, slapping it against his thigh in a cloud of dust. Stepping over Henrietta's crumpled body, he aimed the rifle at her head. "You've been a boil on my dick from the start. Nobody gets the better of Edward Honey."

The blast of a gun ripped across the prairie.

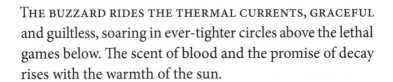

THE BUZZARD RIDES THE THERMAL CURRENTS, GRACEFUL and guiltless, soaring in ever-tighter circles above the lethal games below. The scent of blood and the promise of decay rises with the warmth of the sun.

Read It in a Book

-----ꝏꝏ-----

Miriam froze. The gunshot reduced her to three distinct senses: the crisp, sharp, crackle of the blast when she pulled the trigger, the massive, warm weight of the iron in her hands, and the vision of the man she shot—the surprise on his face, the red blotch on his chest, his arms and legs in the air before he slammed to the ground. The sequence played over and over in her mind, the blast, the gun, the surprise on his face. She tried and tried to figure it out, but she couldn't remember anything before the weapon's flash. Everything seemed strange; the wind gusting at her skirt, a baby's cry, the hot sun, bodies on the ground, someone groaning.

Minutes passed as reality settled in on the girl. The groaning was louder now. Fredericka. Horace. She dropped the pistol and ran to the couple tethered to the wagon. Fredericka motioned and groaned. The girl tugged off the gag.

"Get a knife. Cut the ropes," Fredericka's voice was raspy, her tongue swollen. And her throat dry.

Miriam scurried to the wagon and came back with a cooking knife. She sawed at Fredericka's ropes.

Fredericka took the knife from Miriam, struggled to her feet, and over to Edward Honey's body. She found the key to the handcuffs and released Horace, still unconscious from

Danuta Pfeiffer

the blow to his head. They pulled him under the shade of the wagon. Henrietta, though badly bruised, was alive. They pulled her next to Horace. Fredericka's broken ribs screamed in her chest, and every breath was an effort. Miriam fetched water, and Fredericka collapsed next to Horace and Henrietta.

Half an hour later, Horace came to with a massive headache. Henrietta was alert, but quiet, blinking up at the wagon box. Fredericka wheezed in pain next to them.

Horace tried to remember what was he doing under the wagon. Then came the memory of the storm, Fredericka gagged and tied, and the bounty hunter.

"Fred," he said, scooting closer to her side. "Are you hurt?" His hands flailed above her, wanting to help, to heal, but sensing his own helplessness, he could only squeeze her hand. "What can I do?"

"Ribs. Broke. From the storm. I'll be fine."

"What happened? What were you doing out here?"

"Henrietta. I dragged her out. Left her here. Then the storm. I come back for her. Then he showed up."

Horace scrambled into the afternoon sun and walked to the body. Miriam sat on an upturned pail holding the hungry baby who continued to cry.

"What happened?" he asked the girl.

"I shot him." Her voice was little and thin, and she gave him a look that begged for absolution.

Horace turned the man over. He was shot in the shoulder. "How...?"

"He come after Fredericka and you," Miriam said. "But Henrietta wouldn't let him. He was gonna hurt everybody. So I shot him."

Horace leaned over the man. "He's alive, but not for long." He ripped Honey's shirt open. "Gotta get that bullet out."

He grabbed the cooking knife that had been tossed on the ground and stabbed it into the campfire's embers. Fredericka slid out from under the wagon and hobbled over to him, holding her chest.

"What are you doin'?"

"We can't let him die."

"You wanna save him? The man who wanted to kill us!"

From behind her came another voice. "I say let the dog die." Henrietta had crawled out from under the wagon.

"Listen to me, he's been shot. If he dies, no one will believe a nine-year-old girl did it. They'll accuse us of murder. They'll come after us. Not now, not today, but maybe tomorrow or the day after that. There will never be an end to it. We'll always be looking over our shoulders, running for the rest of our lives. Do you want that?"

Fredericka let the words sink in, but they felt like stones.

"Besides, we're better than that. We're not like him. Isn't that why you went back for Henrietta? Isn't that why we're here in the first place? What do you say, huh?"

Henrietta scoffed at the notion. "I'm a better catch than that weasel."

"He don't deserve to live." Fredericka sensed she was losing the argument.

"Fred, if we let him die, then what do we deserve? Revenge is not how we win. Freedom is how we win."

She knew he was right, and she loved Horace more than all the hate in the world. He had strength in his pain and certainty in his fear. He was her compass, and she was never more assured of their place in the world.

"So, get me that knife and let's save this dog. The two of you hold him down," Horace said.

"You ever done this before?" Fredericka asked.

"Nope. But I read about it in a book."

Henrietta held down one arm while Fredericka took the other. Horace sliced into the wound with the sanitized blade. Honey groaned. The bullet came out in a meaty, bloody blob.

"Now we have to seal it. It won't be pretty." Horace thrust the blade back in the embers until it glowed red. He looked at Fredericka and Henrietta. "Ready?" he asked.

They nodded.

"Hold him down."

The blade seared across the wound, sending up steam and ash and the smell of burning flesh.

Honey screamed, wide awake with pain.

Henrietta hollered, "Serves you right, you boot-lickin' bastard." Too weak to hold him down, she let go of his arm.

Honey clutched Fredericka by the throat. Horace threw down the knife and punched him in the face. Honey blacked out.

"Now what?" Fredericka said, the pain in her chest biting more than ever.

"I think we're all agreed. He stays here. We leave him his horse," Horace said.

FREDERICKA NURSED BO WHILE HORACE DREW THE OXEN to the wagon and rigged the broken tongue to take the yokes. He took a sip of water from the side bucket, wiped the sweat off his brow, and rested next to Fredericka.

She touched the blood-caked wound on the side of his head with her fingertips. "Does it hurt?"

"A strong thumping in my head, but otherwise I'm fine, Mrs. Freeman. You?"

"Hurts to breathe, but I be fine, Mr. Freeman." They both chuckled.

"You wanna tell me about Henrietta?" He cast his eyes to where she was sleeping under the wagon.

"I saved her. She saved us. I guess we even now is all."

Horace pressed his parched lips on her cheek. "There's my brave girl."

"I ain't brave." She cast her eyes aside, half-hoping she was wrong.

"You are the bravest woman I know, Mrs. Freeman. You're just coming to believe it." Horace helped her to her feet. "We need to move. Catch up with the others."

Though each step was a little agony, Fredericka paced the wagon with renewed determination and the words ringing in her ears, *The bravest woman I know, Mrs. Freeman.*

As the sun simmered on the western horizon, Horace, Fredericka, Miriam, and Henrietta trudged toward it.

———❧———

It was after dark before they reached the wagon train and set up camp. It was dawn before they saw the full extent of the storm's destruction. Many wagons needed repair for broken carriages, wheels, and torn canvases. Several mounds of freshly turned dirt marked the graves of the newly dead. Half the cattle were missing, scattered by the wind, the wolves, and roving bands of Natives. Possessions thought irreplaceable and indispensable littered the field as too costly to carry: a grandfather clock shipped across an ocean from Ireland, lugged to Connecticut, transported to Missouri, and hauled halfway across the prairie, had run out of time and propriety. It did not stand proud and upright chiming in the hours of the day but lay like a coffin on its side, the glass face shattered, it's once polished wood parched and drying in the sun. A giant walnut bureau carved with angels and filigrees leaned off-balance, its dignity lost to gaping empty drawers and a broken leg. A sheet-iron stove seemed absurd protruding from the woodless landscape. A claw-footed table was upended like a dung beetle. A rocking chair fixed still in the sand, a desolate comfort to no one, a trunkful of clothes—these were the relics of an abandoned civilization cast-off for the impossible journey ahead.

Alexander Ogden spared no mercy on these losses. He hurried past each calamity with a terse determination to keep moving. "We've lost three days of traveling. 'Most sixty miles," he told the assembly of emigrants. "If we don't make the Rockies by September, we don't make it at all. And there's the Platte," he said, with a weary and ominous sound to his voice. "We still have to cross a river section up ahead, and with the rain, I expect trouble."

"What kinda' trouble you think he means?" Fredericka worried aloud.

Where There's Smoke

⎯⎯❦⎯⎯

Emily sat on the pier in the newly named San Francisco, sobbing. Love was supposed to be romantic, but instead, it was a bother, especially for a seventeen-year-old girl, alone, just off the boat in the frontier town, robbed of all her personal belongings, and addicted to laudanum. Love wouldn't help her now.

Emily fell into a state of self-pity. *How stupid could I be leaving my things to the safe-keeping of Toothless?* The thief took everything. September and Jonathan were three months away. Love wasn't going to help her out of this fix.

Late in the day, and she was cold. Fortunately, she had enough good wits to pocket her money and jewelry before leaving her things on the dock to go to the opium den. She sniffed back her tears and dabbed her eyes. Her disappointment would have to wait for another time. Months at sea had not been kind to her, and right now she needed food, a bath, and a change of clothes.

The smell of smoke in the distance brought her to her feet. Where there's smoke, there's fire, she thought, and where there's fire, there's food and people and help. She punched her hair under her bonnet, lifted her skirt, shabby and soiled, and proceeded to follow the smoke and whatever fire the future would bring.

The Smooth Pebbles

It had been three days since the tornado on the prairie, and on the morning of the fourth day, the wagons assembled limp, tattered, and hobbled together with some horses and cows taking the place of dead oxen. Despite the misery, the wagon train moved on.

A day and a half later, Ogden's premonition about trouble was right. A swollen bend of the river obstructed the trail. Torrents of water gushed around sandbanks and bogs, two hundred yards wide from bank to bank. What typically was a shallow, muddy stream had become tributaries of deep gullies and fast currents. Ogden estimated it would take too long to go around it, and the only way was to cross it. But the river was too deep and too wild to drive wagons through it.

The wagon master stood on the river bank with Horace and several other men working out a plan of action. "We take off the wheels and float 'em across," Ogden said.

"But the caulking on the wagon boxes are all dried out," Horace argued. "Wagons will sink."

"Buffalo hides would work. We passed a herd a few miles back. Get a hunting party together. We wrap the boxes in the hides. Should be just watertight enough to get to the other side. Meanwhile, unload the wagons, dismantle the running gears, ferry it all in the boxes, and reassemble on the other side," Ogden said.

"How do we navigate then?" asked Forest Alltucker, a farmer from Vermont.

"We pole and paddle the boxes across and have horses, oxen, and mules tow."

"Jesus," Alltucker said. "That's gonna take days."

"True enough," Ogden said to the man. "Though I don't take kindly to takin' the Lord's name in vain."

He turned to Horace, who stood gazing at the river with his thoughts running as swift as the current. "You got any better ideas, Horace?"

"Forest is right, Mr. Nash. It'll take days to hunt the buffalo, empty and disassemble the wagons, and load and reassemble on the other side. We're running short of time, you said so yourself."

"So?"

"So, we passed a big grove of cottonwoods." He squatted down and drew out his idea in the sand. "We could hollow out two logs, make dugouts, but they're rafts too. Stick logs in the middle. Lash all three together, the width of a wagon. The wheels fit in the canoes, keeping the wagons stable. Then, pole across with the oxen towing by ropes."

Ogden stared for a long minute at the diagram in the sand, his lips creasing into what might be called a smile. "Make it so," he said with a nod. "Put a team together, and let's get to it. We're burning daylight."

Under Horace's tutelage, both men and women helped cut, carve and lash together two rafts. With the wagon train down to half what they started with, it would take sixty crossings there and back, retrieving two wagons at a time.

The first wagon rolled smoothly into the dugouts, but the oxen and mules were not as compliant and had to be led into the water by a man on horseback. Things seemed to go well until the horse had to swim, knocking the rider into the water. Pushed by the current, the raft, wagon, oxen, horse, and rider drifted helplessly half-a-mile downstream, finally tumbling onto the same side of the river they started on, but the worse for wear. The oxen and mules drowned, and the wagon flipped topsy-turvy in the mud.

Fredericka watched from the bank, horrified, as a sickening feeling rattled through her. She had crossed over a dozen rivers, each time more confident than the last, but this felt different.

The next crossings went almost as planned, except for the loss of a cow poorly tethered to the raft with a failing knot. The beast gave a full-throated bawl before the terrified whites of its eyes sank below the turbulence.

By the time Fredericka's wagon pulled up to cross, the day was late. Horace and the other guides had spent hours escorting the rafts and animals back and forth through the cold, rapid river. Horace's lips were blue with cold, and his shirt clung to his back like a wrinkled second skin. He took the lead on his horse to the front of the raft, riding bareback and barefooted, no stirrups, reining the horse with a bitless bridle. He gave Fredericka a wave of his hat.

"That's my brave girl." He flashed a smile that did not betray his worry. "I'll meet you on the other side!"

Fredericka sat in the bucket, holding Bo. Miriam and Henrietta held tight in the back. The wagon rocked back and forth in the scow as it slipped deeper into the water, tugged by two oxen and lead by Horace. Two men steadied the scow on either side with long poles, digging into the silt against the current's thrust. The water looked level from the bank, but from the raft, the broad river churned in great swirling loops that darkened into deep, brown gullies. The muddy green waters tumbled over boulders and rocks, sloshed into drops, and rose over ledges. The racing currents charged at the raft and its cargo, spraying and pitching it in the rolling surge.

Horace plunged his horse into the torrent. At first, the mare stepped timidly across the rocky bottom, but seconds later, the water rose to her chest and neck. The mare's ears perked up as the water crested over her mane. Horace lay prostrate above the horse, holding the reins, floating on his stomach as the horse began to swim. The mare snorted, breathing hard. The oxen plowed behind, their great lungs heaving with effort, tugging the raft behind them.

Halfway across, the mare lurched into a deep chute, the force jerked her down. The horse flailed her front legs and swung around, tangling in the tow rope, pinning Horace's foot. Horse and rider plowed into the oxen. The oxen twisted back and hit the raft. The wagon tilted, rocked, and rolled backward into the water. Fredericka hit the water hard. Bo flew out of her arms. Miriam and Henrietta floundered in the river and drifted downstream, crying for help. Horse, oxen, raft, and wagon swirled in a boiling cacophony of bawling animals, angry waters, and screaming women.

Pulled under with the drowning mare, Horace tugged violently at the snare around his foot. The rope tightened as the current swept the raft downstream, dragging the horse and the oxen. The raft spun out of the chute and careened into an eddy, which slackened the rope's tension. He tugged at the rope one last time. His muscles cramped, his lungs burned for air, and he heard a thin, tinny ringing in his ears.

Finally, tearing his foot free, he exploded onto the surface gasping, disoriented, and cold.

Downriver, the wagon had beached upright, water gushing halfway up through the wheels. Horace followed Fredericka's voice above the torrent's roar and saw her clinging to a snag in the middle of the river. He fought across the current toward her. If he could walk on water, if he could run or fly, he couldn't have been any quicker to get to her. "Let go!" he shouted. "I've got you!"

She wrapped her arms around his neck as they floundered to the shore's safety. Henrietta and Miriam had washed up downriver and were sitting, dazed on the bank.

No sooner had Horace scrambled up on the rocks with Fredericka, she pointed to the water. "Where's Bo? You have to find Bo!"

Horace dragged himself up, shivering, caved in, and breathing hard. He scanned the waters. Debris, branches, and items tossed from the wagon still swirled in the eddy with the raft, now anchored to the bottom by the dead oxen and the horse. Among the flotsam, his eye fixed on what looked like a tiny cross flapping in the water. Baby Bo was on her back, bobbing in the turbulence, swinging round and round in the whirlpool. Crazy on adrenaline, fear overcame fatigue, and Horace plunged back in the water.

Fredericka watched in horror as he fought against the undercurrents lurking below the surface, but the river would not relent, one stroke forward, two strokes back. He could no longer feel his arms or legs, and his endurance was at an end, but the river was a hard master and refused every grievance. Horace plowed ahead and sensed an odd sensation of buoyancy and freedom within his grasp. He reached for the baby and caught hold of the child's garment.

Rather than relief, terror struck Fredericka more fiercely as she watched with the anticipation of safety or peril balanced in equal measure.

The eddy released Horace and Bo from its grip, and they drifted on the current. Bo rested upon her father's chest, and they glided toward the wagon, unchallenged and unrestrained. The wagon seemed to draw closer to Horace, and larger and taller as if he were motionless and the wagon was rushing to him. His noble chariot soon blotted out the sun, his wagon arrayed in a halo of light splintered into shafts of color. He stretched toward it, the baby in his hands, and released the child to its care. But he lost the advantage for himself.

Fredericka plowed into the shoals toward Horace and the wagon, the water hip-deep, her dress weighing against her progress. Before she could reach him, a warm shroud had lapped over Horace and he no longer struggled against the cold. *The sky so blue...Fredericka...and later will come the stars!* As easily as slipping off an old shoe, his strength waned and gave way.

The Platte carried him for another three miles, escorting him past cottonwood trees, banks covered in pinon, and sage, past cliffs speckled with quartz from ancient volcanos, past the dust of ancestors who waded these waters before Moses was lost in the desert, resting him on the smooth pebbles of the river's edge.

Fredericka found the baby cradled in the spokes of the wagon wheel above the river's reach, the full extent of Horace's arms. She stood in the shallows of the unsettled current facing downstream, clutching Bo, but Horace was gone. Had the forces of nature conspired to tear her apart, giving and taking away, a life for a life? That bargain was beyond her capacity to bear, beyond any anguish except to scream.

So she screamed with a mother's roar and a lover's pain. She screamed at the heavens and at the sun, and at the gods of water and air, a scream that carried downriver to the smooth pebbles and the forces of nature that held her beloved Horace.

Battle with God

⊗≋⊘

Pain doesn't stop a wagon train. After his cursory search for Horace along the riverbank, Ogden rode up on horseback to Fredericka. "I'm sorry, but we can't wait any longer," he said.

Fredericka would not be consoled. "You can't just leave him here. You can't!" Her nerves were on fire. Everything moved too fast: the sky and the river and shouting men, wagons and cattle, Miriam's terrified face, Henrietta's tattered bonnet, Ogden's chin-curtain beard, all assembled in a heart-pounding blur.

"Look, this is a fast moving river. There's no chance he's made it out alive."

"But, you don't know that!" Baby Bo wiggled in Fredericka's arms.

"He was a good man," Ogden sighed. "I'll have the riders pull your wagon out, give you a new team and supplies. Horace earned it. But we're movin' on. Burnin' daylight."

"But, but…Horace!" Fredericka cried.

Ogden turned his horse around. "Go or stay. Your choice."

Fredericka handed the baby to Miriam. "Take care of her," she said and she dashed along the bank.

Brambles and thistles scratched Fredericka's legs and tore at her skirt. She climbed over fallen trees snagging the river and scrambled over boulders and rocks. "Horace!" she called, "Horace!" over and over until her throat was raw. But the only answer was the rushing, pushing river, disgorging the bank, leaping and tumbling over boulders, swirling into furious eddies and hissing into the drops.

Fredericka's prayers flew like startled birds. She prayed to find Horace clinging to a tree branch, waving from a rocky shelf, or stumbling toward her from the shore. Surely God must hear! Surely He is listening! She plunged headlong into the terror and denial of his death, to avoid it, overcome it, outwit it. Not his time. She was not ready. She would not allow it.

Fredericka clawed through the underbrush and tore at the decaying limbs of felled trees searching for her Horace. And the questions, so many questions half-eaten by grief, starving without answers. She railed at God: Why? We not good enough? We not suffer enough? What kind of God rips and tears and destroys? Where is justice? Where is love?

Hope seeped through her panic, thinking she would soon see his wide, embarrassed smile for causing such a fuss. How she would scold him for making her worry. And yet, she wanted to rage at him for drowning.

Hours later, Miriam and Henrietta were shocked to see Fredericka scramble from the brush, bruised, bloodied and battered, as though she had battled with God. Her bonnet dangled off the back of her head, her hair bedraggled and wet, and her clothing in shreds. Fredericka stumbled toward her baby. "I need my Bo," she said, lifting the child from Miriam's arms. She inhaled Bo's warm, sweet breath, and caressed the baby's tender skin. A part of Horace to hold.

Fredericka leaned in close to the child and whispered, "I can't find your Daddy, baby. I try real hard. But I can't find him."

Moments later, a flutter of wings, and Fredericka caught a glance of a heron with fierce gold eyes gliding above her. Turning, the bird swooped down the river and disappeared.

THREE MILES DOWNSTREAM, THE SUN-DRENCHED PEB-bles twinkled along the riverbank. Warmed by the stones, the water trickled against the skin, vibrated to the veins, and massaged the muscles of the body that lay there. Tiny tributaries babbled between the pebbles, riffled through the fingers, and surged against the limbs, lifting and settling, swaying and rocking, gently beaching the body higher on the dry bank as the river pressed on.

FREDERICKA COULD NOT SLEEP. THAT PRIVILEGE WAS reserved for those who did not wrestle with the gods and unacceptable outcomes. There was no grave for him. That was the worst torment of all. How could she live not knowing if Horace could have been saved? How could she take another breath, not knowing if he still breathed? Was he alone, or in pain, or eaten by wolves? Just before dawn, she heard birds creak and chirp along the river, warning of a new, hard day. She crawled from her tent to watch the vast prairie emerge beneath a half-hearted light and a cloud-shredded sky.

Despite Henrietta's nagging, Fredericka couldn't eat. She felt gutted and sick. Eating didn't seem fair to Horace. That's what happens when grief sets in—a deep misery that packs down tight, turning insides to stone and making it impossible to move.

As Fredericka nursed Bo, her daughter's eyelids flickered open and shut, the child's cheeks plump and flushed with satisfaction at her breast. Fredericka realized she would never have the peace of this child, she would never sleep again until she knew what happened to Horace.

Fredericka's indulgence did not sit well with Henrietta, who had become a scrawny, unruly woman with a disposition to match. She owed Fredericka her life and she owed the Good Lord her promise to be a better woman.

Henrietta now had to call upon that higher good. Something had to be done. The wagon train had left. She was damned if she was going to be eaten by mosquitoes, beaten by the sun, and without prospects. She hefted her skirt and made her way over to Fredericka who was gazing upon the river. She would have to take a gentle approach with the grief-stricken woman. "You need to get your damned ass up," she said, slapping a mosquito on her neck.

"Did you see that heron yesterday?" Fredericka asked.

"You're talkin' about herons when we're sitting here, with no wagon train? You're getting crazier by the minute. Look, this isn't good for you, Miriam, me, or your baby. We need to move. Horace is dead. He saved your baby. If you think you're gonna sit here and see his sacrifice go to shit, you have another think comin', 'cause I ain't gonna die out here in this godforsaken land because you're weak and helpless. So get your ass up." She crossed her arms and glared at Fredericka.

Fredericka shot her a hard glance. Just then, Miriam let out a full-throttle scream that roused both women from the riverside. They rushed to the wagon where the girl stood petrified staring at the ground. She was standing barefoot on a rattlesnake thick as a man's arm. Henrietta let out a horrified gasp and cupped her mouth. Fredericka fought back a vinegary, sour tang that almost gagged her with fear. The brown-and-white banded snake was coiled and the child's foot was stamped in the center of the spiral. The snake's tail wound about the girl's ankle, beating its manic rattle in the air. The viper's triangular head poked out just beyond her toes, flashing its forked tongue. Neither the snake nor the girl could move.

"I jumped out of the wagon and stepped right on him," Miriam squeaked, holding back tears. "I didn't even see him. He's gonna bite me!"

"Stand still," Fredericka commanded, although hardly a necessary order. She handed the baby to Henrietta.

"Oh dear God! Oh dear God!" Henrietta backed up, still hand to mouth.

Miriam stood frozen in place, her eyes following Fredericka's every move.

"Get him off me!" Miriam wailed, her legs now beginning to wobble.

"Be quiet and hold still." Fredericka circled behind Miriam, then slowly bent down and grabbed the viper's rattling tail.

"Now, you gotta trust me, Miriam. When I count to three, I want you to run. You got that?"

Miriam's eyes were wide and terrified and all she could do was nod.

"Ready?"

Miriam nodded again.

"One, two, THREE!"

Miriam sprinted off the rattlesnake and stumbled forward as Fredericka whipped the snake backward. The rattler lunged at her as she held it upside down.

"No!" she shrieked at it. "No! No more!" and thrashed the snake against the ground like a wet cloth. "No more! No more!"

Over and over, she beat it against the ground, plowing up the dust, a bloody dangling mess in her hand. She was breathing hard, strands of hair stuck to the sweat on her face. Throwing the snake aside, she hiked up to Henrietta, pinning her face up-close. Unwavering and fierce, Fredericka said, "I ain't weak. And I ain't helpless. Horace told me. I am brave. Not you or nobody ever gonna call me less."

"So now what, Fredericka? You're so brave and smart, you tell me, what's the plan?"

"The plan?" Fredericka exploded. "The plan was to get away from the likes of you, and all those other White folks strippin' our minds and our bodies outta who we are. Makin' us so lost that just survivin' weren't enough no more. Tellin' us 'keep your head down, nigger,' while freedom was just danglin' in front of us a bite away like a carrot before a mule. Gettin' punished for what's up here, in our minds, for readin' and writin' and thinkin'. Gettin' punished just for hopin'. And now Horace is dead for all that hopin'. And you askin' me, what's the plan? I ain't got no plan 'cept what you got all along, but you ain't seen it. Dyin' free. That's all I want. That's all Horace wanted."

"Dyin' ain't no plan!" Henrietta shot back.

"No! It ain't! And for this one time, you be right, Henrietta." Fredericka marched to the wagon and grabbed her shawl and stuffed into it several biscuits, a flint, a cup with cornmeal, a knife, and a small handsaw.

"Where you going now?" Henrietta shouted after her.

"I'm gonna find him. If I have to come back with a bag of his bones, it's better than not knowin'." She looped the shawl around her shoulders and headed to the riverbank.

"You just can't leave us here!"

"I'll be back. Take care of Miriam and Bo. But I'm gonna find him."

Fredericka marched to a raft the wagons had used to cross the river. It was lodged near the sandbank where their wagon had grounded. Grabbing the raft's long pole half-buried in the sand, she climbed aboard the log float, threw her satchel into one of the hollowed-out centers where the wagon wheels had found their grip, and shoved off.

The raft wobbled, rocked her off her balance and slammed her onto her back as it slipped into the current. She was at the river's mercy. Spinning in circles and crashing into limbs, the raft propelled her downstream.

One mile down, the river widened into a flat, swampy floodplain where islands and sandbars protruded from the water. Fredericka poled through the shallows calling for Horace. The river's edge was hard to distinguish, and tree roots jutting under the shallows snagged and jerked the raft.

Two miles down, the river curved into a narrow, fast-moving stream that carved out the banks into slick, steep walls. Fredericka took no notice of her bloody knees chafing against the logs, nor did she give in to her fear of water. Her eyes and ears and heart were glued to the banks searching for Horace.

Three miles down, the water flattened again and slowed its pace. The late afternoon sun glanced off the water in stinging shards of white flashes. Gradually, the raft scraped along the rocky bottom to a stop. Fredericka thrust the heavy pole into the river bed and leaned against its resistance, but the raft would not budge. Her grip slipped from the pole drilling her back to her knees.

She was alone on a raft, an island of her own making. Too headstrong. Too stubborn. Too much in love to let go. Losing Horace, she had now lost herself. "Consarn you, for dyin' Horace!" she sobbed.

Alarmed by the sudden outburst, a heron shot up from the bank and flapped across the river, landing in a nearby marsh. Fredericka grabbed her bundled shawl and plunged feet first into the water. Scooping up a handful of pebbles, she threw them at the creature. "No more!" she hollered, done with hope.

The bird leaped into the air with a dancer's grace slow-beating its great wings above her. Fredericka trudged toward the shore and stumbled. On her hands and knees, she crawled to the river's edge, the edge of everything and nothing, her head full of contradictions. She was a slave on the brink of freedom, in a parched desert running with water, plucked from both certainty and doubt, driven by instinct or insanity to follow a bird, searching for Horace who would not be found.

She sat on the shoreline as the sun dipped behind the scrub pines. The light turned gold, then gray and the sun blinked out. Fredericka was exhausted and her passions fled like starlings. She was no longer fueled by active rebellion, nor preyed upon by self-pity or remorse. All resistance had flown.

In light of those losses, something was gained: her resistance to hope allowed hope to flourish. As her tears dried, her senses became enlivened. She detected a change in the air. Jittery glances about the riverbank revealed nothing, yet the space around her felt thick as butter. She turned toward a leafy tree a few yards away. Through the blur of her tear-swollen eyes, she saw a log lying in the semidarkness under the branches. A shiver ran down her back. She scrambled to her feet and drew closer. There, in the shadow of the cottonwood tree, lay Horace.

Fredericka froze as her brain ordered her legs to move. She fell toward him. "Horace!" Her hands waved over his body, not knowing if she should, if she could touch him. "Horace!" she said.

He lay on his back. Still, shirtless, barefoot, cold.

"I's here, Horace." She lifted his head onto her lap. "I's here."

His eyes flickered and opened, tried to focus.

"Horace! Love, I's here!"

"Waited…" His voice was feeble and raspy.

"I's here now, baby."

"Bo…?"

"You saved her, Horace."

"Good…good."

His limp body draped across her lap like a blanket left out in the rain. "You hush now and rest some. We gettin' outta here," she said.

"Promise…"

"What Horace?"

"Promise…keep going…freedom." His eyes closed as though part of him had already flown away.

"I ain't going nowhere without you, Horace." She rocked back and forth, stroking his face, cradling him in her arms. "Come back to me, Horace."

His eyes fluttered open again. "Promise."

"I promise. I promise." She pulled him in tight. "But freedom together. Just like we said."

He lifted his hand up to her and managed a weak smile. She kissed his fingers. They were so cold. "I'm gonna build us a nice fire," she said. "Get you warm."

"Can't make it, Fred…" His eyes closed again.

"Don't you give up on me, Horace. Don't you do it!"

But Horace felt radiant and expansive. Long shafts of light pierced through him and became him. He was the light and the air, absorbed into the thrill of being everything.

Yet earthbound Fredericka held him closer. "You my hero, Horace. We go together or we don't go." She leaned over him. His breath was shallow and slow.

Fredericka scanned their surroundings and spied a few dried branches and leaves, a stand of sage, clumps of dead grasses. She slipped his head gently down and swept the scrub together. Untying her shawl, she dumped out the food and tools, and covered his bare chest. She kissed his forehead. Horace didn't move.

"Horace, you stay with me!" Her hands trembled as she scratched her knife against the flint for a spark. A puff of smoke, a tiny flame and the grasses lit and the branches crackled into a small fire.

Fredericka yanked off her skirt and threw it over his body. She rubbed his arms and legs, massaged his feet, and held him in her arms as the fire built to a roar.

"You waited for me, Horace. Now, I wait for you."

Love, that insubstantial mystery, mingled and twisted with the flames. That mystery took flight and called back the speed of light. The twitch of a thumb, a faint pulse, and life took hold once more in the pursuit of *libertas*.

To Be Continued…

ACKNOWLEDGEMENTS

A book never stands alone, and to quote an old adage, "it takes a village," beginning with the inspiration. That spur came from Robin Pfeiffer, the love of my life. While digging an irrigation pond in our vineyard, he dug up a mystery and connected that curious discovery to a legend. I imagined a backstory to that tale and thus began the Pocket Full of Seeds Trilogy with this first installment, *Libertas*. Many thanks to my dear husband for his insight, ideas, and reassurance as I read every new scene or chapter at the end of the day over a glass of our pinot noir.

The wagon is an enduring character in this story, brought to life by Wade Skinner, a cowboy, a romantic, an artist, and a friend. He would have been right at home a hundred and fifty years ago sleeping under a buffalo robe in the wild—and, truth be told, he sometimes does. As a gift, he drove his covered wagon to a field within sight of my window. The wagon became my muse. I sat in it; ran my fingers over the boards; crawled beneath the undercarriage; fingered the hub, the hounds, the reach; marveled at the wheels; and napped in the box. Wade spoke to me of the beauty of his chariot, the strength of the rims and the fire behind the iron, the pressure of the axles, and the durability of the wood. Thanks to Wade, I became a lover of covered wagons.

Many thanks to my manuscript readers, including Susie Silvestri, who loved Horace and Fredericka so much that she mourned and cheered for them at every turn of the page. Peggy Snyder, whose years of teaching English honed her skills against all my "ands" and "buts" and commas. Deb Wells, who helped with spell-checking and scene development. Rosemary Howe Camozzi, who mended character gaps, and Kathleen Cremonesi, who found herself glued to the manuscript on her cell phone. Thank you to Debra Whiting Alexander for her encouragement, insight, edits, and for recommending the book's title.

As a White woman, I agonized over writing about escaped Black slaves, not being Black, and never having been a slave. But then, I never lived on a cotton plantation nor sailed a steamship around the Horn of South America, experienced a lake tsunami, or walked two thousand miles miles across a continent. But it was the perception of arrogance that concerned me most—how could a White woman cross the bridge to the Black experience of the 1800's? Research could only inch me across that divide. I also cringed over the use of racist language and characters—both as shameful today as they were in the nineteenth century. But in order for this story to unfold, I had to stay true to its historical nature. I sought the voices of Frederick Douglass, Clara Brown, and Harriett Tubman and many other diarists and historians, but I also needed the advice of African-American contemporaries to guide me across this bridge.

And so, a special debt of gratitude goes to Darline Jackson and Perry Adams, who encouraged me with their Black perspectives and a nod to my concerns, offered gentle guidance and, I hope, an absolution for even attempting this crossing.

Multiple thanks to the great professionals at Luminare Press who guided this project to a polished fruition. A writer couldn't have better support.

Although this story is historical fiction, many situations, conditions, and characterizations reflect the journals of the courageous women and men who took the westward challenge against great odds. I have learned so much from the lives of Black pioneers, Native Americans, cowboys, statesmen, farmers, teachers, laundresses, mothers and wives, bankers, builders, prostitutes, and suffragettes who staked out the New World.

Now, more than ever, we need to be reminded of their sacrifices. I hope to be worthy of them with *Libertas*.

Made in the USA
Columbia, SC
16 May 2021

37552818R00212